• Praise for the Onyx Court Novels •

"Brennan fleshes out the primal conflict of love and honor pitted against raging ambition and lust for power."

—*Publishers Weekly* (starred review) on *Midnight Never Come*

"You will swallow this book whole, wishing that it would never end. Brennan is a bright new voice in fantasy fiction, and *In Ashes Lie* is her best effort yet."

—*Sacramento Book Review*

"Brennan has created a fascinating hidden underworld beneath London, and it's enhanced by prose that has an elegance perfect for historical fantasy."

—*RT Book Reviews* on *In Ashes Lie*

A Star Shall Fall

MARIE BRENNAN

TOR®
fantasy

A TOM DOHERTY ASSOCIATES BOOK
NEW YORK

This is a work of fiction. All of the characters, organizations, and events portrayed in this novel are either products of the author's imagination or are used fictitiously.

A STAR SHALL FALL

Copyright © 2010 by Bryn Neuenschwander

A Tor Book
Published by Tom Doherty Associates, LLC
175 Fifth Avenue
New York, NY 10010

www.tor-forge.com

Tor® is a registered trademark of Tom Doherty Associates, LLC.

ISBN 978-0-7653-6450-0

First Edition: September 2010
First Mass Market Edition: October 2012

Printed in the United States of America

0 9 8 7 6 5 4 3 2 1

DRAMATIS PERSONAE

MORTALS

Those marked with an asterisk are attested in history.

Galen St. Clair — *a gentleman, and Prince of the Onyx Court*

Charles St. Clair — *a gentleman of good name and poor fortune; Galen's father*

Cynthia St. Clair — *a young lady in need of a dowry; Galen's sister*

Philadelphia Northwood — *a young lady of great wealth*

Jonathan Hurst }
Laurence Byrd } — *friends to Galen St. Clair*
Peter Mayhew }

Dr. Rufus Andrews — *a physician and scholar; Fellow of the Royal Society*

*George Parker, Earl of Macclesfield — *President of the Royal Society, and architect of the new calendar*

*Henry Cavendish — *a brilliant young scholar; son of Lord Charles Cavendish*

*James Bradley — *Astronomer Royal to King George II*

*Charles Messier — *a French astronomer*

*John Flamsteed — *the first Astronomer Royal, now deceased*

*Edmond Halley — *a cometary astronomer and Fellow of the Royal Society, now deceased*

*Sir Isaac Newton — *former President of the Royal Society, now deceased*

*Dr. Samuel Johnson — *a learned gentleman of very strong opinions*

*Elizabeth Vesey   }
*Elizabeth Montagu }   *— ladies of the Bluestocking Circle*
*Elizabeth Carter   }

Edward Thorne — *valet to Galen St. Clair*
*Kitty Fisher — *a courtesan*

Sir Michael Deven   }
Dr. John Ellin   }
Lord Joseph Winslow }
Dr. Hamilton Birch }

FAERIES

Lune — *Queen of the Onyx Court*
Valentin Aspell — *Lord Keeper*
Amadea Shirrell — *Lady Chamberlain*
Sir Peregrin Thorne — *Captain of the Onyx Guard*
Sir Cerenel — *Lieutenant of the Onyx Guard*
Dame Segraine — *a lady knight of the Onyx Guard*
Dame Irrith — *a sprite, and lady knight of the Vale of the White Horse*
Carline — *an elf-lady, now fallen from grace*

Rosamund Goodemeade — *a helpful brownie*
Gertrude Goodemeade — *likewise a helpful brownie, and Rosamund's sister*
Savennis — *a courtier of scholarly inclinations*
Wrain — *a sprite, likewise scholarly*

Magrat — *a church grim*
Hafdean — *keeper of the Crow's Head*
Angrisla — *a nightmare*
Podder — *a hob, and servant to the Princes of the Stone*
Blacktooth Meg — *hag of the River Fleet*

Ktistes — *a centaur, grandson of Kheiron*
Wilhas von das Ticken — *a good-tempered dwarf*
Niklas von das Ticken — *an ill-tempered dwarf; Wilhas' brother*
Lady Feidelm — *an Irish sidhe, and former seer*
Abd ar-Rashid — *a genie of Istanbul*
Il Veloce — *a faun long resident in the Onyx Hall*

Wayland Smith — *King of the Vale of the White Horse in Berkshire*
Invidiana — *former Queen of the Onyx Court, now deceased*

Greater London

TO: Highgate ↑

Holborn

Mayfair

A.

Lambeth

TO: Vauxhall ↓

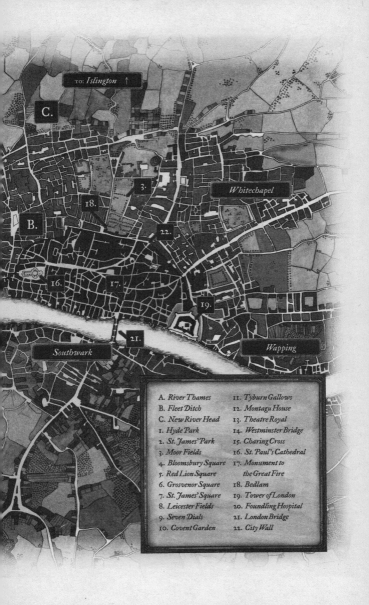

TO: *Islington* ↑

C.

B.

Whitechapel

Southwark

Wapping

A. *River Thames*	11. *Tyburn Gallows*
B. *Fleet Ditch*	12. *Montagu House*
C. *New River Head*	13. *Theatre Royal*
1. *Hyde Park*	14. *Westminster Bridge*
2. *St. James' Park*	15. *Charing Cross*
3. *Moor Fields*	16. *St. Paul's Cathedral*
4. *Bloomsbury Square*	17. *Monument to*
5. *Red Lion Square*	*the Great Fire*
6. *Grosvenor Square*	18. *Bedlam*
7. *St. James' Square*	19. *Tower of London*
8. *Leicester Fields*	20. *Foundling Hospital*
9. *Seven Dials*	21. *London Bridge*
10. *Covent Garden*	22. *City Wall*

A Star Shall Fall

PROLOGUE

Gresham College, London: June 20, 1705

The room was a shabby one to contain the intellectual brilliance of England. Small and scant of windows, it was nearly unbearable in the warmth of an early summer day, and filled with gentlemen looking forward to the pleasanter air of their country estates, away from the stinks of London. Some listened with interest to the letters being read, an exchange between two of their fellows regarding the island of Formosa; others fanned themselves futilely with whatever papers came to hand, wishing they dared nod off. But the gimlet eye of their president was upon them, and though Sir Isaac Newton might be more than sixty years old, age had not slowed him in the least, nor dulled the sharp edge of his tongue.

They gave an impression of agreeable uniformity in their somber-colored coats, so very different from the young gallants of London's *beau monde* who took every opportunity to quarrel. Nothing could be further from the truth. *Nullius in verba* was their motto: on the words of no one. This was the temple of facts, of careful observation and even more careful reasoning; the men of the Royal Society of London, the premier scientific body of the Kingdom of England, were no respecters of ancient authority. They respected only Truth. And when they found themselves in disagreement as to what that Truth was, their arguments could grow very heated indeed.

But there was little to argue in the second piece of that day's business, presented by Oxford's new Savilian Professor of Astronomy. In all honesty, hardly any men there had the capacity to debate it; the proof hinged on Newton's *Philosophiae Naturalis Principia Mathematica*, which fewer of them understood than pretended to. Edmond Halley's calculus therefore meant little to them. The fundamental point, however, was clear.

The orbit of a comet was not a parabola, but an ellipsis. And that meant that a comet, having departed from view, would in the fullness of time return.

A point that held rather a high degree of interest for two members of Halley's audience.

"The measurements made by Flamsteed at Greenwich in 1682 are exceptionally precise," the professor said, with a nod that acknowledged the contributions of the absent Astronomer Royal. "They provide us with a basis for examining the less-precise accounts of cometary apparitions in the past—1607, 1531, 1456, and so on."

Back to the days of the Stuart kings, and the Tudors, and the Lancastrians. Many here today remembered the comet twenty-three years before, but a man's beard would have to be gray indeed for him to have seen any of the others Halley named.

The one member of his audience who could claim that distinction had no beard at all. He was a young gallant more often found haunting the halls of London's fencing masters, and his friends would have been surprised to see him in such sober costume, attending with hawklike intensity to the dull minutiae of astronomical mathematics.

Though not half so surprised as they would have been, had they ever seen their friend's true face.

"A question, if you please," the gallant said, interrupting Halley's presentation of his *Astronomiae cometicae synopsis*, and drawing a swift frown from Newton. "Could anything divert the comet from its path?"

The Savilian Professor's well-rehearsed presentation faltered. "I beg your pardon?"

"You say the comet travels far away from the sun, returning only every seventy-five years, or seventy-six. Could anything prevent that return, sending it out into space?"

Halley's mouth opened and shut several times without anything coming out. "I suppose," he said at last, with bewildered uncertainty, "that a large mass might exert gravitational force upon the cometary body, perturbing its path such that the return would not occur as expected. But to make it depart entirely . . . why, sir, would you be concerned with such a thing?"

Now all eyes in the room were upon the gallant—save for those belonging to Lord Joseph Winslow, who'd brought him there as a guest. Winslow had a most peculiar expression on his face, as if he wished dearly that his companion had not interrupted with such a bizarre question . . . but he also craved Halley's answer.

"It seems to me," the young gallant said, "that the eccentric wanderings of such a body might pose a danger to us here."

A startled voice came from elsewhere in the audience. "If the orbits aligned unfavorably—could a comet strike the Earth?"

"Nonsense." Newton's sharp reply cut them all off like a blade. "The Lord designed the heavens to His purpose; if it should come to pass that anything in them brings calamity to the Earth—as may have occurred at the Deluge—then it will likewise be the Lord's will. We may conclude, therefore, that there is no need for diversion of a comet's path."

The gallant was brave indeed, for he pressed his point, even in the face of Newton's displeasure. "But what of smaller threats? Have not natural disasters been ascribed to the influence of comets? If one should—"

"Enough of this." The President of the Royal Society stood, glaring at Winslow's guest. "Comets are mechanical bodies, obeying the laws of motion and universal gravitation; if they have any effect beyond that, it is beneficial, distributing vapors that fuel the processes of vegetation and putrefaction on Earth, and perhaps supplying the spiritous component of air. Your fears are foolish, and you will waste no more of our time with them."

Sir Isaac Newton had a piercing eye; but so, too, did the

young gallant. He stood, not breaking his gaze from the great man's, and made a curt bow before exiting the room. Winslow murmured his apologies and followed.

Pacing at the base of the stairs outside, the gallant growled a string of curses. "It isn't the will of his divine Master—it's *our* doing, and our fault."

"I wouldn't tell Sir Isaac that," Winslow said, trying for a hint of humor. "He isn't likely to believe you if you tell him there's a Dragon on that comet, and a bunch of faeries put it there."

Dragon. A word not often spoken in the enlightened halls of Gresham College. Neither was the word *faerie*, and yet here she stood: Dame Segraine of the Onyx Court, lady knight to a faerie queen, come in masculine and mortal guise to confirm the warning they'd received.

She put one hand on the corner post of the wall at her side. The architecture was old; this building hadn't burnt in the Great Fire of 1666. It was one of the few that hadn't. Flames had consumed four-fifths of the land within London's walls, and some of the land without them, while the mortal inhabitants of the city fought to stop their progress.

One of two battles that raged during those infernal days. The other was between the city's faerie inhabitants, and the spirit of the Fire itself: a Dragon.

Which, in 1682, they exiled to a star in the sky—not knowing that the star would return.

Inside the chambers of the Royal Society, Edmond Halley was concluding his presentation, saying, "I advise posterity to watch for it most carefully in the year 1758, at which time may science be vindicated in its prophecy."

"We have fifty-three years," Winslow said to Dame Segraine. "Thanks to your Irish seer, we've been alerted to Halley's work, and its consequence for us. We have time to prepare."

And prepare they must—for without a doubt, their banished enemy had not forgotten them. Whether from a desire for vengeance or simple ravening hunger, it would seek out the meat it had before.

London.

Fifty-three years. As Winslow opened the door to the quadrangle of Gresham College, Dame Segraine murmured, "I hope that will be enough."

PART ONE

Congelatio

Autumn 1757

Purged by the sword and beautified by fire,
Then had we seen proud London's hated walls.

—Thomas Gray,
"On Lord Holland's Seat near M——e, Kent"

The blackness is spangled with a million points of light. Stars, galaxies, nebulae: wonders of the heavens, moving through their eternal dance.

Far in the distance—impossibly far—a bright spark burns. One sun among many, it calls the tune to which its subjects dance, in accordance with the immutable law of gravity. Planets and their follower moons, and the brief visitors men call comets.

One such visitor draws near.

The oblong is frozen harder than winter itself. The sun is yet distant, too distant to awaken it to life; the light barely even gilds the black substance facing it. The spirit that dwells within the comet sleeps, driven into torpor by the endless cold of space.

It has slept for more than seventy years. The time will soon come, though, when that sleep will end, and when it does . . .

The beast will seek its prey.

Mayfair, Westminster: September 30, 1757

The sedan chair left the City by way of Ludgate, weaving through the clamor of Fleet Street and the Strand before escaping into the quieter reaches of Westminster. A persistent drizzle had been falling all day, which the chair-men disregarded, except to choose their footing carefully in the ever-present slime of mud and less savory things. The curtains of the chair were drawn, blocking out the dismal sight, and the twilight falling earlier than usual.

Inside, the blackness and rhythmic swaying were almost enough to put Galen to sleep. He stifled a yawn as if his father were watching: *Up late carousing, no doubt,* the old man would say, *gambling your allowance away at Vauxhall.* As if he had much of an allowance to wager, or any inclination to such pursuits. But that was the simplest explanation for Galen's late nights and frequent absences, and so he let his father go on believing it.

Regardless, he would do well to rouse himself. Galen had visited Clarges Street before, but this would be his first formal gathering there, and yawning in his fellow guests' faces would not make a good impression.

A muffled cry from one of the chair-men as they slowed. Then the conveyance tilted, rocking perilously up a set of stairs. Galen pulled the curtain aside just in time to see his chair pass through the front door of the house, into the entrance hall, and out of the rain.

He stepped free carefully, ducking his head to avoid knocking his hat askew. A footman stood at the ready; Galen gave his name, and tried not to fidget as the servant departed. Waiting here, while the chair dripped onto the patterned marble, made him feel terribly self-conscious, as if he were a tradesman come to beg a favor, rather than an invited guest. Fortunately, the footman returned promptly and bowed. "You are very welcome, sir. If I may?"

Galen paid the chair-men and surrendered his cloak, hat, and walking stick to the footman. Then, taking a deep breath, he followed the man to the sitting room.

"Mr. St. Clair!" Elizabeth Vesey rose from her seat and crossed to him, extending one slender hand. He bowed over it with his best grace, lips brushing lightly. Just enough to make her blush prettily; it was a game, of course, but one she never tired of, though she would not see forty again. "You are very welcome, sir. I feared this dreadful rain would keep you home."

"Not at all," Galen said. "My journey here was warmed by the thought of your company, and I shall carry the memory of it home like a flame."

Mrs. Vesey laughed, a lilting sound that matched her Irish accent. "Oh, well done, Mr. St. Clair—well done indeed. Do you not agree, Lizzy?"

That was addressed to a taller, more robust woman, one of at least a dozen scattered about the room. Elizabeth Montagu raised one eyebrow and said, "Well spoken, at least—but my dear, have you not instructed him in the proper dress for these occasions?"

Galen flushed, faltering. Mrs. Vesey looked him over from his ribbon-bound wig to the polished buckles of his shoes, and *tsk*ed sadly. "Indeed, sir, we have a very strict code for our gatherings, as I have told you most clearly. Only *blue* stockings will do!"

He looked down in startlement at his stockings of black silk, and tension gave way to a relieved laugh. "My humblest apologies, Mrs. Vesey, Mrs. Montagu. Blue worsted, as you instructed. I will endeavour to remember."

Linking her arm through his, Mrs. Vesey said, "See that you do! You are far too stiff, Mr. St. Clair, especially for one so young. You mustn't take us too seriously, or our little Bluestocking Circle. We're merely friends here, come together to share ideas and art. Dress as if for court, and you'll put us all to shame!"

There was some truth to her words. Not that he was dressed for court; no, his gray velvet was far too somber for any occasion so fine, though he was very pleased with the new waistcoat Cynthia had given him. But it was true that few of the people present showed anything like such elegance, and in fact one of the two gentlemen present might have been a tradesman, dressed for a day of work.

Galen let Mrs. Vesey conduct him about the room, making introductions. Some he'd met before, but he appreciated her reminders; he always feared he would forget a name. The two gentlemen were new to him. The seeming tradesman was one Benjamin Stillingfleet—who, true to Mrs. Vesey's word, was wearing ordinary blue stockings—and the other, a stout and loud-voiced figure, was revealed to be the great Dr. Samuel Johnson.

"I am honored, sir," Galen said, and swept him a bow.

"Of course you are," Johnson grunted. "Can't go anywhere in this town without being known. Damned nuisance." His head jerked oddly on his shoulders, and Galen's eyes widened.

"If you did not want recognition," Mrs. Montagu said tartly, "you should not have poured years of your life into that dictionary of yours." She took no notice of the gesture, nor of his ill manner, and Galen thought it best to follow her example.

Mrs. Vesey's drawing room was a masterpiece of restrained elegance, its chairs upholstered in Chinese silks that showed to great advantage in the warm glow of the candles. It lacked the ruelles and other accoutrements of the great *salons* in Paris, but this was a modest affair after all; scarcely more than a dozen guests altogether. Mrs. Montagu hosted much larger gatherings at her own house on Hill Street, and she was nothing to the French *salonnières*. Galen was glad of the smallness, though. Here he could believe, as Mrs. Vesey said, that he was among friends, and not feel so conscious of himself.

As he retired to a chair with a glass of punch, Johnson picked up the thread of a conversation apparently dropped when

Galen entered the room. "Yes, I know I said March," he told Stillingfleet impatiently, "but the work takes longer than expected—and there's another project besides, a series called *The Idler,* which will begin next month. Tonson can wait." His manner as he spoke was most peculiar—more strange tics of the head and hands. It was not a palsy, but something else altogether. Galen was torn between staring and looking away.

"Shakespeare," Mrs. Vesey murmured to Galen, not quite sotto voce. "Dr. Johnson is working on a new edition of the plays, but I fear his enthusiasm fades."

Johnson heard her, as she no doubt meant him to. "To do the work properly," he said with dignity, "takes time."

Mrs. Montagu laughed. "But you don't dispute the lack of enthusiasm, I see. What play is it you edit now?"

"*A Midsummer Night's Dream*, and a piece of nonsense it is, too," Johnson said. "Low comedy—quite unappealing, to discerning tastes—full of flower faeries and other silliness. What moral lesson are we to derive from them? Do not tell me he wrote of pagan times; it is a writer's duty to make the world better, and—"

"And justice is a virtue independent of time or place," Mrs. Montagu finished for him. "So you have said before. But must there be a lesson in faeries?"

The writer's eyebrows drew together sharply. "There can be no excuse for them," Johnson said, "if they serve not a moral purpose."

Galen found himself on his feet again, with no sense of transition, and his glass of punch clutched so tightly in his hand he feared the delicate glass would shatter. "Why, sir, you might as well say there can be no excuse for a tree, or a sunset, or a—a *human,* if they serve not a moral purpose!"

Johnson's white eyebrows rose. "Indeed there is not. The moral purpose of a human is to struggle against sin and seek out God, to redeem himself from the Fall. As for trees and sunsets, may I refer you to the Holy Bible, most particularly the Book of Genesis, wherein it tells us how the Lord created the day and the night—and therefore, we may presume, the transition between them—and also trees; and these are the stage upon which He put His most beloved creation, which is that human previously mentioned. But show to me, if you will, where the Bible speaks of faeries, and their place in God's plan."

While Galen sputtered, searching for words, he added— almost gently—"If, indeed, such creatures exist at all, which I find doubtful in the extreme."

Heat and chill washed Galen's body in alternating waves, so that he trembled like a leaf in the wind. "Not all things," he managed, "that exist in the world, are laid out in scripture. But how can anything be that is not a part of God's plan?"

Somehow Johnson managed to convey both disgust and delight, as if appalled at the triviality of the topic, but pleased that Galen had mustered an argument in its defense. "Just so. Even the very devils in Hell serve His plan, by tempting mankind to his baser nature, and therefore rendering meaningful the exercise of his free will. But if you wish to persuade me regarding faeries, Mr. St. Clair, you will have to do better than to hide behind divine ineffability."

He wished for *something* to hide behind. Johnson had the air of a hunter merely waiting for the pheasant to break cover, so he could shoot it down. Oh, if only this debate had not come so *soon*! Galen was new to the Bluestocking Circle; he scarcely had his feet under him. Given more time and confidence, he would have defended his ideals without fear of ridicule. But here he was, a newcomer facing a man twice his age and twice his size, with all the weight of learning and reputation on Dr. Johnson's side.

To flee would only invite contempt, though. Galen was aware of his audience—not just Johnson, but Mrs. Vesey and Mrs. Montagu, Mr. Stillingfleet, and all the other ladies, waiting with great enjoyment for his next move. And others, not present, who deserved his best attempt. Choosing his words carefully, Galen said, "I would say that faeries exist to bring a sense of wonder and beauty into life, that lifts the spirit and teaches it something of transcendence."

"Transcendence!" Johnson barked a laugh. "From something called Mustardseed?"

"There is also Titania," Galen countered, flushing. "Faeries must have their lower classes as well, just as our own society has its farmers and sailors, tradesmen and laborers, without whom the gentry and nobility would have no legs to stand upon."

Johnson snorted. "So they must—if they existed at all. But this has been nothing more than a pretty exercise of the intellect, Mr. St. Clair. Faeries live only in peasant superstition and the inferior works of Shakespeare, where their only purpose is silly diversion."

Mrs. Montagu saved him. Galen didn't know what words would have leapt from his mouth had she not spoken, but the lady brought up *Macbeth,* and diverted Dr. Johnson onto the topic of witches, where he was only too happy to go.

Freed from the transfixion of the great writer's gaze, Galen sagged weakly back onto his chair. Sweat stood out on his brow, until he blotted it dry with a handkerchief. Under the guise of replenishing his punch—for these informal evenings, there was nothing stronger to drink, nor any servants to fill the glasses—he went to the side table, away from watching eyes.

But not away from Mrs. Vesey, who followed him. "I am so sorry, Mr. St. Clair," she murmured, this time taking care not to be overheard. "He is a very great man, but also a very great windbag."

"I came so near to saying too much," he told her, hearing the anguish in his own voice. "It would be so easy to prove him wrong—"

"On one count, perhaps," Mrs. Vesey said. "He will argue moral purposes until they nail his coffin shut, and then go up to Heaven to argue some more. But you would never betray that secret—no more than would I."

Even to say that much was dangerous. Of those gathered in this room, only they two knew the truth. Perhaps in time, a few others could be trusted with it; indeed, that was why Galen had come here, to see if any might. Instead he found Dr. Johnson, who made Galen long to blurt out the words burning within his heart.

There are faeries in the world, sir, more terrible and glorious than you can conceive, and I can show them to you—for they live among us here in London.

Oh, the fierce joy of being able to fling it in the other man's teeth—but it would do no good. Dr. Johnson would think him deranged, and though seeing would convince him, it would also be an unconscionable betrayal of trust. Faerie-kind lived hidden for a reason. Christian faith such as the writer showed could wound them deeply, as could iron, and other things of the mortal world.

Galen sighed and set down his glass, turning to glance over his shoulder at the rest of the room. "I had hoped to find congenial minds here. Not men like him."

Mrs. Vesey laid her hand on his velvet-clad arm. *Sylph,* her friends called her, and in the gentle light of the candles she looked like one, as if no particle of matter weighed down her being. "Mr. St. Clair, you are letting your impatience run away with you. I promise you, such minds exist, and we shall speak with them in due time."

Time. She spoke of it with the placid trust of a woman who had survived her childbearing years, to whom God might grant another two or three decades of life. Mrs. Vesey attributed Galen's impatience to his youth, thinking it merely the headlong rush of a man scarcely twenty-one, who has not yet learned that all things must happen in their season.

She did not understand that a season would come, very soon, when all this tranquility might be destroyed.

But that was another secret he could not betray. Mrs. Vesey knew of faeries; one called on her every week for gossip. But she knew little of their history, the myriad of secret ways in which they touched the lives of mortal men, and she knew nothing of the threat that faced them.

Already it was 1757. With every passing day, the comet drew closer, bringing with it the Dragon of the Great Fire. And when that enemy returned, the ensuing battle might well spill over into the streets of mortal London.

He could not tell her that. Not while standing in this elegant room, surrounded by the beautiful luxuries of literature and conversation and chairs upholstered in Chinese silk. All he could do was search for allies: others who, like him, like Mrs. Vesey, could stand between the two worlds, and perhaps find a way to make them both safe.

Mrs. Vesey was watching him with concerned eyes, hand still on his elbow. He smiled at her with as much hope as he could muster, and said, "Then by all means, Mrs. Vesey, acquaint me with others here. I trust you will not steer me wrong."

Tyburn, Westminster: September 30, 1757

Irrith often claimed, with perfect honesty, to cherish the unmediated presence of nature. Sunlight and starlight, wind and snow, grass and the storied forests of England; these were, in her innermost heart, her home.

At moments like this, though, ankle-deep in cold mud and drizzling rain, she had to admit that nature also had its unpleasant face.

She wiped the draggled strands of her auburn hair from her eyes and squinted ahead through the darkness. That *might* be light on the horizon—not just the scattered glow of a candlelit house here and there, but the massed illumination of Westminster, and beyond it, the City of London itself.

Or she might be imagining it.

The sprite sighed and pulled her boot free of the sucking mud. She was a Berkshire faerie at heart; her home was the Vale, and though she'd spent some years in the city, she'd left it long ago—and for good reason. Yet it was so easy to forget when Tom Toggin showed up, with all his persuasive arguments. She could take over his return journey; let the hob spend time with his cousins in the rustic comforts of the Vale, and relieve her own boredom with the excitement of London. It sounded like such a fine idea when he said it, especially when he offered bribes.

Maybe he'd known what awaited her on the road. The rain started just after she left, and accompanied her all the way from Berkshire.

As she walked, Irrith entertained herself with a vision of stumbling onto some farmer's front step, drenched and pathetic, begging shelter from the night. The farmer would aid

her, and in exchange she'd bless his family for nine genera-
tions—no, that was a bit much, for mere rain. Three genera-
tions, from him to his grandchildren. And they would tell tales
for the remaining six, of the faerie traveler their ancestor had
saved, of how magic had touched their lives for one brief
night.

Irrith sighed. More like the farmwife would screech and
call her "devil." Or they would stare at her, the whole farm
family of them, wondering what strange creature had come
to their door, and what she could possibly want from them.

She knew she was being unfair. Country folk had not forgotten the fae; the burden she carried was proof of that. But
whether Westminster was on the horizon or not, she was near-
ing the city, and she didn't have much faith in their knowledge
of their proper duties toward faerie-kind.

How long had it been, since she last saw London? Irrith
tried to count, then gave up. The time didn't matter. Mortals
changed so rapidly, especially in the city; whether she was
gone for six months or six years, they were sure to have invented strange new fashions in her absence.

She hitched the sack Tom had given her higher on one
shoulder. Yes, those were definitely lights ahead, and something looming in the center of the road. Could that possibly
be the Tyburn gallows? The triangular frame looked familiar,
but she didn't remember there being so many houses near it.
Ash and Thorn, how big had the city *grown*?

A rustle in the hedgerow to her left was her only warning.

Irrith dove flat against the mud as a black shape burst toward her. Its leap carried it clear over, so that it skidded and
went down in the muck. A black dog, she saw as she scrambled to her feet. And not an ordinary hound, someone's mas-
tiff escaped from its keeper; this was a padfoot or skriker,
a faerie in the shape of a dog.

And he was not there to welcome her back to London.

The dog lunged forward, and Irrith dodged. But she realized
her mistake as she went: the beast wasn't aiming for her. His
jaws closed around the oiled cloth of the satchel she carried,
and dragged it free of the mud.

Irrith snarled. Her blossoming fear died beneath the boot

of fury; she had *not* hauled that bag all the way from Berkshire in the rain just to lose it to a padfoot. She threw herself forward and landed half on the creature's back. His feet splayed under the unexpected weight, and down they both went, into the mud again. Irrith grabbed an ear and yanked mercilessly. The black dog snarled and tried to bite her; but she was on his back, and now he'd lost the bag. The sprite snatched at the strap, and quite by accident managed to kick her opponent in the head as she slid across the ground. He shook his head with a whimper, then lunged at her again, and this time she was flat on her back with no way to defend herself.

Just before the beast's massive jaws could close around her leg, a sound broke through the patter of the rain, that Irrith had never thought she would be grateful to hear: church bells.

The black dog howled and fell back, writhing. But the peals broke harmlessly over Irrith, and so she seized her advantage, and the bag; clutching it in her filthy hands, she aimed herself at the Tyburn gallows and ran.

By the time the bells stopped, she was well among the houses that now crowded the once rural road. Irrith slowed, panting for breath, feeling her heart pound. Would the dog track her here? She doubted it; too much risk of someone hearing the disturbance and coming out to investigate. And now the other faerie knew she was protected, as he was not.

Then again, Irrith would have said if asked that no local faerie would dream of assaulting a fellow on the road, so close to his Queen's domain. A mortal, perhaps, but not a sprite like her.

Perhaps he wasn't local. But then what was he doing on the Tyburn road, waiting for her to pass with the delivery from the Vale?

It was a good question. She knew the fae of London had their problems, but she might have underestimated them. How much had changed here, besides the landscape?

She hadn't thought to ask Tom Toggin. Unless she felt like walking all the way back to Berkshire—past the black dog who might still be hunting her—the only way to answer that

question was to continue onward, and present herself, looking like a rat drowned in mud, to the Queen of the Onyx
Court.

The Onyx Hall, London: September 30, 1757

The crowded and unfashionable environs of Newgate, in the
central City of London, were an unlikely destination for a
gentleman so late at night, but so long as Galen paid the chair-
men, they had no reason to ask questions. With the rain finally ended, they deposited him at the front of a pawnbroker's,
closed for the night, and went on their way. Once they were
well out of sight, Galen tiptoed around the corner, trying and
failing to protect the shoes and black silk stockings Mrs.
Montagu had derided, into a narrow alley.

The door he sought stood in the back wall of the pawnbroker's, and if anyone noticed it—which they should not—they
no doubt assumed it let into the cramped room where the
shopkeeper stored wares he could not fit in the display out
front. Instead, it admitted Galen to a tiny alcove barely large
enough for him to squeeze into and still shut the door behind
him. Standing in that stifling space, he murmured, "Downward," and felt the floor drop away.

It was a vertiginous feeling, no matter how often he experienced it. Galen always tensed, expecting a bruising impact,
and he always touched down as lightly as a feather. He would
have preferred a more ordinary staircase. But with that word,
he shifted from the ordinary world into one that was anything
but.

His feet settled onto a roundel of black marble, and cool
light bloomed around him. The chamber in which he now
stood was a lofty dome—nothing to the soaring heights of St.
Paul's Cathedral, but it felt so after the confines of the alcove
above. The walls formed slender ribs that seemed inadequate
to the weight, and no doubt they were; something other than
the architect's art kept the shadowed ceiling up.

It was far from the greatest wonder here.

Country folk still told tales of faerie realms hidden away in hollow hills, but few if any would expect to find one beneath the City of London. So far as Galen knew, the Onyx Hall was unique; nowhere else in Britain, or possibly in the entire world, did fae live so close with mortal kind. Yet here they had a palace that was a city unto itself, crowded with bedchambers and gardens, dancing halls and long galleries of art, all protected against the hostility of the world above. It was a mirror of that world, casting a strange and altered reflection, and one that only a select few could enter.

Galen sighed to see the muddy track he left behind as he stepped clear of the roundel. He knew that if he left the chamber and came back a minute later, he would find the dirt gone; there were unseen creatures here, more efficient than the most dedicated servant, who seemed to treat the slightest mess as a personal affront. Or they would if they had any sense of self; as Galen understood it, they had very few thoughts at all, scarcely more than the faerie lights that lined the delicate columns along the walls. Still, he wished for a boot-scraper on which to clean his feet, so he would not trail bits of mud around so miraculous a place.

No help for it. Galen was about to abandon his concerns and proceed, when a sudden swirl of air tugged at the hem of his cloak.

Another figure descended from the aperture in the ceiling, dropping swiftly before floating to a halt on the roundel. Galen's own muddy prints were obliterated by an enormous smear as the dripping and filthy figure shifted, slipped, and landed unceremoniously on his backside.

"Blood and *Bone*!" the figure swore, and the voice was far too high to be male. Galen leapt forward, reflexively offering his hand, and promptly ruined his glove when the newcomer took the assistance to rise.

That she was a faerie, he could be certain; the delicacy of her hand—if not her speech—made anything else unlikely. But he could discern little more; she seemed to have rolled in the mud for sport, though some of it had subsequently been washed off by the rain. Her hair, skin, and clothes were one

indeterminate shade of brown, in which her eyes made a startling contrast. They held a hundred shades of green, shifting
and dancing as no human irises would.

She in turn seemed quite startled by him. "You're *human*!"
she said, peering at him through the dripping wreck of her
hair.

What polite answer could a gentleman make to that? "Yes, I
am," he said, and bent to pick up the satchel she had dropped.

The faerie snatched it from him, then grimaced. "Sorry.
Someone has already tried to take this from me once tonight. I'd rather carry it myself, if you don't mind."

"Not at all," Galen said. Sighing in regret, he pulled off the
ruined glove and the clean one both, dropping them to the
floor. The unseen servants might as well take those, too, when
they came to mop this up. "May I escort you to your chambers? This marble is treacherous for wet feet."

He thought she might be a sprite, under all that mud; she
didn't carry herself with the courtly grace of an elfin lady.
Slinging the bag over her shoulder, she sat down again—this
time deliberately—and pulled off her dripping boots, followed by her stockings. The feet beneath were incongruously
pale, and as delicate as her hands. She set them down on a
clean patch of floor, then levered herself to her feet. "I'll
drip," she said, making a futile effort to wring out the hem of
her coat, "but it's better than nothing."

Her efforts with the coat revealed a pair of knee breeches
beneath. Galen suppressed a murmur of shock. Fae viewed human customs, including notions of proper dress, as entertaining diversions they copied or ignored as they pleased. And he
supposed knee breeches more practical in this weather; had
she been wearing skirts, she would not have been able to move
for all the sodden weight. "Still, please allow me. I would be a
lout if I abandoned you in such a state."

The sprite took up her bag once more and sighed. "Not to
my chambers; I don't believe I have any, unless Amadea's
kept them for me all this time. But you can take me to see the
Queen."

This time the murmur escaped him. "The Queen? But
surely—this mud—and you—"

She drew herself up to her full height, which brought her muddy hair to the vicinity of his chin. "I am Dame Irrith of the Vale of the White Horse, knighted by the Queen herself for services to the Onyx Court, and I assure you—Lune will want to see me, mud and all."

The hour was late, but that scarcely mattered to the inhabitants of the Onyx Hall, for whom the presence or absence of the sun above made little difference. This, after all, was London's shadow: a subterranean faerie palace, conjured from the City itself, where neither sun nor moon ever shone.

Which meant, unfortunately, that people were around to see the unlikely progress of Irrith and the young man at her side. She carried herself defiantly, ignoring them all, and telling herself it wouldn't help much if she *did* go in search of a bath first; given the tangled layout of the Onyx Hall, she would pass as many folk on her way there as she would going to see the Queen. At least the observers were common subjects, not the courtiers whose biting wit would find her disheveled state an easy target. They bowed themselves out of her way, and stepped carefully over her muddy trail once she passed.

Her intention was to go first to the Queen's chambers, in hopes of finding her there, but something stopped her along the way: the sight of a pair of elf-knights standing watch on either side of two tall, copper-paneled doors. Members of the Onyx Guard, both of them, and as such they owed salutes to only two people in the whole of the court.

They saluted the young man at her side. "Lord Galen."

Lord— Too late, Irrith realized the bows on the way here had not been for her. Of course they hadn't—how long since she'd been in the Onyx Hall? And who would recognize her beneath the drying shell of mud? Turning to the gentleman, she said accusingly, "You're the Prince of the Stone!"

He blushed charmingly and muttered something half-intelligible about having forgotten his manners. More likely, Irrith thought, he was too self-conscious to bring it up. New, no doubt. Yes, she remembered hearing something about a new Prince. The Queen's mortal consorts came and went, as mortals so often did, and this one clearly hadn't been in his position long enough to grow accustomed to anyone calling him "Lord." She pitied him a little. To be consort to a faerie queen, living proof of her pledge to exist in harmony with the mortal world, was no small burden.

"Irrith?" That came from the guard on the right. Dame Segraine peered at her, pike drifting to one side.

"Yes." Irrith shifted uncomfortably. If Segraine and Sir Thrandin were on watch at this door, then it meant the Queen was on the other side of it. Irrith couldn't remember what room lay beyond, but it wasn't Lune's chambers, where she'd have some hope of a private audience, or at least one with only a few ladies in attendance. Common sense said she should wait.

Common sense, however, was for hobs and other such careful creatures. "I have something for the Queen—two things, in truth. Both of them important. The Prince, being a gentleman, offered to escort me."

Segraine eyed her dubiously. The lady knight had always been one of Irrith's closest friends among the fae of the Onyx Court, but she cared more about propriety than the sprite bothered to. "You'll ruin the carpet," she said.

Which was, Irrith had to admit, more than a simple matter of propriety. In the Vale, the "carpets" were of ground ivy and wild strawberries, which did not mind a little dirt. Here, they were likely to be embroidered with seed pearls or some other foolishness. She settled the matter by stripping off her coat and wringing the last of the water from her hair onto the damp heap of cloth. "Give me a handkerchief to wipe my feet, and I'll be safe enough."

Galen averted his eyes with another furious blush, and Segraine's fellow guard was staring. Irrith had to admit she'd done it on purpose; she had a reputation in the court for being at best half-civilized, and it amused her to live up to it.

Or down to it, one might rather say.

Standing barefoot on the marble, in nothing more than a damp pair of knee breeches and a linen shirt, she had to struggle not to shiver. Then a square of white lace appeared in her vision: a handkerchief, offered by the Prince, who still would not look directly at her. Irrith dried her feet, looked ruefully at the dirty lace, and scrubbed a little at the bottoms of her breeches to discourage further dripping. The Prince was hardly going to take the handkerchief back after that, so she deposited it gently atop her filthy coat and said, "I'm sure someone can return that after it's been cleaned. May I see the Queen now?"

"You'd best," Segraine said, "before you scandalize Lord Galen any further." She knocked at the door. After a moment, it cracked open, and she conferred in a brief whisper with someone beyond. Irrith could hear noise: the lively murmur of conversation, and a clinking she couldn't identify. Then Segraine nodded and swung the door wider, and the usher on the other side announced, "The Prince of the Stone, and Dame Irrith of the Vale!"

Galen offered his arm, and together they went in.

Irrith cursed her choice the moment she walked inside. What purpose that chamber had served before, she couldn't recall; but now it held a long table well filled with silver and crystal and porcelain dishes, and well lined with the favored courtiers of Lune's realm. A formal dinner, and Irrith in her bare feet and damp shirt, come to face the Queen of the Onyx Court.

Who sat in a grand pearl chair at the head of the table, eyebrows raised in honest surprise. Diamonds and gems of starlight glittered across the stomacher of Lune's dress, brilliant against the midnight blue of her gown. Her silver hair was swept up into a flawless coiffure, crowned by a small sapphire circlet. Even had Irrith been dressed in her finest, Lune would have made her feel shabby, and the sprite was far from fine. If she could have fallen through the floor right then, she would have done it.

But the Onyx Hall did not oblige her with a pit, and so she had to walk forward, following the guidance of Galen's arm. Past the seated ranks of the courtiers, elf-lords and elf-ladies, and the ambassadors of other faerie courts, down the length of the impossibly long table, to a respectful distance from

Lune's chair, where Irrith dropped to one knee while Galen went forward and kissed the Queen's hand.

"Dame Irrith." Lune's voice, silver as the rest of her, was unreadable. "What brings you to London?"

There was nothing for it but to offer up the bag she still clutched. "Your Grace, I bring payment from Wayland Smith, King of the Vale of the White Horse. In exchange for two clocks, one telescope, and one thing I've forgotten the name of, as delivered by the hob Tom Toggin."

"An armillary sphere," Galen said, accepting the bag on behalf of the Queen. The oilcloth was as filthy as its bearer, but he opened the flap, wiped his hand clean on a second handkerchief, and pulled out a small loaf of bread.

Lune took it from him and inhaled the scent as if appreciating a fine wine. Irrith understood the impulse; one could almost smell the mortality in the bread. A peculiar heaviness, but it attracted as much as it repelled. In that simple mix of flour, water, and yeast lay safety from the human world, tithed to the fae by human hands. The food on her courtiers' plates was for pleasure, but this, in its way, was life: the ability to go among mortals without fear of iron or other banes.

Nodding, Lune handed the loaf back to Galen. He surrendered the bag to the usher, who took it in white-gloved hands and bowed his way out of the room. "We thank you, Dame Irrith," the Queen said, with just enough dryness to hint that she hadn't the faintest notion why Irrith had interrupted their dinner with a simple delivery.

Irrith wasn't about to admit she'd done it merely to live up to that rash declaration of her own importance. She glanced up enough to see that yes, everyone was watching her; the Lord Keeper, Valentin Aspell, had his thin mouth curled in disdain. "I have something further to tell you, that maybe should be said in private."

"Very well," Lune said after a moment's consideration, and rose. Chairs slid back all down the room as her guests rose in echo. "Please, continue your meal. Lady Amadea, Lord Galen, if you please."

Galen waved one hand at Irrith, and she followed him,

Lune, and the Lady Chamberlain into an adjoining room. It seemed to be a parlor of sorts, with chairs grouped for intimate conversation, and the carpet—while lacking in seed pearls—was luxuriously soft against Irrith's feet. Amadea murmured a brief charm at the door, so their words wouldn't be overheard by those in the next room, and then they were alone.

Lune seated herself. She made no gesture for anyone else to do so, but in this more private setting, her expression showed greater warmth. "Irrith. This is an unexpected pleasure; I had no idea you were returning to London. Amadea, if her state bothers you, then have a cloth brought to protect the carpet."

Amadea went to the far door as Irrith curtsied, feeling a proper clown. "Tom Toggin convinced me to bring Wayland's payment back for him. What in the name of most ancient Mab has been going on in this place, your Majesty? There's houses out by Tyburn gallows, and the River Fleet has vanished!"

Amusement danced in Lune's silver eyes. "The Fleet is still there, just underground. They built a culvert over it, oh, how long ago, Galen?"

The Prince thought it over. "The most recent stretch? Not long after I was born. Perhaps nineteen years? The river can still be seen, Dame Irrith, from Ludgate to the Thames."

Which gave her some idea of how long she'd been gone. "And how does Blacktooth Meg feel about that?"

Lune's amusement faded. "As you might expect. River hags are not pleasant creatures under the best of circumstances, and these are rather worse."

Irrith had seen the hideous creature once before, well before the culverting of the river. Shuddering, she said, "I'm just as glad I didn't have to cross her, then. But that isn't what I need to tell you—" A hob popped through the door, interrupting her, and laid down a piece of sturdy canvas, all but lifting Irrith's feet so the cloth could be placed more quickly. The carpet duly protected, she waited until the hob was gone, then said, "You almost didn't get that bread. A black dog ambushed me at Tyburn and tried to steal it."

"What?" The Queen came to her feet in a swift rustle of silk.

"I didn't roll in the mud for fun—madam." She added the courtesy address belatedly. Being in the Onyx Hall was bringing back the old manners she'd forgotten in the Vale. "He leapt out at me near the gallows, and tried to take the bag. Fortunately, Wayland gave me leave to take a bite of the bread when I neared London, so I could enter the City unharmed; the black dog wasn't so lucky. I escaped when the church bells rang."

Lune pressed one slender hand to her brow, then lowered it. "We do not begrudge you that grant from your King. Did you recognize the dog?"

Irrith shook her head. "Maybe if I'd seen his other face. But it was raining; I can't even tell you what kind he was— padfoot, skriker, or what."

The Queen exchanged a glance with her Prince. Irrith didn't miss Galen's helpless shrug. New, indeed. But there was something more in his manner, that she didn't have the time to puzzle out; she didn't want to compound her rudeness by staring at the Prince. Not in front of Lune.

Well, she'd done her duty, handing over the mortal bread the Onyx Court relied on, and telling of the one who'd tried to steal it. Few people in the vicinity of London tithed bread or milk to the fae any longer; Lune had to trade human curiosities to more distant courts, in exchange for their surplus. Those fae with the sense to live in places less riddled with iron and churches had much less need for protection.

But Irrith knew it didn't end there. Nineteen years since the Fleet was culverted, the Prince said. Tom had hinted at the passage of time, but Irrith had refused to ask for a number. Now she couldn't hold the question in. "Your Majesty—how long until the comet gets here?"

The Queen sank into her chair, as if suddenly weary, and gestured for her Prince to answer. Galen said, "We don't know exactly. 'Getting here' . . . we know the time of the comet's perihelion, but not the point at which the Dragon will make its leap."

What Irrith knew about astronomy would fit into an acorn cap, so she merely rephrased her question. "How much time do you have left?"

"A year and a half," he said. "Maybe less."

She shivered. *So little time.* They'd had more than fifty years, when the seer's warning first came. Where had it all gone?

"It will be enough," Lune whispered. She sounded as if she believed it, and perhaps she did; the Queen of the Onyx Court had faced down challenges before. Her face, however, was more than usually pale. Irrith couldn't imagine what it must be like, living under such a threat for decades, counting the time like a mortal. Knowing that it was running out. Fifty years of that could, it seemed, sap the life from even a faerie queen.

Seeing that weakness, even for a moment, made Irrith uneasy. "With your permission, madam," the sprite said, "I should like to clean myself up now. I didn't want to delay getting that bread to you—"

"I appreciate your care," Lune said, straightening in her chair, either banishing or hiding her weariness. "Amadea will provide you with a suitable chamber. Unless you intended to return to the Vale?"

Irrith thought about the culverted Fleet, and the houses around Tyburn, and the court under the patronage of a new and inexperienced Prince. So many changes. And little more than a year until the comet returned, possibly bringing this all to an end. "I will stay, at least a while."

"Good." Lune smiled, but it was a tense thing, carrying a tremendous weight of care. "This court needs all the friends it can find."

When the muddy and half-clad sprite was gone with Lady Amadea, leaving Galen alone with the Queen, Lune rose once more. Instead of returning to the dining room, though, she went to the fireplace, and laid her hand upon the stone.

"So," she said, her voice musical and quiet. "How did your evening go?"

Galen wished Dr. Johnson could see her now, shining with all the regal glory so absent from Britain's Hanoverian King.

There was transcendence in the polished gleam of her hair, and a portraitist might have wept for the opportunity to render her serene likeness on canvas. She was the reason he dwelt between worlds, the hidden Prince of a hidden court—despite the threat they faced.

A threat that was never far from anyone's mind. "Pleasantly, but not productively," Galen was forced to admit. "We may be able to find other allies among them, open-minded gentlemen, or ladies like Mrs. Vesey. But their interest lies primarily in literature, art, and similar topics; I doubt anyone there can offer much help. Not against a Dragon."

The word came out hushed. Lune's hand tightened along the edge of the mantel. A slender hand, long-fingered and pale—but all Galen had to do was look to its mate for a reminder of the danger they faced. A glove concealed the blackened, paralyzed claw of her left hand, the mark left upon her in battle with the Dragon of the Fire.

Her timeless face made it easy to forget that she was there when it happened, nearly a hundred years ago.

Distant history, for the city's mortal inhabitants. A few old half-timbered buildings still dotted the streets, past the margin of the Great Fire's reach, and the Monument near London Bridge commemorated the disaster. Beyond those few reminders, who gave thought to it now?

The fae did. No amount of time could dull their memories of those desperate, infernal days, struggling against a beast too powerful for them to kill. In the end, they could only imprison and exile it—and both, in time, had proved imperfect solutions.

The sight of Lune's gloved and ruined hand spurred Galen's determination. She would suffer no second wound from the Dragon; he would protect her from it.

Somehow.

He searched desperately for inspiration, and came up short. "Madam—surely fae know better than any mortal how to battle a creature like this. I'm told you had some weapon against it before—"

Her swift turn whisked her skirts out of her way. "We

did. And my first act, when Feidelm warned me the comet would return, was to seek it out again. I've spent decades chasing the possibility of some weapon, from one end of Europe to the other—Sweden, the Germanies, across the Mediterranean, my ambassadors asking everywhere for some means of destroying the Dragon. I would pay any price for a surety of doing so. So far, unfortunately, all we have are possibilities."

"But if you cannot kill it," Galen said, "with all the enchanted power at your command—what makes you think mere mortals can do better?"

He tried not to let the desperation through; it was contemptible of him to show it, especially when she had laid this great honor and great burden upon him, making him her Prince. But it fluttered in his throat, like a panicked bird trying to win free, and rattled his voice as he spoke.

Incredibly, Lune smiled. More emotions than he could name lived in that smile, but none of them were contempt. She said, "Everything of great import done in this place—*everything* that has made the Onyx Hall the wonder it is, and preserved it against threats—has been done by mortal and faerie-kind together. Without your people, we would not be here. So when I heard the Dragon was to return, my first thought was not of weapons. It was of the Prince at my side."

A Prince who had aged and passed away without ever finding an answer. And others had come after him, as the years marched in their inexorable course, all of them the bearers of Lune's trust, all of them—ultimately—failures.

Now it was Galen's turn, to carry that burden, and to fall beneath it.

I should never have agreed, he thought miserably, clenching his hands until his knuckles ached, *when she offered me the title. She deserves better.*

"I haven't the slightest idea," the Queen said, unaware of his dreary thoughts, "what meeting of worlds will save us this time. But I am certain it will need us both to do it. Whether it is some effect of the Onyx Hall's nature, or simply the consequence of my governance these centuries, that has always been the case. I will contribute what I can, and you will do the same, and out of that will come the answer."

She did not sound complacent; she had struggled against this question for too many years to be complacent. But the confidence in her voice gave Galen heart.

Though what my kind can do, when so few even believe in magic now . . .

His sudden inspiration must have produced an audible sound, for Lune raised her arching eyebrows. "Yes?"

"I," Galen said, and hesitated. "I don't know how this could be of help."

"We have tried everything that might be," she said, with a hint of weary amusement. "We might as well try the things that *can't* be."

It seemed thinner and weaker the longer he thought about it, but the Queen was waiting. Galen said, "Natural philosophy."

She didn't laugh, or dismiss it out of hand. It was something mortals could contribute, that fae knew little of: the rational understanding of the world, as achieved through observation and experimentation. Every day, new discoveries, sending beams of light into the dark mysteries of nature. It had warned them of their impending peril; perhaps it could also save them.

Lune followed the thought to its inevitable conclusion even as Galen did. If such knowledge were to aid them, there was but one place to seek it out. "The Royal Society," she said.

A fellowship of the most learned men in Britain, with allies all over Europe. Lune's growing smile made Galen's heart soar—until a new thought dragged it down once more. For him to gain entrée into the Royal Society, he would have to beg a favor of the last person to whom he wanted to owe a debt.

She knew it as well as he did. She said, "Can you get your father's assistance?"

I don't know. But he made himself smile, because this was what the Queen needed of him, her Prince, and he would pay any price she asked. "Yes, madam, I can."

Memory: September 12, 1682

In the ordinary way of things, night was the ideal time for sneaking and subterfuge. Honest men were in their beds, with only the occasional watchman to sound an alarm, and darkness provided a friendly veil against such eyes.

The Royal Observatory at Greenwich did not operate according to the ordinary rules of society. Here, men slept during the day, and woke at night to observe the stars and moon and the distant planets.

Which became something of a problem when others wished to use their instruments, in secret, without their permission.

But the Onyx Court played home to many creatures that took pride in their stealth. If it was strange for them to operate in sunlight, they adapted. They had good reason to wish for success in this undertaking. So they went to Greenwich in the light of day, and moved either disguised or unseen among the astronomers and clerks and servants who worked there, bearing with them tiny vials of crystal. In those vials lay the essences of faerie herbs, gathered from the gardens of the Onyx Hall, to prepare for the coming night.

The contents of the vials went into food, into wine, into the bitter coffee drink some of the men swore sharpened their wits and kept them alert during their vigils. One by one, the men of the observatory slept, and dreamt the dreams provided to them.

Lune reached the top of the hill as a puck bent to drip visions on the eyelids of the last sleeper, a man who had curled up on the grass at the foot of Flamsteed's great telescope. Behind her, three stocky yarthkins lugged a heavy crate up the slope. One man in his forties, hair thinning on top but still hale, wheezed theatrically as he staggered through the courtyard gate. "I swear it gets steeper every time."

"This is the last time you have to climb it, Jack." Lune stepped from the cobbled courtyard onto the grass, then stood gazing up at the telescope, and the stars beyond.

She could not see the one she sought. But that was what telescopes were for.

Jack Ellin, Prince of the Stone, nodded cheerfully. "Indeed. Either we exile this beast beyond the boundaries of the world—or it gets free and burns us all to ash. Either way, I won't have to climb the hill again."

For all his levity, he showed nothing but precision as he directed the various fae to their tasks. Once he'd taken the necessary sights through the telescope of the Astronomer Royal, he sent a few of his more agile assistants up the mast, where they unhooked the ropes that held the sixty-foot tube in place. Others pried open the crate, revealing another, shorter telescope—this one unlike any other in the world.

Lune paced impatiently while her subjects rigged this one to the mast and set up a platform for them to stand next to its eyepiece. Jack ignored her restlessness. Hauling their telescope hither and yon would have jarred the mirrors from their careful alignments, and any error in that respect could lead to disaster. Under his direction, a delicate-fingered sprite tapped them into place, first the great, then the little.

At last he said, "We're ready."

"Are you sure?" Lune asked.

His wry face reached for, but did not quite achieve, carelessness. "Am I sure that an inverted model of a revolutionary design of telescope, crafted out of faerie wood and faerie metal, will succeed at focusing and directing the spirit of a Dragon through the aether and onto a comet so far distant it can only barely be seen with the aid of the most advanced astronomical equipment in England? Of course, your Grace. I would never suggest it otherwise."

Despite the gravity of their task, Lune smiled. But Jack knew the danger quite well, and so he added, too quietly for the others to hear, "What will we do if this fails?"

Lune's left hip carried the London Sword, the central piece of the Onyx Court's royal regalia. She touched its hilt with her good fingers. "I yet have another hand. And the prison might hold a while longer."

Both of them turned to watch the approach of a second crate, this one of hawthorn. Once it was laid in the grass at their feet, all the fae retreated, leaving Queen and Prince alone at the foot of the telescope. All of them drew weapons—as if they would do much good. Jack offered his arm to Lune with a courtly bow, assisting her up onto the platform.

Then he knelt and lifted the top from the hawthorn crate.

Inside that shielding wood lay a small box of black iron, unadorned save for a flame-marked shield on its lid. It had been cold the first time he touched it, sixteen years ago. Now gloves barely protected his hands from the heat. The prison into which they had forced the spirit of the Great Fire of London could not hold it forever. The strange enchantments of the iron were weakening under its power.

He prayed—silently, so the fae would not hear—that this would work. Even if Lune sacrificed her other hand to trap the Dragon once more, it would leave them in hopeless straits. They could not kill the beast, and it seemed they could not imprison it, either. Exile was their only remaining option.

Jack lifted the box free and climbed up to join Lune next to the eyepiece. "Let us hope," she said, "that Isaac Newton is as great a mind as you say."

"He is," Jack promised her, and opened the box.

A radiance like the heart of the sun blazed forth, into the waiting eyepiece. An ordinary telescope gathered up the faint light of space and brought it in small to the human eye; this one, adapted from the reflective design of Professor Newton, took the intense light of the Dragon's spirit and sent it out into the void. That unbearable blaze struck the flawless craftsmanship of the mirrors and ricocheted outward, in an unerring line, straight to the bearded star Flamsteed had been observing these many months.

Jack could hear nothing past the silent roar of the Dragon. Lune might have been screaming; so might he. But then the light was gone, and the box crumbled to rust in his hands, blistered even beneath the leather of his gloves.

And Lune swung the London Sword, cutting the ropes that held the telescope in position. It fell to the ground, severing the last link between the Dragon and this place.

In the aftermath, the only sound was the steady wind off the Thames.

Lune whispered, "It worked."

Jack looked upward. He thought he could discern something in the sky, that had not been visible before: the departing comet, glowing unnaturally bright. Then it faded, and was lost to his eye.

The Dragon of the Fire was gone.

The Onyx Hall, London: October 1, 1757

When she first came to the Onyx Hall, Irrith had found the subterranean palace an incomprehensible maze, through which she could follow only a few memorized paths.

In the century since, that opinion had not changed much.

But there was one chamber to which she could find her way blindfolded, for she'd fallen in love with it the first time she stepped through one of its arching entrances. There were many small gardens tucked into odd corners of the Onyx Hall; this, the night garden, was the grandest by far. Here the Walbrook, London's long-forgotten stream, wound through grassy plots and shadowing trees. Here flowers bloomed, in changeless defiance of the seasons above, blossoms drawn from both the mortal world and the deeper reaches of Faerie. It wasn't pure nature—with its fountains and charming pathways, the night garden was more like a poet's notion of the countryside—but Irrith loved it nonetheless.

And so when she left her chamber after a fitful rest, it was to the night garden that her disconsolate steps took her.

She glanced up as she entered the green, breathing space, to see the faerie lights twinkling in artificial night above. Sometimes they shaped themselves into patterns that reflected the current mood of the court, but at present they drifted aimlessly, forming no identifiable shape.

Irrith sighed and walked on. Then she saw something ahead that lifted her spirit, and provoked her into a run.

A pavilion stood near one end of the night garden, surrounded by a wide swath of grass, and a figure moved within that should be—was—utterly out of place in the airless stone galleries of the Onyx Hall. Hooves clopped a startled tattoo against the polished boards of the pavilion floor as Irrith vaulted the ramp, and then a pair of arms caught her at the apex of her leap.

"Ktistes!" she cried in delight. "I thought you had gone!"

"That was my intent," the centaur said, setting her down gently. "But her Majesty asked me to stay. It has been many a long year, Dame Irrith."

"Fifty, I think. I lost count in the Vale."

Ktistes laughed. "And you so often beneath the stars, but so rarely watching their dance."

He gestured upward as he said it, not to the ceiling of the night garden, with its false constellations, but to the roof of his pavilion. The structure was new, by the standards of the Onyx Hall; Lune had it built following the Great Fire, for Ktistes's use, when he came from Greece to help repair the damage done to the Onyx Hall. The centaur cared nothing for shelter—he was happy to sleep on the soft grass of the garden—but the roof was valuable to him. It had once been the ceiling of some chamber elsewhere in the Hall, and the chips of starlight set into its surface moved in perfect reflection of the hidden sky above.

Irrith dismissed it with a wave of her hand. "Years. Why should I count them?"

"Only for the sake of your friends, who regret your absence. But you thought I was returning to Greece, and so I forgive you. Come, sit with me in the grass." Ktistes descended the short ramp into the garden.

Next to him, Irrith felt tiny. His sturdy horse body, a gray so dark it was almost black, was as tall as she; his olive-skinned human torso towered over her. But he folded his white-socked forelegs down onto the grass, and she sat a little distance away, and then it was not so bad.

Irrith said, "Amadea told me my chamber is gone. Not 'given to someone more important than you'—*missing*. Ktistes, what's happening here?"

One lock of his black hair, curled in an old style, fell forward as he bowed his head. "Ah. The Onyx Hall is fraying."

"It's *what*?"

"The wall," Ktistes said. "That surrounds—or rather surrounded—the City of London, separating it from the towns beyond, that are now part of the city as a whole. The mortals have been tearing it down, because it impedes the flow of their carts and riders. A portion near Bishopsgate was removed not long after you left, and when she saw its effect, the Queen asked me to stay."

Irrith felt obscurely as if she'd betrayed the Onyx Hall—as if her departure had introduced that crack. "Without the wall, the palace falls apart?"

The centaur made a gesture with his hands, that seemed to indicate it was complicated. "The wall is the boundary of the Onyx Hall. When the boundary fragments, the edges of the fabric begin to fray. But because the reflection is not direct, the fraying occurs in unexpected places—such as your old chamber."

She had liked that chamber; its pillars were carved in the fashion of trees, with leaves of green agate. She wanted it *back*. "So mend it."

"I am trying," the centaur said, with a touch of grimness.

He had repaired the palace entrances, after they burnt in the Fire. No faerie of the Onyx Court had been able to do it, until Lune finally sent an ambassador to Greece to ask for help. Ktistes, grandson—grandfoal?—of the wise centaur Kheiron, had done what they could not.

He could do this. He *had* to.

Her disconsolate mood was back, and worse. Rather than think about the Onyx Hall, Irrith diverted her attention to a more personal wound. "I even lost my cabinet."

Ktistes' strong white teeth flashed in an unexpected smile. "Do you think me so poor an architect, to be caught unawares by the disappearance of your chamber? Or so poor a friend, to let your prized possessions vanish with it?"

"You saved them?" Irrith leapt to her feet in hope.

"Yes, I did, little sprite. I will have them brought to your new quarters—what, you thought I kept them here, to clutter up my pavilion with all your odds and ends?" Ktistes laughed. "I've never understood your fascination with them."

"They're *mortal* odds and ends," Irrith said, dropping to the grass once more. She had little interest in the gems and fossils others kept in their cabinets of curiosities, but anything

made by humans was intriguing. Leaving her collection behind when she went to Berkshire had been a terrible mistake.
"Actual mortals are better, of course, but I can't lock them in
a drawer. On that topic—did you know this new Prince is in
love with the Queen?"

The centaur stilled, his profile as somber as one of the statues from his homeland. He said carefully, "We do not speak
of it."

"But you know."

"Everyone knows." Ktistes didn't have to tilt his head to
meet Irrith's gaze, even though she was standing. His dark
eyes were liquid, more like a horse's than a human's. "But no
one speaks of it. Lord Galen believes it a secret, known only
to his heart."

Irrith wrinkled her nose. Secret? Hardly, when Galen's eyes
followed Lune's every movement. "That won't end well."

Ktistes nodded, though he managed to make the gesture
equivocal. How *could* it end well? Fae rarely loved, and Lune
had already given her heart, a very long time ago. Galen
could pine after her all he pleased; it wouldn't win him anything. And though that was a story as old as the fae themselves,
it rarely led to anything good for the mortal.

It would, however, be interesting to watch. Love was something Irrith didn't understand, any more than she understood
mortality, but she found both fascinating: stories in cipher, of
which she could translate only fragments. And there was no
place in the world better suited to hearing those stories told
than the Onyx Hall, where fae lived unseen among mortals.

Or at least below them. Restlessness seized Irrith, a desire
to make use of the time she had. But she would need protection before she went above—and thanks to Tom's bribe, she
could afford to buy some. "Ktistes, who could I wheedle bread
out of?"

The centaur shook his curled head. "I have no part in that
trade, as you well know. It may be difficult, though; from
what I hear, people demand more than they once did in exchange."

Perhaps that was the reason for the black dog: some faerie

badly in debt to others, and desperate enough to risk attacking the courier. Despite Ktistes's discouraging words, Irrith bounced to her feet. "Then I'd best get started. I have fifty years' absence to make up for, after all, and I'm eager to get on with it. Shall I bring back anything for you?"

"A nice bundle of hay," Ktistes said gravely.

It was an old joke between them. Laughing, Irrith went in search of bread.

Leicester Fields, Westminster: October 1, 1757

The morning was far enough progressed that when Galen disembarked from his sedan chair, the sun had risen above the rooftops, spilling its excessively bright light into the open square of Leicester Fields. He winced and covered his eyes with one hand while he fumbled out coins for the chair-men, then stood for a moment as they picked up their burden and trotted off, hoping that fortitude might find him.

That proved to be an unwise choice. A disagreeable smell drifted from somewhere, and someone's housekeeper was haranguing a delivery boy with language more suitable to a Billingsgate fishwife. Swallowing back the sick feeling in his throat, Galen hurried down the narrow steps into the area of his family's townhouse, and through the door into the cellar.

Inside, someone made a startled noise, and there was a shadowy movement like a curtsy; when his vision cleared, he saw Jenny, with her arms full of linen. Galen tried to edge past her in the narrow corridor, but the maid curtsied again and said, "Beg pardon, sir—your father told us all to tell you. He wants to see you."

And knew his son's habits well enough to guess by what door Galen would come in. "Thank you, Jenny," he said, and abandoned his plan of creeping up the servants' staircase.

Edward was in his bedroom, laying aside newly polished pairs of shoes. When Galen entered, he rose, bowed, and said, "You look terrible."

"I feel terrible." Galen found his way to a chair by memory, and collapsed into it. "And that was *before* I heard Father wanted to see me."

"Someone else broke that to you, I see." Edward didn't bother to hide his relief. The elder St. Clair deplored the casual manner of his son's valet, but not enough to sack him; it was miracle enough that Edward had been in their household for more than a year, without wandering off in the usual manner of servants.

At least it seemed a miracle, to the outside observer. Galen knew why the fellow had become a footman in the St. Clair household, and why he stayed: Lune had sent him, after the passing of his previous master, the late Prince. Though not himself a faerie, Edward Thorne was the natural son of one of Lune's knights by a mortal woman, and as such was a perfect go-between for the two worlds.

It also meant Edward, unlike Galen's father, did not assume Galen had spent his night carousing in a Haymarket brothel. "Late night at court?" he asked, only a little too briskly, whisking the peruke from his master's head.

Galen leaned forward in the chair to let Edward slide the tightly fitted coat from his shoulders. "I only wish it were," he said. "No, for once Father's assumptions will be something like right: I spent my night drinking, and haven't slept."

His eyes were closed, but he heard the brief silence as Edward paused, before laying his coat aside and fetching a fresh shirt. "You don't sound as if you enjoyed yourself."

"I didn't." The strength he took from Lune's confidence had vanished like the morning dew after he left her presence. He'd sought inspiration in brandy, and not found it.

A cool glass pressed into his hand. Galen sniffed, eyes still closed. Water, carrying a dose of Dr. Taunton's Fortifying Drops. He drank the mixture down, sighed, and addressed himself to the washbasin, which Edward had just filled. It had the salutary effect of waking him, though the chill splash made his headache worse.

"He had his electrical treatment last night," Edward warned, helping Galen into another shirt. "But it doesn't seem to have taken well. It's been a devil of a morning already."

To that, there seemed no suitable response other than a groan.

But delaying would not help anything except the progress of his hangover, and so a short while later, with fresh clothes and wig alike to give him a semblance of dignity, Galen descended the stairs to his father's study, to beard the lion in his book-lined den.

Charles St. Clair had none of the appearance of a lion, being fat and gouty, with a somber black bagwig and a coat of brick red. He was in his most comfortable chair when Galen entered, with one shoeless foot propped up in front of him—a sure sign that his leg pained him. At the sound of the door, he did not look up from the ledger balanced on his other knee, but made Galen wait in silence for several long minutes, before finally clapping the ledger shut and fixing his son with a gimlet eye.

"When you are married," St. Clair said, biting off each word, "then you may keep the hours you please, and your wife will suffer the consequences—but while you still live under my roof, boy, you will behave like a civilized man. I won't have you creeping in the servants' entrance after cockcrow, after wasting your night in God knows what debauchery."

There was nothing Galen could say to this. He could hardly tell his father it was a faerie court, not a brothel, that occupied his hours, and no other response had done much good. Galen had tried them all. So he simply waited, head bowed, for his father to move past the opening pleasantries and into the reason for this summons.

St. Clair snorted in disgust. "Can't even speak up for yourself, just stand there like a spineless worm. I pity the woman saddled with you: she'll find herself with a wife, not a husband."

Marriage. Unease churned the medicine and lingering spirits in Galen's stomach. He should have guessed this might be his father's purpose. They scarcely talked, save on a small number of unwelcome topics. "I should not want to make myself a burden on any woman," he ventured to say, "until I was sure I could be worthy of her."

"Too bad for her, whoever she is." St. Clair creaked his way to his feet, grunting as his stockinged toes touched the floor, and went to his desk, where he dropped the ledger with a thud. "You will find yourself a wife, boy, and you will do it soon."

Galen flinched. That was even blunter than usual. "Sir—I cannot simply go through London, weighing women for their dowries, and make my offer when I find a purse heavy enough."

"Why not? The St. Clair name is a good one, even if its finances are somewhat more tattered. London throngs with rich men eager to marry their daughters into a better family. Your youth will hardly signify—some might consider it a selling point." St. Clair snorted again. "I dare say you can even find a pretty one, if you look hard enough."

The words came out before he could stop them. "And affection?"

His father didn't say anything; the silence was enough. Less than it could have been, in fact; the last time Galen had said anything of the sort, he'd been clouted over the ear for it. But he was not foolish enough to mistake the silence for any kind of softening on his father's part.

"I know," Galen whispered, staring at his shoes. "Affection doesn't enter into it; what matters is money." Cynthia was nearly twenty, and needed a dowry to attract a worthwhile husband; and behind her waited Daphne and Irene, with the same need. The burden fell to Galen, the eldest, and their only brother, to repair the family's finances.

Bitterness stung him. *Yes, it's my responsibility to repair them—as it was Father's to destroy them.*

That, at least, he managed to keep behind his teeth. The thought of Lune saved him from speaking: if he angered his father badly enough, he might be confined to Leicester Fields, and then he would be no use to the fae at all. But that was the source of his pain: how could he shackle himself to a wife— how could he shackle a young woman to *him*—when his heart was already given elsewhere?

Few men would see a problem with it. Men kept mistresses all the time, sometimes under the same roof as their wives; their name and their affection need not go to the same recipient. But Galen could not stomach the dishonesty, especially when his wife could never know of the second world he inhabited. And Lune . . . she would despise him for it.

It was hopeless, and Galen knew it. He could worship the faerie Queen until the sun grew cold, but he would never have her, neither as mistress nor wife. His mind could not even conceive of such an outcome. In which case, he must fill that void with thoughts of Cynthia, and Daphne, and Irene. However much he detested his father, he loved his sisters. If their futures depended on this sacrifice from him, then he must harden his resolve and do as his father bade.

St. Clair was awaiting his answer, with increasing disgust and impatience. Galen gritted his teeth, and prepared to embrace the black satisfaction of martyrdom.

But inspiration touched him as he opened his mouth. He'd come here with a purpose, one he almost forgot under his father's assault—and now he had a means of addressing it. "If I am to do this, sir, for you and for my sisters—then I must ask a favor in return."

A flush leapt up toward the edge of St. Clair's wig. "You are in no position to make demands, boy."

But he was; Galen could hardly be wed against his will. And he held a bargaining position now, that he hadn't foreseen when he came home this morning. "I don't ask much. Simply this: give me letters of introduction to your acquaintances in the Royal Society."

Now it was the eyebrows leaping upward. "What possible business could you have with them?"

His surprise was understandable. Galen enjoyed learning rather more than the next young gentleman, but he'd never shown any interest in his father's connection with the Royal Society. The truth was that the connection embarrassed him; Galen knew quite well that Charles St. Clair had bought himself a fellowship because he wanted the prestige and they wanted the money. This, of course, had been when the St. Clairs *had* money. But his father had never done much with the privilege, and neither had Galen. He said, "I cannot be certain of my business—not until I speak with men better able to advise me. But marriage, sir, is hardly the only way I can be of use to our family."

"You think to make your fortune with some kind of speculative venture?"

Why not? After all, that's how you destroyed yours. Galen again flung the thought of Lune between those words and his mouth, and lifted his hands with a faint smile, letting his father draw what conclusions he would.

St. Clair growled under his breath, then said, "I'll consider it. They're adjourned until November regardless. In the meantime, you can prove to me you're serious about your duty to this family. Start hunting a wife."

It was a miserable time to go looking; with the aristocracy and landed gentry departed to their country estates for the summer and autumn, London's social calendar offered few prospects for success. The St. Clairs only stayed because Aldgrange, their Essex estate, was too expensive to maintain for residence. "I can offer you a promise," Galen said, seeing a way to postpone his fate. "I'll make an offer to a suitable young lady before the end of the next Season. Will that suffice?"

His father regarded him with a cynical eye. "If you fail to make good on it, you'll suffer the consequences." The presentation of his back dismissed Galen. Suppressing a sigh, the young man headed for the door.

That gave him until early summer. If London's safety was achieved by then, did he dare defy the old man, and break his promise? But there was Cynthia to consider, and his younger sisters; he could not pay their dowries in faerie gold.

No, there was no escape to be had. In this, his father was right: he had a duty. *Come what may, I must find myself a wife.*

Central London: October 7, 1757

The clamor and stench of the city struck Irrith full in the face as she slipped out of a nonexistent gap between two buildings on Cloak Lane. She wrinkled her nose, but grinned despite her distaste. That was the smell of humanity, true enough, right down to their coal smoke and shit.

The street to either side of her teemed with a solid mass of people—none of whom noticed her sudden appearance, thanks to the enchantments that protected the Onyx Hall. A giant wagon sat at rest just to her right, its driver standing on the seat and swearing at whatever blocked his way. Things might change, but obscenity wasn't one of them: he insulted the offender's parentage, cleanliness, and sexual habits as his father and grandfather had done for ages before him.

Yet something seemed wrong. The street was full, but it didn't seem like day. The sprite glanced upward, trying to determine what time it was. Though Onyx Hall didn't stand outside of time as some faerie realms did, its unchanging gloom made it seem as if it did.

The sky above glowered with unnatural darkness. Heavy, smoke-stained clouds sat low in the air, but it wasn't merely an impending storm; the light had a strange quality, ominous and weird, like nothing she had ever seen before. Irrith couldn't even tell whether it was morning or afternoon.

Unease rippled down her spine. Around her, the city went about its business—but now she noticed that others shared her discomfort. They cast nervous glances skyward, or fixed their eyes upon their shoes, trying to ignore this upset to the natural order.

Frowning, she began to make her way along the street, ducking under a low-hanging shop sign and slipping into the stream of passersby where they eddied around the halted wagon. Despite pavements on either side of the street, and the ragged boys with their brooms at the crossings, her stockings and coat were spattered with mud before she went twenty paces; she had forgotten to think of pattens, when she put together the glamour that disguised her.

Up ahead, a knot of people stood talking, tin cups in their hands. These they seemed to have purchased from a shop crammed into a narrow alcove on the ground floor of a larger building. Upon drawing close, Irrith caught a surprising evergreen scent.

"Drunk for a penny!" the man behind the counter called out, when he saw her looking. "A small price, to lose your cares."

Irrith generally found it simpler to look like a man, when she went above, but she hadn't bothered to make it a gentleman. Most of the fellows standing about were rough sorts, who probably had little more than a penny to spend. Irrith fished a leaf out of her pocket, charming it as she went, and handed the resulting silver two-penny piece over to the seller. "Only one," she said hastily, wrinkling her nose at the spiritous evergreen reek. He gave her a tin cup and her change, and Irrith, seeing the barrel, finally realized where she was: a gin shop.

She'd heard of the drink in Berkshire, but never tasted any. One sip later, she decided a single taste was enough. The gin seemed determined to eat away at her mouth, throat, and nose. Coughing, she nodded her thanks and stepped aside.

The sallow-skinned fellow next to her was staring at the blackened sky with a grim expression. "What's causing it?" Irrith asked him.

He had the cadaverous face of a potter, which went all too well with his reply. "Why, the comet, of course."

Irrith dropped her gin cup. "The comet?"

Her informant waved a hand skyward. "The one that smart cove said would be coming back. Halley. It's here."

"And now," someone else slurred, "the world'll burn right up."

The disguised sprite retrieved her cup from the dirt. Most of the gin had spilled, and now she wished she had it back. "But—I thought it wasn't supposed to come for another year." Her heart beat double-time. *It can't be true.*

A woman dressed like a maidservant nodded agreement. "My mistress was reading the *Gentleman's Magazine,* and she told me not to be afeared, as this was a different comet. Though how they can tell, God only knows. Them stars look all the same to me."

"Then how d'you explain the sky?" the potter demanded.

No one could. But Irrith discovered, to her startlement, that the mortals of London had not forgotten Halley's prediction, any more than the fae had. They even seemed to have a presentiment of its danger. "Mark my words," the potter said, "this comet or the next, one of them'll crash right into us, and then it'll be Noah's Flood all over again."

"Fire, not flood," the maidservant insisted. "We'll pass through the comet's tail and burn, just like this fellow said."

Irrith listened with wide eyes. Not everyone shared that fear; someone started an argument with the maidservant, quoting some other magazine to prove they were in no danger. No one mentioned a Dragon. Still, she wondered whether the black sky was in truth a sign. Even if this wasn't the same comet—which it didn't appear to be, as London wasn't on fire—it seemed a terrible omen.

When the argument faded out, she abandoned the gin shop and wandered onward. Her intent had been to enjoy herself today, swindling shopkeepers and picking up new curiosities for her cabinet, but in the grim light she just didn't have the heart. Irrith stopped in the middle of Cheapside, surrounded by fine shops, and made a face of equal parts frustration and worry.

She'd left for Berkshire fifty years ago because there were things she hated about London. Mostly the faerie courtiers: vipers, all of them, saying one thing and meaning another, then biting you when your back was turned. The longer she stayed, the greater her risk of getting caught in their political coils.

But she also loved the City. She loved it for the smart stone and brick buildings that stood where plaster and timber had once been. For the gin shops, with the poor and working folk standing around drinking poison and talking of what their mistress read in the newspaper today. For the little boxes people rode in, carried along on long poles, and the bewildering variety of their wig styles, and the Chinese wallpaper being sold in the shop in front of her.

A few days here would not be enough to scratch that itch. Not after fifty years of absence, and not if this might all come to an end in a year and a half.

She could always run for Berkshire at the first scent of politics.

Irrith jumped sideways to avoid a carriage forcing a path through the crowd, and found herself against a wall plastered with advertisements. One of them caught her eye, with a word that did not belong on a sheet of paper stuck to the wall of a Cheapside shop.

DR. RUFUS ANDREWS
presents
His MARVELOUS MENAGERIE
featuring many Strange and Rare
Half-Breeds and Homunculi
including the
ORONUTO SAVAGE,
two
RED INDIAN MAIDENS,
born joined at the Hip,
and most wondrous strange,
the half-Man, half-Goat
OLYMPIAN SATYR

She stared at that last word, then scrubbed her eyes. It did not oblige her by vanishing.

There was more, in smaller print, crammed in toward the bottom of the sheet; it seemed these wonders could be viewed for a fee at some place in Red Lion Square. Ladies were coyly advised that the satyr might be shocking to their delicate constitutions.

Irrith was prepared to be more than shocked, if this Dr. Andrews had an actual faerie in his menagerie. Could he? The Greek fae were not like English ones; iron didn't bother them. Maybe a satyr could survive in mortal captivity, without wasting away to nothingness.

Her fingers scrabbled at the edges of the sheet. Half stayed behind when she tore it free, but the satyr stayed, as did the address.

Irrith had no idea where Red Lion Square was, and she wouldn't go there on her own even if she did. Should it be true this man had a captive satyr, she would need help to get the prisoner free.

The Onyx Hall, London: October 7, 1757

The pure ring of silver echoed off the polished stone of the walls as Irrith approached the set of chambers collectively known as the Temple of Arms. Hidden in the heart of London, where outsiders could not easily attack them, the fae of the Onyx Court rarely saw battle. Still, those among them with a martial bent yet practiced their art, no more able to abandon it than rain could stop falling downward.

They had all the accoutrements of war at their disposal, short of siege equipment: axes, maces, swords both large and small, centuries of armor. One long gallery had been converted into an archery range; another was dedicated to pistol practice. But the room Irrith sought was the central one, a large, octagonal chamber, its sleek floor covered with a hard-packed accumulation of dirt and straw the masters of the training ground refused to let anyone clean away. Here she found what looked like the entire fighting contingent of the Onyx Hall, watching two of their number at work.

For the second time that day, Irrith's heart leapt into her mouth. They were fighting the Dragon.

Her common sense caught up a moment later. When she blinked, she recognized the terrible beast as nothing more than a glamour, roaring silently in the center of the room. But there were plenty at court who remembered their foe; the illusion was uncomfortably lifelike. The serpentine creature, if it reared upward, would nearly strike the chamber's high ceiling, and its flesh was black char over molten flame. There were salamanders in the Onyx Hall, lizardlike spirits of elemental fire, but they were to the Dragon as a brook was to the mighty sea.

The two facing the beast, a blocky gnome and an elf-knight, were wrestling with a strange weapon. It was nearly invisible, except where the light struck a gleam off one smooth facet or another; Irrith didn't appreciate its full length until the knight swore and lost his grip, letting the enormous spear collapse to the dirt. He tucked his hands under his arms, shivering and ignoring the gnome's harangue, and Irrith realized what the weapon must be.

"Elemental ice," Segraine said, startling her. Irrith hadn't heard the lady approach. "From Jotunheim, or so the Swedes who sent it to us claim. Whether that's true or not, it makes a terrible weapon—terrible for *us*, not our enemy."

Now Irrith understood the gathering. "You're preparing to fight it."

Her friend shrugged. "What else can we do?"

Something new, Irrith thought. She would never say it, though. Under the command of Sir Peregrin Thorne, Captain of the Onyx Guard, Segraine and her fellows had faced the Dragon once already, battling it amidst the flames of the Great Fire. Their willingness to do so a second time showed just how brave they were—or how foolhardy. Irrith herself, though brave on occasion, had no intention of going anywhere near the creature a second time. Love for the city aside, if the appointed day came and they had no better plan than facing down the Dragon in battle, she was going back to Berkshire. London could burn just as well without her as with.

Segraine didn't seem much more enthusiastic. The lady knight cut an impressive figure, even in a plain silk shirt and old slops; the severity of her tightly queued hair drew attention to her strong profile, and the breadth of her shoulders. She had been Lieutenant of the Onyx Guard, before she gave her place to Sir Cerenel. Irrith wondered if it was because her friend had looked ahead just as she had, and had seen the specter of defeat.

Then Segraine noticed her scrutiny, and the mere touch of her gaze made Irrith feel ashamed of that thought. "Mind you," the knight added, "this all assumes there's a Dragon to *fight*."

Irrith blinked in confusion. "What? You think the Queen's lying, that Feidelm made the vision up?"

Her friend's lip curled in something not quite a laugh. "We should be so lucky. No, we have an enemy; the question is whether it will have a body we can attack. Remember, what they imprisoned was its spirit. And that's a hard thing to stab."

The shard lay on the floor, steaming a little in the cool air. The practice was breaking up, and the audience with it; a small group went with Sir Peregrin out the far door, the gnome and another collected the ice, and the rest drifted away, grumbling. "That's it for today," Segraine said, "but I doubt you came here to watch us wave a piece of ice around anyway."

It recalled Irrith to her purpose. "I saw an advertisement in Cheapside," she said, pulling the torn paper from her pocket. "Do you think this man has a real satyr?"

Segraine took the fragment and studied it. A few of the fae who hadn't yet left came closer, reading over the lady knight's shoulders. "I don't know," she murmured, peering at the small print near the bottom. "Though it's happened before."

Hempry, a short and thick-limbed yarthkin, was reading not so much over Segraine's shoulder as under her elbow. He said in his broad Yorkshire accent, "That centaur fellow, six years ago."

"Ktistes?" Irrith said, alarmed.

"No, a friend of his." That came from a second northerner, a duergar Irrith didn't know. "Some fool come over from the continent. Got himself snatched at the docks, maybe, or off the ship he came on—never did get the story out of him."

"What happened to him?"

"Nothing bad," Segraine said, handing the sheet back to Irrith. "We rescued him before the man who meant to display him was able to make good on his advertisements. Adenant, has Il Veloce gone missing? Or any other fauns or satyrs?"

The questions were directed to one of the knights who had gone with Peregrin, now on his way back across the chamber. He paused, eyeing them in puzzlement, and said, "Not so far as I know."

"Could be another visitor," the duergar suggested.

Segraine's chuckle was dry. "Or just a man in goatskin breeches. That's happened before, too."

"Trouble?" Adenant asked.

Irrith shifted her feet when everyone's attention fell on her. "How should I know? I saw this, advertising a satyr like some kind of Bartholomew Fair show, and thought at the very least that you should see it." It seemed like a very small matter, after watching their efforts against the illusion of the Dragon—though the possible satyr, if he existed, might disagree.

Adenant and Segraine exchanged looks, and she said, "We should at least look into it."

"I'll go with you," Irrith said, barely ahead of Hempry and the duergar.

"It doesn't need an entire regiment," Adenant said dryly. "Ask Peregrin, but I expect he'll say two is enough."

Hempry grumbled mutiny, only giving in when Segraine promised to include him in any rescue attempt. Once the others had dispersed, the lady knight said to Irrith, "Arrange a showing. I'll tell the Captain, and the Queen."

"And the Prince?" Irrith asked. "This is a mortal thing, after all."

Segraine's hesitation was barely visible, but not quite absent. "And the Prince," she agreed.

Why the pause? Anything having to do with the mortals of London fell under the Prince's authority; Lune would probably tell Peregrin and Segraine so. That was how it was done with the Princes Irrith had known. But this one was new, she remembered. Perhaps Segraine didn't fully trust him yet.

She didn't really want to ask. That was politics, and something she intended to stay far away from. Instead she flicked the advertisement in her hand and offered Segraine her most impudent grin. "Only one question, then."

"And that is?"

Irrith's grin got wider. "Which of us has to be the lady?"

Crane Court, London: November 10, 1757

Letters of introduction, unfortunately, were insufficient to bring a man into the hallowed chambers of the Royal Society. To come among that august body, Galen needed his father to bring him in person.

He had, with extreme reluctance, begun attending what small social events offered themselves in this season, when most people who could afford to—and who, therefore, presented suitable targets—had retired from London. He did not enjoy it, and Charles St. Clair growled at the lack of results; in consequence, neither was pleased.

But it achieved what Galen needed: together, he and his father went to Crane Court, a narrow lane off of Fleet Street, to the home of the Royal Society of London for the Improvement of Natural Knowledge.

Whatever Galen expected of the place, he didn't see it. The facade in front of him might have belonged to any one of a thousand townhouses in London, with a narrow front, three windows across, and a short staircase leading up to the door, all in simple Palladian style. But the fellowship that met within its walls counted among its past number some of the greatest minds in all of Britain: Robert Boyle; Robert Hooke; Sir Christopher Wren, the guiding genius that rebuilt London in the aftermath of the Great Fire. Edmond Halley, whose calculations had called the spirit of that Fire home to roost. Sir Isaac Newton himself.

Charles St. Clair said nothing to his son, either during the journey or once they arrived. He merely went up the stairs and rapped on the door with the head of his walking stick. A footman in livery welcomed them in and directed them up to the *piano nobile,* where a spacious room overlooking the garden would be the stage for tonight's meeting. It held an assortment of cabriole-legged chairs, an abundance of candles with mirrors to reflect their light, and a small number of gentlemen, all respectably dressed in gray powdered wigs and cravats.

His father introduced him around with a brusqueness bordering on rudeness. Galen bowed, made pleasantries, and was somewhat relieved to be rescued by the beginning of the meeting. Perhaps after it was done, and he had more to converse upon, this would become less awkward.

The meeting, alas, no more displayed the marks of intellectual brilliance than the building did. Galen could forgive it the routine business with which it began: every society that wished to survive for more than a brief time must conduct itself in an orderly fashion. He soon found himself struggling, however, against the urge to yawn, as someone read an interminable extract from what was presumably even more interminable of a lecture on the lymphatic vessels of animals. Galen lost the thread of it a few minutes in, and returned to alertness only when he realized the group was ordering thanks to the doctor who had delivered the lecture.

He made a better effort to stay alert for the letter that followed, and was rewarded with a name he recognized: Dr. Halley. For a moment, he thought someone might mention the comet. But no; the topic was magnetism, and Halley's work on charts of the same. Which might be of great use to navigators at sea, certainly—just not of use to Galen.

Be patient, he told himself, and put down the hand that wanted to fidget with the cuff of the opposite sleeve. *This is only one meeting.* The impatience that plagued him at Mrs. Vesey's had returned; his heart kept beating faster, his breath shallowing, as he thought of his purpose. What did he care, if some laborer had grown extraordinary tumors on his head? No doubt it was a great inconvenience to the laborer himself, and Galen mustered what sympathy he could, but that sentiment was in short supply.

By the time one of the Fellows produced a stone dug up by the New River Company, in which Galen could see no interest or value at all, he was nearly beside himself with impatience. Fortunately—but also frustratingly—that seemed to be the end of the evening's business. After ordering thanks to the man who presented the rock, the Society broke up, leaving Galen afraid that his inspired suggestion was, in fact, a waste of time.

But there was more to the Society than merely its lectures. The real wealth was the members, whose interests ranged across every field of philosophical inquiry. If there was help to be found, it would be among them—and that meant Galen must not leave yet. Bowing to his father, he said, "I thank you, sir, for bringing me here tonight. I should like to stay a while longer; there are gentlemen I would like to speak with."

St. Clair grunted. "Hire a chair, not a carriage." And with that miserly advice, he took his leave.

Drawing in a deep breath, Galen squared his shoulders and surveyed the room. His best prospect was a man he had greeted before the meeting, the closest of his father's acquaintances here. Galen approached before he could grow too nervous. "Dr. Andrews, if I might trouble you for a moment?"

The doctor was an older gentleman, almost the inverse of Galen's father: pale instead of ruddy, thin instead of stout, thanks to long illness. "Yes, Mr. St. Clair?"

"That reference to Dr. Halley's work made me think—did I not read something in the *Gentleman's Magazine* a while ago, regarding some predicted return of a comet?"

Andrews gestured to the front of the room. "There, Mr. St. Clair, is the man to ask: Lord Macclesfield is twenty times the astronomer that I am."

Galen felt like he'd swallowed that supposedly interesting rock. Though the St. Clairs might be a good family, they were nowhere near the rank of the Society's President, the Earl of Macclesfield. When he formed his intention to speak with men here, he hadn't aimed *that* high.

"Come," Andrews said. "I will introduce you." When he moved, Galen had no choice but to follow.

The earl was in conversation with another man, but turned as Andrews approached. "My lord, may I introduce to you Mr. Galen St. Clair?"

Galen bowed deeply as Andrews presented him to the earl and to Lord Charles Cavendish, the Vice-President of the Society. Then the doctor said, "Mr. St. Clair was inquiring about this comet business."

A look of mingled pity and annoyance crossed the earl's face. "I could damn that Benjamin Martin to the depths of Hell—yes, and John Wesley, too—for filling people's heads with such fears. No, my boy, the Earth will *not* pass through the cometary tail on the twelfth of May. And even if it did, there is no reason to suppose it would result in the end of the world. While Halley may have suggested that a comet was the cause of the Deluge, it does not necessarily follow that *his* comet will be of equal consequence."

Galen cursed his fair skin, which advertised his slightest embarrassment to all the world. "My lord . . . that was not the intent of my query."

"Oh." Macclesfield's expression was the stuff of comedy. "My apologies, Mr. St. Clair. What did you wish to know?"

Whereupon Galen realized he'd failed to prepare anything like a coherent question. "I—that is—the state of affairs regarding the comet, my lord; the expectation of its return, the preparation for sighting it, anything about the nature of cometary bodies that was not known in Halley's time . . ." *Anything we might use to keep the Dragon upon its chariot, such that it cannot come down to plague us once more.* Segraine had tried this, but fifty years ago. Surely astronomers had learned new things since then.

The earl sighed. "Truth be told, Mr. St. Clair, I fear the French will steal a march on us where the comet is concerned. I've spoken to Bradley at the Royal Observatory, but at the moment his attention is much occupied with other matters. The most crucial issue, of course, is the timing of the comet's perihelion—"

"Its closest approach to the sun," Cavendish supplied.

Galen covered his irritation with a smile. "I am familiar with the term."

"Good!" Macclesfield said. "And also with Newton's *Principia*?"

"In principle, my lord," Galen said, drawing scattered laughter at his pun, "but not in application. I am no great mathematician."

"But you know the ideas. The problem is one of gravitation: the comet's progress will be retarded by its approach near Jupiter and Saturn. And the equations to calculate that, sir, are devilishly hard."

Hard, but not impossible. The fae had undertaken it already, out of necessity; in fact, that had been the major work of Galen's predecessor. Perihelion would occur in March of 1759. Their danger, however, might arrive sooner.

"Is Mr. Bradley likely to search for the comet when it comes?" Galen asked. In the best opinion of Wrain, one of the Onyx Hall's faerie scholars, observation would be their doom: just as the beast had been exiled via telescope, so would it return. It had taken special equipment to banish the creature against its will, but ordinary lenses and mirrors might suffice to draw it back down. And the Astronomer Royal, with his superior instruments, stood the greatest chance of sighting the comet early, at least in England.

"No doubt he will," Macclesfield said carelessly, "but as I said, he has other things on his mind."

Cavendish asked then after Bradley's health, which was not good, and the conversation moved on from there. Disappointed, but mindful of his duty, Galen took a moment to draw Dr. Andrews aside. "Thank you, sir, for that introduction."

"Not at all," Andrews said. "It pleases me to see you take an interest in such matters, Mr. St. Clair. Do you intend to go on attending our meetings?"

Galen couldn't hide his wince. "As much as I may, Dr. Andrews. Dependent upon the goodwill of my father."

He didn't have to say any more. Andrews and his father were acquaintances, not close friends; the man had treated Charles St. Clair for gout, before his own illness forced him to retire from active practice. Their degree of familiarity was enough for Andrews to understand, and not enough for him to take offense. "I see. If you would like, Mr. St. Clair, I could serve as your patron in his stead; I attend every week, and would be more than happy to aid you in the same."

Gratitude warmed Galen to the soles of his feet. "I would be much obliged to you, sir."

"Then it is easily done," Andrews said. "I will write to him tomorrow."

Red Lion Square, Holborn: November 11, 1757

The hackney carriage circled the green lawn in the center of Red Lion Square and rattled to a halt in front of No. 17. The coachman leapt down to open the door, and a tall gentleman in a sober red coat stepped out with a graceful motion, then turned back, one hand extended to help his lady companion maneuver her skirts out the narrow portal.

She needed the help. The false hips that bulked out her

dress to either side had been folded up like wings to fit her into the carriage, and now impeded her ability to reach the gentleman's hand. When she twitched her cloak out of the way to ensure a secure footing on the step, the quilted dimity of her gown caught against the frame of the door. The coachman saved it before it could tear, and with a stumble and an unladylike curse, she was free.

While her companion paid their fare, the young woman sorted her skirts and cloak back into something resembling order. And then they were alone, and Irrith had the freedom to be herself for a moment, rather than the meek mortal girl she was impersonating—and badly at that. "How in the name of Ash and Thorn does anyone manage these things?"

Segraine shrugged, looking every inch the gentleman. "Practice, I presume."

"Right. Just as you winning our bet was 'luck.' There's magic in both, I'm sure of it."

The lady knight's grin was fleeting. Irrith was convinced her friend had cheated at dice, but her best efforts had failed to catch it happening. As a result, she was the one wrestling with yards of fabric and undergarment architecture that would do a cathedral proud, while Segraine got to play the role of her indulgent elder brother, bringing her to see the Marvelous Menagerie.

Which apparently dwelt behind the innocent facade of No. 17 Red Lion Square. The house was like any other in the row: three stories of red brick, with a servant's attic above and cellars below, and to Irrith's eye indistinguishable from a thousand others they'd rattled past on their way out of the City. Horsemen rode through the square, on their way to important business no doubt, dodging past a handful of carriages and sedan chairs, scattering folk on foot as they went.

Arranging this visit had taken far longer than it should. The proprietor of the Marvelous Menagerie had been ill this last month—or so his butler claimed—and only now recovered enough to do business. Lune had forbidden them to break in without evidence of a real satyr, and so they'd been forced to wait. But now that the time had come, Irrith was reluctant. She eyed the blue-painted door as if it were the maw of a beast, waiting to swallow her. "Shall we go in?" Segraine asked.

Irrith took a deep breath. "Whatever we find in there—it isn't as if he'll know what *we* are. So we're quite safe."

"Quite," her friend agreed.

They stood a moment longer on the hard-packed dirt of the street. Then Segraine said in a breezy voice, "Come along then, Pru; you were the one who wanted to see the Oronuto savage," and strode across to the house.

Irrith followed with as much grace as she could manage. Segraine rapped smartly on the door, then waited with her hands folded behind her back. When a footman opened the door, she announced, "Mr. Theodore Dinley and Miss Prudence Dinley. We have an appointment with Dr. Andrews."

"Yes, sir, you are expected." The footman bowed them in, took their cloaks, and led them upstairs to the drawing room. Irrith had little to compare it to, but it seemed an odd place; the furnishings were sparse, leaving one half of the room entirely empty except for the carpet upon the floor. This, she supposed, was where Dr. Andrews conducted his exhibition.

Andrews himself came in a moment later. Seeing him, Irrith had to believe the reports of his illness; he was pale, with a hectic flush about his eyes. Old enough to look right in his gray wig, and thin as a birch tree, he could have dropped dead on the spot and she wouldn't have been surprised. But he greeted them with pleasant composure, shaking Segraine's hand and bowing over Irrith's. "I am delighted to welcome you to my exhibition. You understand, of course—this is no simple spectacle for the common people. I am a scholar, and I aim to share with those of discerning minds the many wondrous permutations the world holds. Please, be seated. The display will begin momentarily. Would you like some coffee?"

One servant poured for them while another drew the drapes, leaving them in semidarkness. Candelabras illuminated the bare space where the specimens were to stand. Irrith accepted her bowl of coffee with a grimace. In her opinion, the stuff was only slightly better than gin.

The first marvel to come out, disappointingly, was not even alive. "A mummified pygmy of the African continent," Dr.

Andrews said, and began to drone on about its conformation. Irrith peered at it, wondering if it might have once been a faerie, but no; it seemed that humans really did grow that small.

The Oronuto savage came in next. The dramatic candlelight of the shadowed drawing room seemed designed to give his pitch-black skin and foreign features a sinister air, but the man himself seemed bored, and went out quickly when dismissed. He was followed by more preserved specimens, these not even of entire bodies but only pieces, and Dr. Andrews forever looking to Miss Prudence Dinley to see if she was about to faint. Irrith peered with gruesome curiosity at a skull with a hole cut into it—according to Dr. Andrews, while the owner was still alive.

Large sketches accompanied the young Red Indian sisters, who like the Oronuto were clothed according to their native practices, with some allowances for English sensibilities. The sketches depicted other pairs of twins born with body parts stuck together, and Dr. Andrews lifted the drape that covered the sisters' hips to show his audience that their strange, awkward manner of walking, with their arms about each others' waists, was no mountebank's trick; their flesh truly did meld together. Segraine poked it with one finger just to be sure.

And finally, just when Irrith had almost forgotten their purpose there, a servant ushered in the Olympian satyr.

Her bones melted in relief. The sickly creature who limped to the center of the floor was no satyr, and had probably never been closer to Greece than the south bank of the Thames. His ginger hair made him look more like an Irishman. But there was something odd about his gait, and when Irrith looked more closely, she saw there was a strange deformity in his stocking-less lower legs, clearly visible below the button of his breeches.

Deformity, but no goat fur; they were done. Segraine, however, had more concern than Irrith for their Dinley personas, and showed no sign of leaving. Dr. Andrews steadied the ginger man in front of them and began to explain about the warped bones of his legs.

"Pardon me, Dr. Andrews," Irrith said, interrupting him. If they weren't leaving yet, she might as well have some fun. "Is this what you advertise as an Olympian satyr? I was expecting goat hooves, panpipes—that sort of thing." Fauns were the ones with goat hooves; according to Ktistes, satyrs had human feet. But it sounded better this way.

Dr. Andrews looked disgruntled. "My apologies, Miss Dinley. I'm afraid the advertisement you saw is the work of a man I hired, who persuaded me that such language is necessary to attract attention. Were it not for him, I assure you I would have described this fellow in more scholarly terms."

"So he *isn't* a satyr."

Evidently the good doctor saw the specter of disappearing profits looming near. He hastened to say, "As it happens, Miss Dinley, I think he may be—in a manner of speaking. The orgiastic behaviors attributed to the satyr in the art of the Greeks and Romans may well be an echo of the practices of those two societies, but why the description of goatish features? I theorize that it owes something to deformities such as those seen here: just as the myth of centaurs may have arisen from a race of horse-mounted men, so may instances of this deformity have become the basis for an entire race of goatish creatures, upon whom men laid the burden of their own licentious behavior."

"So you don't think there's any such thing as a real satyr." She tried very hard to keep the laugh out of her voice.

"Miss Dinley," Andrews said in a condescending voice, "I traveled Italy and Greece as a young man, and saw no such creatures. This is the closest I have come." He gestured at the poor, forgotten man beside him.

Irrith blinked innocently. "But just because you never saw them doesn't mean they don't exist."

Segraine intervened before Irrith got a chance to find out what kind of annoyance she could provoke. "Come, Pru; we've taken up enough of the good doctor's time."

Sighing, Irrith gave in. "Very well, Teddy. I'm famished anyway. We've seen the satyr; now I want my dinner."

Segraine gave Dr. Andrews their polite thanks, and accepted

his offer to send a man for a carriage. Once Irrith was safely inside, skirts and all, she said, "Wouldn't it be something if we sent Ktistes in to prance all over his fancy carpets?"

"It would be something," her friend agreed, "but nothing good. Let's go back; the Queen is waiting for our report."

The Onyx Hall, London: November 11, 1757

"Weekly meetings," Galen said, "and I shall attend as many as I can. I fear the time itself will be less than fruitful, unless the quality of presentations improves greatly—"

"But it is worth it, for gaining the acquaintance of the men there." Lune nodded. "I would be very much surprised if anyone were to stand up and deliver a lecture that contains the solution to our problem, tied up with a bow."

Harpsichord music formed a pleasant background to their conversation, Lune's attendant Nemette playing for her mistress's relaxation. Various other ladies sat at their leisure, playing backgammon or embroidering; one fed bits of candied fruit to a human child. With some of them, he knew, the distraction was a mask. The Queen's ladies of the bedchamber were not merely for decoration; she made excellent use of them in her political negotiations with other courts. But some of them, he suspected, paid little attention to anything that went on around them.

A knock at the door brought Lady Yfaen to her feet. She spoke briefly to someone outside, then turned to curtsey. "Dame Segraine and Dame Irrith, your Majesty, returned from Red Lion Square."

"Send them in." Lune set down the fan she had been toying with and straightened in her chair.

The two had dropped their mortal glamours, leaving behind clothes suitable for their visit above. Masculine garb was a common sight on Segraine, though usually not so fine. But the delicate sprite at her side . . .

The muddy, sharp-tongued creature he'd brought in to see Lune last month had vanished. In her place stood a modest young lady in stays and skirts, her auburn hair neatly pinned up beneath a lace-edged cap, with two curls escaping to dance above her shoulders. The gown, Galen thought, belonged to Nemette; he'd seen that pattern of peonies and bees before. Irrith looked startlingly demure.

At least until the Queen said, "Sun and Moon—I almost did not recognize you," and Irrith snorted in a manner decidedly at odds with her attire.

"Lost my bet with Segraine," the sprite muttered, and smacked one false hip with her palm, setting the whole structure rocking.

"I am the taller of us two," the lady knight said tranquilly, though a smile lurked at the edges of her mouth. "It would have looked odd for you to play the part of my brother."

"Glamours can cover that, as you know very well. Your Majesty," Irrith went on, as if eager to escape and change her attire, "the Marvelous Menagerie has nothing of faerie in it. Dr. Andrews says someone else wrote that handbill, to bring audiences in."

Galen straightened. "Did you say Dr. Andrews?"

Lune raised her delicately arched eyebrows. "You know him?"

"An acquaintance of my father's, who has offered to be my patron in visiting the Royal Society. That menagerie you went to was his?" They hadn't mentioned the name, only the location.

"There might be two Dr. Andrews in London," Irrith answered, shrugging. "This one looked like he had one foot in the grave."

Blunt, but not inaccurate. "Indeed—he's a consumptive. I fear his health is very poor indeed."

"Could he be of use?" Lune asked.

The idea had already occurred to him. Galen bit his thumbnail in thought—a habit his mother had tried and failed to break him of. "I confess, when I thought of the Royal Society, I was considering astronomers more than anything. But I'm not certain they can do much for us; it seems unlikely there's any effective way to trap the Dragon upon its comet. Which means we are looking for some means to defeat it on the ground. Dr. Andrews is a physician, and also perhaps something of a chemist—well, intellectual men learn about all kinds of things, and I imagine he's no different. His primary learning, however, is in medicine."

The Queen folded her fan one stick at a time, fingers trailing over the edge. "It would not be the first time a physician's been of use to us. My preference, I admit, would be to kill the Dragon; at this point it seems the only way to ensure it never troubles us again. And perhaps this Dr. Andrews might know something that could help."

"He seemed pretty clever, madam," Irrith said, with a curtsy that proved she did not often wear so elegant a dress. "And he knows about all kinds of strange things."

"I will try, madam," Galen promised the Queen. Visions danced before his mind's eye: a gathering of fae, like a second Royal Society, and himself standing before them, presenting a scientific plan for the slaying of the Dragon. He would never be able to ride at it in armor, lance in hand, like a hero of old—but this, he could do.

And then Lune would look at him, and those silver eyes would warm, and then—

Irrith was watching him. Suddenly afraid that his thoughts were showing on his face, Galen blushed and took his leave. Dreams of heroism did no one any good if he did not put them to action.

PART TWO

r

Destillatio

Winter 1758

If the Scale of Being rises by such a regular Progress,
so high as Man, we may by a parity of Reason
suppose that it still proceeds gradually through those
Beings which are of a Superior Nature to him; since
there is an infinitely greater space and room for
different Degrees of Perfection between the Supreme
Being and Man, than between Man and the most
despicable Insect [. . .] In this System of Being, there
is no Creature so wonderful in its Nature, and which
so much deserves our particular Attention, as Man,
who fills up the middle Space between the Animal and
Intellectual Nature, the visible and invisible World,
and is that Link in the Chain of Beings, which has
often been termed the *nexus utriusque Mundi.*

—Joseph Addison,
The Spectator, no. 519

With stately grace, the planets mark the passage of time, scribing out the different arcs of their years. The ellipses contract as the comet moves inward, the years growing ever shorter, as if time itself runs faster. They cluster about the sun, the little planets do: round balls of stone and stranger things, Mercury, Venus, Mars.

And in their midst, Earth.

It is scarcely a speck in the distance. Scarcely even that. The sun is god to the comet, the beacon that calls it home and bids it farewell as it leaves, and the sun is bright in the void. But for the creature that rides the comet, the sun is nothing: only the spark that will set it alight once more.

Earth is everything. For while the beast sleeps, it dreams, and remembers the City where it was born.

Red Lion Square, Holborn: January 13, 1758

A light snow began falling as Galen disembarked from his chair outside Dr. Andrews's house. He welcomed the sight; it had been a gray, dreary Christmas, and a bit of sugar frosting might make London more attractive—at least until the coal smoke turned it to black crusts.

He paid the chair-men and hurried across to the door, shivering. The footman took a dreadfully long time to answer, and bowed deeply as he let Galen in. "My apologies, Mr. St. Clair. Dr. Andrews is in his laboratory at present. If you would be so kind as to wait in the parlor, he will be with you shortly."

Galen agreed, and was led upstairs to the back parlor. While he waited, he chafed his cold hands in front of the fire and surveyed the room. It had the kind of vague ordinariness that characterized the homes of many bachelors; Andrews put out sufficient effort to furnish his parlor with chairs, tables, and so on, but with no wife to make it fashionable, the result was utterly forgettable.

"Ah, Mr. St. Clair." Dr. Andrews entered behind him, still buttoning his waistcoat. "I was unaware of the hour, or I would have been more ready to receive you."

"Quite all right. Your footman said you were in your laboratory . . ." Galen's voice trailed off as he noticed a smear on the back of Andrews's hand.

The doctor saw it and hastily fetched out a handkerchief with which to scrub it away. "Yes, in my basement. I have a room down there where I conduct dissections. My apologies;

I don't usually come upstairs with blood on my hands. Shall I have the maid brew coffee for us?"

He rang a bell, and gestured Galen to a chair. "I never touch spirits myself, and only occasionally take wine," the older gentleman confided, "but coffee has become my great vice."

Faced with that admission, Galen didn't try to hide his own guilty smile. "Mine as well. Its effects are most wonderful: it clears the mind, steadies the hand, aids digestion—"

"It's fortified my own health wondrously," Andrews said. "Indeed, just last week I advised a certain lady to adminster regular doses to her sickly child, to fend off infections."

"Very wise," Galen said. "But I was under the impression you don't practice medicine any longer?"

Andrews made an indeterminate gesture that could have been meant to convey anything at all. "By and large, no. But I make exceptions for a few trusted families."

No doubt the most influential and respectable ones. Galen quite understood. "Your time is mostly taken up with your studies?"

"And illness," Andrews said bluntly, as the maid entered with the coffee tray. Judging by the speed of her return, the doctor had not been lying about his fondness for the drink; it must have been nearly prepared already when Galen arrived. She laid the tray on a pillar-and-claw table to one side, then curtsied out of the room again when Andrews waved her off. He poured the coffee himself. "You will have guessed, I am sure, that I suffer from consumption."

"My heartfelt sympathies," Galen said. "I had an aunt taken by the same disease, and two of her children."

Andrews passed him a coffee bowl. "With so many diseases in the world, I sometimes wonder that any of us reach maturity. But it produces this happy coincidence in my life, that my time is occupied by two facets of the same issue."

"You study your own illness?"

"What else should I do, with the time I have left? Particularly if I wish to increase the amount of that time."

"Then that is why you remain in London," Galen said, understanding. Most consumptives who could afford it went to more healthful climates, where the air was warmer and drier, and might prolong their lives. The damp, chilly rains of London were not good for such men.

But Andrews looked puzzled. "What has London to do with it?"

Now uncertain, Galen said, "The Royal Society. I presumed there were men among its number who shared your interest, and that you wished to remain here to work more closely with them, without the delay of letters."

The doctor was drinking coffee as he responded; Galen could not tell whether a routine coughing fit struck him just then, or whether the answer caused Andrews to choke on some of his drink. Galen hovered at the edge of his chair, not certain what he should do, as the gentleman hastily put down his bowl and snatched out a handkerchief.

"I would to God that were true," Andrews said. "Come, Mr. St. Clair, you've seen what our meetings are like. Nice, orderly business, suitable for gentlemen, and occasionally someone from the Continent, or elsewhere in Britain, performs a bit of experimentation that actually *does* 'improve our natural knowledge,' as the name would have it. But the weekly activity is often tedious and trivial in the extreme."

Galen took refuge in the contemplation of his coffee. "I would not say so, Dr. Andrews."

"Of course not. You're a polite young man. No, I go to Crane Court because I must leave my house occasionally or go mad, and it seems as good a destination as any. But I have a very convenient arrangement here, and no desire to disrupt it by going elsewhere. Besides," the doctor added with blunt honesty, "I had rather die in England, not in some foreign city."

Shame left a sour taste in Galen's mouth. He was cultivating this friendship in the hope of some benefit for the Onyx Court; he'd never thought to consider Andrews's own problems. The fae could not, so far as he knew, cure diseases. Still, there might be some chance that they could aid the man. "I'm no physician myself, Dr. Andrews, but I'll gladly lend you any assistance I may. It would be a grand thing indeed, if we learned more about consumption, that would allow us to save others from it."

The red tinge that rimmed all late consumptives' eyes lent

a strange cast to Andrews's expression. "Not just that disease, Mr. St. Clair. England has already produced Sir Isaac Newton, who unlocked the mysteries of the mechanical universe. He touched but little, though, on the mysteries of living bodies. We need a second genius."

"And you intend to be that man?" Galen asked, before he could consider how rude the question was.

Andrews's mocking smile seemed to be directed at himself. "I'm unlikely to succeed. Newton was younger than I am now when he turned the world on its head with his *Principia Mathematica*. But I can think of no higher purpose than to dedicate what remains of my life to pursuing that star."

Indeed, the fire of that purpose burnt in his eyes. It sparked an idea within Galen—one far enough beyond the scope of his original plan that he hesitated to even consider it.

If Andrews worked *with* the fae—directly, with full knowledge of what they were . . .

That would be quite a risk. Galen would have to make very certain the man was trustworthy. It could be worth the gamble, though. Otherwise Galen himself would have to translate what he learned from Dr. Andrews to a faerie context, with much danger of error. He'd been doing that for two months now, with little result. Wouldn't it be far more productive to bring the two together?

Not today, of course. Still, that inspiration put Galen on his feet, hand over his heart. "Dr. Andrews, I owe you a debt for your patronage at the Royal Society. I repeat my offer of a moment before, foolish though it may be. The work you undertake, sir, could be the salvation of more people than you know. I will do *everything* in my power to aid you."

The Onyx Hall, London: January 17, 1758

Ktistes, as royal surveyor and architect, had taken great care to explain to Irrith which parts of the Onyx Hall were fraying due to the piecemeal destruction of the wall, so that she might avoid them.

She figured out for herself that one of the places on that list was nowhere near the wall.

Most people wouldn't have noticed. The Onyx Hall was a rabbit warren, tangled threads with even less rhyme or reason than the streets above; moreover, the warped reflection from above to below meant the bad patches weren't at the edges of the palace, but rather snaked tortuously through its middle. But there was an inconsistency in the centaur's list, and it wedged itself into a corner of Irrith's mind like a bit of grit in her shoe, chafing her. And when she realized what was bothering her—why, then there was nothing to do but seek out the cause.

Not Ktistes. He would only lie again. Irrith went to the source.

The passage toward the supposed bad patch ran behind the bathing chambers, where salamanders curled beneath great copper boilers of water that could be tipped into the pools. The entrance to the passage was barred by two waist-height bronze pillars supporting a rowan-wood beam. It was no real barrier; rowan might not like the fae, but a simple branch could hardly stop anyone continuing on. The point was to warn the idle traveler that she should go no farther.

Irrith was not an idle traveler. She was bored beyond the telling of it: the bribe Tom Toggin had given her to bring the delivery to London was all but spent, leaving her with no bread to go safely above, and little to amuse her down here. Investigation at least promised a bit of entertainment. She ducked under the beam, and continued down the passage.

The blackness closed in around her, broken only by the faerie light she'd brought along, and carried doubt with it. Maybe this *was* a bad patch. Maybe she was about to find that out the hard way.

Upon that thought, disorientation struck her, and Irrith staggered. When she straightened, she found herself staring at the rowan-wood barrier, and the ordinary corridor beyond.

Ktistes had warned her of this. One of the first effects of the fraying was that fae might enter one part of the Onyx Hall and end up in another one entirely, though the centaur feared worse might happen in time. This, clearly, was what he meant.

Or perhaps it was just meant to seem that way.

Some of the pucks in the Vale adored this charm, disorienting a traveler so that he wandered into a stream or a bull's enclosure. But there were ways around such tricks—if it was indeed a trick.

Irrith squared her shoulders and began walking backward, searching for the floor with her toes, one careful step at a time.

She felt the unease—the vertigo—but this time it was like rain, slipping off an oilcloth cloak. Irrith grinned in satisfaction. *Caught you.*

Then the floor gave way beneath her and she fell.

Her chin smacked against the lip of the hole and she tasted blood, but she managed to stop her fall, fingers straining along the edge of the black stone. Irrith waited until her head cleared, then dragged herself painfully upward until she could fling a leg onto the floor and roll to safety.

She lay panting for a moment, then spat out the blood and peered over the edge. The bottom of the pit was well-padded with cushions. *Definitely the Queen's work. Most of the people who keep secrets in this place would fill it with spikes instead.*

The pit crossed the corridor from one side to the other, but it wasn't so wide that an agile sprite couldn't leap it. Irrith took the precaution of a silencing charm before she made her attempt, and tucked into a tidy somersault on the other side. Two obstacles cleared, and she was careful as she went onward, lest she run headlong into a third. But the remainder of the passage was clear, and then it turned a corner, into a short, pillared vault with old-fashioned round arches, the antechamber to a larger, well-lit room beyond. From that room came an angry voice.

"Dieser verdammten Federantrieb brechen andauernd!"

The words were abrupt and loud enough that Irrith almost jumped from her skin, before she heard them properly. Once she did, she blinked—for that was certainly not English.

Nor was the second voice that answered him. *"Aber natürlich! Ich sage dir doch, dass er soviel Zugkraft nicht aushalten werden."*

The tone was bickering, and resigned; the words weren't directed at her. Concealing herself behind a pillar, Irrith peeked into the chamber Ktistes and the Queen did not want her to find.

Two fae grumbled over a pair of worktables strewn with unfamiliar oddments and tools. The tables would scarcely have been knee-height to a human, and even for Irrith they were low, but they perfectly suited the two, who were hob-size and thick with muscle. The implements they held were incongruously delicate in their blunt-knuckled hands, and both, she saw, had tied their long beards out of the way, the better to see the tiny things they peered at.

What *were* they working on? Irrith risked a longer look. The faerie lights above the tables reflected off minute bits of metal, too small to identify at this distance. But she noticed something odd: a quiet, regular rattle, underlying the humming of the blond-bearded faerie.

The chamber, she realized, was filled with clocks.

One perched atop a bracket on the wall behind the strangers. Two pendulum clocks stood in opposite corners, and a very small piece teetered on the edge of a table, a breath away from falling. A pocket-watch on the floor below it seemed to have fallen already.

Tom Toggin had brought clocks to the Vale. And Irrith had heard rumors, about the crazy German dwarves that came to England with the new German king, and now made clocks and watches for the Queen.

But what were they doing, hidden away down here?

She was still trying to figure that out when every clock in the room began to chime the hour. It wasn't just the ones she could see; from the sound of it, the entire wall to both sides of the entrance, invisible from her concealment behind the pillar, was covered in clocks. And the two dwarves literally dropped the pieces they were working on in order to hurry to a door on the other side of the chamber.

Its face held what looked like sundial, though what use one could be in the sunless realm of the Onyx Hall, Irrith didn't know. Its blade spun without warning, making her twitch; then the red-bearded dwarf seized hold of it, and two things happened at once: first, the bronze-bound door creaked open, and second, a sound too deep to hear shook the very marrow of Irrith's bones.

A sound like the single *tick* of the Earth's own clock.

Her teeth ached with the force of it, and her skull rang like a drum. Irrith had heard many tremendous sounds in her life, up to and including the roar of the Dragon itself, but she'd never encountered anything like this—as if she'd just heard one of the numberless moments of her immortal life tick away.

She was still standing there, jaw hanging slack, when the door finished opening and a puck stepped out and saw her.

"Hey, you! What do you think you're doing here?"

The looks on the two dwarves' faces would have been comical, if only she could have stayed to appreciate them. But instinct set in, as if she were running wild in the forests of Berkshire, and Irrith bolted.

She didn't get very far. Three strides took her to the far end of the pillared vault, and then she ran full-force into something that felt remarkably like an invisible wall.

A voice came through the ensuing fog, but she couldn't have said whether it spoke German or English. By the time she had her senses back, she was surrounded: the two dwarves and the puck stood over her, where she had collapsed on the floor. All three wore identical expressions of suspicion.

The red dwarf demanded, "Vy vere you spying on us?"

Resisting the urge to mock his thick German accent—she was, after all, caught in their trap—Irrith said, "I wasn't spying."

"Vat do you call it ven you hide and vatch vat others are doing?"

Could he have chosen a question with more Ws in it? Irrith stifled a laugh. Her face felt too bruised for laughing, anyway. "I call it curiosity."

The third faerie scowled. He, at least, was English: a lubberkin, though surprisingly warlike. "Curiosity. Right. You just happened to slip past the defenses because you were curious."

Did he expect those defenses would make her *less* curious? They just made it obvious there was something to find. The red-bearded dwarf was much more menacing. He cracked his knuckles and said, "Ve vill dispose of her."

"Now see here," Irrith said hastily, climbing to her feet and mustering as much dignity as she could manage, so soon after knocking herself silly. "I'm a lady knight of the Onyx Court."

"So?" the dwarf said, unimpressed.

The lubberkin drew the blond one aside and bent to mutter in his ear. Irrith, losing a staring match with the other dwarf, could still overhear the whisper. "She might be a Sanist. Watch her; I'll go inform the Queen."

A Sanist? Irrith didn't ask. The puck searched her for weapons and found none, then said, "I'll be back soon to deal with you. Don't try anything foolish." Then he walked out through the same pillars that had stopped Irrith before, leaving her with two German dwarves and a suspicion that maybe she should have asked Ktistes after all.

"Interesting," Lune said, one slender fingertip tapping against her cheek.

She said nothing more, but Galen relaxed. Family affairs had kept him from coming below for several days after his encounter with Dr. Andrews, and in the interval he'd had more than enough time to question his notion of working directly with the man. If Lune agreed, though . . .

"The decision is in your hands," she said. "If you believe it would be useful to bring this man into the Onyx Court, that is within your prerogative as Prince."

Which he knew, full well. Lune had explained it when she chose him for the position. He had authority over all matters involving the interaction between mortals and fae, including the decision to bring them below. This was the first time, however, that Galen had attempted to exercise that prerogative.

The prospect made him nervous in the extreme. There were ways to repair the mistake if someone chose poorly—but far better, of course, not to err in the first place. The watchful gaze of Lune's Lord Keeper, Valentin Aspell, made him dreadfully aware of that. "I won't do it yet," Galen said, and made himself stop twisting his fingers. "I don't know the man well enough—and it's worth exploring his knowledge further, to be sure it's worth the effort. But I'll inform you before I reveal anything to him."

One of Lune's gentleman ushers entered the privy chamber, then, and bowed deeply. "Madam, the lubberkin Cuddy is here, but will not tell me his business. He insists it is worthy of your attention."

The usher had doubt writ large on his feathered face, but Lune and Galen both straightened. Cuddy was out already? A quick count in his head told Galen that the timing was right; it had been eleven days, though just barely. And anything he had to tell them so soon after his emergence was certainly worthy of the Queen's time.

Lune gestured Aspell out. "We will hear Cuddy alone, Lord Valentin. Make certain we aren't disturbed for anything less than the Dragon itself."

The serpentine lord bowed himself out. A moment later, Cuddy entered, and the usher closed the door behind him. "Majesty," the lubberkin said, going to one knee, "there was a spy, outside the dwarves' workshop, who observed me coming out. I fear the Sanists have found the room at last."

Galen's gut tightened. "Who is the spy?"

The lubberkin shook his head. "I don't know her name. I could describe her—"

"No need," Lune said. "We will go see her ourselves. Is she secure?"

Cuddy leapt to open the door for her, but took care to answer before he turned the handle. "The brothers are watching her, in the pillar trap. I don't know how she made it past the others; I came immediately to you, madam."

Then they were out into the more public space of the presence chamber, where some of the more favored courtiers congregated in idleness. All surged to their feet as the usher announced, "The Queen, and the Prince of the Stone!" A wave of bows and curtsies eddied around them as they passed, and curious whispers rose in their wake.

They went by a secret path, one of many that honeycombed the Onyx Hall, until they reached the entrance to the main passage. Cuddy moved the rowan-wood barrier aside, and Lune laid a palm upon the stone of the floor. The defenses, recognizing her touch, let them pass unhindered.

Two stocky figures waited at the edge of the pillar-trap, and one slender one that leapt to her feet as they approached. Galen recognized her instantly, and was surprised at himself; there were many fae in the Onyx Hall, and he'd seen her only twice. But Irrith had made a vivid impression—though that impression consisted mostly of mud.

"Your Grace!" she exclaimed, and dropped back down.

Galen winced. Her knees must have struck the floor hard, though she didn't make a sound. Lune said, in a tone both startled and wary, "Irrith? Sun and Moon—what are you doing here?"

"Proving that Ktistes is a bad liar," the sprite said. Then, belatedly noticing her own impudence, she added, "Madam."

"The centaur?" Galen shook his head in confusion. "What do you mean, he's a liar?"

She hesitated, one hand going to the stone as if to push herself upright, before remembering no one had given her permission to rise. "He told me this was a bad patch. Because of the wall. But it isn't near the wall at all, is it? I think we're somewhere around Fish Street. My lord."

Her accuracy startled Galen. Few fae attempted to trace the connections to London above, beyond the entrances. Only he and Lune, bound into the sovereignty of the Onyx Hall, understood them instinctively.

"The way was barred with rowan wood," Lune said. Since that first exclamation, the emotions had drained out of her voice, leaving it cool and unreadable. "Even if you believed the reason to be false, you knew you were forbidden to pass. And if that had not made it clear, the other defenses must have. Yet you continued on. Why?"

Galen wondered at her coolness. Cuddy had accused Irrith

of being a Sanist, but he doubted it; the sprite had been gone from the Onyx Hall since before that problem began. There was no reason to think she'd been swayed by them in the few short months since her return. He doubted Irrith even read a newspaper.

Those shifting green eyes held an echo of old hurt. "Madam . . . nobody sent me. I really was just curious. And I suppose it was foolish of me, but I—I've learned my lesson. I know better than to tell anyone anything I've seen."

The weary bitterness of it took him aback. It didn't fit with the Irrith he'd seen before. She and the Queen were clearly having a conversation of their own, separate from the four who watched them; and glancing around, he saw that Cuddy and the dwarves understood no more than he did.

A division that only sharpened when Lune waved one hand in dismissal. "That doesn't matter anymore, Irrith. It's been moved. This, however, is a different matter."

Whatever "it" was, the revelation of its movement was enough to make Irrith's eyes nearly start from her head. Then the rest of the Queen's reply sank in, and the sprite twisted enough to glance over her shoulder, at the dwarves' workshop behind her. The sundial door hung slightly ajar, but gave her no glimpse within. "I've hardly seen anything—but of course that doesn't matter, does it, your Grace? I know there's *something* here. Though . . ." She curled her fingers halfway in, as if stopping short of fists, then said, "I won't be the last to come down here. Those defenses didn't stop me, and you rule over a court of very curious fae, madam."

She was right. It had worked so far—and, with any luck, would only need to work a little while longer—but the defenses were not remotely enough. Galen could hardly tell her why there weren't more: the massive enchantment just a short distance away, behind the sundial door, made it unwise in the extreme to place many other charms nearby. If they tried, Ktistes feared this might become a broken part of the Onyx Hall in truth.

Very quietly, Irrith said, "I could give you my word."

Galen happened to be looking directly at Lune when she said it; he therefore caught the minute narrowing of the

Queen's eyes, the tightening of her sculpted lips. Fae could not break their sworn words, which made Irrith's offer the perfect solution. If she swore, she would be *incapable* of telling what she'd seen. Why did that prospect disturb Lune?

He didn't know, any more than he knew what Irrith had almost told in the past. The one thing he *did* know was that this entire affair risked being magnified far beyond its merits. Finding Irrith here had clearly disturbed Lune, enough that her response might be too harsh.

Saying that, however, was more than a little difficult. "Madam," Galen began diffidently, then choked on the rest.

Lune's lips pressed together again, before she turned her attention to him. "Yes?"

Now he had to say *something*. Holding his hands out in placation, Galen went on, "I know that Dame Irrith, as a faerie, falls under your authority instead of mine. But if I may . . . offer a suggestion . . ."

The Queen gestured him onward, with a hint of impatience.

He felt like a very sharp stone had lodged in his throat. Around that obstruction, Galen said, "It may be that in this instance, there is more to be gained by revelation than by secrecy. Not just as concerns Dame Irrith, but the court as a whole."

Cuddy failed to repress a snort, and Lune's eyebrows rose into two doubtful arches. "What gain do you see?"

Galen spent little time among the fae outside of the Queen's company, but Edward Thorne heard things, and passed them on to his master. "There's a great deal of fear in your realm that time is running out. We have a year—perhaps less, if an astronomer makes an early discovery. If your subjects were to know there's more time—"

He stopped because he could see Lune working through the complications and counterarguments. "It hasn't harmed the Hall," she murmured, almost inaudibly. "Though some, of course, will try to say that it has. But if we leave unspecified the details of its operation—to silence, or at least confuse, those who would demand to know why we haven't disposed of the cometary threat already—"

"They're asking that anyway," Galen reminded her. Then he wished he'd found a more tactful phrasing. "But this, at least, is a concrete step, something they can point to when they ask themselves whether—"

The rest of that sentence was swallowed, courtesy of more belated tact, but Lune finished it for him. "Whether we've accomplished anything at all."

Everyone else had stayed well out of this exchange. Irrith looked to be holding her breath. Galen said, "If the question of secrecy is removed, then Dame Irrith has nothing to betray, whether by accident or design."

Lune smiled. The sun might have risen in that small portico, by the warmth it gave him. And Irrith, too, was beaming at him with undisguised gratitude. *This place keeps too many secrets,* Galen thought, heaving an inward sigh of relief. *I am glad to unveil at least one of them.*

"I will draft an announcement," Lune said. "In the meantime, Irrith, you might as well see what you came for. Galen, if you would be so kind as to show her the Calendar Room? I shall be in my chambers." With a swirl of rich skirts, she was gone.

Irrith wasn't entirely certain how pleased she was to see the pale figure of the Queen depart, leaving her with two crazy dwarves, one unfriendly-looking puck, and a very youthful Prince. But Galen stepped forward, all courtesy, to lift her to her feet, and though she didn't physically need the aid, she accepted it gladly.

"This way," the Prince said, and left the pillars for the broader space of the workshop beyond.

Remembering her previous experience, Irrith prodded the gap between the pillars with one finger. It encountered a familiar wall. "Er—Lord Galen—"

He turned, saw her still there, and flushed enchantingly. "Ah. Yes." Galen came back and extended one hand, courteous as a dance. Irrith took it, and he led her into the chamber.

Peculiar equipment and half-finished projects crowded the space. Not just clocks and watches, either: she spotted the cousin of one of the objects Tom Toggin had brought to the Vale, that Galen had called an armillary sphere. This one, however, had far too many rings, set at cockeyed angles to one another, as if someone had tried to wrench the heavenly circuits they represented into a more useful configuration.

Perhaps they had. Like everything else that occupied the Queen's attention nowadays, Irrith guessed this had to do with the return of the comet.

"What's *that*?" she asked, pointing past the armillary sphere to something even more peculiar.

"An orrery." The answer came from the blond-bearded dwarf, who appeared to have discarded all animosity once the Queen was done with Irrith. His red-bearded friend, unfortunately, seemed less easily won over.

Irrith peered at the object. It had gears like a clock, and thin arms that held balls of various sizes. "And an orrery is . . ."

"A model of the heavens. It is more useful than an armillary sphere." He came over to demonstrate, cranking the arms around so they circled the gold ball in the center. Irrith guessed that represented the sun, but that was where her comprehension ended.

The dwarf smiled when she looked at him, though it was hard to find behind the beard. "I am Wilhas von das Ticken. This is my brother Niklas." Beard or no beard, it was easy to tell when the other dwarf scowled.

Well, if he didn't like her, she might as well go directly to the question she *really* wanted answered. Pointing at the door with the sundial on it, Irrith said, "So what's *that*?"

Galen cleared his throat and said, "Er, yes. Dame Irrith—I don't know what news reaches you out in the Vale, but perhaps you recall the measures taken a few years ago, to correct the calendar?" Irrith nodded. Berkshire mortals were *still* confused by it, checking their almanacs to see which fairs and festivals were being held on the same date as before, and which ones on the same day, regardless of the calendar. "Parliament took great pains to make sure everyone understood that this was merely a change of style, to correct for the inaccuracies that had accumulated through the centuries, and that although September second, 1752, would be followed by September fourteenth, they would *not* lose any genuine time."

Wilhas snickered quietly into his beard.

Grinning a little himself, Galen said, "That . . . wasn't entirely true."

Irrith's eyes went to the heavy door, with the sundial nailed to its surface. "So that . . ."

"Is the Calendar Room," the Prince said. "It contains within it the eleven days skipped over when the adjustment occurred. *All* of the eleven days: those lost by every man, woman, and child in the whole of Great Britain."

The sprite hadn't the faintest clue how many mortals dwelt in the kingdom, but even her most inadequate guess was staggering. "How much time is *in* there?"

"The von das Tickens could tell you," Galen said. "I don't bother to keep count. More than the Onyx Court is ever likely to use, even given the way the room operates. Once the door is closed, it won't open again until eleven days later—from the perspective of one standing outside. Within the chamber, however, it's a different matter. If you spend one day inside, you will come out eleven days later. If you spend fourteen years inside, you will *still* come out eleven days later."

When Irrith stared at him, he shrugged, with an embarrassed grin. "No, I can't tell you how it works. This was made before I came to the Onyx Hall. You can ask Wilhas if you like, but I fear the explanation would make your head spin."

The dwarf answered with his own cheerful shrug. "Ve could go inside and shut the door. I am sure that vith enough time, I could make her understand."

By the time Irrith realized she was moving, she'd already drifted several paces toward the door. "May—may I see?"

Galen bowed and swung the door open. One half-eager, half-reluctant step at a time, Irrith rounded the obstacle of his body and looked into the room.

And saw the clock.

Movement and stillness: somehow both at once. Irrith knew without question that the pendulum was swinging in a broad arc across the floor, though its motion was so slow as to be imperceptible. She stared at it, unblinking, *incapable* of blinking, because the stone describing that arc was too large to look away from, inescapable, oppressive in its weight, as if she faced a rough-hewn chunk of Time itself—

Then something else filled her vision, because Galen had taken her by the shoulders and wrenched her around, putting the clock behind her. His face was so *young*—his whole life less than an eyeblink in the great duration of the universe, less than the *thought* of an eyeblink. Mortal. Ephemeral. That was how *Irrith* felt, and if she was ephemeral, then what did that make him?

The Prince was talking. Words. She focused on them. "—strikes most people like that, at first," he was saying. "You become accustomed, eventually. As much as anyone can. I cannot say *I* have. Not entirely."

Words. Tongue, and lips, and air. "That weight—"

"Twenty-five tons, or so they tell me. But it isn't the physical burden you feel. The clock ticks once a day, and when it does . . . it's like hearing the heartbeat of the Earth itself."

She'd heard it, when they opened the door and the puck came out. Irrith might be a faerie, and immortal, but the Earth was far older than she. No wonder that sight, that sound, made her feel like a mayfly.

"Now you understand one of the limitations of the room," Galen said ruefully. "Even faeries don't find it comfortable. Mortals . . ." His eyes darkened with something deeper than fear. "But it gives us more time, and so we use it."

His hands were still on her shoulders. Irrith suspected Galen was, in the ordinary way of things, a gentleman much concerned with propriety, but he seemed to have forgotten such things in the urgency of distracting her from the clock. The two points of warmth, seeping through her coat and shirt, were comforting against the chill that had sunk into her bones.

It would be easy to stay turned away, to go out through the pillars and never look back. But that would mean letting her fear win. And if this boy of a Prince could face the clock, then so could she.

Irrith disengaged gently, squared her shoulders, and turned back to the doorway.

This time she was prepared; this time, it wasn't so bad. She was able to drag her attention away from the terrible inexorability of that pendulum and up to the clock face above it. Flawless gold gleamed in a disc the height of a giant, its face marked with twenty-four hours. Behind it lay an incomprehensible mass of gears, ruled over by a device like an inverted V, and a sharp-toothed wheel. *Actually* toothed, so it seemed to Irrith—or were those claws? The mechanism was much too high up for her to be sure.

And then there was the pulley, a massive cylinder wrapped with a cable unlike any she'd ever seen. From it hung an absurdly little ball. "As it falls, it helps drive the clock," he said over her shoulder. "Once a year, they pull it up to the top again."

Against her will, she turned back to the pendulum. It hung, not from a cable, but from a softly glowing pillar of light, that vanished into the darkness above. "And where does that go?"

"To the moon." Galen spread his hands when she eyed him suspiciously. "If it's a lie, Dame Irrith, then they've lied to me, too. It has to do with the mechanics of the clock. They had to hang the pendulum from something very far distant, and so they drew down a beam from the moon."

Irrith shivered and turned elsewhere. The rest of the room was ordinary by comparison: tables, shelves, every flat surface crammed with books and paper and bottles of ink and flocks of quill pens. She tried to imagine staying here for days, let alone years, and shuddered again.

Unnerving—but also fascinating. Faerie magic was a familiar thing. This, with its gears and pulleys and calculations, was unlike anything she'd seen before. A collision of two worlds, with results she could only imagine.

And I thought it strange when fae began carrying guns.

Galen bowed her out of the room as she exited. "So now you've seen it. I expect the Queen will put a guard on this room, to prevent any interference by others . . . but if you'd like to assist with our efforts against the Dragon, I am certain I can arrange for you to be permitted back here."

Irrith wasn't sure she wanted to set foot across that threshold again. She wasn't even sure she didn't want to run back to the Vale, where there was earth instead of the Earth, and the fae lived as they had for ages. The Prince meant so kindly, though, that she said, "Thank you, Lord Galen. I—I'll think about it."

He bowed again, and offered his arm. "Then let me guide you back to the rest of the Onyx Hall."

Memory: September 2–14, 1752

In the dark of night on September second, they moved the last components into place.

Gold drawn from the sun itself, hammered into a perfect disk fifteen feet in height, its face marked with twenty-four engraved hours. The hands were starlight, glittering and cold. Behind it, gears of metal, catching pinions of stone, riding arbors of wood, all taken from every corner of Britain. The toothed escapement wheel was the stuff of nightmares itself, for this theft would happen while most of the kingdom slept: every human who lay at rest when the hour passed midnight would add eleven days to the total stored in this room.

And that hour had almost come. The von das Tickens hauled on a rope, snarling German curses to each other, lifting the pulley into place. The block was a tree trunk, perfectly circular, its rings marking off a hundred years. The tree was native; the cable wrapping it was not. Lune had bargained hard with the svartalfar for it, a length woven from the roots of a mountain, the noise of a cat's footfall, the breath of a fish. Nothing less could hold the stupendous burden of the driving weight: a sphere of old age, heavy all out of proportion to its size. The Welsh giant Idris stood ready to wind the pulley for the first time. He would return every year on this date to wind it again, as long as the Queen could persuade him, for only a giant's strength could achieve it.

"Hurry," Hamilton Birch, Prince of the Stone, whispered under his breath. His pocket-watch lay clutched in one sweat-slick hand. If they missed their moment, there would be no second chance.

The pulley was slotted into place. The giant bent to the crank, grunting. The driving weight began to rise from the floor.

And the Queen of the Onyx Court stood, dressed in silver, waiting with both healthy and crippled hands outspread.

The driving weight reached the top of its drop and hung there, too heavy to sway, while Idris braced himself against the crank. "One minute," Lord Hamilton called out, glancing through the sundial door to check his pocket-watch against the more accurate regulator in the dwarves' workshop.

Lune tilted her chin up and raised her arms toward the black ceiling above.

Far, far above; the dwarves and Ktistes had altered this chamber, raising its ceiling to make room for the clock. And there was something in the stone now, not quite an entrance, more like a hatch, that would permit only one thing through.

Moonlight.

The quarter moon hung low in the sky above. Its light struck a lens placed at the top of the Monument to the Great Fire, then a mirror behind; the silvered metal reflected it downward, through the hollow shaft of that great pillar, into the chamber at its base—and then still farther. Obedient to Lune's call, the light passed through, and shone down into the chamber of the clock.

Onto the second stone waiting on the floor, just in front of the Queen.

As the pocket-watch's hands reached midnight, and the regulator outside struck the hour, the dwarves dragged the wooden supports free. The pendulum bob, a sarsen stolen from Stonehenge, hung in midair, suspended by only a beam of moonlight.

And then it began to move.

Idris had let go of his crank, releasing the driving weight to begin its imperceptible drop. Lune stepped back, hands dropping to her sides. Hamilton watched, breath held tight in his chest.

When the regulator began tolling, it was September second in the world outside this room. When it struck the final chime, the date was September fourteenth.

And all the days in between, the dates never lived by a single soul in Britain, came flooding into this room. Hamilton *felt* them come, slipping past like the wasted days of his youth, scented with the experiences that might have been. An enormity of time, and none at all, shivering him to the core of his soul.

When the last of them had passed, Niklas von das Ticken hauled the sundial door shut, and spun its inner face to lock the mechanism.

Leaving the five of them alone with the clock.

"Vell," his brother Wilhas said, "ve have eleven days, before ve may open it for the first time. Who vould like to play chess?"

Rose House, Islington: January 23, 1758

For the most part the economy of the St. Clair household was the province of Galen's mother, who did her best to reduce expenditures while still presenting a respectable face to the outside world. There were a few points, however, upon which his father had strong opinions, and one of them was the greater expense of a hired carriage over a sedan chair. But Islington was a miserable distance to go on such a cold day, and so Galen paid for the greater shelter of a carriage, riding with foot-warmer and heavy cloak past the grasping edges of the city and through the still-green fields to the village north of London.

He came this way every month to spend an afternoon in the company of the two people he trusted to teach him what he needed to know, without censure for his ignorance.

The driver deposited him on the icy ground in front of the Angel Inn. After paying the man, Galen deposited his foot-warmer in the inn; then it was back out into the cold, ostensibly to do business with someone in town.

His path, however, took him away from the houses, to the back of the coaching inn, and the winter-dead rosebush that stood behind it.

Rubbing his hands together in a vain attempt to restore circulation, Galen said to the bush, "I don't suppose a lost and freezing traveler could beg for a hot drink?"

The rosebush didn't answer him. After a moment, though, the branches shifted and wove themselves into an ice-gilded arch, over steps that beckoned him inside.

The warmth of the chamber below enveloped him like a loving embrace. Galen let his breath out in a moan of pure pleasure. "Ladies, I would steal you for my father's house if I could. Or, better yet, make my home here, and never leave."

Galen's fashionable friends would have dismissed this place as "rustic," and so it was. Fashion had never touched the furnishings here. Bare wooden beams held up the ceiling, and the furniture was heavy oak, its primary decoration being the years of oil rubbed into its surfaces. The chairs were ridiculous things, their upholstery stuffed with far too much padding, but Galen doubted more comfortable seats existed in all of Britain. Flowers bloomed here and there, despite the cold above, and the smell was of all good things: fresh-baked bread, gentle woodsmoke, and the sweet honey of the sisters' excellent mead.

The sisters themselves looked like a pair of poetic country housewives, rendered in three-foot miniature. At least until Gertrude Goodemeade advanced on him with the demeanor of an overwhelmingly friendly army sergeant. Then Galen laughed and fumbled with numb fingers at the neck of his cloak, surrendering it with a bow.

Her sister Rosamund, almost Gertrude's twin save for the embroidery of their aprons, handed him a cup of mead once his gloves were gone. "Drink that up, Lord Galen, and come sit by the fire. You look frozen through."

Dr. Andrews's belief in the curative powers of coffee was nothing next to the sisters' opinion of the mead they brewed. It warmed Galen down to his toes. These were, in his estimation, the two kindest fae in all of Britain. A pair of Border brownies, resident here in Islington for long enough they should have lost their northern accents, Gertrude and Rosamund Goodemeade called nearly everyone friend, and suited action to word.

While he drained the cup, Rosamund stoked the fire, and Gertrude fetched out the tea set. With her resolutely country mode of dress, it was comical to watch her go through the refined ritual of serving the tea, for all the world as if she were the Duchess of Portland, and drinking from porcelain bowls. He would not have laughed at her for all the world, though.

Because these two were his best support, better even than Cynthia, who could only advise him in one half of his life. Ever since his investiture as Prince, he had relied upon the sisters to teach him the many things about the Onyx Court he should and did not know. Galen hardly imagined the Prince of Wales ever turned to countrywomen for such things, but the Goodemeades were different. Beneath their cheery and provincial exteriors lurked two very alert minds indeed.

"Now," Rosamund said when they were all supplied with tea, "what shall it be this month, Lord Galen?"

He'd been sitting on this question for nearly a week, awaiting his chance to ask it. "What can you tell me about that sprite from Berkshire, Dame Irrith?"

"Oh, we've known her since the end of the war," Rosamund said. It took Galen a moment to realize which one she meant. Would he ever grow accustomed to their habit of referencing the previous century's civil wars as if they were recent memory? They cared little for battles in foreign lands, but remembered those at home quite well. "She's been by to see us once—"

"Twice," Gertrude corrected her. "Oh, but you were in the city the second time; I'd forgotten."

Galen frowned over the dark surface of the bohea in his tea bowl. "I . . . Dame Irrith found the Calendar Room. I convinced the Queen it would be better to admit the place's existence than to punish her. But there seemed to be something between them, and I was hoping you knew what it was."

That last was merely a bit of politeness; sometimes he wondered if there was anything in the Onyx Hall the Goodemeades *didn't* know. Rosamund sighed unhappily. "Aye, we do. Old history, from your perspective, and not a piece we share with most people; it can lead in dangerous directions. But since it's important to the safety of Lune's throne, you should probably know." Her brow furrowed. "Indeed, Lune should've told you. I wonder . . . well, no matter."

She wondered why Lune hadn't. There'd been no reason to, of course, before Irrith's return. Since then—"I think her Grace is more concerned with the comet."

Two curly heads nodded acceptance, if only for the sake of his pride. Rosamund said, "The nasty details of it are neither here nor there, but the heart of it is this: some troublemakers in the Onyx Hall almost tricked Irrith into telling them the location of the London Stone."

Galen's heart skipped a beat. The London Stone . . . it was easy enough to find, if one meant the ordinary lump of lime-stone that stood on the north side of Cannon Street. Nowa-days it was more an obstruction to passersby than anything else, its history as the heart of London forgotten by most. In the Onyx Hall, however, its function as the site of oaths saw very specific use, every time a new Prince was crowned.

The Stone held both Galen's sovereignty and Lune's. What-ever oaths the chosen man swore, whatever rituals the Queen conducted, no one became Prince in truth until he laid his hand upon the faerie reflection of the London Stone. That was why it was hidden away, concealed from all eyes: if someone gained access to it, he could, in theory, try to take the Onyx Hall for himself.

Rosamund was nodding. "You don't need *me* to tell you the danger. This was right after we had word of the comet's return, and right after they passed that law making England and Scotland one kingdom, too. Which Lune's enemies used against her. They—"

"Wait," Galen said, startled. "The Act of Union? How could that be relevant?"

Gertrude made a huffy noise, and crossed her arms. "It got rid of the Kingdom of England, and you think it's nothing?"

She wasn't really angry; he'd never seen either of the brown-ies truly angry. She did seem offended, though. Still baffled, Galen said, "But the two lands have been ruled by the same monarch for over a hundred and fifty years. It hardly makes any difference, except in government."

He regretted the words as soon as he spoke them. Galen never would have thought such friendly hazel eyes could *blaze*, but there Gertrude was, arms clamped down hard, lips pressed white, and child-size though she might be, there was nothing childish about her expression. *This* was real anger.

Rosamund laid a calming hand on her sister's knee, for all the good it did. "Faeries are . . . provincial creatures, Lord Galen, even those that live in London. And Lune's whole purpose—well, part of it, anyway—is to protect England. So how does it look if suddenly there's no England anymore?"

Galen was still half-distracted by the seething Gertrude. He managed to catch himself, though, before he pointed out there *was* still an England; it was just part of the United Kingdom of Great Britain, now. He also managed to catch the undoubtedly disastrous impulse to ask what they thought of Britain's new German kings. Though had the Scottish Stuarts been any better, in their eyes?

It's a strange day, when faerie politics seem the safer *topic,* he thought ruefully. "Lune's enemies, then, were using that, and the return of the comet, as an argument to . . . remove her?" That sounded unpleasantly familiar.

Gertrude had recovered her temper enough to speak. "Yes. Ungrateful bast—"

"Gertrude!" Rosamund exclaimed, going scarlet.

"Well, they *are*!"

"That doesn't mean you *call* them such—"

"Ladies!" Galen was off his chair, whisking Gertrude's tea bowl out of the way before she could hurl it to the floor for emphasis. They were Rosamund's favorite pattern—with roses around the rim, naturally—and he did *not* want to discover whether that would tip the sisters over into a real fight. "I'm sorry I asked. I thank you very much for the explanation, but had I known—"

Rosamund's ire vanished as if it had never been, and she began assuring him that it wasn't his fault, he was welcome to ask as many questions as he liked, whenever he liked. Gertrude, apparently still smarting from his comments about the Act of Union, retrieved her bowl and drained its contents, slops and all. By the time she was done, she'd calmed down enough that Galen ventured one last query. "Did the Queen banish her?"

"Irrith?" Gertrude shook her head and began gathering up the tea things. "No, Lune knew she meant no harm. As Rose said, she was tricked. But Irrith left because it was too much of everything she hates about this place: politics, and deceit, and folk stabbing each other in the back."

Galen sympathized. Were it not for Lune, he would gladly spend all his time among the common fae, and avoid the intrigue of the courtiers.

Were it not for Lune.

"Thank you," he said. "It makes more sense now. Cuddy thought Irrith was a Sanist, and I believe her Grace suspected it, too, at least briefly."

"Irrith?" Rosamund shook her head emphatically. "She's loyal to Lune. Has been for a hundred years. She would never do anything to hurt her."

He was glad to hear it. Then Gertrude said, "We'd love to have you stay longer, but I think you should be going, my dear; it's started to sleet."

How she could tell, with her home buried underground, Galen didn't know, but he emerged into the bitter air to discover she was right. He rode back to Westminster with fresh coals in the foot-warmer fighting back the chill, and brooded upon Irrith all the way.

The Onyx Hall, London: February 11, 1758

Raucous laughter advertised Irrith's destination before she could see it. This was the underbelly of the Onyx Hall, far from the elegant diversions of the courtiers; here, the dank chill of the river pervaded the stones, and the comforts of upper society were rarely seen. The furnishings of the room Irrith sought were nothing like the delicate mortal fashions that surrounded the Queen and the Prince. Spindle-legged chairs that had been stylish at the restoration of the monarchy clustered around heavy tables that had seen old Elizabeth Tudor's day, and all of them blackened with ages of use.

But a few novelties reached this place. The fae gathered in the Crow's Head—common folk, all—drank coffee and tea and gin, alongside the familiar beer and ale. It was a fashion in its own right, though one few courtiers would gamble with; those were mortal drinks, and not given in tithe. Consuming them could change a faerie. Irrith, catching a human serving-boy by the shoulder, chose the safety of faerie ale.

Magrat, she saw, was not so cautious. The church grim sat hunched in a corner, watching the world through the gap between her bony knees, a gin cup clutched in her skeletal hand. It was her usual posture, and Irrith could understand why; the church Magrat had haunted was destroyed back when fat Henry chose a new wife over loyalty to the Catholic Church. She was hardly the only grim dispossessed of her home during those times, either. Some, Irrith heard, had taken to haunting Quaker meetings and the like. It rarely turned out well, though; the white-hot faith of the Methodists and Baptists and other dissenters was too uncomfortable, even for a church grim's tolerance. Many abandoned the mortal world entirely, fleeing into Faerie itself.

And a few, like Magrat, made new homes elsewhere. The goblin, who had once known whether the dead were destined for Heaven or Hell, now traded in different sorts of information. It wasn't political; Magrat didn't give a priest's damn what use those secrets were put to. She only cared if she got paid.

Irrith slid onto the bench across from her and got a nod. "You cost me a child's first nightmare," the goblin said, without much rancor. "I bet Dead Rick you wouldn't return, after that business over the Stone."

The sprite's stomach turned over. Blood and Bone—how had that become public knowledge? It had been a state secret when she left.

"Don't worry," Magrat told her, after a swig of gin. "No one'll be after you for that anymore. Your knowledge turned to worthless dust when the mortals moved the thing to the north side of Cannon Street. Mab only knows where it is down here, now."

Moved the *Stone*? Irrith did her best to keep the shock from her face. The London Stone was the heart of the Onyx Hall. If the mortals had moved it . . . she was surprised *any* of the palace was holding together anymore.

Secrecy now was rather like closing the stable door after the horse had bolted, but she owed it to Lune anyway. "I came to buy, not sell," Irrith said. "Tell me about the Sanists."

Magrat had no eyebrows, but the gray-tinged skin above her black eyes rose into furrows. "Sanists, is it? That'll cost you."

It always cost her. But Irrith knew it didn't have to cost as much as Magrat made out. "What do you want?"

"Bread. Three pieces."

Irrith laughed in the goblin's face. "For that, I could buy the name of the next Prince. This isn't worth bread, Magrat, and I don't have any to give anyway. It's more valuable than oaths, these days." An exaggeration, but not by much. "How about the memory of a kiss?"

Magrat rolled her eyes in exaggerated disgust. Irrith added, "Not just any kiss. The last one given by a young man to his lady love, before he went off and got killed by the Jacobites." It was all that remained of Tom Toggin's bribe, and Irrith had been saving it for special use. The lady had feared, when her lover went off, that he was going to die, tinging the memory with a presentiment of grief.

"Done," the grim said without hesitation, and spat in her hand. Irrith did the same, and they shook. She hadn't brought the captured memory with her, of course; too many fae here had wandering fingers. The handshake was enough to secure the deal. "It's cheap information," Magrat admitted. "Lots of people know about the Sanists. But I can tell you more than most. It's funny you should ask me, really, when you've dealt with them yourself."

"I have?" It gave Irrith an unpleasant start. She'd wondered at the lubberkin's whisper—had he somehow hit the mark?

Magrat waggled her over-long fingers in the air. "Not under that name. They didn't start calling themselves Sanists until after you'd left. And Carline doesn't let herself be seen anywhere near those folk—not publicly."

A second start, more unpleasant than the first. *Carline.* Formerly one of the Queen's ladies of the bedchamber, and the reason Irrith had left the Onyx Hall, intending never to return. "You're talking about people who want to replace the Queen."

The church grim unbent one spindly leg to shove something across the floor toward Irrith. "See for yourself."

The thing turned out to be a torn, filthy sheet of paper. Irrith picked it up and found a title printed across the top in large block letters. *The Ash and Thorn.* Dated February 10, 1758.

"A *newspaper*?" Irrith lowered it to stare at Magrat. "There's a newspaper in the Onyx Hall?"

"Two, actually. What good's one newspaper, if it doesn't have another to argue with? *The Sun and Moon* is the one loyalists read. This one publishes Sanists."

Irrith's stare shifted outward, to swing around the Crow's Head. She'd noticed other fae reading things that looked like newspapers, but she'd assumed they'd been brought down from above. No doubt some of them had—but not all. She couldn't concentrate enough to read the one in her hand, so she dumbly echoed Magrat's words. "Sanists. Published in a newspaper. You're saying they make their treason *public*?"

The grim waggled her hand. "Yes and no. Mostly they don't talk about replacing her. They just mention what a shame it is, the Queen wounded and unhealing, and look how the Hall suffers, too, bits of it fraying away. And then, if they're feeling bold, they wonder how it might be made well."

Irrith's fingers clenched in the filthy paper. This wasn't Carline's old treason; that had been simple, damnable ambition, using things like the comet's return as an excuse to gather support against Lune. This time—*Blood and Bone.*

This time, they had a point.

"*Mens sana in corpore sano,*" Magrat said. "That's Latin, you know. 'A sound mind in a sound body'—not that anyone in this black warren's terribly sound, but nobody asked me before picking the name. What the Sanists want to know is, how can we make the palace strong when its Queen isn't?"

She didn't have to say anything more. Irrith knew exactly what she meant. Lune had taken two wounds in the past: one from an iron knife, and one from the Dragon. Neither would ever heal properly. Which meant the faerie realm was ruled over by a Queen who wasn't whole.

The Queen *was* her realm. It was the basic principle of faerie sovereignty; the bond between the two was the foundation for authority. Carline had tried to find the London Stone because that was the focal point, the place where she could, perhaps, wrest authority away. Now, it seemed, she was trying something else: the force of popular opinion, and the weight of faerie tradition.

What if the Sanists were right? What if what London needed, for its own sake, was a new Queen?

Irrith glanced away, to keep Magrat from reading her expression. Not a good plan: the Crow's Head was filled with other fae, some of them eavesdropping, some not, but all of them probably willing to sell rumors if offered a price. The galley-beggar sliding past her in the close quarters of the tavern had no ears to hear with, nor eyes to see—nor, for that matter, a head to put such things in—but that wouldn't stop him. If he could drink the coffee in his hand, he could carry tales, too.

"Welcome back to London," Magrat said dryly. "A nest of vipers, all with their tails tied together, because nobody's quite willing to give this place up. Except you, fifty years ago."

When she'd abandoned Turkish carpets and dirty rushes in favor of clean dirt and wild strawberries, politics and spying and insurrection for hunting beneath the summer moon. It would be easy enough to escape this snare again; all she had to do was put down her ale cup, walk out the nearest entrance, and return to the Vale.

Easy enough to leave. Staying away was harder. All it had taken was Tom Toggin, and the recollection of the coming threat, to drag her back into the city. Because, as Magrat said, she wasn't quite willing to give it up.

Out of the corner of her eye, Irrith saw the church grim's lipless mouth twitch. Suddenly suspicious, the sprite demanded, "Have you made another bet with Dead Rick?

Maybe one about how I'll go crawling back to the Vale before the season is out?"

The grim's smile was all teeth. "That's what *he* thinks. I'd be obliged if you didn't; I stand to win a pair of eyes off him."

Gambling, at least, was something Irrith understood. So was a challenge. She returned Magrat's grin fiercely. "All right. I could see my way clear to obliging you . . . if you give *me* something in return."

"Iron blast your soul," the goblin said, but the venom was only halfhearted. "I should've known better than to tell you that. All right, what do you want?"

"More information. Not now; I'll save the debt for later. And I'll make it something small."

Magrat thought it over, then spat in her hand again. Wet palms joined, the church grim said, "I'm counting on your stubbornness. Don't you disappoint me."

The Onyx Hall, London: February 12, 1758

My own court should not be a distraction to me.

Lune recognized the foolishness of that sentiment, even as she thought it. Political difficulties did not resolve themselves just because there was an external threat; some might, but others worsened. For every faerie who decided a wounded Queen was a problem for later, after the defeat of the Dragon, there was another who felt that now more than ever, they needed a sovereign who was whole.

The best she could do was to keep one finger on that pulse, and try to anticipate where real trouble might break out. To that end, she met in private with her Lord Keeper, Valentin Aspell.

"As you might expect, madam," the lord said in his quiet, sibilant voice, "the reaction is mixed. Some take it as a hopeful sign: if you can achieve something as great as the Calendar Room, then surely you can mend the Onyx Hall."

He let a hint of reproach through. The major responsibility of the Lord Keeper, at least publicly, was the maintenance of enchanted items; the Calendar Room, while hardly something that would fit into the royal treasury, might have fallen under his authority. Lune had shared the secret only with those few who needed to know, however, and Aspell had not been one of them.

Hopeful signs were good. She knew better than to believe they comprised the majority, though. "What of the rest?"

The Lord Keeper picked up a neatly bound stack of newspapers, grimacing as the cheap ink came off on his fingers. "Sanist reactions are as you would expect. The profound lack of logic and reasoning on display is nothing short of astounding; some have leapt to the conclusion that the Calendar Room operates by draining *your* life, madam, and that you are therefore mortal now."

Lune sighed. She knew better than to think the common subjects of her realm were all stupid; some goblins and pucks were very clever indeed, just as some of her courtiers were utter fools. But many of those common fae were uneducated, knowing nothing beyond what their own natures inclined them to, and that made them easy prey for rumors.

Some of which, she knew, were spread deliberately.

Aspell shook his head before she could ask. "I do agree with you, madam, that there is a leadership of some kind among the Sanists—a group actively seeking your replacement. But they are more careful than the fools who drink in the Crow's Head. I doubt we'll be able to find them until they make a clear move."

The fact that he was right made it no easier to swallow. And even if she broke up the Sanist leadership, the sentiments would remain; it might give her a brief respite, but nothing more.

She lifted one hand to pinch her brow, then made herself lower it. While there was no great warmth between the two of them, she couldn't fault Aspell's effectiveness; he'd served her almost continually since her accession to the throne, and proved his use more times than she could count. Sooner or later he would find the right thread to pull, and unravel this knot.

She just hoped it came sooner. It would be pleasant to have one less problem to deal with.

"Keep watch over Carline," Lune said at last. "If she isn't involved, they may yet approach her. Inform me if you uncover any signs of trouble."

Ordinarily she put the Lord Keeper's spies to a variety of uses, but they were useless in the matter of the comet, and the Sanists were by far her second greatest worry. Anything else could wait. Valentin Aspell bowed deeply and said, "Madam, I will do everything I can."

St. James, Westminster: February 14, 1758

Miserably chill rain washed across Westminster in sporadic waves, but the interior of Gregory's was warm, and laden with the competing scents of coffee, wig powder, perfume. The close of the Christmas holidays, the sitting of Parliament, and the prospect of approaching spring meant the quality were returning to London from their country estates, and marshaling themselves for the beginning of the Season.

Of Galen's companions, two had retired in such fashion, while one—like him—had stayed in London, for lack of money to make that country estate habitable. Today was the first renewed gathering of their usual club, which Mayhew had dubbed the Feckless Scions. It was more a joke than anything else. They were just a small group of friends meeting in a coffeehouse; nothing like so organized as White's, or even the clubs of the whores or the Negroes. It was, however, the only one Galen belonged to. There was one for men associated with the fae, but it was an awkward thing; they were too mismatched of a lot, and as Prince, he felt very self-conscious in attending.

Besides, those men would not have been able to help him with his current problem. Galen drained his coffee cup, clapped it onto the table, and said, "Friends, I need your assistance. I have to find a wife."

His declaration met with appalled looks. Jonathan Hurst, eldest of their coterie at twenty-five, said, "What for? By any decent standard, you've got at least five more years of free whoring ahead of you, before being shackled to a wife."

"Don't tell me you've sired a bastard," Laurence Byrd said suspiciously.

Peter Mayhew smacked him on the shoulder. "He said *find* a wife, idiot. If he had a bastard, logic says it would come with a woman attached."

"Not if the mother's dead, or unsuitable! He might need another woman to raise the child for him."

"*I don't,*" Galen said, before their speculations could saddle him with enough scandal to occupy society gossips for a week. "There's no child—at least not that I know of. But my father is forcing my hand."

Noises of comprehension sounded around the table. All had met his father, and knew Charles St. Clair's manner. "It had to happen sooner or later," Byrd agreed, his countenance now sympathetically gloomy. "Well, there's one silver lining: the sooner you're married, the sooner you get out from under his thumb. You have that to look forward to, at least."

For what it was worth. Galen knew better than to believe his wedding and departure from Leicester Fields would mean freedom from his father. He knew men of thirty years' age who still flinched when their sires spoke.

None of his companions suffered quite so much under the patriarchal hand. Byrd's and Mayhew's fathers were both of a more amiable nature, and Hurst's had died seven years ago—though that had the unfortunate effect of making him responsible for two headstrong younger brothers, both of them disinclined to respect him as the patriarch of their household.

"My round," Mayhew said, and got up to buy more coffee, threading his way through the room.

Hurst tugged the folded cuffs of his coat straight with a precise motion and said, "All right. You've asked our aid, and we shall give it. What do you need?"

"A wife," Byrd reminded him.

"And any female creature of marriageable age will do?

Provided, one imagines, that she has two legs, two eyes, and all the other parts customary to such a creature—"

Galen laughed. "I took your meaning, Hurst, and he did, too. He's just being an ass. As to your question . . ." Laughter turned to a sigh. "The primary requirement, as you might imagine, is wealth."

Hurst nodded. "Your sisters."

Mayhew had just come back, and the bowls rattled against the table as the he set them down. He was the youngest of their group: eighteen, and precisely Daphne's age. Galen knew full well that his friend harbored a not-so-secret tendre for his middle sister. He also knew, unfortunately, that the May-hews were in even worse straits than the St. Clairs. Regardless of what wealth Galen acquired with his marriage, his father would never consent to let Daphne wed someone of such low status.

"How large of a settlement do you need?" Byrd asked. If he noticed Mayhew's discomfiture, he gave no sign, but simply took one of the cups.

Choosing a number left a bad taste in Galen's mouth, but he'd promised himself, while Edward shaved him that morning, that he would approach this in precisely the same way he did the threat of the Dragon: identify what needed to be done, evaluate potential methods of achieving it, and then pursue them one by one until he attained success. It was a wretched manner of seeking marriage, but it was also the only way he could bring himself to do it at all.

"Five thousand," he said at last. "More, if possible." Which made it unlikely he'd snare the daughter of a gentleman. Those with good fortunes were seeking better prey than him.

His companions nodded, and Hurst said, "Anything else?"

Now it became a matter, not of necessity, but of desire. And that was far more treacherous territory. "The usual," Galen said, trying to make light of it. "An agreeable nature, good habits of cleanliness, no insanity in the bloodline—"

"No fondness for lapdogs," Byrd suggested. "Can't stand the damn things. I'll never visit if you marry a woman with a dog."

But Hurst didn't break his gaze from Galen. He, too,

sought a wife, though less urgently; as head of his own household, it was now incumbent upon him to secure an heir. "You're a romantic, St. Clair," he said, over Byrd's complaints about useless dogs. "Surely you must desire more in a wife than a moderate fortune and a clean bill of health."

Byrd ceased his tirade. Mayhew, too, was watching. They would not let it go, he knew; they understood him too well.

A faerie queen, he thought, images of Lune filling his mind. Seated on her throne, or taking her ease in the garden, ethereal as the moon.

He closed his eyes. "A serene manner," he said, releasing the words one by one, as if laying treasures on the table. "Well-educated, not just in languages and music and dancing, but history and literature. And above all, a quick mind, curious and clever. Someone I can converse with, in more than mere flirtation."

Silence greeted his description. Galen made himself open his eyes once more, and found himself facing three very different expressions. Byrd, ever the cynic, recovered his tongue first. "You'll have to keep such a wife on a leash; curiosity and marital stability rarely go hand in hand." Mayhew smacked him again.

"I'm quite serious," Galen insisted, flushing. "Fortune is well and good, but that is my father's requirement, not mine. And he isn't the one who will be living with her until death do us part. I'm damned if I'll take a wife I don't respect."

It silenced Byrd, and put a thoughtful look on Hurst's face. "It narrows your field, at least, and that is a virtue; you'll be pursuing specific targets, which they often appreciate. Judith Chamberlain might do."

"Too old," was Byrd's immediate verdict. "He can't take a wife half again as old as he is."

Which was an exaggeration, but Hurst let it pass. "Abigail Watts. Cecily Palmer. Northwood's eldest—what's her name—"

"Philadelphia," Mayhew supplied, after a moment's pause.

Byrd had objections to them all. "Abby Watts would never tolerate a mistress. The Palmer girl's mad for another fellow;

she'd be the one straying from *you,* St. Clair. And Philadelphia—phaw! Can you imagine a more unwieldy name?"

"Well, damn it all, Byrd; you'll shoot down every girl in England if we give you half a chance!"

He met Mayhew's accusation with a shrug. "As they merit, my friend."

"Every marriage is a compromise," Hurst said—a declaration so authoritative, it could almost make one forget he was still unmarried himself.

"I'll compromise on beauty," Galen said; none could meet the standard of Lune, anyway. "But not upon fortune, nor upon respect. If that means there end up being lapdogs, then Byrd, you'll just have to endure." He drew a small book and pencil from his pocket. Opening it to a blank page, he asked Hurst, "Which names did you suggest, again?"

The Onyx Hall, London: March 11, 1758

Irrith didn't have the temperament for spying and intrigue, nor the inclination to publish her thoughts in either of the Onyx Hall's newspapers. But reading *The Ash and Thorn* for a few weeks vexed her enough that she did the one thing she was good at, which was to go after the source of her problem.

Carline.

Not Lady Carline, not anymore; she'd lost her position in Lune's bedchamber after her ill-fated attempt to trick Irrith. She still occupied the same rooms as always, though, and that was where Irrith sought her out, pounding on the door with an impatient fist.

A mortal servant opened the door, a wrinkled old woman quite unlike the beautiful youths that had waited on the elf-lady before. The woman eyed her dubiously. "What do you want?"

"Carline. And my business with her is serious, so don't even—"

"Irrith?" The surprised call was unmistakably Carline's velvety tone.

The woman scowled and let Irrith pass. The chamber beyond was embarrassingly luxurious, with red-cushioned benches in some Oriental style; Carline lounged upon one of these, wine in hand. She rose as Irrith entered. "Why, it *is* you. I'd heard you were in London once more, but I confess, I never thought you would come to me."

The fallen lady's lush body showed to great advantage even in the relatively plain gown she was wearing, and she towered nearly a head over Irrith. Undaunted, the sprite put her hands on her hips and glared upward. "I wouldn't have, except that I have something to say to you."

The black eyebrows rose. "I see you haven't changed. Or rather, you've changed back to what you were before I tried to refine you. Very well, be blunt: say what you have come for."

"Stop trying to overthrow the Queen."

The previous rise had been an elegant affectation; this time, Carline's brows shot upward like startled crows. "I beg your pardon?"

Irrith dug a folded copy of the most recent *Ash and Thorn* out of her pocket and waved it. "You didn't stop, did you, even after Lune found out. I told you fifty years ago, Carline: you don't just *vote* your monarch out."

"The mortals did," Carline said. She'd recovered from her surprise, and set her wineglass down with a *clink*. "Seventy years ago. And now the Jacobite pretenders try to regain the throne through the votes of swords—which is better? But I have no wish to debate political philosophy with you, Irrith, as entertaining as it would be to watch the result. Since I have somewhere I must be, let me say this instead: come with me. I'd like to show you something."

Irrith recoiled, sensing a trap. "No."

"What do you expect—that I'll knife you and leave you in an alley? I promise, I mean no harm."

Carline might be taller, but she'd never be able to kill Irrith, especially not when Irrith had a pistol in her other pocket. "I've learned my lesson about trusting you."

The former lady sighed in disappointment. "I confess, that was an error on my part. I didn't think you clever enough to realize what I was doing. Well, *I* have learned *my* lesson; no more tricks." She tilted her head and looked down at Irrith with an expression that might almost be called fond. "You had a certain charm, though. Unlettered, uncultured—I enjoyed introducing you to the *beau monde* and watching you scandalize them. Consider this a favor, in repayment for that diversion. I'll even give you bread. And when it's over, I'll answer the demand you came to make."

That Carline was dangerous, Irrith had no doubt. But it was danger of a sort that could be avoided, so long as she kept her eyes open. And the offer, she had to admit, had aroused her curiosity. "Very well. But if you're deceiving me after all, you'll find out just how uncultured I can be."

Covent Garden, Westminster: March 11, 1758

Carline led her above and west. At first Irrith thought this more of her usual *beau monde* business, entertaining herself with society's high-born and beautiful people. But their destination lay in a warren of narrow streets just north of the Strand, where a crowd of people both fine and not waited outside a large building. "Three shillings for a floor seat," Carline said. "I will find you afterward."

It was a theater. "Where will you be?" Irrith asked, but her companion had already vanished into the crowd.

If this was a deception, it wasn't Carline's usual style. Irrith frowned, paid, and went inside. There she found herself a seat on one of the backless benches that covered the floor. The theater being crowded, she had to fight for a place, but being in London made her remember the use of her elbows. Soon she had a patch of green cushion large enough for her rump, just in time for the play to begin.

She'd been to the theater before, though not this particular one. It amused her to watch mortals invent and play out stories that never happened. With their studied gestures and bombastic delivery of lines, they almost became something other than humanity, strange beasts in a ritual pageant.

She'd never seen anything like this before.

It was as if real people were on the stage, unaware of the audience observing them. They laughed and shouted and wept, for all the world as if these things were happening to them in truth. If their words were more eloquent and their lives more strange than any real person's would have been, it only heightened the effect, like a polishing cloth bringing out the fine grain of wood.

It was magic. The charms and enchantments of faerie-kind were nothing to this. During one of the pauses for applause, Irrith realized she'd even seen this play before; it was an old one, *The City Heiress,* written by a woman last century. But this new style of acting made it all seem fresh. They wove an illusion with nothing more than the tools of ordinary life, until the audience vanished and there was nothing but the story on the stage. Here was a rich heiress, and here, the two men who would woo her, and Irrith had to struggle to remember they were simply mortals playing a part.

Mortals—and one faerie.

Irrith's jaw fell slack when Carline walked onto the stage. That it was the elf-lady, she had no doubt; Carline looked almost exactly like herself, the glamour only serving to remove the faerie cast from her features. But she was dressed in sumptuous clothes befitting a wealthy man's mistress, for that was the role she was playing: Diana, mistress to the younger of the two would-be suitors.

It broke the magic, and for that, Irrith resented her. In the scenes that didn't include Diana, she could briefly lose herself once more, but every time the faerie actress reappeared Irrith was back in a noisy and boisterous theater, watching people in costumes pretend to be something they were not. And Carline was no good at it: she could not counterfeit emotion, not as the humans could. For fae, there was little distance between pretense and feeling, and without the latter it was hard to manage the former.

When the play ended, Irrith turned to the drunken young

gentleman at her side. "What was that woman doing up there?" she demanded.

"Mrs. Pritchard?" He seemed to have forgotten Irrith's use of her elbows, for he peered at her in a friendly enough manner, albeit an unsteady one. "Too old for the role of Charlot, but she's so splendid that—"

"Not the heiress," Irrith said impatiently. "The other one. The mistress. Diana."

"Oh, her." The gentleman blinked, then turned to his companion. *Her* occupation was obvious enough, for he seemed to have forgotten her name. The woman, painted an inch thick, merely shrugged. He echoed the shrug back at Irrith. "She plays here on occasion. Don't know why Garrick lets her; she isn't any good."

Irrith could guess. Further application of her elbows got her through the crowd and out the lobby once more, and then she followed two gentlemen around to the back of the theater.

They had come to see Mrs. Pritchard, but were turned away at the door. Irrith loitered a little distance off until Carline emerged, dressed once more in plain clothing.

The sprite shook her head in disbelief as Carline came toward her. "All right, so you've charmed the manager into letting you make a public display of yourself. Why did I have to see this?"

Carline looked hurt—genuinely so. "Mr. Garrick knows my worth. Some of the best people in London have come to see me perform. Did you not enjoy the play?"

She sounded like she truly believed it: that the rich gentlemen and their ladies came to see *her*, rather than the splendid Mrs. Pritchard. "I enjoyed it," Irrith said grudgingly. "But what did this have to do with anything?"

She jumped back when Carline tried to grab her arm. "Stop that," the lady said through her teeth. "We've drawn attention, Irrith, and unless you want to make new friends, you'll come with me, quickly."

Glancing around, Irrith saw they were almost alone in the alley, save for two pipe-smoking actors, one prostitute trying to drum up a bit of business, and a rough-looking fellow taking far too much interest in herself and Carline. They went swiftly around a corner, then another, then a third; the elf-lady clearly knew her way through this warren. They emerged without warning into an open space, edged with taverns doing roaring business: Covent Garden Market, Irrith realized, much seedier than when she last saw it.

There were prostitutes and thieves here, too, but being out in the open gave them a measure of safety from the latter, and Carline's company deterred many of the former. Not all, though; one half-fed wretch asked through bruised lips if the gentleman might perhaps like the company of *two* ladies. "No, thank you," Irrith said, and hastened past.

Carline breathed deep of the reeking air, then let it out in a gusty sigh. "I brought you here so you could see the truth. This is what I'm doing these days—not scheming, or plotting, or egging on the Sanists. You've no reason to believe me, Irrith, but I swear to you: I don't want Lune's crown."

She was right; Irrith had no reason to believe her. "You wanted it before."

"That's true." She looked thoughtfully across the riotous square. "But with Lune's crown come Lune's problems, don't they? It was one thing fifty years ago: the Dragon's return just announced, and all that time in which to figure out how to get rid of it. Now we've scarcely a year left. The Queen can say what she likes about that Calendar Room, but I know the truth; she hasn't got a plan. The Onyx Hall will burn, and maybe London, too. Why should I make that my fault, instead of hers?"

Irrith tasted bile. "So you'll wait until afterward. Until it's all been destroyed."

Carline gave her a pitying look. "And how would that profit me? I have no desire to rule over ashes. No, little sprite: my political ambitions are finished. My intention is to spend this last year doing everything I've always wanted to, everything that can only be done in London, and then when that bearded star appears in the sky, I will go someplace where it is not." Now her eyes fixed on a distant point—a point, Irrith suspected, not in this world. "Faerie, I think. I have no desire to exile myself to some rustic hovel like your Vale. But I haven't decided; it may be France instead."

Her words cut close to the bone. Hadn't Irrith thought almost the same thing, when she arrived in the autumn? Enjoy the Onyx Court while it lasted, then abandon it to its doom.

Now the bile in her throat was for herself. She'd never thought to feel kinship with Carline.

As if hearing those thoughts, the elf-lady laughed softly. "I'm not the only one, either. It was different when the Dragon took us by surprise, birthing itself out of the Great Fire; we were trapped, with little choice but to fight. Now we know it's coming. Only the foolhardy wish to stand in its path."

Despite the evidence of the past, Irrith found that she believed Carline. The lady really was done. "So what do the Sanists want?"

She got a shrug in reply. "Precisely what they say they want, I imagine. A new sovereign—presumably one who has both health and a plan for defeating the Dragon. But it won't be me. In truth, I think they'll get only half of what they want, and they know it; they can build whatever court they please after this one is gone."

If that was true, Irrith despised them. Lune was wounded, yes, and that was a problem in need of an answer. Letting the Dragon destroy the court, though, was no answer at all. "What about the mortals?"

"What of them?"

That sounded like honest confusion, not artful innocence. Irrith said, "If the Dragon destroys the Onyx Hall, and the court is broken—what will become of mortal London?"

"It will continue on, as it always has," Carline said dismissively. "Even if their city is destroyed again, they'll simply rebuild; they've done it before. But you don't mean that, do you?" Her eyes regarded Irrith with cool irony. "What you mean is, however will they cope, without faeries beneath their feet?"

They were speaking far too frankly, in far too public of a place; even if nobody nearby had reason to understand or care, it still made Irrith twitch. Back in the Vale, fae did not stand in the village square discussing Wayland's affairs. But Carline's sardonic question demanded an answer. "We've done so much for them."

The twist of Carline's lips mocked her assertion. "Have we?"

"We stopped the Dragon. Without us, it would have burnt down the rest of London."

"And with us, it only burnt down *most* of London. Such a gift to the people of this city! It isn't just that we failed to stop it sooner; *we fed it*. With our wars and our magics. Without us, would it even have *become* a Dragon? Or would it have stayed a simple fire, the kind London has seen before? Consider that, Irrith, before you speak so righteously of what we've done: it may be that our very presence in this city, the enchantments that bind the world above to the world below, transform London's troubles into something more than they can handle alone . . . or create trouble where none was before." Carline's smile was poisonous. "Without us, the comet would be nothing more than a light in the sky."

Irrith felt as if she'd swallowed fire. Carline was wrong; she had to be. The Onyx Court was important—

To whom? To fae like Irrith—and yes, like Carline—who wanted to be close to mortals, to observe them and talk to them and bask in the reflected glow of their passion. Brief lives, flickering in and out like fireflies, and all the more brilliant because of it. But what benefit did the fireflies gain?

Carline recognized the selfishness of it, as Irrith had not. And far from repenting, she embraced it, reveled in it. But when the music stopped, she would leave the dance.

Would Irrith do the same?

"Think about it, little sprite," Carline said softly, leaning in uncomfortably close. "Decide whether you believe the Queen, that this place, this court, is so grand as to be worth preserving. Or admit the truth of it—use these mortals while you can—and then move on. You have eternity to live; do you want to risk it for those who would be better off without us?"

She didn't wait for an answer. Perhaps she knew Irrith didn't have one to give. Without a backward glance, Carline left Irrith standing in the clamor of Covent Garden Market, surrounded and alone.

New Spring Gardens, Vauxhall: March 11, 1758

Galen paced the deck of the barge with restless strides, staggering occasionally when the river slapped its side and tilted the vessel without warning. It didn't disturb the consort of viols who entertained the barge's passengers, seated as they were midway down the deck, but he had taken refuge in the bow, where the small turbulences of the river were felt most strongly.

Better that than to take a carriage. As the barge drew near the western bank and the waiting stair, he could see an unmoving line of conveyances clogging the road to the entrance of the Vauxhall Spring Gardens. Had his family gone that route, he would have spent even more time listening to his parents quarrel about the respectability of the place, with even less opportunity to escape it.

A footstep behind him, coming down unexpectedly hard as the barge juddered in the rough water. It was a windy night, and when Galen turned, he saw Cynthia clapping one hand to her gypsy hat, lest a sudden gust carry it away. He came forward and retied the bow beneath his sister's chin, and she smiled her thanks. "The barge-men hardly need to row," she said, brushing one hand over her sarcenet skirts. "They could just get the ladies on deck, and we'd sail all the way upriver."

Galen offered his arm to steady her. From farther down the boat, he heard his father say to his mother, in a tone that ought to brook no argument, "I don't give a damn what goes on in the bushes, so long as the father has money to hush it up."

He winced. Cynthia tightened her hand on his arm, and they stayed where they were as the other passengers crowded the rail in anticipation of arrival. "That's *his* sentiment," she reminded him, rising on her toes to murmur it in his ear. "Not yours."

As if he could so easily disown his relations. "I'm tarred with it regardless," Galen said. He tried to summon some enthusiasm for this night, and failed. "I've come in search of a fortune, and everyone will know it. What young lady wants to wed such a man?"

Another squeeze of Cynthia's hand. "I don't see such a man at all."

"You're my sister, and partisan."

"Yes—but that doesn't mean I'm wrong. *I* see a man determined to do what's best for his family, particularly as it concerns the future happiness of his sisters. Young ladies find that sort of thing very touching."

The barge thudded gently into the lower end of the river stair and was made fast. Passengers began to disembark, gentlemen assisting ladies to solid land once more. "Touching," Galen said, amused despite himself. "So I'm a charity cause, now."

"*Everything* is a charity cause, to a kind-hearted young lady," Cynthia answered brightly, not so much accompanying as steering him toward the barge's rail. "It's our profession, you know, and being touched in the heart is our foremost skill. I myself got very poor marks in it, burdened as I am with too much sense—but then, you aren't looking to marry *me*."

That last comment got an alarmed and confused look from their mother, who clearly was not certain what they were talking about, but was just as certain it showed too much levity for the occasion. "Cynthia, do not hang upon his arm," she admonished her eldest daughter, making shooing motions with her folded fan. "From a distance it will look as if you two are in company, when people cannot see you are related, and then they will not approach."

Galen could hardly blame his mother for her concern. She had a nervous disposition to begin with, and his agreement with his father had put her into a pother. Nothing would do but that both Galen and Cynthia were promised to be married by the end of the Season; only then would she rest easy. She might not like the pleasure gardens as a hunting ground for spouses—there were far too many opportunities for illicit liaisons, in the dark byways of the walks—but the charity event tonight was respectable enough, and likely to draw the sort of man and woman both he and Cynthia needed.

Bracing himself, he helped his sister to the stair, then his mother. The elder St. Clair glared away any prospect of aid, so he waited until the old man had passed, before following like a docile sheep.

On the roadway above, Cynthia contrived to fall back so they could walk together, following the line of people to the waiting carriages, and the building that marked the entrance to the Spring Gardens. "All will be well," she assured him, letting their parents draw a bit ahead. "If it helps, think on this: you may believe you're the hunter, but in truth you're hunted. All those mothers with unwed daughters, looking to trap you in their snares. You hardly stand a chance, poor boy."

A hint of pain hid behind those light words. No such happy snares awaited Cynthia; she had no profit to offer a prospective husband, beyond her good nature. "Then I shall hunt on your behalf," Galen promised.

She hadn't Daphne's beauty, but Cynthia was the only one of the St. Clair children to inherit their mother's dimples. They flickered briefly in the lantern light as the garden entrance drew near. "We can work together, like a pair of hounds. I'll bring suitable young ladies to you, and you shall find gentlemen for me. With such an alliance, success cannot be far away."

Galen smiled down at his sister, feeling his spirit lighten. "If there are any young men here worthy of your good heart, my dear, I shall not fail to lay them at your feet." And with those words, they passed through the building into the Spring Gardens beyond.

Despite the windy night, the Grand Walk was well lit by globes hung from the trees. Beneath those lights circulated the cream of London's society, from wealthy merchants to the aristocracy itself, to the accompaniment of music from the orchestra in the grove.

And half of them at least were hunting spouses, for themselves or for their offspring.

At least he needn't winnow the grain from the chaff. Tonight's ridotto al fresco was a charity event, to benefit some worthy cause or another—the Foundling Hospital, perhaps, or soldiers wounded in the Jacobite Rebellion. On an ordinary night, anyone who could afford the shilling entrance fee could come inside. Poorer folks saved their pennies, then dressed in their shabby best to gawk at the music and the paintings and the splendor of their betters.

His mother had a point, Galen was forced to admit; the place *wasn't* entirely reputable. Hopefully Cynthia knew to keep far away from the Druid Walk and other such dark corners, where young bloods laid snares for unchaperoned young ladies. It should be safer tonight, with the prostitutes chased out, but not every peer's son respected a woman's dignity as he should.

Food was laid out in the Rotunda to their left, slightly better than the usual overpriced fare of the gardens. Peter Mayhew lurked there, and his face fell when he saw that Daphne hadn't accompanied them. "Hurst is about somewhere," he told Galen, gesturing vaguely at the expanse of the gardens. "If I see him, I'll tell him you're here; I believe he intends to spend the night hunting on your behalf."

It seemed Galen would have all the assistance he could stomach, and more. He was grateful to spot Dr. Andrews near the orchestra, the one man in London with whom he could talk something other than marriage prospects.

The stick-thin man turned when Galen called his name. "Ah, Mr. St. Clair. Here to support the good efforts of the Marine Society?"

So it was the Navy they were benefitting. "Yes, of course," Galen said, as if he'd known. Andrews's mouth compressed, not quite concealing amusement. To prove he wasn't *entirely* ignorant of the evening's design, Galen added, "Mr. Lowe will be singing later, I believe. Have you had the pleasure of hearing him? A fine tenor indeed."

"A fine voice, but an inferior grasp of musical art," Andrews said. "One would think the latter could be taught, and the former could not, but it seems beyond Mr. Lowe's capacity. Nevertheless, a splendid singer—I do not mean to belittle him. Hanway would not engage him for this event, otherwise."

"How go your studies?" Galen asked, and they spent an enjoyable if gruesome few minutes discussing the medical arts. This entirely inappropriate conversation, however, was interrupted by the arrival of Cynthia, with another young lady in tow. "Oh, I do apologize—Galen, I wanted to introduce you to my friend Miss Northwood."

He bowed, sighing inwardly. *From one duty to another, this one less pleasant.* Northwood; that was one of the names Hurst had suggested. The one whose given name Byrd had derided.

Philadelphia certainly was a grand name for its bearer. She was excessively thin, and had the kind of plainness that showed its worst in fine dress; elegance merely heightened the lack of it in her face. Not ugly, just very unexceptional—the sort who attracted compliments for her fine straight teeth. And even those only appeared briefly, in an awkward smile.

"We'd be poor gentlemen indeed if we objected to the company of two pretty girls," Galen said, substituting courtesy for truth. "And if you overheard our topic—I promise you, we *can* be more civilized. Just a few minutes ago Dr. Andrews and I were discussing the singer, Mr. Lowe. Have you heard him, Miss Northwood?"

"Once," she said, in a soft contralto. "Not the most subtle in his interpretation of the melody—but you hardly notice that fault, past the glory of his voice."

Which earned her Dr. Andrews's instant approval. The two of them immediately commenced a debate over whose musical interpretation was superior to Lowe's, while Cynthia cast Galen a look he could interpret all too easily. So this was her assistance to him: Miss Northwood as a prospective target. He had not known they were friends.

She seemed pleasant enough. And Galen *had* said that beauty was not his chiefest requirement. In fact—noting the colorful chiné silk of her gown, the intricate cording around its neckline—he recalled now why Hurst would have suggested her. Philadelphia Northwood's father was one of the Directors of the Bank of England. Wealthy, and eager for his daughter to marry into a better family. In short, exactly what Galen was looking for.

He marshaled his courage and waited for an opportune moment. When it came, he said, "Miss Northwood—do you dance?"

She raised her eyebrows at him. Galen had the distinct impression this was not a question she was often asked; young men, seeing her, no doubt assumed that plainness on her part meant bruised toes on theirs, and inquired elsewhere. But the musicians were striking up a contredanse, and a platform had been built in the Grove for the purpose. She said, "I do, Mr. St. Clair—when invited."

"Then please allow me to extend my invitation," he said, proffering his arm to accompany the words.

Cynthia's encouraging smile pursued them as they went to join the other dancers. This was easy enough, easier than conversation; he'd been through many hours of dancing lessons, and no doubt she had, too. He settled his hat more firmly upon his head, so the trickster wind could not snatch it away, and gave his hand to Miss Northwood, who accepted it with a curtsy.

She danced like an instruction book, every movement precisely as her own dancing master must have dictated it to her, without any particular flair or grace. But neither did she step upon his toes, and once he was certain of that safety, Galen realized he must make conversation after all. "I was not aware you were friends with my sister," he began, seizing upon the first safe topic that came to mind.

"Cynthia and I share certain charity interests," Miss Northwood replied, as they circled each other in an allemande. "The Society for the Improvement of Education Among the Indigent Poor."

A perfectly respectable thing for polite young ladies to do. "And do you fill all your days with the improvement of one thing or another?" he asked, with a smile to show he meant no disdain. "Or do you spare an hour here and there for more frivolous pursuits?"

Her careful mask of pleasantry briefly deepened to something more genuine as they joined hands for a promenade. "I am no Methodist, Mr. St. Clair. If I filled every day with nothing but good works, I would soon burn my candle to a stub.

The occasional frivolous diversion, I find, restores some of its lost wax—if I may be forgiven my execrable choice of metaphor, which I fear has taken a wrong turn somewhere. I should have gone with lamp oil."

It startled a laugh out of him—a real one, not the polite chuckle every gentleman cultivated for genteel conversation. "Forgiven, Miss Northwood. What manner of diversion do you prefer?"

She hesitated for only the most fleeting of instants; had the dance oriented him away from her at that moment, he would have missed it. "I enjoy reading."

As many plain young ladies did, their time unoccupied by the demands of flirtation and social intrigue. "Novels?"

Her answering look was sharp, before she moved to change places with the lady of the neighboring couple. By the time they were rejoined, the careful mask was back. "Sometimes. Also history, philosophy, translations of classical works—"

Galen realized his mistake. He should have detected it sooner; Cynthia knew him, and knew where his priorities would be in courting. "I apologize, Miss Northwood. Were it not at our estate in Essex, I would show you my own library, and you would see I'm of your mind. These days, I must make do with a circulating library." It was the only way he could get new books; his father firmly condemned the expense of purchasing them.

"Make do?" She laughed. "They are a wonderful institution, for if I purchased every book I wished to read, my father would put me on bread and water to make up the expense."

Not just the refuge of a plain girl who could get nothing better; she had actual passion for learning. *Vauxhall is a terrible place for her,* Galen thought. It advertised every good quality she did not possess, while hiding those she did. *She would do much better in another context.*

The dance was ending, which was a good thing for them both. Their inattention had caused their steps to degenerate, his as well as hers. "Miss Northwood," he said as he made his final bow, "have you been to see the curiosities of the British Museum?"

"I thought it wasn't open to the public yet."

He smiled. "It isn't, but they can be persuaded to admit the occasional select visitor. I would be delighted to arrange a small party." Cynthia would help, he was sure. And for the chance of snaring such wealth, his father would not begrudge the expense.

Having uttered those words, he saw that the smile Miss Northwood had offered upon meeting him was a false thing, her attempt at the coquetry expected of a marriageable young woman. *This* was the real Miss Northwood, and the frank honesty of this smile was much more charming. "Mr. St. Clair, I would walk barefoot to Bloomsbury for the chance."

As they approached the edge of the crowd, Galen saw Cynthia raise an inquisitive eyebrow. He nodded at her, gratitude warming his heart. *There may be other prospects. Nothing is certain yet. But thank you, beloved sister—this is a very good place to start.*

The Onyx Hall, London: March 11, 1758

There were two elf-knights at the chamber door, members of the Onyx Guard, but it was the valet Irrith couldn't get past. "Lord Galen is occupied," he said.

Irrith scowled ferociously. The servant didn't so much as blink. He was faerie-blooded, that was obvious; it showed in the set of his eyes. Clearly he'd seen enough of fae to be less than impressed with the scowl of one slender sprite.

She had nothing to bribe him with, either. Flirtation was out of the question; Irrith was not Carline, in inclination or skill. She had to resort to something like the honest truth. "It has to do with the Dragon."

The word was practically a magic key, opening doors throughout the Onyx Hall. But not this door, it seemed. "Very good, ma'am," the servant said with a bow. "If you would care to leave your message with me—"

"I would not. Listen, nocky boy; I have a question for the Prince, and until I get an answer—"

The door suddenly swung farther open, revealing Lord

Galen, in a state of half-dress. His shirtsleeves billowed silk-white out of his unbuttoned waistcoat, and his wig was missing. Irrith fought not to goggle. He looked very different without its carefully styled curls—somehow both older and younger, and definitely less foppish.

Galen ran one self-conscious hand over his cropped scalp, as if only just now realizing that perhaps it did not do to meet a lady at his door with his head so very bare. His hair was chestnut brown, darker than her own. "Dame Irrith. Come in."

He did not say, *So I don't have to listen to you and my man argue forever.* Irrith didn't much care why he let her in; she obeyed with speed, slipping past the servant, and even restraining herself from smirking at him.

The Prince's chambers were much changed from the last time she saw them—which was, after all, more than fifty years and several Princes ago. They were *light*! Someone, perhaps at Galen's instigation, had covered the black walls with some kind of paint or paper in an agreeable shade of pale blue. Carpets softened the stone floors, and elegant chairs stood about, as well as a few sturdier pieces. No doubt those were there for the convenience of the Onyx Court's more massive fae.

Irrith bowed, but Galen dismissed it with a wave of his hand, gesturing her to sit at a small table. "Would you like anything to drink? No? Thank you, Edward; that will be all."

The man bowed and retired to an inner room. If he was a proper Onyx Court servant, he'd be eavesdropping at the keyhole. *Well, let him,* Irrith thought. Lune wouldn't let him serve the Prince if she didn't trust his discretion.

It was hard to attach that title to Galen, young as he was, and so uncertain. He seemed to breathe easier, though, away from Lune. He hesitated for a moment, before apparently deciding not to retire and dress properly; instead he seated himself across from Irrith. "So. You have something to say about the Dragon."

"I," Irrith said, and stopped. "Um. That is—"

A grin lurked at the corner of his mouth. "It was something you said to get past Edward." Irrith looked down in embarrassment. "It's all right; my time isn't so precious as he thinks. What did you want?"

She felt very odd, sitting in this light and delicate room. It didn't feel like the Onyx Hall at all—more like some fashionable gentleman's parlor, that happened to have no windows. A little piece of the mortal world, brought down here intact. "You're mortal," Irrith said.

The grin came back, lurking more obviously. "I am," Galen agreed.

"And you're a part of the Onyx Court. The Prince, even. So you must believe this place is worthwhile. Right?"

It didn't quite kill the grin, but Galen's eyebrows rose. "Of course I do."

"Why?"

He stared at her, lips slightly parted. Watching the play of emotions across his face was entrancing. Galen had a very expressive face, wide-eyed, with a sensitive mouth and skin that easily betrayed a blush. And his mood changed so quickly, so easily! She could observe him for a week without pause and never grow bored.

That sensitive mouth opened and closed a couple of times, as Galen searched for words. At last he said, "Her Grace told me you fought for the Onyx Hall during the Great Fire. Did you not think it worth preserving then?"

"I did."

"Have you changed your mind?"

Irrith squirmed on the padded seat. "I . . . don't know. It just seems to me—like we, the fae, *cling* to you. To mortals. Because you give us things, feelings, experiences, that we can't get otherwise. But what do *you* get in return? Oh, sometimes we inspire the occasional artist—but is a painting or a piece of music that important? And sometimes a mortal falls in love with a faerie, but how often does that turn out well for them?"

Irrith damned her thoughtless tongue even as the words came out, too late to be stopped. Galen flushed a fascinating, fragile pink. Did he really believe no one in the Onyx Hall knew of his unrequited love, when his every mannerism shouted it to the world?

Out of pity for his discomfort, Irrith said, "I agree with the Queen, as far as it goes. I like the idea of mortals and fae having some kind of harmony . . ." She sighed. "Even in the Vale, we're drifting apart. People are more concerned with London newspapers, the latest fashion or gossip about the aristocracy, the next ball or concert or whatever gathering is planned. It doesn't touch Wayland's realm, of course; we're perfectly safe inside. But fae are going out less and less. And if we don't go out, then what's the point of being there at all? Why not just go into Faerie?" Or to France. Like Carline.

"Because we need you," Galen said.

"Do you? Why?"

He sighed and ran his hands over his scalp again. One of his fingernails was bitten down to the quick. "I don't know if I can explain it."

If he couldn't, then who could? "You're Prince of the Stone," Irrith reminded him. "The mortal half of the Onyx Court's rulership. You of all people should have an answer."

The compression of his mouth, the shift in his eyes, illustrated a welter of emotions. Embarrassment, nervousness, frustration. Irrith had clearly reminded him of something he knew, and tried not to think of. *He's a very odd Prince,* she thought; she had seen enough to compare. *And it isn't just him being new, either.*

Galen said, seemingly out of nowhere, "There is such beauty here—and such ugliness, too."

Magrat's face suggested itself. "And that's somehow good for mortals?"

"In a way." He rose from the table, hands half-raised, cradling empty air as if trying to grasp the idea in his mind. "Whatever a faerie is—beautiful or ugly; friendly or cruel; amusing or appallingly rude—you're *pure.* They say evil exists in the world because without it, good would have no meaning. I wonder sometimes if that's what the fae are. Not evil—I don't mean that—" Galen's half-distracted words stuttered into apology, before he saw Irrith hadn't taken offense. "More like the, the pigments a painter works with. The pure colors, before they're blended. When you hate, you *hate.* When you love—"

"We love forever." Or at least Lune did. Irrith had never given her heart, and had no intention of ever doing so. "But how does that help *London*?"

"How does water help, or air, or the downward pull of gravity? Those things simply *are*, and without them, there is no London."

Irrith shook her head impatiently, hopping off her own chair. "There *was* a London, though, before there was an Onyx Court. It hasn't always been here, you know. I never saw the city until a hundred years ago, but I can't imagine it was somehow less *real*, less full of life, back when they didn't have a bunch of mischievous, meddlesome faeries being friendly and ugly and all the rest of it beneath their feet."

"A hundred years," Galen said, on a breath of startled laughter. "The charms and enchantments, you know—those I can accept, without much trouble. It's the immortality my mind can't encompass. You don't look a hundred years old."

She was far older than that. She suspected, though, that Galen didn't need to hear her talk about the Black Death, or any of the other fragments she remembered from humanity's long-distant past. Instead she went back to the original point. "What would happen, if we all left? Not just London—all of Wayland's court, and Herne's, and every other faerie realm in England. No more faeries. What would you lose?"

Galen looked as if the mere thought was enough to break him into splinters. "I—"

He would lose Lune. A more thoughtless young man might have said it; Irrith had known many mortals who scarcely thought past their own desires. Galen, for all his youth and uncertainty, had a larger heart than that. But *why*? It frustrated her, that she could not understand. What made him care so much about the fae?

At some point his hands had curled into helpless fists; now they relaxed, one joint at a time. Galen's eyes—nearly the same blue as the walls—were unfocused, gazing off into the distance, and in them was a well of feeling deep enough for Irrith to drown in. Then he blinked, and so did she; the spell was broken. Galen said ruefully, "You want a single answer, one thing I can name that will account for all the fae at once.

I don't know if it's that simple—if it *can* be that simple. The good comes in many diverse ways. Some of it is grand, like the saving of England from the Spanish Armada; some of it is slight, like the rescue of a single child from starvation in a gutter. If I must name a single thing . . ." He turned to her, and the longing in his eyes made Irrith shiver down to her toes. "You are our bridge to Faerie. If you leave, then it goes beyond our reach. And that would be a terrible loss."

He believed it. He really did. Irrith was used to fae hungering for the brightness of mortals, but to see that hunger reflected back in his eyes . . .

"I'm not leaving."

Her own voice, speaking without instructions. But the words, Irrith realized, were true. She repeated them. "I'm not leaving. Others probably will, because it's easier than fighting. But I'll stay. If nothing else, London deserves this much good of us: that we mend the things we broke."

That sounded good. And it was easier than saying the other thing in her mind, the one called forth by Galen's eyes. *I cannot refuse you.*

Odd as it was, a mortal wanted something from her—and she wanted to give it, if she could.

Galen caught up her hand and kissed it, then gripped her fingers as if holding fast to a rope. "Thank you, Dame Irrith."

Common words, a courtesy tossed back and forth a thousand times a day. But the words, and the touch of his hands, stayed with her long after she departed.

PART THREE

Fermentatio

Spring 1758

I court others in Verse, but I love Thee in Prose;
And They have my Whimsies, but Thou hast my
Heart.

—Matthew Prior,
"A Better Answer to Cloe Jealous"

In certain lights, there might almost be a face within the dark mass. A long snout here; two indentations there, that might be eyes, set predatorlike in the dust and ice.

Hunger stirs within the dream. The sun's radiance is warming the comet: heat, light, fire. Things the sleeper remembers. Like calls to like, and it is kindred to the sun, a wayward child sent farther than it was ever meant to go. There is nothing to burn, out here in the black; even the strongest spirit is vanquished by this absolute cold. They crafted better than they knew, those enemies, those jailers, when they banished their foe; this prison is a torture beyond any it has ever known.

But release is coming. Heat, light, fire. Things the sleeper remembers.

Things it will know again, and soon.

Niklas von das Ticken glared at Irrith as she came through the pillars into the antechamber of the Calendar Room. She could never tell whether he hated her particularly, or whether he turned that expression on the world as a whole. Even his conversations with his brother sounded like arguments—though admittedly, *everything* sounded like an argument in German. Either way, the red-bearded dwarf soon turned his scowl back to the half-built contraption on his worktable, ignoring Irrith as if she weren't there.

That suited her just fine. Wilhas was far more pleasant to talk to anyway. "What's he building, a birdcage?" Irrith asked, not caring if the other dwarf overheard.

"*Drachenkäfig*. A Dragon-cage," Wilhas said. His fierce and bloodthirsty grin faded a moment later. "That is the idea. So far, though . . ."

"It doesn't work." Irrith didn't ask why he wasn't working on it inside the Calendar Room. She'd made that mistake precisely once, and gotten as her reward a half-hour diatribe from Niklas—she'd timed it by the assorted clocks—all throat-hacking consonants and spittle, the gist of which was that the chamber's time out of time was only useful if you didn't need to keep coming out to fetch things or question someone or test your results. And apparently that happened often.

Someone was in the Calendar Room right now, to judge by the closed door. Or more than one someone, perhaps. Wilhas talked endlessly about *Körpertage*, which Irrith didn't fully understand; it had something to do with each person inside using up one day for every day the group remained in the room—but the sum of the collected time was great enough that no one other than Wilhas was overly concerned about how many they might be using.

If they didn't find a solution, they'd never get a chance to use the remaining days anyway.

Irrith gave the Dragon-cage a dubious look. So far it was little more than a haphazard assortment of metal strips, like a barrel that had sprung all its staves, then lost about two-thirds of them. Whatever metal Niklas was using, it didn't seem like much of a prison.

"That isn't iron, is it?" she asked. Ktistes had made a passing comment about the dwarves trying to find a way to forge iron so it wouldn't bother fae, but so far as she knew, nothing had come of it.

Wilhas shook his head, and she breathed a little more easily. Iron would seem like the logical choice; after all, the Dragon was just a kind of salamander—a really, really overgrown salamander—and therefore a creature of faerie-kind. But the box Lune had imprisoned the beast in at the end of the Great Fire had been solid iron, and that only worked for a little while. The Dragon's power was just too great to be confined so easily.

Still, the box had given them ten years of peace, and its weakening structure held together for another six, until they hit upon the idea of exiling the Dragon to a comet. If Niklas could achieve half that result, it would still be more than they had now.

She hopped up onto the edge of Wilhas's table, and got a scowl like his brother's as he moved various tools to safety. The dwarves fascinated her almost as much as mortals did. They'd come to England when the crown passed to a German cousin, George I, and as near as Irrith could tell, they considered Lune the counterpart of the Georges: Queen over all of faerie Britain. So long as they didn't say that where any of faerie Britain's other monarchs could hear—or their ambassadors—Irrith supposed it didn't hurt. At least it meant they worked hard on Lune's behalf.

On various things, some more plausible than others. "What do you think?" Irrith asked.

"Of vat? Of my brother's cage?" Wilhas shrugged, which was probably a wise move when Niklas was standing right there. Not listening, or at least not appearing to, but Irrith had already broken up more fistfights between them than she wanted to.

"Of the current plans," Irrith said. "Or lack of same."

The blond dwarf fiddled with a mirror, mouth twisted into a grimace. "There are plans. Many plans. Keep the *Drache* on its little star; trap it ven it comes down; kill it if ve can. Any of those vould be good, *ja*? If ve can make them vork."

Which made them no plans at all, as far as Irrith was concerned. "Wayland made a sword once, ages and ages ago, that— Hey!" She gestured at the two stocky faeries. "You two are dwarves!"

Niklas spun to face her, a tiny hammer clutched in one meaty hand. "You are going to ask about Gram."

"I'm from the Vale of the White Horse," she reminded him. "Our King, Wayland Smith, was the one who made that sword. But he said Gram was broken and reforged before it was used to kill the dragon Fafnir—and that a dwarf did the reforging. Can't you do something similar?"

"Reginn vas *Nordmann*," Niklas said, face reddening to almost the shade of his beard. "*Nicht Deutscher.* You understand? Not from our land. Ve are not all the same, happy little *Schmiede* hammering away in—"

Wilhas clapped a hand over his brother's mouth to stop the flood of words, fewer and fewer of which sounded like English, and Irrith threw her hands up. "I'm sorry I asked! I just thought— Never mind."

Niklas had by then clawed free of his brother and gone back to his work, snarling more German under his breath. "Honestly," Irrith said, "I'd rather it stay on the comet, or get trapped here, and we avoid battle entirely."

Shaking out his hand—Irrith rather thought Niklas had bitten it—Wilhas said, "There is nothing wrong vith fighting."

"There is when you don't have a weapon! Segraine tells me they're still wrestling with that jotun ice, but they haven't gotten very far. Bonecruncher wants to hack chips off for shot."

Wilhas chewed on an available bit of mustache, before shaking his head. "Even if you could make it round enough, I do not think the bullets vould survive the explosion. Too much fire, and ice is too brittle." The chewing turned into a meditative sucking, and he rolled his eyes up to contemplate the ceiling. "Unless you could do it vithout fire . . ."

"Afraid of a little battle?" That came from Niklas, though he didn't bother to turn around.

He sounded like he was trying to needle her. Irrith, however, felt no shame about her cowardice. "Have you *looked* at me? I'm not one of those fae who look like twigs and feel like stone giants; the Dragon broke my arm at Pie Corner, with just a swat of its tail. If battle comes . . ."

He turned his head far enough to sneer at her. "Vat? You vill run away?"

Run away . . .

"Or hide," she said, eyes widening.

Wilhas came out of his contemplation and shook his head. "You vould be safer to run. Hiding—"

"Not me," Irrith said. "London."

Now both dwarves were staring at her.

"Hide the city!" she said. Inspiration goaded her off her perch on the table; she had to pace. "The Onyx Hall is a place of power, right? The Dragon ate a little of it back then, and wanted more. Everybody's pretty sure it will come looking for us again. But what if it can't find us?"

"Then it vill go elsevere," Wilhas said.

Then it will be someone else's problem. Irrith didn't say it, though. What if the Dragon went for the Vale, instead? "Hide all of England, then."

She didn't know if it was possible for someone's eyes to literally bulge out of his head, but the dwarves' were certainly trying. Irrith grinned. "I know, I know. A whole island—might as well toss in Scotland while we're at it—I'm insane. You might have noticed, though, that we're standing in a rather insane place. Ash and Thorn—who looks at the biggest city in England and says, I think we need a faerie palace underneath it? Who steals eleven days from millions of people and traps them in a *room*? If anyone can hide us from the Dragon, it'll be someone in this court, if only because they're too mad to realize it'll never work."

Niklas crossed his arms belligerently. "Say it vorks. Say ve hide England. Say the *Drache* stays on its comet instead of going somevere else—it's a lot to suppose. But even then, it only delays the problem. The beast still comes back."

He was just saying it to be contrary; the set of his glare had shifted. Irrith answered him anyway. "And in the meantime, you've had seventy-five more years to figure how to chip jotun ice into usable bullets."

She got to enjoy a brief moment of pride; then Wilhas deflated her with a single word. "How?"

"Don't ask *me*," Irrith said, putting her hands up in protest. "I said *someone* would be mad enough to figure it out. I haven't been here in fifty years; my lunacy's out of practice."

Wilhas was still looking at her. "What? You need a puck for this, not a sprite! They're the ones with all the tricks!"

"Then ve vill get you pucks," he said, with a decisive nod. "How many do you need?"

"None. I came up with the idea; my work is done."

Wilhas smiled. "Ve shall see vat the Queen says."

Irrith realized, far too late, that she should have kept her mouth shut.

The Onyx Hall, London: April 3, 1758

Remembering Irrith's first visit to his chambers, Galen had told Edward to let the sprite through if she came calling again. When Irrith tried to barge past him without even the barest courtesy, though, the valet stopped her with one efficient arm. "Dame Irrith, I have *told* you—"

Her undoubtedly obscene response got swallowed when she saw Galen standing a few feet away, dressed save for his shoes and hat. Galen said, "My apologies, but I'm afraid I have an engagement. Can your matter wait?"

She answered with her usual impudence. "As long as you don't mind losing another day."

Edward dropped his blocking arm with a scowl. Like all good valets, he could read his master's mind: if this had to do with the comet, then it couldn't be postponed. The days ticked steadily away; already it was spring, and once winter came, astronomers would begin searching the skies.

His engagement was to escort his mother, Cynthia, Miss Northwood, and Mrs. Northwood through the British Museum's collections in Montagu House, and Galen was looking forward to it, but he had a little time before he must depart. "Have you come up with an idea?"

"Yes," she said, passing Edward with an expression just this side of sticking her tongue out at him. "And I told the dwarves, and that should have been the end of it. But now Lune wants me to make it *happen*."

Her tone and posture clearly proclaimed that there was a problem somewhere in this. Galen could not see it. "What is it you wish me to do?"

"Convince her to have someone else do it!"

"Dame Irrith . . ." Edward was hovering with his hat and shoes, but Galen gestured him back for the moment. "I was under the impression you were interested in helping us."

She shifted, not meeting his eyes. "I am."

"Then where's the problem?"

He heard the catch in her breath, before she turned and became very interested in the porcelain figure of a hound on a nearby table. "I can't possibly do it. Because I haven't the slightest idea *how*."

That hound might have dragged the admission from her, it came out so strained. Galen bit his tongue. He was so accustomed to Lune, who rarely betrayed anything of her inner state, even when it was in turmoil; or her closest courtiers, who followed the model of their Queen. He wasn't used to someone like Irrith, whose attempts at guile fell as flat as his own.

It gave him a sense of kinship with her, though. *Neither one of us is half so polished as this place would like us to be.*

"What is the idea?" Galen asked, and listened as Irrith summed it up. No one, to his knowledge, had suggested hiding from the Dragon; he had to admit the notion held some appeal. As for how to make it happen, though, he was forced to admit he had no more notion than she did.

Floundering for a starting point, he said, "Don't fae have some means of hiding from mortals? Charms and the like?"

"Yes, but we aren't trying to hide from a mortal, are we?" Irrith gesticulated with the porcelain hound, and Galen spared a moment to hope she wouldn't throw it into a wall for punctuation. The piece was a gift from the French ambassador, the faerie one—though in truth, Galen wouldn't miss it all that much.

What protected mortals against faerie-kind? Iron. Christian faith, whether expressed through prayer or church bells or other signs. But London was already armored with those—and besides, they didn't *conceal* anything.

Edward coughed discreetly. Galen looked up, ready to insist on just a few more minutes' delay, and found his servant had put aside the hat and shoes. "Begging your pardon, sir, but I believe there's a way for mortals to hide from faeries. Dame Irrith—if a man turns his coat inside out, doesn't that give him a measure of invisibility?"

Her shifting green eyes went wide. Irrith stood, gaping, and then a grin split her face. "You're a genius," she announced. "What's your name, anyway? Geniuses should have names."

The servant gave her a shallow bow. "Edward Thorne, ma'am."

"Edward Th—" Curiosity flared to life. "Are you Peregrin's son?"

A second, deeper bow. "I have that honor, yes."

"Hah! You're cleverer than your father, Mr. Thorne. Ask me sometime about when he first came to Berkshire, the adventure he had with a milkmaid. Just don't ask when he's around." Irrith bounced on the balls of her feet. "Inside-out clothes! I should have thought of that." Her face fell as she turned to Galen. "But London isn't wearing any clothes."

He didn't have an answer to that, but Edward had at least given him a notion of what advice to offer. "Her Majesty may have instructed you to make this happen, Dame Irrith, but I doubt she meant you must do it on your own. May I suggest recruiting help? Others may have useful suggestions, which you can coordinate into a proper plan."

Irrith wrinkled her nose at him. "Do I look coordinated to you?"

"You are a model of grace."

"That isn't what I meant, as you well know," Irrith said, but she colored a little. Galen had spoken the words in jest, but they were also true; she moved like a young fox, with natural rather than studied elegance.

Edward had picked up the shoes and hat again. Galen sighed and beckoned him forward. "I have every confidence you can make this happen, Dame Irrith, and it may do us crucial good. If time in the Calendar Room would aid your thoughts, I'm sure her Grace will approve it. In the meantime, I must beg your forgiveness, but—"

She was nodding before he finished. "Right. Sorry I kept you. But this helped a lot."

"I'm glad," he said, settling the hat upon his head. "Let me know if I can be of further use."

The Onyx Hall, London: April 6, 1758

Ktistes might have been a statue of a centaur, his hooves planted foursquare on the grass, looking off into the distance where several courtiers were chasing each other around a fountain. Their giggles and false shrieks of surprise made Irrith want to bellow at them to be quiet, but she had no illusions as to the weight her knighthood carried. Even if she told them she was trying to save their frivolous little lives.

"Difficult enough," the centaur finally said, "to hide London. The City itself, within the walls, that could be done; it is only a square mile or so. Since that is the part reflected in the Onyx Hall, and the power of this palace is what the Dragon craves, it might be enough."

Irrith shook her head. "Do you really want to wager that it *will* be? It's already burnt enough, Ktistes. I'm not going to let it do the same thing again."

He sighed, hooves shifting restlessly, breaking the illusion of the statue. "Then will you hide the entire world? There are cities elsewhere, and faerie realms, too. You cannot be certain it will not strike the Cour du Lys, or my brethren in Greece, or folk in lands you've never heard of. Folk who are not prepared."

"It might," she admitted. That was the worry that, as the mortals said, kept her awake at night—or would, if she slept. The nervous intensity of Galen and all the rest had infected her, making sleep a luxury for later. "I don't think it will, though."

The centaur rarely wasted words; he merely studied her patiently, awaiting an explanation.

Biting her lip, Irrith said, "You never saw it, Ktistes. I did. I was there when it tried to eat the Onyx Hall. After it's eaten London, it will turn somewhere else—all those other places you named. Because it can never eat enough. But it won't move on until it has *this* place." It had the scent—or rather the taste—like a bloodhound. And it needed no huntsman to chivvy it on.

"Then as I said before: you need not cover the entire island."

She grinned. It was better than showing her uncertainty. "Well, I don't want to bet it wouldn't gobble up Oxford on its way to London. Better not to let it get a foothold, right?" The grin faded, though she tried to hold on to it. "Never mind the scale. Help me figure out *how* to do this, and then we can argue over whether it can be done so widely. What counts as clothes?"

Ktistes lifted one hand, letting the quaking leaves of an aspen trail over his fingers. "What clothes the land," he murmured to himself.

Then his horse part swung around sharply, so that he faced his pavilion. A dazzling smile split his face. "There is your answer, Dame Irrith."

She stared. "Your . . . pavilion?"

"Buildings! Towns. Houses, and churches, and all the things mortal kind has built upon the face of the land. Do they not clothe its nakedness?"

Irrith blinked once, then a second time. Her voice seemed

to have gone missing. When she found it again, it came bearing words. "You want . . . to turn London . . . *inside out.*"

Ktistes paused, hands in midair, where he had swept them in a grand gesture. "How would that be done?" he mused. The note in his voice was pure curiosity, a clever mind given something to play with. "The Onyx Hall—but no, this place is not the inside of London, and to put it 'outside' would only deepen our problems. Perhaps an earthquake, though, to open the buildings themselves? We caused two some years ago, quite by accident, but if we arranged one deliberately—"

"Then it would *destroy London*," Irrith said. "And every other town you want to hide. Ktistes, the idea is to *prevent* destruction."

His face fell. After a moment, so did his hands. "True," he admitted. The powerful centaur briefly sounded like nothing so much as a little boy, chastised by his mother. "I did not think of that."

This is why Lune has a Prince. The thought flew out of nowhere and lodged in Irrith's mind like an arrow. Ktistes was Greek, and had spent most of his life somewhere in that Mediterranean land; the differences between him and the English fae were many. In the final weighing, however, he had more in common with Irrith than Galen. They might hover on the fringes of mortal places, drinking the intoxicating wine of mortal passions, but that was not the center of their world, the first thing their minds went to; human life, human society, was an afterthought.

That was why Lune kept at her side a man for whom it was the *first* thought. However much effort she devoted to considering mortal needs, there would always be these moments, when they slipped from her mind. As they had slipped from Ktistes's. And only a mortal could be trusted to always do as Irrith had done this once, and catch the Queen when she slipped.

The centaur was still thinking, oblivious to Irrith's distraction. One front hoof tapped a restless beat against the ground. *Does he miss galloping?* Irrith wondered. The night garden was large, but nothing like the open grass of Ktistes's land. Or did he, as a learned centaur, live so much in his own mind that it hardly mattered where he made his home?

Maybe that was why she'd thought to stop him, when he spoke of earthquakes in London. The prospect of losing her home—either of them—horrified her to the depths of her faerie soul.

"We'll think of something," she said. Perhaps she should take Galen up on his offer of the Calendar Room? The thorough shudder that followed the possibility was answer enough. Locking herself in the same room as that clock, for days on end . . . fae were capable of madness, in their own way. She had no desire to experience it herself.

"I will continue to ponder," Ktistes said, still repentant.

So would Irrith. But not here, with all these black shadows stifling her spirit. The Queen had commanded her to find a solution to this puzzle; surely that would be good for squeezing a bit of bread out of the royal stone.

If she was to turn London inside out, she would have to go study it in person.

London below and above: April 9, 1758

Irrith could not quite believe her ears when the Queen told her to go ask the Lord Treasurer.

She had enough experience of the Onyx Court to know that Lune, like England's mortal rulers, surrounded herself with a circle of people who were both advisers and deputies, dealing with various matters who were so the Queen herself didn't have to. Wayland did the same thing, though without the fancy titles and so on. But Irrith thought she'd heard of them all, and the Lord Treasurer had been nowhere on the list.

It seemed, however, that the problem of tithed bread was serious enough that Lune had taken the precaution of appointing someone to oversee it: what came in through the Onyx Court's trade with other lands, who it was paid out to, and—as much as anyone could track this—what happened to it after that. Trade wasn't the only source of bread, of course; some fae kept mortals on a string just to provide them with a regular tithe. And all of it, regardless of source, was hoarded, wagered, gifted, stolen, used as bribes, and given over in underhand deals, before eventually being eaten; attempting to record those transactions was nothing short of madness.

"Come to think of it," Irrith said to the clerk behind the desk, "Ktistes told me a story once, of a fellow damned to roll a stone forever up a hill . . . have you heard it?"

The clerk, an officious little wisp of a thing, was unimpressed. "I do as her Grace and the Lord Treasurer bid me. At the moment, they have given me no orders concerning the disbursement of bread to you. But if you would like to present your case to my master—"

"I would." It came out through Irrith's teeth. *Mab have mercy: they're treating it like coin.* Irrith had always thought secrets the most valuable currency in the Onyx Hall, but it seemed that was changing, as the mortal world did its best to shake off the faerie superstitions of its past.

She presented her case to the Lord Treasurer, who surprised her by being a stolid, methodical dobie named Hairy How. Most of the officers of Lune's court were elfin types, but she supposed that when it came to careful bookkeeping, a hob was ideal. This one seemed more sensible than your common dobie—too sensible, in fact. Convincing him was none too easy. But the magic key word of *Dragon,* combined with a believable explanation for how her use of bread could benefit the court, finally talked him around, and he commanded the clerk to give her a week's worth.

Irrith would have liked more; she owed more than seven pieces to various fae already. Segraine might be willing to let the debt go for a century, but others would not. Unfortunately, this was obviously as much as she would get today. She watched, bemused, as the clerk counted out the seven pieces with excessive care, then counted them a second time before making his tally and wrapping them in a handkerchief. When Irrith tried to pick it up, he swatted her hand. "All disbursements from the royal treasury must be recorded," he said, getting out a pot of ink and a moth-eaten griffin feather for a quill. "It's the law."

"Law!" The clerk, by his glare, didn't appreciate her scornful laughter. "That's a mortal thing."

"And a faerie one, too, Dame Irrith. By order of the Queen and Lord Alan."

One of the old Princes. Irrith waited, not attempting to hide her impatience, as the clerk made a note in his ledger, then wrote out a receipt, which he handed to her.

The slip read, *Seven (7) pieces from the Treasury, as follows: three (3) rye, two (2) barley, one (1) brown wheat, one (1) white wheat. Disbursed to Dame Irrith by Rodge, Clerk of the Treasury, on 4 October 1757.*

Irrith threw it away in disgust. "You might as well be a mortal clerk, with your dates and numbers." A small clock sat on the desk in front of him: probably the work of the von das Tickens, and the reason why the clerk could date the receipt. The Onyx Hall wasn't detached from human time as the deeper realms of Faerie were; it would render interactions with the mortal world too difficult. But in the unchanging darkness of those stone halls, most fae lost count of the date. And few of them cared.

Rodge apparently saved his lack of care for the fae he dealt with. He didn't even look up as Irrith took the bread and departed.

She stowed six pieces with Ktistes; the centaur was always near his pavilion, and few would risk stealing from him. But the safest place in the world was her stomach, where it could do its inexplicable work, shielding her from threats. Irrith ate the white bread, grimacing at its chalky taste, and went into the streets above.

Darkness greeted her, but this time it wasn't the strange murk of last fall; just ordinary nighttime. The sky was overcast enough that she couldn't guess the hour, though. Irrith had chosen the Billingsgate door, which put her in a less-than-savory part of the City; after a moment's consideration, she cloaked herself in a charm that would encourage strangers to look past her. Cutpurses and other criminals were as fascinating as any other part of mortal society, but not one she wanted to experience right now.

Voices from the direction of the fish market told her it must not be long until dawn. Soon boats would crowd the little harbor, unloading the day's catch; then the fishwives would go to work, with their powerful arms and vivid profanity, hawking their wares to the cooks and cooks' servants, laboring housewives, and finally the poor on the edge of starvation, who would buy what no one else wanted, after it had begun to smell.

She drifted, silent and invisible as a ghost, in the direction of the wharves, for they showed more life than the predawn streets. The river was little more than a black sloshing sound, wavelets receding from the mudflats of its banks, their tops gilded by the occasional bit of torchlight. Here, in the darkness, it was easy to forget about all the changes that entranced her; Irrith could half-convince herself she'd stepped out into the London she first saw a hundred years ago. Many things stayed the same.

Indeed, that was what made the changes so entrancing.

The sun gradually emerged as a flat gray disk on the eastern horizon, barely penetrating the clouds. It allowed Irrith to see the buildings around her, the eighteenth century replacing that fleeting illusion of the seventeenth. Brick and stone, not the timber and plaster of the past, which had burnt in the Fire. But some places were familiar, beneath their new clothes; rich men still gossiped in the Exchange, the Bow Bells still rang out over Cheapside, and a cathedral still crowned the City's western half.

How was she supposed to turn all this inside out?

The streets slowly filled with people. At this hour, London belonged to its lower classes: the servants and laborers, porters and beggars. Men thick with muscle, and men wasted down to skeletons from illness and starvation. Women in the drab clothes of maids, hurrying to buy for the day's meals. Yawning apprentices, surly cart drivers, a half-grown girl with a flock of chickens. Watching them go by, Irrith thought of her words to Ktistes. The buildings didn't matter so much, but the people . . . they were the ones Lune, and Galen, and all their allies were trying to protect.

Ktistes thought like an architect. He saw the land, whether he was on top of it or inside it, and the structures that could be shaped to it. People mattered because they would use what he built, but that was the only point at which they entered into his plans. When it came to hiding England, he didn't think of them. He thought only of the land.

It won't be enough, Irrith realized. London wasn't its fabric; it was its people. Lune had taught her that. And surely it was true for other places, be they Berkshire or Yorkshire or Scotland.

She had to hide *all* of it: the ground, the trees, the houses and shops and churches, and most especially the people.

If the buildings weren't the clothing, then what was?

Something smacked her shoulder hard, and knocked Irrith sprawling into the chilly mud.

"Blood and Bone!" she swore, and got baffled stares from the porters carrying kegs into a nearby tavern. Irrith swore again, then threw a hasty glamour over her faerie face, so that they blinked in confusion and went back to their work. A charm of concealment could make people look away from her, but it did nothing to protect her from collision, and the attention that brought.

Time to get below, or to find a quiet place where she could improve her glamour and continue her wanderings.

But before she could climb to her feet, something caught her eye—and then she began to laugh.

Flat on her back in the mud, with the porters staring again and carts rumbling past her unprotected toes, Irrith laughed and laughed, because the answer was right there, wrapping England in a gray and frequently rainy cloak.

Clouds.

The Onyx Hall, London: April 18, 1758

Lune laid her head against the back of her chair in a rare gesture of frustration. "I don't suppose any clever mortal has designed a scheme for influencing the weather?"

"Designed one?" Galen said. "Almost certainly. Executed it successfully? That, I fear, is another matter."

She sighed in acknowledgment. "Then it must be faerie magic." One pale hand rose to rub at her eyes. "We have some ability to call rain when we need it, but nothing of sufficient force, nor duration—not to hide this entire island, certainly not for months on end."

Silence ruled the chamber for a few minutes. They were not alone; Lune had called a small convocation of her closest companions: Amadea, the Irish lady Feidelm, and Rosamund Goodemeade, whose sister was occupied elsewhere. With an air that suggested she knew her words would be unwelcome, the little brownie offered, "We *do* know folk who might manage it."

Lune winced. Rosamund, upon Galen's quizzical look, said, "Those who live in the sea."

"Mermaids?"

"And stranger things," Lune replied, lifting her head. "You're right, Rosamund, and if we must, we will ask them. But I would very much like to find another way. For aid of this kind, we'd be heavily in debt to them, and the folk of the sea are strange enough that I cannot begin to predict what they would demand in return."

A faerie was calling someone else strange? Galen bit down on the urge to ask whether that meant they were of surpassing normality. The unease Lune showed at the thought of dealing with them told him now wasn't the time for such a jest.

The chamber door opened, and Lewan Erle slipped through. The foppish lord bowed in meticulous apology before approaching the Queen, a sealed letter in his hands.

She broke the seal and perused it, first with a disinterested eye, then with a very interested one indeed. Upon finishing her second reading, she turned to the waiting lord. "He's in the Onyx Hall?"

"Yes, madam. But he waited at the Crutched Friars entrance until Greymalkin found him—I believe he was there at least an hour."

"Very courteous." Lune folded the paper again and turned to Galen. "This is a letter of introduction from Madame Malline le Sainfoin de Veilée, formerly the ambassadress of the Cour du Lys. It recommends to our attention a certain foreigner now waiting—"

"Still at Crutched Friars, madam," Lewan Erle supplied, when Lune paused.

She passed the folded letter to Amadea and rose. "We shall receive him in the lesser—no, the greater presence chamber. And Lord Galen and myself will take the time to dress more formally. If he is the first faerie of his land to set foot in England, then we can at least make his initial impression a grand one."

Bewildered, Galen likewise rose from his chair. "What land is that, madam?"

He heard an echo of his bewilderment in Lune's answer. "Araby."

Galen couldn't help but wonder whether Lune, like him, drew some strength from elegance of dress, and for that reason had ordered a delay while they both changed into more suitable clothing. Whether she did or not, he was grateful for the deep-cuffed coat and powdered wig Edward put him into; they helped him stand proud as the massive bronze doors of the greater presence chamber swung open to admit the traveler.

The chamber itself was such a wondrous space that Galen might have thought any additional wonder would seem at home. Soaring black pillars served as a frame for panels of silver filigree and faceted crystal, bestowing a degree of lightness on what otherwise would have been a grim and ominous space. The figure who entered, though, brought with him a different kind of wonder entirely.

It wasn't that his countenance was especially grotesque. His bearded face was darker skinned than Galen expected of an Arab, more like a Negro, with a powerfully hooked nose, but beyond that he looked almost human. His dress was moderately odd, being a long, straight robe confined at the hips with a broad sash, and of course his head was wrapped in a neatly folded turban; that was not the cause, either. In the years Galen had been among the English fae, their alien natures had become almost familiar—but this fellow awoke that *frisson* again, the awareness that there was always more strangeness beyond his ken.

The lords and ladies assembled for this audience rustled and murmured amongst themselves, watching him approach. When the visitor reached a courteous distance from the dais upon which Lune and Galen sat, he sank gracefully to both knees, bowing his head just shy of touching the floor. "*Assalamu alaykum,* O fair Queen, O wise Prince. Peace be unto you. I am called Abd ar-Rashid, Al-Musafir, At-Talib ul-'ilm, of the land known to you as Araby."

"Welcome to the Onyx Court, Lord Abd ar-Rashid," Lune said, smoothly enough that Galen suspected she had practiced the foreign name while dressing. "Never before has our realm been visited by one of your land. Do you come to us as an ambassador?"

"I do not, O Queen." The stranger had risen from the lowest part of his bow, but remained on his knees. The stone of the presence chamber carried his voice to them, clear despite the distinct and oddly French-tinged accent. "I an individual only, traveling the faerie Europe courts these many years."

Galen, content to let Lune manage the niceties of welcome, had been studying that hook-nosed face, chasing a wisp of memory. It was the French letter of introduction that did it; his tutor had given him several books for practicing the language, years ago, and one of them had mentioned something like this creature. Galen's mother had confiscated the volume in horror once she saw the title—too late to protect him from the scandalous bits—but he'd read enough to remember the word. "If you will pardon me for asking, sir—are you a genie?"

Abd ar-Rashid's white teeth flashed a startling contrast against his dark skin. Smiling, he said, "A genie indeed, O Prince. Read you the *Thousand and One Nights*?"

Floundering for useful memories beyond the bare word—and succeeding only in recalling more and more of the scandalous bits—Galen caught sight of Lune, out of the corner of his eye. Without ever so much as uttering a word or changing the serene pleasantry of her expression, she somehow communicated her intentions to him. *You know more than I do of this stranger. Deal with him as you will.*

God help him. Galen had stood at Lune's side on various state occasions, fulfilling his duties as her mortal consort, but never before had he been the chief voice in such a matter. And now to hand him an Arabic faerie, sent to them by some French lady he'd never even met . . .

Well, it could not hurt to be polite. He hoped. "What brings you to England, Lord ar-Rashid?"

The smile flickered out of existence a heartbeat before the genie bowed again. "I beg your kindness, O Prince. I am not Ar-Rashid, The One Who Knows, being his servant only. I am called *Abd* ar-Rashid, meaning this: I serve the Most Merciful, the Most Compassionate."

Apparently his attempt at politeness *could* hurt. Galen had no choice but to forge ahead. "No, the apology should be mine; I did not realize." Then, belatedly, he took note of the way the faeries had whispered amongst themselves at his words. *The Merciful and Compassionate—does he mean God? Did this faerie just claim to be a servant of God?*

That question seemed even more likely to drop him into a pit than the simple use of Abd ar-Rashid's name had. Galen fled back to his original query. "Is it some task set by your sovereign that brings you to our shores, Lord Abd ar-Rashid?" Did genies even *have* sovereigns?

The Arab's answer didn't enlighten him. "It is not, O Prince. These years have I been journeying across Europe in the service of my own curiosity, and it brings me now to England."

At the distance that separated the genie from the dais, it was unlikely he noticed Lune stiffening; Galen, at her side, could not miss it. "Curiosity of what sort, my lord?" she asked.

"That of a scholar, O Queen." His accent made subtleties of intonation difficult to discern, and in the cool light of the chamber, Galen had equal trouble making out the expressions on the dark face. "I come here to ask of your Prince introduction to the Royal Society gentlemen."

Had he asked for an introduction to King George II, Galen could not have been more surprised. "The Royal Society? The philosophers?" Perhaps it was some error in the genie's English.

Abd ar-Rashid soon disabused him of the notion. "Once a

great flower of wisdom grew in my land, but in recent centuries it has withered under the hand of the soldiers and the officials. Araby was the mother of medicine and alchemy, astronomy and the making of clocks; now the infant she reared has grown to manhood, and traveled to Europe, where he finds a more friendly home. Taqi al-Din has been succeeded by your John Harrison and James Bradley and Isaac Newton. I have no interest in war and the operation of government; therefore I come here, following in the footsteps of knowledge."

It had the sound of a rehearsed speech; indeed, Galen suspected the genie had delivered it in French to the Cour du Lys—with, of course, suitable replacements for the English scholars he'd named. Bemused, Galen said, "And you believe I can grant you admittance to the Royal Society."

The Arab hesitated. "Out of your kindness—if French would be possible—" Lune nodded, and Galen thought he saw relief flash across that dark face as the genie bowed again. In much more fluent French, he said, "In the Cour du Lys, I heard that the Queen of London kept a mortal man at her side, who governed all matters relating to the human world. When news came that this man had become a Fellow of the Society, I made arrangements to come here."

His French was good enough that Galen, far more rusty in the language, had trouble keeping up; but he was able to catch where rumor had gone astray. "I am not a Fellow, sir," he said, painfully aware of his own bad accent. "Only a visitor among them."

The genie's stillness came as a surprise, after all the bowing. "Was I in error, O Prince? Have I asked something not in your power to give?"

A tiny shift in Lune's body told Galen she'd been about to speak, then stopped herself. He could guess why. She never turned visitors away from her court empty-handed; unlike most faerie realms, this one was composed of strangers who had come from a dozen other homes, some merely visiting, others resettling themselves within its dark shadow. Interaction with the mortal world was not the only thing that separated this court from others in England.

She didn't turn visitors away—but neither did she give gifts without hope of something in return. "An introduction is within my power," Galen said, wishing to Heaven that he'd been given some warning of this, so he could think through his reply without the genie, Lune, and the assembled courtiers watching his every move. "But it is no small thing, sir, to bring you into company with the gentlemen and lords of my acquaintance there. You are a stranger to me as much as to them, and a foreign stranger at that. I don't know how these things are done in your land, but here, if a gentleman introduces another in that manner, he risks his own good name; he vouches to his friends that the new man is a trustworthy fellow, and worthy of their company. I mean no insult to you, but I cannot in good conscience give such assurances for someone about whom I know virtually nothing."

He realized too late that he had lapsed back into English. Perhaps it was just as well; he would have embarrassed himself, trying to say all that in French. The genie's eyes had narrowed, but whether it was a sign of hostility or merely difficulty understanding him, Galen didn't know.

He hoped the latter, and that Abd ar-Rashid understood enough to see the opening Galen had provided. And indeed, after a silent moment, the genie bowed. "I would die a hundred times, O Prince, before I bring shame to you by my behavior. I am content to wait. Perhaps in that time I find some service for yourself or your Queen, and prove my character to you?"

Now Galen turned to Lune, gratefully handing off the burden of this negotiation. The notion of introducing, not just a faerie, but a *heathen* faerie to the philosophers of the Royal Society was a staggering absurdity his mind could scarcely encompass, but perhaps it would be possible to disguise Abd ar-Rashid with a glamour of an Englishman, and to improve his English. Or just to conduct the entire affair in French. In the meantime, Lune could decide what price she wanted to put on Galen's help.

With a rueful quirk of her lips, Lune asked, "Do the powers of a genie, by any chance, extend to the weather?"

The Onyx Hall, London: April 28, 1758

The effort to find a weapon against the Dragon had sent Lune's ambassadors farther than ever before—but never beyond Europe. For the first time in her reign, she found herself with a visitor about whom she knew precisely nothing.

A state of affairs she did not permit to last for long. A week and a half after the genie's audience, she convened a small meeting of fae: Sir Adenant, Lady Yfaen, and the puck Beggabow.

Sir Adenant had not even brushed the dust off his boots, so recently had he returned from France. "My report, madam," he said, handing over a sheaf of papers with a bow. "I judged it more important to get this information to you rapidly than to uncover every detail, but this is the essence of it."

He was far from her best spy, but he'd gone to France before, and had friends in the Cour du Lys. "What did you learn?"

"He's definitely a traveler, madam. Before France, it was Italy and Athens; his home, inasmuch as he has one, is Istanbul. But he seems to have gone there with that fellow he mentioned, Taqi al-Din, nearly two hundred years ago, and they met in Egypt."

Beggabow whistled. Lune felt like doing the same. Most fae looked oddly even on those who served as ambassadors; travel was not something they did much of. But perhaps genies had a greater fondness for it. "Why all the movement?"

Adenant spread his hands. "It seems to be as he said, your Grace. A thirst for information. Madame Malline told me those later parts of his name mean 'the traveler' and 'the seeker of knowledge,' or some such."

"What about the first part? 'Servant of He Who Knows'?"

The faerie knight shuddered. "That's the strangest part. They say he's a heathen—that he follows the Mohammedan deity. And he isn't the only one, either. He claims several genies are 'of the Faithful.'"

Lady Yfaen laughed, a bright, disbelieving sound. "Surely you don't mean they *pray*."

"They do," Beggabow said. "Or at least he does. Five times

a day. I've been watching him the last week, wondering what in Mab's name he thinks he's doing."

The puck was one of Aspell's spies, diverted from the Sanists to follow Abd ar-Rashid. "Where is he living?" Lune asked.

"In Wapping," the puck said. "Bold as you please. Makes himself look like a Turk, and rents a room from some Lascar near the Frying Pan Stairs, right by the river."

Now it was Adenant's turn to whistle. "Does the Lascar give him bread?"

Beggabow shook his head. "Not as I can tell. He don't seem to *need* it. Iron don't bother him, and neither do holy things, him praying and all. Wish *I* could learn that trick."

It explained why he hadn't asked for shelter in the Onyx Hall. Lune had been uneasy about that, not certain whether she wanted to offer it to him or not. Strangers were common enough, but not strangers whose capabilities and motives were entirely opaque to her. And while it seemed, at least so far, that this genie's motives were honest enough, his capabilities were still a dangerous unknown.

Adenant's report might contain something of that. So, too, might Yfaen's contribution. The sylph had a tall stack on the table at her side, books and loose papers alike. "This is all I could find, madam," she said, with an apologetic duck of her head, as if she hadn't assembled a month's worth of reading. "The *Thousand and One Nights* he mentioned—a French translation, and two English ones. Also a few other books, and a manuscript from Lady Mary Wortley Montagu. I don't know if it says anything about genies, but her husband was the English ambassador to Istanbul about fifty years ago, and she went with him; this is what she wrote about her experiences. It may help."

Anything that chipped away at Lune's ignorance would help. She sighed, foreseeing a great deal of work ahead. "My thanks to all three of you. If you learn more—"

Beggabow snapped his fingers, then blushed and tugged his forelock in apology for interrupting her. "Sorry, your Grace. I just remembered. There's a Jew around the corner from where he lives, a lens-maker named Schuyler; your Arab has him and a silversmith working on some kind of mirrored bowl. Not sure what that's for, but it's big." The puck held out his arms, indicating something at least a yard across.

A chill ran down Lune's spine. "I'll have the Lord Treasurer disburse more bread to you. Watch him, and watch this Jew. We need to know what that bowl is for."

Mayfair, Westminster: May 16, 1758

"Mr. St. Clair," Elizabeth Vesey said in a disapproving voice, "I am beginning to think you left the better part of yourself at home."

One of the ladies let out an unregenerate cackle. She was an older woman, and not one Galen knew, but their brief introduction had made it clear she had a filthy mind, and no shame about it, either. Though she hadn't voiced her interpretation of Mrs. Vesey's words, Galen still blushed, and got another cackle for his pains.

"My apologies," he told his hostess, shaking himself to alertness. "My mind was indeed elsewhere—though I assure you, in a place more pleasant than home."

He realized too late how that would sound to the scandalous old woman. Her third cackle was even louder than the first two. *Ah well,* he told himself, resigned. *Learn to do that on purpose, and you might pass muster as a wit.*

But social reasons were the least part of his purpose here tonight. At one end of the room, Dr. Andrews was preparing his materials for a presentation. This was not the Bluestocking Circle per se, but a gathering of learned ladies and some gentlemen, and Galen was attending to continue his evaluation of the man. The days were passing, and he was painfully aware of them; but he was also aware that the consequences of trusting the wrong man could be severe.

In the meanwhile, other plans were proceeding apace, and that was reason he had come. Across the room, a redoubtable woman in her early fifties conversed with Mrs. Montagu. Galen waited for a suitable moment, then approached and bowed to her. "Mrs. Carter, good evening. My apologies for interrupting, but I was wondering if I might beg a favor of you."

He didn't have to feign respect. Elizabeth Carter's learning and skill with words shamed that of most men; her translations of Stoic philosophy were renowned, and they said Greek was only one of the nine languages she spoke.

Of the other eight, one—according to rumor and Mrs. Montagu—was Arabic.

She gestured with her fan for him to continue. "I've recently come into possession of a strange item," Galen said, "which the former owner claims comes from somewhere in the Ottoman lands. It's a mirrored bowl, quite large, and bears an inscription in a language I believe to be Arabic. Might I prevail upon you to examine it, and translate the words if possible?"

If Abd ar-Rashid was telling the truth, the bowl would aid them in their attempts to veil the sky. No one wanted to use it, however, until they had some confirmation of that. Mrs. Carter said, "It might be a 'magic bowl,' as some call them; they have been used for centuries in that part of the world, and not just by the Arabs. Though usually they are quite small. I would be delighted to study it for you, Mr. St. Clair."

Should the bowl prove to be what the genie claimed, it would be a great boon to Irrith's plan. Galen thanked Mrs. Carter profusely, and made arrangements to have the bowl delivered to her house. These were scarcely completed when Galen felt a delicate hand upon his arm. "Mr. St. Clair, I believe you are acquainted with Miss Delphia Northwood?"

Galen was at the nadir of his bow before he realized he knew that name . . . sort of.

"My lady of the mixed metaphors," he said, straightening in time to see Miss Northwood stifle a laugh. "Indeed, Mrs. Vesey, we met at Vauxhall, and have had the pleasure of each other's company several times since then."

Delphia. Had Cynthia used that nickname? It suited the young woman far better than the ponderous weight of "Philadelphia," as did her gown tonight. The pale rose gave warmth to her complexion, and while nothing could transform her plainness to beauty, the simplicity of her dress at least suited her scholarly air. Miss Northwood smiled and said, "Indeed we have. Mama has been most . . . eager to see me in the company of new friends."

"Is she here?" Galen asked, glancing about. A foolish question; his one previous encounter with Mrs. Northwood had established her as a woman not easily overlooked. She lost no opportunities to scrutinize any young man that came near her daughter.

"No, indeed. Our dear Sylph is a good friend of the family, and therefore, in Mama's opinion, a sufficient chaperone for my good behavior." Miss Northwood smiled at Mrs. Vesey.

The girl's mother would probably not think that if she knew their dear Sylph kept company with an actual sylph, Lady Yfaen. Their hostess, smiling as if she had precisely that thought, excused herself to make certain Dr. Andrews had everything he needed. Watching her go, Miss Northwood added, "Of course, Mama thinks tonight is a harmless card party, with no topic more mentally strenuous than, say, the current fashion in hats."

"You lied to her?"

She smiled at his shocked reply. "And do you tell your family the truth of everything you do, Mr. St. Clair? No, I thought not."

He wanted to say he kept secrets for greater cause, but that would open him to far too many questions. Making comparisons between his father and her mother struck him as invidious, so instead he asked, "She would not approve of tonight's presentation?"

"She fears—quite rightly—where it might lead me. As she has reminded me on many occasions, neither grasping for patronage nor battling with publishers is a suitable pastime for a young woman desiring respectability, and if I hope to make a worthwhile match, I should lay aside such dreams—at least until after my marriage, whereupon it will be my husband's decision as to whether I may write or not." Miss Northwood shrugged, with no particular rancor. "She is correct, of course. But I still flout her as I can."

Galen could only gape. "You—you write, Miss Northwood?"

Her rueful smile came with a bit of a blush. "I put pen to paper, Mr. St. Clair. I do not publish. Not yet, at least."

He could understand her mother's concern. Learning in a woman was not a shameful thing—at least he did not think so—but the public activity that went with it could be, particularly when it involved wrangling over business like some common Grub Street hack. Elizabeth Carter had done it, but Galen suspected her quiet and retiring life at least partly a stratagem for maintaining her respectability. And was it coincidence that she had never married?

Grasping for some fragment of wit to lift the shadow from Miss Northwood's face, he said, "If you would like, I can pretend I do not see you here, so as to preserve at least one of your marriage prospects."

In the pause that followed, he realized what he had just said. It should not have mattered; Miss Northwood knew he was looking for a wife, as he knew she—or at least her mother, on her behalf—was hunting a husband; to say it out loud should change nothing. Yet it did, introducing a sudden and palpable awkwardness broken only by Mrs. Vesey's voice. "Ladies and gentlemen, please be seated; we are ready to begin."

Normally their hostess preferred to arrange her guests into scattered groups, the better for them to enjoy conversation with one another, but for Dr. Andrews's presentation she had set the chairs in rows. Galen, fleeing embarrassment, took a seat next to Mrs. Montagu; Miss Northwood ended up two rows behind them. He tried not to wonder whether she was staring at his back as Dr. Andrews began his lecture.

He began by thanking Mrs. Vesey, but soon embarked upon his topic. "The French philosopher René Descartes," Dr. Andrews said, "spoke in his writings of the division between Body and Mind. The body operates like a machine, according to the laws that govern physical things, while the the mind is immaterial, insubstantial, and is not constrained by physical laws. But each can influence the other: if I raise my hand, thus, it is because my mind directed my body to do so. The passions of the body can likewise influence the mind, as when anger leads a man to make a rash decision.

"But what is the means by which this interaction occurs?"

Mere abstraction would have been weighty enough for an evening's lecture, but Dr. Andrews soon proceeded to detail, speaking first of Descartes's obsolete notion that the pineal gland was the point of connection between Body and Mind. From there it was on to the ventricles of the brain and other matters Mrs. Northwood certainly would not have considered appropriate for ladies of any age.

And indeed, Galen saw some expressions of distaste when Andrews delved too far into anatomy. For others, though, fascination was the much stronger force. These were the same kinds of women for whom Mrs. Carter had translated *Sir Isaac Newton's Philosophy Explain'd for the Use of Ladies*, from the Italian. Physics might be a cleaner subject, but their curiosity did not end there.

"There are times," Andrews said, "when no physician can tell what has brought life to an end. No discernible cause explains it. Or one man suffers a wound that defeats him; another, wounded just the same, lives on. The ultimate cause of mortality, perhaps, lies not in the body, but in the mind: if it can transcend the body's control, and become the sole master of the self . . ." He broke off with an embarrassed, affected laugh. "Well, short of a reversal of the Fall, that isn't likely to happen. But we can at least dream of such a day."

Weaken the mind, Galen thought, not even certain what he meant by that phrase. *Perhaps that's why the Dragon could not be killed. Its mind is more powerful than its body.*

The lecture was done. Distracted, he rose from his chair and went to the table at the side of the room, where he poured a cup of punch for himself. Then he stood with it forgotten in his hand, biting one thumbnail, still thinking.

Mrs. Vesey found him there. "Well, Mr. St. Clair, inquiring busybodies wish to know—when do you intend to offer for her?"

Her question was so unexpected, and so little in keeping with his current thoughts, that he almost didn't understand the words; she could have been speaking Arabic. Once her meaning became clear, he glanced across the room to Miss Northwood, who stood in animated conversation with Mrs.

Montagu. "I have until the end of the Season, as you well know."

"She is free," Mrs. Vesey said, "but not likely to remain so forever. Not with parents so ambitious to see their daughter matched well."

Galen liked to believe that Miss Northwood looked kindly upon him. He might not be the only man so favored, though. He sighed. "Free—as I am not. Mrs. Vesey, whatever shall I do? How can I, in good conscience, take a wife? It's one thing to have interests and business separate from marriage and one's wife—every man does so—but when they must be kept secret . . ."

Mrs. Vesey pursed her lips, then said, "You *could* tell her."

"About—" Far too loud, especially for the words that had nearly come out of his mouth. Galen waited until he could speak more moderately, then whispered, "You must be mad."

"Must I?" She seemed unconcerned by the prospect. "I know you aren't the first man to be in your position. They cannot have all been bachelors, and surely some told their wives."

Galen had no idea whether they had or not. It was not something he'd ever thought to ask the Queen. On the surface of it, there was no reason Mrs. Vesey should be wrong; after all, as Lune had reminded him, if he wanted to reveal the secret of the Onyx Court to some mortal, he had the authority to do so. Yet in his mind, *mortal* had always meant *man*. Even standing here, within whispering distance of a woman who had tea every week with a faerie, he'd never thought to include the gentler sex.

But of course Mrs. Vesey's suggestion only addressed the objection of secrecy. She knew nothing of his love for Lune, that would make him unfaithful to his wife from the moment they were wed.

Galen gritted his teeth. *I thought I left that objection behind in my father's study.* Apparently his conscience would not let go so easily.

Mrs. Vesey said, "Well, do consider it. I think Miss Northwood is a proper match for you; she, of all girls, might be able to accept that truth. And if you wait until the end of the

Season, Mr. St. Clair, you may well lose her to another gentleman. Think on *that*, too—and while you do, please take this punch to Dr. Andrews."

The Onyx Hall, London: May 18, 1758

On her way to the night garden, Irrith passed a surprising number of fae in the corridors of the Onyx Hall. They fell neatly into two groups: the rough-clad, non-elfin ones were going to the arena to watch a mortal boxer stand up against the yarthkin Hempry, and the elfin ones in fanciful dress were on their way to one of the greater halls, for a masquerade ball.

Near the branch that led to the Temple of Arms, she ran into and almost did not recognize Segraine. For once the lady knight looked more lady than knight, in a dress woven of mist that complemented her eyes. "You aren't going to watch the boxer?" Irrith said in surprise.

Her friend scowled. "A pair of mermen showed up in Queenhithe this morning, come to negotiate with her Majesty about the clouds. She didn't expect them; this might be the first time they've deigned to come so far upriver. The hope is that it's a good sign. But it means she wants a big retinue at the ball, to impress the sea folk."

The speculation on Segraine's face made Irrith say hastily, "I have *nothing* suitable to wear, and couldn't possibly find anything in time."

"And if I go looking out a gown for you, you'll vanish while my back's turned." Segraine made a frustrated noise. "Rumor has it Carline will be showing up in a dress made of *flame*. I liked her better when she was scheming; then she wanted something, and was willing to display the tiniest bit of tact in order to get it."

The reasons for Irrith not to attend the ball kept mounting. She said, "I was going to the night garden, to talk to Ktistes. He says his people have ways to talk to the winds, and I think that might help me with the clouds."

"Better the Greeks than the merfolk. Their desires are far more comprehensible." Segraine brushed her hands across the false hips of her dress, sending mist eddying outward, and said, "Her Grace is waiting for me. If she asks, I'll say I didn't see you."

Irrith barely waited to express her gratitude before bolting for the night garden.

The place was eerily silent. Normally there were fae scattered around enjoying the fountains or the flowers or conducting an assignation under a bower, but tonight Irrith had it to herself—except for Ktistes, of course, who showed no interest in masquerades, and preferred wrestling to boxing. On her way to his pavilion on the far side, though, Irrith realized there was one other person in the garden.

Galen sat on a low bench next to a slender white obelisk. What he was doing there, Irrith didn't know; he should have been with Lune, preparing to greet the ambassadors from the sea. Certainly he was dressed for court, in a deep blue coat heavily crusted with silver embroidery and a diamond-buttoned waistcoat. He sat unmoving, though, and his expression was a complex blend of melancholy and speculation, and it drew her like a moth to a flame.

She made enough noise that he heard her coming and rose. "Dame Irrith. Is her Grace calling for me?"

"Probably," Irrith said. "I came to visit Ktistes. What are you doing?"

The Prince gestured toward the plaque at the base of the obelisk. "Just . . . thinking."

Irrith drew closer and knelt in the grass, the better to read the inscriptions at the base. They turned out to be a list of names and dates.

Sir Michael Deven	1590–1625
Sir Antony Ware	1625–1665
Dr. John Ellin	1665–1693
Lord Joseph Winslow	1693–1724
Sir Alan Fitzwarren	1724–1750
Dr. Hamilton Birch	1750–1756

And above them, in large letters, *PRINCES OF THE STONE*.

The numbers made her feel very odd. It was such a human thing—of course, the men commemorated here *were* human. But to see the years of their reigns laid out in marble like that . . . it was as if she normally flew above the landscape of time, and this forced her briefly down to earth.

From behind her, Galen said, "You knew some of them, didn't you?"

"Three." Irrith reached out with an uncertain hand, brushing her fingertip along the names. "Lord Antony. Jack—he rarely used his title. And Lord Joseph." After that, she'd been in Berkshire.

"How many were married?"

Irrith twisted around to stare at him. Galen still had that look on his face, the melancholy and the speculation. And a bit of apprehension, too. "Of the ones I knew? Lord Antony and Lord Joseph."

Now melancholy was winning out. "And the first one, too, I think. Even if they were never wed in a church, I know he loved the Queen. And she loved him back."

Irrith glanced past him, to the canopy of ever-blooming apple trees on the other side of the path. The greenery in between hid the second obelisk—the one that marked Sir Michael Deven's grave. "Yes."

Galen let out his breath as if trying, and failing, to banish his gloom with it, and sank back down upon the bench. There being nowhere else to sit but next to him or on the grass, Irrith stayed where she was. She could almost *taste* the sentiment churning in his heart, and perhaps it was that which led her to speak recklessly. "She won't stop you from marrying, you know. Even if you *are* in love with her."

The transformation to shock, horror, and embarrassment was instantaneous. Galen sputtered out several half-finished words before he managed a coherent sentence: "I'm not in love with her!"

"Ah." Irrith nodded wisely. "Then I misunderstood. I thought the fact that you watch every move she makes, light up when she smiles, grovel like a kicked dog when she's disappointed, and would do absolutely anything she asks in a heartbeat meant you were in love with her. But I'm a faerie; I know little about such things."

She managed not to laugh at Galen, even though he was staring at her like the very spirit of the word *aghast*. It *was* funny, but she also felt a pang of sympathy for him. It could not possibly be pleasant, tying your heart to someone else's heels like that.

Sunset still flamed in his cheeks when the strangled whisper emerged from his frozen mouth. "Please tell me she doesn't know."

"She doesn't," Irrith agreed. After all, he was the Prince; she had to do what he told her. Also, he wouldn't be able to help Lune with the mermen if he went and buried himself under a rock to die of shame.

"You *cannot* tell her," Galen said. For the first time since she met him, he sounded authoritative—if a little desperate. "My . . . sentiment is my own concern. Her Majesty will not be burdened with the knowledge of it."

Irrith hardly listened to the last of that; she was distracted by something else. "No wonder you almost never use her name. Other Princes have, you know. She doesn't require formality of them. Are you afraid she'll guess, if she hears you say it?" It would be hard, she supposed, to sound like an ardent lover while wrestling with cumbersome forms of address.

Galen said stiffly, "Until such time as I can show her the proper respect in my heart, I must rely on the respect of speech."

Good luck, Irrith thought. "How did it happen, anyway?" She wrapped her arms around her knees, like a child awaiting a story. She'd once spent a few years spying on such children, trying to understand the nature of family. It still escaped her, but she'd learned some entertaining tales.

His teeth caught his lower lip, a charming bit of off-center uncertainty. "I caught a glimpse of her one night, returning from a journey outside of London. She shone like the moon . . ."

Irrith shivered. That was it, right there: the sound of adoration. It thrummed in his voice like a low string, plucked once.

Galen took sudden and intense interest in his fingernails. Seated below him, Irrith could still see a little of his face: the wings of his brows, the clean slope of his jaw. Not his eyes. "I knew nothing of the Onyx Court, and scarcely more of faeries; our nursemaid told other kinds of stories. But I searched London high and low, seeking hints of my vision, and ended up following Dame Segraine to an entrance." He laughed quietly. "Which wasn't my cleverest decision ever. But it worked out in the end."

"You must have been terribly young."

"Nineteen," Galen said defensively.

Irrith blinked. "And you're how old now?"

"Twenty-two."

There was a profoundly tactless response to that, and Irrith might have made it had a puck not come running down the path just then. He ran past the two of them, slid to a halt, and came leaping back almost before he'd gotten his body turned around. "Lord Galen. The Queen needs your presence urgently—the masquerade—"

Galen was already on his feet. Despite the messenger's obvious hurry, the Prince offered a hand to Irrith, and helped her up from the grass. "Are you attending the ball, Dame Irrith?"

It would almost be worth it, just to watch Galen try not to sigh over Lune, but even that could not drag her into so elegant an event. "No, I must talk to Ktistes. But I hope it goes well."

He bowed, and then followed the twitching messenger out a nearby arch.

Left alone, Irrith knelt again and touched the plaque. *Dr. Hamilton Birch: 1750–1756.* It was . . . 1758 now, she thought. Galen was twenty-two. Nineteen when he came to the Onyx Hall.

She didn't know when his birthday was, nor when in 1756 he'd succeeded Lord Hamilton, but he couldn't have been in the Onyx Hall for more than a year or two before he became Prince of the Stone.

Quick elevations had happened before. Usually it was because something had happened to the previous Prince. And Hamilton Birch had reigned for only six years.

Then gave way to an uncertain young man whose chief qualification seemed to be adoration of the Queen.

Irrith *liked* Galen well enough. He clearly had a generous heart and an overwhelming desire to serve Lune faithfully. He was, however, also naïve enough to make Irrith feel like a jaded politician. Why had the Queen chosen him? Especially at so crucial a moment, with the Onyx Hall itself in mounting danger. Lune must have her reasons, but Irrith could not fathom what they were.

But then, Irrith didn't know Galen all that well. She'd managed to accumulate a little bread, though—enough that she could spend some time sniffing around in the world above.

The time had come, she decided, to take a closer look at this new Prince.

Memory: September 16, 1754

Leaving behind the seventh draft of a note explaining the necessity of his decision, Galen St. Clair rode south out of London.

Darkness and the threat of tears obscured his vision as he crossed the new Westminster Bridge, descending into the open fields of Lambeth. Galen tried to force the latter down. He'd wept enough already; all of them had, from his mother down to little Irene.

All except his father.

Fury made his best guard against misery. Charles St. Clair had refused to share the details of the disaster, but Galen had gotten them from Laurence Byrd; he now knew to an excruciating degree of fineness how his father had gambled his fortune on a series of dubious investments, and lost it through the same. They were not penniless—his father kept saying so, louder every time, as if that made the situation more palatable. Not penniless, but they would have to practice a great deal of economy, and even that would not save the three St. Clair daughters. Their marriage portions would be small indeed.

Unless money was found, somehow. And so Galen wrote a letter, sealed it, and left it on his father's desk, then took horse for Portsmouth and the Royal Navy. Britain was fighting

France in the Ohio Country; there was hope of proper war, and with it, prize money.

In the madness of his desperation, this was the life Galen had chosen for himself.

He pulled his horse to a stop in the middle of a narrow lane, bracketed by hedgerows. His breath came hard in his chest, almost crossing the line into sobs. Could he do this? Abandon his mother, and his sisters, and the soil of England itself, to go to sea and court death in hopes of a brighter future?

It seemed to him that the darkness lifted a bit, as if the clouds had cleared, uncovering the moon. Galen's breathing slowed when he realized two things: first, that the night was already clear, and second, that the moon was new.

He looked up into the sky.

High above, silver-radiant against the tapestry of the stars, rode a goddess. Her hands rested lightly on the reins of an enchanted steed, and her hair streamed free like the tail of some glorious comet. No road bore her weight, nor wings; the horse galloped upon the insubstantial air.

Behind her came a host of others, but Galen had no eyes for them. He sat rapt, his own mount forgotten beneath him, and turned in his saddle to watch the goddess go by. His memory, trained since childhood by a mother who loved the stories of the pagan Greeks and Romans, whispered names in his ear: *Artemis. Diana. Selene. Luna.*

Perfection, beyond the reach of mortal kind.

And she was riding to London.

There was no mistaking it. The enchanted host changed their course, lowering to the grassy fields just before Southwark's edge. His heart ached to see them descend to earth. They were airy things, and *her* most of all, that should not be contaminated by the heaviness of the world.

Yet they were of London. He'd seen it in the serenity of her beautiful face: she was coming home. Somehow that filthy city, choked with dung and coal smoke and the cries of the poor, that maw that ate up fortune and spat out ashes, was beloved to her. Wherever she had gone, she rejoiced at her return.

I must know who she is.

Galen tugged unthinking at his reins. Nothing happened.

His horse, he saw, had bent to graze on a thick tuft of grass. Growling, he yanked harder, and dragged the reluctant beast onto a neighboring lane. But however much he spurred it onward, he wasn't fast enough; by the time he reached Southwark, the enchanted host had vanished.

His heart pounded with passions that could not be put into words. That vision—who she was, *what* she was, and why she dwelt in London—

He could not leave.

A few moments ago, he'd been uncertain. Now there was no question. He could not turn his back upon the glory he had seen. Galen would stay, and search the city from Westminster to Wapping, tearing up the very cobbles of the streets if need be, until he found the lady again. And when he did, he would offer her his services, even unto death.

With tears once more upon his face, Galen turned his weary horse homeward.

But this time, they were tears of wonder.

The Mitre Tavern, Fleet Street: June 15, 1758

The crowds of Fleet Street were bad enough in the evening; at four o'clock in the afternoon, they were nothing short of absurd. This time, Galen's choice to ride in a sedan chair had little to do with economy, and a great deal to do with common sense; as slowly as he was moving, a carriage would have gone even slower. Andrews had chosen the same mode of conveyance, and as they crawled through the press, the doctor's rear chair-man was able to carry on an entire conversation with Galen's forward man.

By the time he and the doctor stepped out at their destination, the early heat had called forth sweat from every pore of Galen's skin. Andrews had gone so far as to take off his wig, and was fanning himself with his hat as Galen rejoined him. "God, I hate London in the summer," the man said with feeling. "But the food will make up for it, I assure you; we've had a gift of turtle recently. Come, follow me."

They escaped the clamor of the street for the quieter—though by no means quiet—interior of the Mitre Tavern. Men sat at their dinners all along the tables, and waiters scrambled to attend to them; Galen was almost run over by one plate-laden fellow as Andrews led him toward the stairs. The private room above was a relief by comparison, even if the air within was stuffy with pipe smoke, and the gentlemen there distinguished enough to put Galen to shame.

Most of them were members of the Royal Society, but this, the similarly named Society of Royal Philosophers, was a much more select group. According to Andrews, their membership was limited to forty, and the dues collected to pay for their weekly dinners would have sent Galen's father into an apoplexy. Though it was far from the most expensive or exclusive club in London, it was more than enough to intimidate Galen, who once again was attending only as a guest.

Andrews made the rounds of introductions. Encouragingly, a number of the gentlemen remembered Galen; those who didn't came rarely or never to the meetings in Crane Court, which took place after this dinner every Thursday. And there was another young man there, perhaps five years older than Galen, who was likewise a newcomer and a guest. "Henry Cavendish," Dr. Andrews said by way of introduction, when they came face-to-face. "Son of— is your father here, Mr. Cavendish?"

The answer came in the form of a gesture toward a man Galen remembered from his first Royal Society meeting. Once again he stood in conversation with Lord Macclesfield, who was president of both societies. "You are the son of Lord Charles Cavendish?"

A nod. Galen glanced fleetingly at Dr. Andrews, perplexed by the other's silence. But his companion was distracted. "Ah, Mr. Franklin! Good to see you again. Hadley was telling me your thoughts on evaporation—"

When everyone sat down to dinner, Galen found himself with Andrews on one side and Henry Cavendish on the other, with Franklin—who, it transpired, was a Society Fellow visiting from the colonies—across the table. His conversation with

Andrews had moved on to electricity, about which Galen knew very little. While the waiter brought out the first course, Galen addressed himself to the challenge of drawing Cavendish into conversation. "Your father is the Vice President of the Royal Society, I believe. Do you have an interest in natural philosophy as well?"

Another nod, as the fellow piled his plate high with pheasant, cod, and pork. What was it going to take, to make him open his mouth? Perhaps it was simple snobbery; if Galen remembered lineages correctly, Henry Cavendish was the grandson of not one but two dukes. On the other hand, it was hard to ascribe snobbery to a man so shabbily dressed; his coat, to choose but one example, was not only plain but frayed at the cuffs and collar.

Faced with the prospect of eating in silence, or else of ignoring his companion to join in conversation elsewhere, Galen opted for a third course of action: he began to talk about whatever came into his head, with frequent pauses that invited Cavendish to contribute. Taking his cues from those around him, he kept his focus on matters philosophical, but within those constraints he gave his curiosity free rein. From Lord Charles's work on thermometers he went on to something Franklin had said about electricity, and thence to astronomy, which—as it always did—led his tongue to fire.

"It's a topic of great interest to me," Galen admitted. Somehow he'd managed to empty his wineglass, wetting his throat; he would have to be more careful, lest he inadvertently make a drunken fool of himself. "I'm fascinated by an account I just read of the work done by a German, Georg Stahl—do you know of it?" He paused for the now expected nod. "I'd never considered that the calcination of metals and the combustion of wood might be the same thing, the release of phlogiston from the material. And who says it ends there? After all, the transmission of electrical fluid can cause fires, as lightning strikes have shown; perhaps that fluid is phlogiston in pure form, or at least contains it in high proportion."

With the general chatter filling the room, Galen almost didn't hear the response. "If it w—if it w—" Cavendish stopped and tried again, with better success. "If it were pure phlogiston, we should expect to see electricity leap into the air as a log burns."

It was two answers in one: a refutation of his notion, and an explanation for why Henry Cavendish had not opened his mouth before. The gentleman's high-pitched voice squeaked like a nervous girl's, and strain showed in his eyes and jaw as he forced himself past the awkward pauses.

Galen felt instant remorse for having thought the man a snob. Nothing could change that unfortunate voice, but surely a gathering of this sort, filled with strangers and free-flowing conversation, made his stammer worse. No wonder Cavendish was quiet.

Having achieved the tiniest bit of success, though, Galen was not about to abandon the effort. "I suppose that's true. I confess, I've only just encountered Stahl's phlogiston theory; a friend gave me the book last week." One benefit to Cavendish's reticence; he wouldn't ask about the friend, and therefore Galen wouldn't have to come up with a lie with which to disguise Wilhas von das Ticken. "Have you done any experiments on the matter?"

The conflicted expression in Cavendish's eyes was familiar to Galen: a profound desire to indulge in his passion, warring against an equally profound reluctance to speak of it. Their respective situations might be very different, but the result looked remarkably similar.

"Hard to do," Cavendish finally mumbled, after another excruciating set of attempts to get the words out. "Need to isolate phlogiston. Might be able to do it with iron filings and acid—Boyle's experiment. Drive the phlogiston out of the metal and ca—and ca—"

Galen stopped himself just short of saying "capture it." Interrupting someone of Cavendish's stature would be rude in the extreme. Besides, even as the words formed in his mind, the association they called up startled him so badly he dropped his fork. *Perhaps it's already been captured.*

Captured—and exiled to a comet.

Salamanders, according to the fae, were the embodiment of fire, and the Dragon was that same concept writ large. And what was phlogiston—the substance that escaped wood when it burnt, and metals when they calcined—but the fundamental stuff of fire?

"Dangerous," Henry Cavendish said, in an overenunciated squeak, apparently responding to some speculation he'd made while Galen wasn't listening.

He was far more correct than he knew. "I think," Galen said, his thoughts racing ahead almost too quickly for his own mind to catch, "that I might have a notion of another way to do it. To obtain a pure sample of phlogiston—or close to pure, at any rate. If I brought such a thing to you, would you—"

He didn't even have to finish the sentence. Henry Cavendish's eyes blazed from the phrase *pure sample* onward. Behind the awkwardness was revealed the sort of mind Galen had hoped to find when he first came to the Royal Society. This grandson of dukes might not be another Sir Isaac Newton, bringing fundamental revelation to the world, but neither would he be a mere dilettante scholar, writing rambling letters to the Society about the curious rock he found on his estate. The passion for knowledge was there, and the intelligence necessary to seize it.

From the other side of Galen, Andrews said, "Pure phlogiston? If you obtain that, Mr. St. Clair, you must share it with the Royal Society at once! Not merely the substance, but the means by which you isolated it. This could be a tremendous advancement."

Far too much attention was falling on Galen now. Bring a salamander to Crane Court? It was unthinkable. Using his dropped fork as an excuse to hide his face, Galen mumbled, "Well, I—I am not confident it will work. And I would have to, ah, repeat my results, to be certain they're reliable. You understand."

The waiter saved him. He entered the room just then, followed by two of his fellows bearing a large silver platter. With a flourish, they lifted the cover to reveal the promised turtle, and Galen's reckless declaration was forgotten in the ensuing approval.

By most. Andrews, however, did not forget. While the dish was being served, he leaned closer to Galen and said, "If you need any assistance, Mr. St. Clair, do not hesitate to ask. I know this is quite aside from my usual studies, but I would be extremely interested to see that result."

"You shall," Galen said, arriving at a decision without warning. *I've dithered long enough. There are minds here who can help the Onyx Court—but only if they have information to work with.* Cavendish was too new; Galen had known him for less than an hour. Andrews, on the other hand, he'd been studying for six months. The time had come to make a decision.

Andrews saw the change in him. Softer yet, he asked, "What is it, Mr. St. Clair?"

Galen shook his head. Not here, and not until he had a chance to notify the Queen. But once that was done . . .

"Might I call on you tomorrow, Dr. Andrews?" The older man nodded. "Excellent. I have a few things to share with you, that I think you will find very interesting indeed."

Holborn and Bloomsbury: June 16, 1758

Galen half-wondered why no one commented on the strange drumbeat coming from within the sedan chair. Surely his heartbeat was audible all the way to the river. Lune's encouraging words last night had fortified him enough to propel him out the door, but now that he was here, the magnitude of what he was about to do threatened to overwhelm him.

Momentum alone carried him out of the chair, up to the suddenly menacing door, into the cool entrance hall of Dr. Andrews's townhouse. The words he'd carefully rehearsed all through the Royal Society meeting last night, through the hours when he lay unable to sleep, through the breakfast he didn't eat and the journey to Red Lion Square, now ran about like frightened mice in his head, scattered and incoherent. Telling himself that others had done this before him didn't help; he hadn't taken the time to study preferred methods of revealing the Onyx Court, and now it was too late.

The obvious solution—fobbing Andrews off with some

other topic, and trying again later—was out of the question. Galen knew himself an occasional coward, but that was a retreat he could not accept.

"Coffee?" Dr. Andrews offered, once he'd emerged from his laboratory and washed his hands clean in a basin the maid brought. "Or brandy, perhaps?"

That his host should offer spirits told Galen just how visible his nervousness was. Licking his lips, he thought, *Delaying will only make it worse. I must do this now, or not at all.*

"No, thank you," he said, and somehow those commonplace words of courtesy steadied him. "Dr. Andrews, I do not wish to give offense, but—are your servants the sort to listen at keyholes?"

The older gentleman's eyes hardened. "They are entirely loyal to me, Mr. St. Clair, and they know I will not tolerate indiscretion."

The frostiness, Galen thought, was not directed at him. A household like this, without a wife to manage it, was often an ill-run menagerie; it took a wise choice of housekeeper and a stern disciplinary hand to prevent gossiping, pilfering, and general shabbiness of service. Dr. Andrews, it seemed, had achieved that success.

"What I have to say to you is very private," Galen said, unnecessarily; he'd already made that much obvious. His nerves would not rest, though. "I don't mean to impugn your control of your servants, but it would be disastrous for many people if word were to slip out." No doubt it had happened before, in the centuries of the Onyx Court's existence, and no doubt the fae had methods of dealing with it; otherwise all London would know of their presence. But they could be ruthless in protecting their secrets, and Galen had no desire to provoke a demonstration.

Andrews gestured toward the door. "If you're truly worried, Mr. St. Clair, we could walk in the fields around the Foundling Hospital. It's a pleasant day, and we should have no worries of being overheard."

Only when relief broke in a cold wave over Galen did he realize how much the servants had been worrying him. "That would be ideal."

With no further ado, Andrews bowed him through the doorway. Red Lion Street, lined with rows of smaller houses, opened without warning into placid fields, just a few blocks to the north. A broad avenue led to the brick heights of the Foundling Hospital, but Galen and Dr. Andrews went left, along a footpath into the Lamb's Conduit Fields.

He breathed much more easily out here, and not just because the nearest people were well distant, hard at work in the little market gardens that served London with fresh vegetables and flowers. The sunlight was warm without being oppressively hot, and the buttercups blooming along the sides of the path unknotted his shoulders just by their cheerful color. In such surroundings, the existence of a dark and hidden world beneath London seemed more like a point of curiosity than a threat. That was the greatest risk: that someday the Onyx Court would be exposed to one who saw them as an enemy. Galen was determined to protect himself, and the court, from that error.

Dr. Andrews gave him the time he needed to marshal his thoughts. They ambled along in silence, until Galen took a deep breath and launched into the speech he'd so carefully prepared.

"I must confess, Dr. Andrews, that while I've been grateful for your patronage in the Royal Society, from early on, I had an additional motive in cultivating your acquaintance. I hoped you might be able to provide me with a touch of assistance on a rather pressing matter. The questions you pursue—the nature of mortality, and the relationship between mind and body, spirit and matter—those have very direct bearing upon my concerns. I saw in your quest the opportunity not just to solicit assistance, but to offer it to you in return. You see, sir, I have these several years now been closely involved with a number of individuals upon whom mortality has no hold."

Andrews had been walking this entire time with his hands clasped at the small of his back and his eyes raised to the sky, enjoying the scents of summer. Now he lowered his chin, so that his face fell into shadow, and turned a look of astonishment upon Galen.

He said nothing, though, for which Galen was grateful. If

interrupted now, he might lose the thread of his explanation for good. "I'm well aware of the extraordinary nature of that claim. I assure you, Dr. Andrews, that I am entirely serious, though what I'm about to say to you may seem otherwise. These individuals live in London, but in secret; they never go about in public undisguised. Some of them have been here for centuries, and could tell you at first hand what it was like to live under the Tudors. They aren't perfectly immortal—they can be slain—but in the absence of violence, they live forever."

Here he paused to swallow, wishing he had some drink to wet his terribly dry mouth, and in that pause Dr. Andrews responded. "And who, may I ask, are these extraordinary immortals of which you speak?"

Dr. Johnson's scornful face rose, unbidden, in Galen's memory. He'd avoided the word deliberately, putting the meat of his explanation first, because he recalled the mockery of that great man, and did not wish to invite it a second time. But the word must, inevitably, be said.

"I speak, sir, of faeries."

Andrews didn't laugh. He didn't make any sound at all.

"They aren't the silly creatures of Shakespeare's fancy," Galen said. Well, some of them were—but those didn't matter. "They exist in many varieties, from regal to foul, and not only might they teach you the very secrets you wish to learn . . . Dr. Andrews, they need your help."

They had drifted to a halt in the middle of the path, surrounded by foxgloves and sunshine and the hard-packed dust of the ground. In the near distance, ordinary Londoners went about their work, blissfully free of the screaming apprehension that gripped Galen's throat again, strangling him more with every moment in which Dr. Andrews did not respond.

He has to believe me. He must.

"Mr. St. Clair," Andrews said, then stopped.

His chin was down even farther now, the brim of his hat concealing his expression. His hands were still behind his back, and in the set of his shoulders Galen saw rigid tension. It was to be expected; no one could take such a revelation in stride. But once he had a moment to assimilate it—

Andrews raised his head, and met Galen's eyes with sober

concern. "Mr. St. Clair, I'm not certain what possessed you to bring me out here with such a story. My guess is that you have been deceived by a mountebank—perhaps one offering wild promises of restoring your family's fortune; perhaps one merely preying on your admirable heart, with these tales of faeries in need of a savior. I shudder to think what assistance he has asked of you."

"There is no mountebank!" Galen exclaimed, horrified. "Dr. Andrews—"

The gentleman's mouth hardened. "If no one has deceived you, then I must conclude that *you* are attempting to deceive *me*. I do not wish to know what your request would have been. Should I learn that, I would be forced to go to your father and share the news of this unfortunate encounter. As it stands, Mr. St. Clair, I offer you this much: I will *not* tell your father, nor will I bring any trouble upon you for wasting my time and goodwill. But in return, I must insist that you cease to attend the Royal Society. I can no longer in good conscience admit you as my guest, and should you persuade your father to do so again, I will speak against it to Lord Macclesfield. Have I made myself clear?"

He could have torn Galen's heart from his chest and stomped it into the dust and he would not have been more clear. Galen wished he could sink into that dust, or leap into the sky and flee on the wings of a hawk—*anything* that would remove him from this sunny lane, and the disgusted gaze of Dr. Andrews.

Like an automaton's, his mouth opened and formed words, without the instruction of his brain. "Yes, sir."

"Good." Andrews made a curt bow, barely more than a slight twitch forward. "I believe you can find your way home from here. Good day, Mr. St. Clair."

Around the point when Irrith followed Galen to Red Lion Square, she had to admit she was spying on him.

How else was she to satisfy her curiosity? He was ludicrously easy to follow; a simple glamour, and she could shadow him wherever he went. Not into Royal Society meetings, where she would have to pretend to be one of the members, but other places were open to her. She visited his favorite bookshop, and saw what titles interested him. She loitered in his favorite coffeehouse, drinking the foul, bitter tonic while he played games of chance with his friends. She even investigated his house, with his three sisters and his tyrannical father.

It wasn't spying. It was . . .

Very well, it's spying.

And it sounded a bit shameful when she admitted that. Especially since she was neglecting the task Lune had set her, the concealment of England. Well and good to say she was waiting on the Queen's negotiations with the Greeks and the folk of the sea, but Irrith had better things to do with her time than spying on the Prince.

She'd been considering sneaking into the house of the Marvelous Menagerie, to overhear what Galen might be saying, but now it didn't seem like such a good idea. She was on the verge of convincing herself to go home when Galen emerged once more, this time in the company of that man. Dr. Andrews. The one with the fake satyr.

Following someone through green fields wasn't shameful; it was one of her favorite pastimes in Berkshire. And she was very, very good at it. Freed from her doubts, Irrith crept close enough to hear Galen's unbelievable speech, and Andrews's unbelieving reaction.

She bit down on a curse. While the two men took their leave of each other, going separate ways, she fought the urge to chew on the brambles that concealed her. *I should have warned Galen. I knew, when I asked him about satyrs—this isn't a man who wants to believe in faeries.* But she hadn't realized that was what the Prince had in mind.

If she hurried, she might catch Andrews before he came among the houses once more, and then she could make certain he never reached them. Never had the chance to repeat what Galen had revealed.

But no; the Prince thought Andrews would be useful. She couldn't simply kill him, even if he'd proved his lack of use.

It gave her another idea, though.

Irrith cut across the open ground, relying as much on the cover of hedges as faerie charms to keep herself concealed.

Andrews was almost to the back of those big buildings near the town's edge. She had only an instant to wonder if this was truly a good idea before she flung a glamour over herself, then flung herself into the path.

The mortal stopped abruptly. He drew a surprised breath, but it set off a fit of coughing; disgruntled, Irrith waited, as he fished out a handkerchief and spat something into it. Once his wind had returned, he looked up, and said with some confusion, "Miss Dinley?"

She'd remembered the look she put on for that visit to the menagerie, but not the name. *What a helpful fellow.* "Are you all right, Dr. Andrews?"

He waved his free hand at her, tucking the handkerchief away with the other. "You startled me, is all. What—" Now he looked around. "Are you out here alone?"

The temptation to play an elaborate role tugged at her. Under the circumstances, though, it was best to dispose of this quickly. "I saw you walking with Galen St. Clair." She paused, holding Andrews's gaze. "I know what he told you."

The man scowled. "If you are a friend of his, Miss Dinley, then I would ask that you advise him to stop playing games."

"But I like games," Irrith said—from behind him.

She almost ruined it all by laughing when he squawked and spun around. It was an easy trick, the sort of thing pucks dismissed as beneath their efforts, but she hadn't planned for this; she had to work with what she had.

Which was enough to impress Andrews. Or to frighten him, which was just as good. "What—how did you—"

"Get back here?" Irrith gave him a mocking curtsy. "Perhaps I moved faster than your old eyes can see."

She read his intentions with plenty of time to spare. Andrews didn't get two steps farther down the path before she moved again, blocking his way. "Of course," she said, "I'm older than you are. *Far* older. But you don't believe in creatures such as me, do you, Dr. Andrews?" She had to pause to concentrate, but that was all right; the man wasn't going anywhere. His feet seemed rooted to the ground as the glamour masking her rippled, replacing Miss Dinley with a red-haired young gentleman in a foppish coat. "I'm just a mountebank, preying on his admirable heart."

And then her final move, that went so hard against her instincts she had to grit her teeth to make it happen. Standing in the open, with the townhouses of sprawling London less than a quarter mile behind her, Irrith dropped her glamour entirely, and showed her true face to Dr. Rufus Andrews.

"I assure you," she said. "Every word Galen St. Clair spoke was the truth."

Galen had no thought in his head as he walked away, except to go somewhere Dr. Andrews was not.

The enormity of his failure was like a drowning sea around him, and nothing he could do would lift his head above the waters. It was no consolation at all to think that his caution had served him well; since Galen betrayed nothing of the Onyx Hall's location, and brought no faerie as proof, Andrews had no way to cause them harm.

But that same caution had made it all too easy to dismiss Galen's words.

Had I gambled more, would I have won?

Galen lifted his gaze and found he'd wandered across to the New River Head, the reservoir glittering incongruously bright. Beyond it lay a road, one direction leading to London, the other to Islington. He should have solicited the help of the Goodemeades, who would have been only too happy to advise him.

Yet he was the Prince. There had to be a point at which he could handle such matters on his own.

I certainly must do so now. However I mend this—and mend it I must—I don't dare ask for help.

Pounding footsteps made him whirl. Despairing as he was, Galen's first, overwrought fear was that some footpad had decided to murder him for the gold he wasn't carrying.

Instead, he saw Dr. Andrews.

The old man stumbled on a stone and crashed to the ground, wheezing and coughing. His pallor was worse than ever, and his cheeks flushed with hectic spots. Throwing their argument to the wind, Galen rushed to his side. "Dr. Andrews! What has happened? Are you all right?"

Stupid questions. The man couldn't tell what had happened, because of course he wasn't all right; he was a consumptive who had just run much too far. Galen shuddered in horror when he saw the bright red spots on Andrews' handkerchief.

Even before he had regained his breath, though, Andrews began trying to answer him. "F—f—"

Galen's heart dropped like a stone.

"*Faerie,*" Andrews said, rasping the word out on an indrawn breath. "Near the—Foundling Hospital. A g—" More coughing. "A girl."

Lune? Not a chance. Galen could not have been walking for more than a few minutes, though; who could have been so nearby, to cause such an immediate change?

Andrews was whispering something else. Galen bent close to hear.

"I'm sorry," the older man said, addressing the dust between his hands. "I'm so sorry. I didn't believe you. But she—her eyes—" He spat bloody saliva into the dirt, and spoke more clearly. "Not human. No one's eyes are so green . . ."

Irrith.

Galen straightened with a jerk, staring wildly about as if the sprite would come sauntering up behind Andrews. Irrith, of course, was nowhere in sight. "What did she do to you?"

"Showed me." Andrews was trying to get to his feet; against his better judgment, Galen helped him. "What she was. Is. I—" His spectacles had been knocked askew; he took them off, then stopped just before he could rub his soiled handkerchief over the lenses. Galen offered him a clean one, which he took with gratitude. "I'm ashamed to say I ran like a child."

Galen didn't want to ask further, but he had to know. "What did she *do?*"

A breath huffed out of Andrews, not quite a laugh, not quite a cough. "Nothing to warrant me running. Oh, a bit of trickery, to make her point. You—you did not send her?"

"Certainly not!" Galen exclaimed. "I would never do anything to frighten you like this." *I'm going to kill her.*

Or possibly kiss her.

Because the look Andrews turned upon him held no more doubt. It was eradicated utterly, replaced by hope as fragile as a butterfly's wing. "She said you spoke the truth. Can they truly help me?"

With the bloody handkerchief in his hand, the possibility took on a sharper edge. Galen didn't want to foster it falsely. "They may. I cannot be sure. Lest you think them altruists, however—I can promise you they'll want your aid in return, with a problem they face." He took in Andrews's disheveled appearance, and realized he was being an ass. "Let me fetch you a chair, for returning to your house." He hated to leave the man here on his own, even for a few short minutes; but conveyances did not make a habit of idling around the New River reservoir, waiting to rescue consumptive gentlemen frightened by faeries. Unless Andrews were to ride a cow home, Galen would have to go in search.

But the doctor stopped him with one hand on his arm. "I am well enough to walk," Andrews said, "if we go slowly. And you were right; this is something my servants should not hear. Come, Mr. St. Clair, and tell me more."

The Onyx Hall, London: June 16, 1758

Irrith sat with her back to the wall, eyes trained on the opening that led to Newgate above, waiting for Galen to fall through.

She couldn't be certain he would come this way—at least not any time soon—but she preferred waiting to facing the Queen with news of the Andrews incident. Galen could do that part. It was his duty anyway.

So why am I waiting for him? He can thank me later. But she wanted a chance to explain herself, before he questioned too much why she'd been following him. Assuming she could think of a believable explanation that wasn't the truth.

She'd been waiting only a short while when Galen came

floating down into the chamber, confirming her guess. Before Irrith could say any of the things she'd thought of, though, the Prince saw her—and flared into sudden fury.

"What were you *thinking*?" he demanded, with no prelude. "The man could have died, Irrith; he's a consumptive! And what were you doing out there in the first place?"

Anger made sense, on the face of it—but she'd never seen *Galen* angry. His mild blue eyes took on a fire she wouldn't have believed possible; Irrith had to stop herself before she could retreat. Summoning up what she could of her usual confidence, Irrith said, "You needed an example. Something he couldn't ignore. If you'd told me you were planning such a thing—"

"I didn't tell you," Galen said through his teeth, "because I didn't need your help."

She confined her doubt to her eyebrows, and tried to make her spoken answer more conciliatory. "It was helpful, though, wasn't it?"

Galen bit down so hard she swore she could hear his jaw creak. It wasn't anger, though—or if it was, his eyes were lying. As was his reply. "I'm the Prince of the Stone, damn it. I should be able to do these things *without* help."

"And who told you that?" she asked, bewildered.

"Lune trusts me—"

"To do everything yourself?" Irrith snorted. *Ash and Thorn, he really* is *young.* "She cares about results, Galen, not methods. So long as you don't bring half of London down here on a Grand Tour, she doesn't care *how* you do it. Or whom you ask for help."

But he did. That was painfully obvious. The notion that Lune might be more impressed by a few shreds of common sense than some heroic determination to do everything himself was clearly very foreign to him.

Galen asked the floor, "Did she send you to follow me?"

"No," Irrith said. Now they were both embarrassed. "I, er, was keeping watch over you. For the good of the Onyx Court." That was close enough to the truth to pass.

He laughed soundlessly. "And so you saved me from my own mistake. I suppose you were worried he would say things he shouldn't, tell someone about that mad St. Clair boy and the nonsense he spouts. Well, I have his assurance of secrecy now, so you can rest safely."

"He didn't believe you," Irrith said. That still rankled. The need to make Galen understand why drew her closer to him, across the black stone floor. "Men like him don't, not anymore. As far as they're concerned, I don't exist. And someone like you, who does believe . . . if he weren't so angry, he would have laughed at you. I couldn't let that stand, for me *or* you."

Galen's head came up, and only then did Irrith realize just how near she'd drawn. They stood bare inches apart, and then his gaze flickered, in a way she'd seen countless times across the countless ages.

But he didn't move. So she did it for him, closing that last gap and capturing his lips with her own.

He wrenched back an instant later. "Dame Irrith—"

"What?" she asked, confused and a little hurt. "I saw your eyes move. You wanted to kiss me."

"No! Well, yes, but—" He shook his head, hands up in midair as if warding something off. "It isn't right."

"Why not?"

He opened and closed his mouth a few times, like a man with several explanations competing to come out first, none of them entirely satisfactory.

Irrith sighed. "You aren't married. You aren't even betrothed. Are you a virgin?"

"*What?* I—no—it's none of your business!"

As if he were the first gentleman to make use of a whore's services. Irrith guessed it was a whore; the sort of young man who seduced servant girls or the neighbor's daughter usually didn't blush like that. "So fornication isn't the problem. Do you think it's especially sinful, with a faerie woman? But you don't mind being in love with—"

He didn't have to stop her; she stopped herself. The answer was so *obvious*. But Irrith wasn't used to accounting for such things. "But—she doesn't even know how you feel." Or so he liked to think.

Galen said, very stiffly, "That doesn't matter. *I* know, and would feel ashamed."

"But why should you?" Irrith advanced; he retreated. Step by step, they crossed the roundel beneath the entrance; mercifully, no one chose that moment to fall from the City above. "She doesn't love you back, and you know it. You'll never be with her, and you know that, too. Why not have what you can?"

Galen halted just before he would have hit the far wall. "Do *you* love me?"

Of course he would ask that. Irrith couldn't remember the entirety of her existence, but surely she would remember if she'd ever encountered another man ruled so deeply by his heart. It defined him—and that, of course, was why he fascinated her so much.

"No," Irrith said. "But I don't need to."

This time when she reached for him, he didn't try to escape.

PART FOUR

Conjunctio

Summer 1758

Mankind have a great aversion to intellectual labor;
but even supposing knowledge to be easily attainable,
more people would be content to be ignorant than
would take even a little trouble to acquire it.

—Dr. Samuel Johnson,
quoted in *The Life of Samuel Johnson, LL.D.*
by James Boswell

The first vapors wisp free. Tenuous as ghosts, they soon vanish into the blackness; but they are there.

The comet's surface is warming.

Inert blackness converts to a radiant glow. Encouraged by the sun, the subtle matter bursts forth, creating something like air around the solid core. For the first time in more than seventy years, the beast begins to breathe.

Cold. Still too cold. Its awareness is sluggish, stupid, like a lizard left too long in shadow. Once it was mighty, a beast of flame and char, consuming all within its path. The efforts of humans were nothing, a mockery, a mere game for the creature they fought. To be reduced to this, drinking in the sun's nourishment like a babe at the teat, is a terrible fall indeed.

But with every passing moment, its strength returns, and its mind. Dreams resolve into thoughts. Memories of the past, and plans for the future.

Wisps, as yet. But growing stronger, as the sun draws near.

"How appropriate," Dr. Andrews said, with an unsteady laugh. "You're taking me to Bedlam."

"What? Oh—no, I assure you," Galen hastened to say, once he'd pieced together Andrews's meaning. In the darkness beyond Edward's lantern, the broad expanse of the Hospital of St. Mary of Bethlehem—Bedlam—was nothing more than a shadow against the stars, hulking above the old City wall. "Though some of the lunatics may be, er, joining us." Londoners liked to go and poke at them with sticks for entertainment; the Onyx Court took it further, and invited them to participate in the fun. Tonight of all nights, the mad had a place among the faeries.

Midsummer Eve was swelteringly warm this year. Galen wished it wouldn't be against the royal dignity of a Prince to shuck off his coat and wig and dance in his shirt. Andrews would probably look askance at him, though, even if Lune didn't.

And then there was Irrith to consider.

As if his thoughts had summoned her, the sprite appeared in the gap that had once been Moorgate. Her apparel was an alarming blend of styles, masculine and feminine, mortal and faerie. On top she wore something like a woman's riding habit, with a short jacket that showed off her tiny waist and sleeves that fell open at the elbows, but beneath it were tight-fitting breeches of doeskin, and on her curls perched a charming little three-cornered hat. And in bright colors, too: for occasions such as this, the Onyx Court laid aside its love of dark colors, and decked itself in all the splendor of summer. Whatever bird had sacrificed its feathers for her jacket, it came from nowhere in this world.

Irrith curtsied as they drew near, an incongruous motion that had the virtue of displaying the glimmering spiderweb lace of her sleeves. "Lord Galen," she said, "Dr. Andrews. Her Majesty sent me to make sure you don't get caught by the enchantments." Her smile twinkled even in the darkness. "She would hate for you to be wandering lost for a year and a day."

Galen simply nodded; his throat had gone too dry for anything else. The sly glance Irrith delivered to him was more restrained than it might have been, but it still set off half a dozen conflicting reactions within him. One of them made him glad for the length of his waistcoat. Others made him want to run away, fast.

Instead he gestured Dr. Andrews forward, while Edward extinguished the lamp. They all joined hands, Irrith letting out a sigh that indicated just how much she regretted forgoing the opportunity to play with the newcomer, and went forward. Dizzying vertigo gripped Galen for a moment—brief visions of other streets, moonlit forests, a muddy village—and then they were around the corner of Bedlam's western wing, and standing in the lower Moor Fields.

London had long since burst the confines of its wall to consume the land to the north, but this place remained, defended by tradition less visible but far more enduring than the stones of that wall. By day, Moor Fields was a shabby stretch of much-abused grass, stretching from Bedlam's entrance up to the artillery ground; nearby laundresses still staked their washing out to dry there. By night, it was a haunt for prostitutes and molly-boys. But on Midsummer Eve, it belonged to the fae, as it had since the founding of the Onyx Hall.

Faerie lights danced through the branches of the trees that marked off the lower field, casting colorful light upon the improbably vibrant grass. A great bonfire burnt where the paths came together, without need of wood to feed it, and all around that beacon danced the revelers, faerie and mortal alike. Some wore outrageous mockeries of the most excessive mortal fashions, rendered in moss and mist and leaves. Others wore nothing at all. Galen blushed away from a lushly rounded apple maiden wearing only a few soft petals from her tree, none of them covering anything significant. Rural fae from miles around flocked to London for Midsummer and May Day, and they brought their rural customs with them.

Lune had offered a splendid escort to bring the Prince and his visitor to the celebration. Ordinarily Galen would have entered with the Queen, accompanied by all the pomp appropriate to their joint stations, and she'd frowned at the notion of him coming virtually alone. But he thought it best for Andrews to have an escort he recognized, and an entrance that would draw less attention. Seeing the doctor's wide, unblinking eyes, he rather thought he'd made the right choice.

And there would be pomp soon enough. Irrith was leading them north and east, skirting the crowd around the bonfire. A filthy, unshaven man lay on his back in the grass, hips bucking, rutting with nothing while a pair of pucks watched and laughed. *At least he's enjoying himself,* Galen thought. The tricks played on this night were usually of a benevolent sort, or at least not permanently harmful. All Hallows' Eve was a much less pleasant story.

Something more like dignity reigned in the northeast quarter of the field. There, two long tables stood arrayed before the trees, with dozens of mouthwatering dishes laid upon their white silk. "Remember," Galen whispered to Andrews, "eat nothing whatsoever. There is food here that is safe, but there are also a great many fae who would think it sport to lead you falsely."

"And they can even disguise themselves to make me think you are vouching for its safety," Andrews said. He smiled tensely. "I am not likely to forget."

Then there was no more time for warnings, for Irrith had brought them into the presence of the Queen.

Lune sat in a gap between the two tables, in a chair of estate carved from birch and horn, with a canopy of starlight above her head. Galen's own chair was at her left hand, awaiting him. A truly tiny hob stood with a crystal platter above his head, piled with strawberries and a bowl of cream for the Queen's pleasure, but he backed away with careful haste when he saw their approach, leaving Lune alone.

Galen bowed, and nudged the momentarily paralyzed Andrews into doing the same. "Your Grace, I bring a guest to these revels. Dr. Rufus Andrews."

Even had he not loved her, Galen would have thought the Queen the most radiant star of this night. What fabric her dress was made of, he could not begin to guess; it floated like the wind itself, weightless and pure, with shades of blue shifting through it like living embroidery. Her stomacher glittered with gems, and someone had threaded brilliant blue flowers into her silver hair, creating a style that was somehow both regal and carefree, as if the coronet grew there by nature.

"You are welcome, Dr. Andrews," Lune said. Galen shivered at the sound of her voice. It carried distinctly, muting the noise of the dancers into distant murmuring, without her ever having to raise it. "You come to us on a special night. We are not so festive the year round; even faeries—perhaps especially faeries—need variety. But we hope you will not abandon us when we return to our more sober ways."

Andrews stood open-mouthed for a moment before he realized she was waiting for him to reply. "I—have no fear that I will grow tired of your company, in any form."

"We are glad to hear it." Lune gestured with one graceful hand at the revelry all around. "We've made it known that you are our especial guest here tonight, and under the patronage of both myself and Lord Galen. No one will visit mischief upon you." Her smile took on a roguish edge. "Save that which you ask for, of course."

Clutching his hat in his hands, Andrews bowed his thanks. "If I may, your Grace—curiosity prods me—"

Lune motioned for him to continue.

"How do you prevent interference?" He nodded over his shoulder, at the elegant sweep of Bedlam, belying the squalor within. "Your handmaiden mentioned enchantments, but surely it cannot be easy, keeping such a crowd as this from drawing the attention of the guards there, and the people who live in the houses alongside."

Galen said, "The simplest part of it is an illusion, deceiving all those who look this way. Moor Fields appears to be deserted for the night. More difficult is persuading those who sometimes haunt this space to take themselves elsewhere until tomorrow."

"And then there are the ones who blunder forward anyway," Irrith added. "But those are mostly the mad, who can see through our illusions, and are welcome here regardless."

Andrews shook his head, then froze, apparently fearing he'd offended the Queen. "Those illusions alone—the implications for optics are astounding."

Irrith muttered to Galen, in an exaggerated whisper, "Don't let him anywhere near the dwarves. They'll be talking until half-past the end of the world."

Galen hazarded a glance at the Queen. She was, as usual, neutrally pleasant, but he thought he discerned in the set of her eyes, the line of her swanlike throat, that she understood and shared his sudden thought. *That is* exactly *who we must put him with*. *The dwarves, and more*. There were scholars in the Onyx Hall, faeries who turned their thoughts to their own world. Not many, but Wrain would be ideal for this—or perhaps Lady Feidelm, the Irish faerie who warned them of the comet's return. She'd been exiled from Connacht for being too loyal to London interests, and stripped of her prophetic gifts in the process, but she still had a remarkable mind. Bringing them all together with Dr. Andrews might be very useful indeed.

"You have the freedom of this field," Lune said, in a clear tone of friendly dismissal. "Lord Galen will see to your needs."

Andrews bowed, backed away, and then walked apart with the stiff and rapid strides of a man who wants to reach safety before his knees give out.

Galen followed, and so did Irrith. It was disconcerting to have the sprite there, so close. They hadn't touched since that first night, had scarcely seen one another for ten minutes altogether. He wasn't at all sure how to behave. Whores were a different matter; one didn't encounter them at social events. At least not the class of prostitute Galen could afford, on his allowance from his father.

Someone had set out a cluster of India-back chairs, a bizarre note of middling domesticity amidst faerie extravagance. Andrews sank into one, then looked up wryly at the still-standing Galen. "If I don't miss my guess, then among these folk, I ought not to sit without your leave; I should be deferring to you as I would to the Prince of Wales."

"More like the King," Irrith said. "If the King were the Queen—that is, if he had his throne because he married her. And if he weren't some stupid German."

"Dunce the Second," Andrews said. He seemed bemused enough to take Irrith's rambling and impolitic answer in stride. "Son of Dunce the First. Given the elegance of your Queen, I'm not surprised at your low opinion of him. I don't suppose I might be tucked away into a safe corner where I could enjoy a good conversation with, say, one or two faeries of less intimidating mien? I confess that, in coming here, I expected more creatures the size of my thumb, and fewer who might credibly pass as some of the Greeks' ancient goddesses."

Galen had already anticipated that desire. "Since you mention the Greeks—there is one here, a fellow by the name of Ktistes, who has already expressed an interest in making your acquaintance. Though his own interests lie more in architecture and astronomy, he is quite a scholar in his own right."

"Because of his grandsire, Kheiron," Irrith added.

Andrews blinked once, very deliberately. Then again. Then he said, "Was not Chiron a centaur?"

"And still is," the sprite answered him, with blithe innocence. "I *think* Ktistes said he's still alive. But he retreated from this world after the Romans' little empire fell apart."

The older man buried his head in his hands, knocking his hat to the ground. "Good God."

Galen yelped, but too late. The word rolled outward from where Andrews sat, dimming the faerie lights and withering the grass to its usual dusty brown. The music faltered, and from all around the fields, fae stopped what they were doing and turned to stare in their direction.

Andrews felt it. He sat up, and a moment later the understanding of what he'd done dawned upon him. "I—I'm sorry—"

I have to do something. Galen held up his hands and called out as loudly as he could, "Carry on. It was an error, and it will not happen again. Please, continue dancing."

The music picked up again, sounding thin at first in the suddenly quiet air, but slowly the noise grew as the fae returned to their diversions. Galen let out the breath he'd been holding, and turned back to see Irrith sitting on the grass, pale and wide-eyed. "I hope," Galen said, trying to make the best of it, "that this demonstration will help you remember in the future why such words are not appreciated here."

Chastened, Andrews nodded. Galen picked up his hat for him and knocked bits of grass off it before handing it back. "Come. I think it might be best if I brought you to Ktistes." The centaur would be somewhere on the edge of the festivities, away from the venomous looks of the nearby fae, who had taken the brunt of that careless word.

Once Ktistes and the doctor were settled, Galen left them to their conversation, intending to go apologize to the Queen. Before he got that far, though, the sylph Lady Yfaen accosted him. "Lord Galen—I understand from Mrs. Vesey and her Grace that this Dr. Andrews of yours is a member of the Royal Society."

"He is," Galen said. "I'm very sorry for his mistake—"

She waved it away. "That isn't what concerns me. Rather—" She bit her lip. "To put it very bluntly . . . how can we be certain he won't tell them about us? Isn't that what they do there? Learn about new things, and then tell others about them?"

To ask him that called into question his judgment as Prince. But Galen knew very well how green he was, in the eyes of the fae; he would do better to answer her concern than to object to her speaking of it. "That is what they do," he agreed, "but do not fear Dr. Andrews. I've impressed upon him the need for secrecy—and indeed, I think his error here tonight has helped with that.

"More to the point, I know what he wants. He has no interest in running to anyone with his first, unformed thoughts; he prefers to keep matters secret until he can astound the world, as Isaac Newton did, with a singular work that will change their thinking forever. If he begins such a work, I will know about it, in plenty of time to convince him to keep silent." His duty to the Onyx Court made him add, reluctantly, "Or to prevent him from speaking, if need be."

Yfaen lowered into a small curtsy. "You know him far better than I, Lord Galen. If you trust his discretion, then I will trust you."

She said it, but he wondered if she meant it. Yfaen, though friends with Mrs. Vesey, and therefore hardly an enemy, still had doubts. How much worse must it be among the Sanists, and those who scorned him as Prince?

He doubted the answer was one he wanted to hear. And there was no cure for it but to do his best, and pray that would be good enough.

The Onyx Hall, London: June 28, 1758

Irrith's cabinet was her favorite solace, almost as good as going among mortals themselves, and far cheaper when it came to bread. She ran her hands over the shelves and little drawers, picking objects at random: an embroidered handkerchief, a toothbrush, a locket with a curl of hair inside. A child's doll, with one arm missing. The polished buckle of a shoe, blood stiffening its hinge. Every one of them a fragment of a story, a life, reeking of passion or mortal ingenuity. She could spend hours studying them and never grow bored.

Unless she was interrupted. When a knock came at her door, she closed the panels of her cabinet, sighing, and went to see who it was.

She would have been less stunned if a poleax had been waiting outside to fall on her head. Valentin Aspell said, "Dame Irrith. If I might have a moment of your time?"

What in Mab's name is the Lord Keeper doing here? Her immediate, suspicious answer was, *nothing good.* Irrith had never liked Valentin Aspell. As far as she was concerned, he was an oily, untrustworthy snake. But he'd served the Queen for a long time, and might be here on her business. Grudgingly, Irrith opened the door wider and let him in.

He surveyed the room as he entered. It wasn't as nice as the chamber Irrith had lost; this one was plain black stone, with only her scant furnishings for contrast. The cabinet was nice, though. It, too, was a mortal thing, built of lacquered wood, with brass fittings on its many drawers and doors, and Irrith had long ago fitted it with a detector lock. Fae had ways around charms, but few of them knew how to defeat the complicated mechanism—and if they tried, the lock would tell her.

Aspell said, "I am sorry for the loss of your previous chamber. It was one of the more unusual in the Onyx Hall, and the Queen had shown you great kindness in bestowing it."

Now she *definitely* didn't trust him. Irrith had never once seen Aspell use compliments or sympathy without intending to get something in return. But he was used to people who played the same game, dancing around the target before finally stabbing it. Not people like her. "Why are you here?"

It didn't discomfit him as much as she'd hoped. "To ask you a question," the Lord Keeper said. "May I sit?"

Irrith wanted to refuse, but that would be petty. She waved him to one of her two chairs—both of them old and uncomfortable, since she didn't entertain guests often. He flicked his coat clear with a smooth gesture and coiled onto the more battered of the two. "Thank you. Dame Irrith, you absented yourself from the Onyx Hall for about fifty years, and that gives you a certain perspective that we who dwell here lack. You also know the Queen moderately well."

"Not so well," she said warily. "I'm not one of her ladies."

"Well enough for my purposes. Tell me: do you find her as she once was?"

The question was both perplexing and worrying—the latter mostly because it was Aspell who asked it, and Irrith distrusted everything he said. "What do you mean?"

He shook his head. "I would prefer not to prompt you. Your uninfluenced opinion is what I need right now."

Irrith bit her lip and perched on the edge of the other chair. *Had* Lune changed?

"Lots of people are different," she said, after some consideration. "That's one of the odd things about this place. Fae don't often change, not in so short a time as fifty years, but the folk here do." She gestured toward Aspell. "When I left, you were wearing one of those enormous long wigs with all the curls. Now it's—I think they call that kind a Ramillies? Which, by the way, looks less ridiculous. Guns and cricket and backgammon . . ."

Despite his assertion that he wouldn't prompt her, Aspell said, "I do not mean our activities or dress."

"Ways of thinking, too," Irrith said. She suspected what he was after, and didn't want to say it. "This business of having a treasury—who ever heard of something like that in a faerie court? It's so *orderly*. And—"

"Dame Irrith," Aspell said, and it was enough.

She stared down, biting her lip, digging one bare toe into the ragged rush mat that might have covered this floor for the last two hundred years. "I suppose she's tired."

"Tired," he repeated.

"With all that's going on—trying to make arrangements with someone in Greece so we can hide ourselves with the clouds, and I know she's still searching for a weapon against the Dragon; and then of course there's all the usual affairs of the court, people scheming against one another and causing mischief above, and it's a good thing we don't always have to sleep, because when would she find the time?"

The Lord Keeper let out a slow sigh. "Dame Irrith . . . I do not ask out of malice. I am concerned for the Queen, and for the Onyx Court. If you think it simple weariness, then that is one matter; within a year, one way or another, the threat of the comet will be ended, and her Majesty can rest. But if you think it something more, then for the good of the Onyx Court, I beg you to tell me."

All the suspicion that had been wafting through her mind since he asked that first question hardened into a leaden ball. "Why do you want to know?"

Aspell lifted one elegant hand. "I mean no trap, Dame Irrith. Yes, I have some spies in my keeping, but I haven't come to lure you into indiscreet speech, which I can then clap you in prison for. Her Majesty knows that not all fae who speak of such things would call themselves Sanists, and not all who call themselves Sanists are treasonous. There can be loyalty in opposition. The ultimate concern of most on both sides is the preservation of our shared home, though they differ on how."

She'd been on the verge of throwing him out. His mention of loyalty, though, loosened the knot around her heart. *I don't mean any harm to Lune, or the Onyx Hall. But the situation . . . it does worry me.* She'd been carefully avoiding such thoughts ever since talking to Magrat in the Crow's Head, for fear they would make her a Sanist.

And maybe she was. But that didn't have to be treason.

"Maybe," she said, the admission as grudging as any she'd ever made. "It might be affecting her. The palace. With the wall going away. They're connected, after all, and she's used that in the past—against the Dragon, for example. The damage might be sapping her strength."

The Lord Keeper's mouth had thinned into a frown when she began speaking; now the frown deepened. "Or she is *giving* her strength, in an effort to slow the damage. She might even be doing it unconsciously."

That sounded like Lune. The question slipped out of Irrith's mouth. "What happens when her strength runs out?"

He said nothing, merely lifted his narrow brows.

She scowled at him as if it *had* been a trap. "It won't. She's strong. Fifty years of this has barely made a mark on her; she could go for a hundred more. And Ktistes is working to mend the palace, anyway."

"I wish him all the good fortune in the world." Aspell sighed again, looking melancholy. "I could also wish her Grace had better support to sustain her in these crises."

"Support?"

He opened his mouth, then hesitated. "It isn't my place to question the Queen's choices. The selection of the Prince is and always has been her prerogative."

Galen. In some respects, he was the best support Lune could hope for; the young man worshipped her, and would do without hesitation anything she asked of him.

But that wasn't enough, was it? Lune needed someone who wouldn't just *react*, but *act*. Someone who thought ahead, or sideways, and came up with ideas she never would have dreamt of. Someone she could trust to address problems on his own, so that she didn't need to handle it all herself.

And Galen was not that man.

He *wanted* to be. Perhaps someday he would be. He'd shown signs of it already; this notion of Dr. Andrews and the Royal Society was different, at least, and might bear fruit. But he was more a Prince-in-training than an actual Prince.

Irrith remembered the obelisk in the night garden, with its names and dates. "Lune didn't expect to lose the last Prince so soon, did she?"

Aspell shook his head. Six years. The least of them had gone for decades longer. She would have expected more time, to find and educate a suitable successor.

Was Galen really the best she could do?

"I have said too much," Aspell murmured, shaking his head again. "Such matters are the Queen's affair, and none of mine. I thank you, Dame Irrith, for speaking honestly with me. Uncomfortable as it may be to consider such matters, I feel it's vital to face them, and to consider possible solutions."

Like replacing the Queen. The wounded mistress of a wounded realm. Irrith shuddered inwardly. She didn't want to see Lune deposed, but with the Hall fraying . . .

Aspell reached into one pocket and pulled out a small mother-of-pearl box that he laid atop her cabinet. "For your aid, Dame Irrith. Good day."

She ignored the box for hours after he left, before curiosity finally overcame her reluctance and spite. Inside lay two items: a locket containing a miniature of some fellow's beloved and a snippet of her hair, and a piece of mortal bread.

Irrith shut the box, shoved it into her cabinet, and wondered if she'd done the right thing.

Rose House, Islington: June 30, 1758

Islington seemed much closer than it had been. The Aldersgate entrance was still just as far from the Goodemeades' home as ever, but the land in between had changed; the streets now stretched well beyond Smithfield and the Charterhouse, before suddenly giving way to the market gardens and green grass Irrith expected. After that, Islington was only a brief walk. It didn't seem right—as if someday she would leave the Onyx Hall and walk past houses and shops, churches and manicured little parks, and find herself at the Angel Inn without ever having left the city at all.

Her mood didn't help with such discontented thoughts. Ordinarily a visit to the Goodemeades was a happy occasion, for they were always eager to feed guests. Today, however, she had a purpose in mind, and it was not a happy one.

Only the Queen herself knew why she'd chosen Galen St. Clair as her Prince. But if there were two souls in London who could guess at Lune's reasons, their names were Rosamund and Gertrude.

The brownies had guests when she arrived, two apple maidens and an oak man from the fields around London. They welcomed Irrith, though, settling her down with a plate of food and a mug of their excellent mead, and perhaps it was a good thing; the hospitality loosened her tight muscles and made her questions easier to face. By the time the tree spirits were bid farewell, Irrith felt prepared for whatever the Goodemeades might say to her.

"Now, my dear," Rosamund said, as Gertrude whisked away the dishes. "You came in here with a face as long as a week of mourning, and though it's brightened up since then, I'm guessing you didn't come just for cakes and mead. What troubles you?"

Irrith licked crumbs from her fingers. "Something I have no right to ask, but I will anyway. It's about the Prince."

"And the way he's in love with Lune?" Gertrude asked, coming back in. Her plump hands tugged her apron straight. "Poor lad. He'd make a fine ballad, but it must be dreary living."

"Did Lune know how he felt before she chose him?" The brownies nodded in unison. "Is that why she chose him?"

Gertrude went still. Rosamund busied herself with brushing the last few crumbs from the tabletop. Glancing from one to the other, Irrith said, "I promise, I'm not malicious. I just—I don't understand. He isn't political, and he doesn't have connections in the mortal world, not like some of the men before him. I know the previous one died awfully fast; is it just that Lune expected to have more time to educate Galen?"

Rosamund pursed her lips, then tossed the crumbs into the fire. "Well, for questions one has no right to ask—but that's hardly ever stopped us, now, has it? Irrith, my dear, a little whisper has reached our ears that you're sharing Lord Galen's bed."

If she'd stopped to consider it, she never would have believed they could keep it secret, not in the Onyx Hall. But she hadn't, and so the mention surprised her. "I am. I didn't think the Queen would mind."

"She doesn't. He's hardly the first Prince to enjoy a little dalliance among his subjects. It's more a matter of how it affects *you*. Do you love him?"

Irrith laughed, incredulous. "Love? Can you really imagine me shackling my heart to some mortal who will be dead in a few years? Not hardly. He interests me, certainly." That mild description fell far short of the truth. *Fascinated* would be closer. *Entranced.*

The brownies exchanged one of their usual inscrutable glances. After untold ages of practice, they were very good at them. Rosamund said, "But you're on his side."

With Valentin Aspell's oily concern fresh in her memory, Irrith didn't have to guess what she might mean. "Well, he seems determined to hurt himself with this adoration of the Queen—but no, I don't want to add to it."

"Good," Gertrude said, with unexpected firmness. "Because the truth of the matter is something Galen must never learn."

Irrith's eyes widened. Rosamund laid a reassuring hand over hers and said, "Now, Gertie, it isn't so bad as all that. Just that things have changed, Irrith, and they've made new problems for Lune, that none of us ever foresaw."

"Isn't that always the case?" Irrith asked sourly, thinking of the comet.

The sisters sighed in rueful agreement. "The problem in this case," Rosamund said, "is that there have usually been three requirements for the Prince, and two of them don't fit together very well anymore."

Three requirements? "He has to be someone Lune likes."

"And he has to be a gentleman," Gertrude said.

"And," Rosamund finished, "he has to be born within the walls of the City."

Gertrude held up a cautionary hand. "Might be within the sound of the bells. But no one's quite dared test that yet."

Irrith thought of the City as it had become—not London as a whole, but the City of London, the central part, and specifically the part within the increasingly broken wall. Galen, when he told her where he lived, said Leicester Fields was no longer as fashionable as it had been, that the better sort of people were moving farther west. No one wanted to be within the narrow, twisty, dirty lanes of the City, which had scarce been changed even by the Great Fire. There was a broad new street cutting up from the river to the Guildhall, called Queen Street south of Cheapside and King Street north, but that was the biggest difference. Most of the City was still as it had been these hundreds of years, and that was not good enough for fashion.

She murmured, "So he was the only gentleman who fit?"

"There have never been all that many gentlemen in the Onyx Hall," Gertrude reminded her. "Well, there aren't that many gentlemen at all, are there? Not compared to ordinary folk. Peers are even rarer. So most of the ones who get brought below are common. Lord Hamilton was the grandson of a viscount; for all that he wasn't what anyone would call wealthy, and that was good enough for them as cared. But then he died, and Lune had to choose someone new."

"Galen was a bit of luck," Rosamund added. "His mother went into labor without much warning, and they couldn't move her; so he was born in the house where she'd gone to have dinner."

Irrith just kept blinking, trying to absorb it all. No, they hadn't foreseen that—who would expect that London would grow so much, and all the wealthy people would move out to its western edge? "She's going to have to stop choosing gentlemen. The place of birth has to do with the Hall's enchantments, doesn't it, and we can hardly ask her to work with someone she doesn't like—but the rank, that's just because no one wants their Queen to be paired with a commoner."

The brownies looked unhappy. Gertrude said, "If she *can*. There was an apothecary a few years ago who might have done, but her lords and ladies didn't much like the idea."

Rosamund snorted. "And then he ran mad and flung himself off Westminster Bridge, so maybe it's just as well. Not a stable mind, I fear."

"Galen isn't bad," Gertrude hastened to say. "A trifle green, to be sure, but that's nothing time won't cure. Especially if those around him help out—give him advice when he needs it, that sort of thing. He's too embarrassed to ask for it, poor dear."

No wonder Gertrude had said he must never know. Hearing this laid out so baldly would only cripple him with doubt. And Galen had enough trouble with that already.

"You *will* help him, won't you, my dear?" Gertrude gave Irrith an entreating look that would have melted the heart of a stone.

Irrith nodded. "Yes. I will."

If I can.

Sothings Park, Highgate: July 7, 1758

Nothing brought home to Galen the importance of this evening like his first sight of Sothings Park.

His mother, seated by his side in the carriage, breathed out her nose in something that was almost a snort of disdain, but the look in her eyes was a mixture of envy, hope, and regret. It wasn't that Sothings Park was especially impressive; Aldgrange, the St. Clair estate in Essex, was much larger and grander, if sadly run down for want of money to maintain it. But the fact that the Northwoods could afford to rent not only a townhouse in Grosvenor Square far superior to anything in

Leicester Fields, but also this little manor, just far enough outside London to be pleasantly situated, made it clear without
words what Miss Delphia Northwood could offer in exchange
for the St. Clair name.

The prospect cheered Charles St. Clair sufficiently that he
had hired out *two* carriages for the evening, and neither of
them common hackneys. Galen's sisters followed in the second one, for the Northwoods had invited them all to dinner
today at Sothings Park.

It was not the first meal shared between the two families.
Since that encounter at Mrs. Vesey's in May, Galen had dined
in Grosvenor Square four times, twice with his mother and
father along, and the Northwoods had come to Leicester
Fields twice. He had met Miss Northwood's younger sister
Temperance, and missed her brother Robert only because he
was somewhere in Italy at the moment. In short, Galen was
perfectly well acquainted with the Northwood family.

He would have been less nervous had he gone to dine with
the lions in the Tower of London.

The carriages pulled to a halt in front of the austere entrance, built in the revived Palladian style. Galen handed his
mother down, wondering if she felt his own arm trembling.
He'd mastered it by the time they were shown in to the parlor
where the Northwoods awaited them, but it still lurked inside, where no one could see.

They soon went into dinner, and the dining room on the
piano nobile was fully as grand as could be hoped. The amiable chatter between Mrs. St. Clair and their hostess revealed
that the furnishings there, from the mahogany table to the
spoons upon it, were the property of the Northwoods, and
not rented with the house. Irene was young enough to gape at
that, before Cynthia nudged her into better behavior.

For his own part, Galen was caught between contradictory
impulses to look at Miss Northwood, and to look everywhere *but* at her. She was once more clothed in a sacque
gown too elegant for her plainness, with ruffles and bows
and sewn-in pearls, but she might as well have been a mag-
net, so difficult was it not to stare. Cynthia made easy conversation with her, and drew Galen into it at convenient times;

he formed a resolution to fall on his knees and thank her as soon as they returned home.

By such means did he survive the interminable courses of dinner, though he ate at little as he could without giving offense.

The Northwoods had chosen to dine at the fashionably late hour of five o'clock, and the drawing room in which the men rejoined the ladies after their drinks had a splendid view of the sunset and Sothings Park's gardens. Galen managed to conduct a credible conversation with Mrs. Northwood on the subject of the roses there, despite a tongue that felt like it belonged to a stranger, and when she said "You should go down, before the light is gone, and see them for yourself," he made his reply without a single stumble.

"That would be delightful. Might I impose on Miss Northwood to guide me?"

Mrs. Northwood's broad smile answered him well enough on its own. "I'm sure she would be more than glad to."

Whether she was glad, nervous, or any other thing about it, Galen did not see; he was too nervous to look at her face. They descended the staircase in awkward silence, went out through the doors the same, and only when they reached the first rosebush did Miss Northwood say anything, which was, "I've always quite liked this one."

They ambled along the paths, here touching a bloom, there bending to sniff one, and if there was any mercy in the world, Galen thought, then eight people were *not* watching their progress from the drawing room windows above.

Perhaps Miss Northwood was thinking the same, for she said, "This arbor is a pleasant place to sit, if you would like to rest."

It also happened to feature a green, leafy roof that would shield them from prying eyes. The sun was low enough now that its light blazed across the bench upon which Miss Northwood had seated herself, making the space quite warm, but if she did not mind then Galen did not either.

He couldn't sit. Galen took a deep breath, considered her upturned face, and let the air out in one swift gust. "You know why we're out here."

That wasn't what he'd intended to say, but the intelligent regard in her eyes, free of all the coquetry and feigned innocence that might have attended this moment, prodded him to discard his more carefully crafted opening. Miss Northwood said, "Quite by ourselves. It isn't hard to guess."

"I will be honest with you," Galen told her, interlacing his fingers behind his back. "Which may not be advisable, not if I wish to meet with success on the other side of it—but my conscience will not permit me to do otherwise. You are aware, Miss Northwood, of my family's situation."

She nodded, and when he still hesitated, laid it out plainly. "A good name, but not the income to support it. Due, if you will forgive me saying it, to your father's financial imprudence."

He could hardly wince at *her* blunt honesty, given what he had said, and what he intended to say. And her assessment was perhaps to be expected from a young woman with both a banker father and a brain. "Indeed. I also have three sisters in need of a future. Because of these things, my father has pressed me not only to marry, but to marry well. Which is to say, richly."

Miss Northwood cast her gaze down with a resigned half smile. "I've always been aware that my marriage portion is the better part of my appeal to suitors."

Galen had to swallow before he could go on. This might have been easier indoors, where he could have a glass of wine to wet his throat. But then he might drink too much, and people would be listening at keyholes besides. "I am a romantic, Miss Northwood. I wish with all my heart that I were on my knee before you now, pouring out a declaration of love that would do a poet proud. Unfortunately, it would be false. I . . . I do not love you."

Her eyes were still downcast, making her thoughts hard to read. Galen hurried on. "I mean no insult to you. The truth is that, did care for my sisters not compel me, I wouldn't be looking to marry at all. But I must consider them, and their happiness, and so I vowed that although money might be my father's foremost concern, it would not be mine. Love might be too much to hope for, but I would not propose marriage to any woman I did not respect."

"Respect." It came out an unsteady laugh. "Do you find that in short supply, where women are concerned?"

"I don't mean the respect any gentleman must have for a decent young woman," Galen answered her. "I mean the sort of respect I have for Mrs. Vesey, or Mrs. Montagu, or Mrs. Carter. Respect of the mind, Miss Northwood."

In the rosy light, he could not tell if she colored, but the sudden, embarrassed tuck of her chin suggested it.

Galen went on with quiet determination. "But while I may have resigned myself to an unromantic future, Miss Northwood, I won't ask you to do the same. Tell me now, and honestly: is there another man for whom you entertain such feelings? I would not be the cause of your permanent separation from the one you love, if such a one exists—or if you prefer to seek love, instead of settling for me."

She snapped her fan open for a few rapid beats, then snapped it shut again and rose to pace a few steps away. "There is no such man, Mr. St. Clair. Whether there would ever be one . . . who can say?"

When she turned to face him, her mouth had settled into a startlingly hard line. Dread curled in Galen's stomach, bringing with it a sour taste familiar from his disastrous walk with Dr. Andrews. Had he stepped so wrong again?

Miss Northwood said, "You aren't the only young man to show interest in my hand. You know that, of course—but do you know which one my father favors the most?"

Galen shook his head, mute.

"William Beckford's illegitimate son," she said, biting each syllable off with her teeth.

He was dumbstruck. Miss Northwood nodded, a tight, stiff motion. "Indeed. He would prefer Mr. Beckford himself, except that Maria Hamilton got there two years ago; and any children they have will take far too long to grow up."

"But—" Words were still slow to come. "I thought your father wanted respectability."

"He does, very ardently. On the other hand, he might forgo a gentleman for me, when plantation wealth could buy Temperance a duke." Miss Northwood's hands balled into fists, fan swinging free from her wrist. "If Mr. Beckford persuades the Prime Minister to attack the French at Martinique, as I know he wishes to, then no doubt my prospective husband would be the happy recipient of a new plantation himself. And I? Would be a slaveholder's wife."

Mrs. Northwood kept a Negro page, in imitation of those fashionable ladies who also had the wealth for such an exotic touch. Galen wondered how Miss Northwood felt about that. "I needn't ask your opinion on this prospect," he said slowly, choosing his words with care. "Do you mean then that you would choose me to escape it?"

The fight went out of her hands, and her shoulders slumped. "I would shame to use you in such fashion—but you've been honest with me, Mr. St. Clair. I thought it only fair to do the same."

Now he did sit, and pull out a handkerchief to blot the sweat from his face. The warm scent of roses surrounded him like a too close embrace. "I—" God, how desperately he wished for something to wet his throat. "I suppose I'm flattered, that I am preferred to the bastard son of a Jamaican plantation owner."

She was at his side, in a rush of silk. "Oh, Mr. St. Clair—I didn't mean it that way. Rather to let you understand what you would be taking me away from. Not a secret love, but a match I would avoid at any cost." Miss Northwood hesitated, then settled herself on the bench across from him, smoothing her skirts over her knees with uncertain fingers. "But before— when you spoke of resigning yourself to an unromantic future—the look in your eyes . . . Mr. St. Clair, is there one *you* love?"

The handkerchief twisted in his hands. Ladies had an advantage, with their fans they could hide behind. "Yes," he admitted, in little more than a whisper. "That honesty, too, I think I owe you. But I will never—*can* never—be with the lady in question."

"Your father won't permit it?"

Galen laughed at the mere thought. "He wouldn't, if he knew . . . but no, Miss Northwood. The reasons go far deeper than a father's disapproval. Nor is it a question of wealth, or any other such thing. If you imagine me in the position of a young fool in love with the moon, you'll have a fair sense of just how hopeless my situation is.

"Given that, there is nothing to be gained by delaying my choice. I promise you that, whatever sentiments repose in my heart, you shall have no cause to reproach me for my behavior. It is all I shall ever be able to offer any woman."

He busied himself tucking away the handkerchief, to regain a modicum of his composure. The task done, he found Miss Northwood sitting with her hands folded, and a look in her eyes that said she was preparing to accept, despite—as he had said at the beginning—the reasons his honesty had given her for refusal.

Before she could answer, he spoke again.

"I suppose there is one thing more I can offer. Should you come under my roof, you will never again have reason to conceal your purpose at Mrs. Vesey's. We shall have a library, and you shall buy what books you like for it; you may attend what lectures will admit ladies, learn what languages your talents suit you for, and if your mind inclines to it, you may write." He thought he would have to force a smile past the lump in his throat, but it came with surprising ease. "I may detest Dr. Johnson on many counts, but in this matter, he and I have no disagreement at all: an educated woman is an ornament not only to her family, but to the nation that bore her. I shall do everything in my power to aid you."

Her lips parted during the speech, and remained open in a small, astonished O; when he finished, she sat without speaking for quite a few moments—and then she answered him, in a strangely breathless voice. "Oh, Mr. St. Clair. I was all prepared to say that unlike you, I am not a romantic, and would willingly accept an offer of stability, respect, and friendship, even were my alternative not so terrible. But then you said those words, and I discovered that some part of me is a romantic after all."

Her voice wavered on the last words, but the waver turned out to be a smile. Galen rose without thinking and crossed to her, then knelt and took her hands. "If talk of books and writing is your notion of romance, Miss Northwood, then we are happily matched indeed. If you will consent to be my wife, then I will go this minute and beg your father for your hand."

The setting sun gave her a halo of fiery splendor. "You will not have to beg hard, Mr. St. Clair. I do consent."

The Onyx Hall, London: July 8, 1758

"*Betrothed?*" Irrith said in disbelief. "The Dragon will be here in a matter of months. Is this the best time to be talking marriage?"

Galen collapsed into a chair, sighing. "Likely not. But if I waited longer, I might have lost Miss Northwood to another—and besides, I promised my father I would find a wife before the end of the Season, which is upon us now."

Irrith hardly cared about that. True, the quality would be departing soon for their country homes; they were the *beau monde,* the folk Carline liked best. Irrith preferred the ordinary Londoners, who stayed in the city all year. "You'll be so busy, though, with the wedding, and setting up away from your father, and all the rest of it."

"As it happens, no." Galen's smile was equal parts amusement and smugness. "Drawing up a marriage settlement can take time, and Miss Northwood and I have both made it clear to our families that we are perfectly content to be wed in the spring. Which gives her time to reconsider."

"Maybe I'm misunderstanding your mortal customs, but I thought the lady reconsidering was considered a *bad* thing."

He shrugged. "Usually. But I want Miss Northwood to be certain she's happy with her choice. If her mind changes before spring—if, for example, she falls in love elsewhere—she's welcome to cry off. I have told her so."

Love. Irrith raised an eyebrow. "What does the Queen say?"

It was a cruel blow, but one he would have taken sooner or later. Galen's qualified happiness faded visibly. "I haven't told her yet."

"You *are* aware that she keeps spies, yes?" Including, Irrith suspected, Edward Thorne, who was currently in an adjoining room, attempting to remove the dirt Galen had pressed into his stockings when he knelt to propose to Miss Delphia Northwood.

Galen sat forward in his chair and put his head in his hands. After a moment, he pulled off his wig, giving his scalp a good scratch. The sight reminded Irrith of the last time she'd seen his head bare—and Galen soon recalled it, too, for he blushed and hastily pulled the wig back on. "Dame Irrith—"

So they were back to titles. "Yes, Lord Galen?" she inquired, too sweetly.

It was so easy to call anguish up in his expressive face. "We cannot—I am promised to another, now."

He never ceased to enchant her, the way different parts of him could say different things, all at the same time. His eyes told a much less certain story than his mouth. It wasn't the manipulative artifice of someone like Valentin Aspell, either; Galen *felt* all these things, honestly and completely, even when they contradicted each other. However did he manage it?

She would not surrender the game, not so long as his eyes were still playing. "Promised, Galen. Not married."

"But her Grace—"

"I thought we dealt with *that* matter already."

"I cannot give myself to three women at once!"

The adjoining room was *far* too silent. Irrith hoped Edward Thorne was entertained. "You aren't giving all of yourself— just pieces. Lune has your love. Miss Northwood has your promise. I don't ask for either of those things; your body is enough for me."

He turned *very* red, and shot up out of his chair like a jack-in-the-box. "You would treat me like some kind of male prostitute?"

Where had this anger come from? Irrith rose to her own feet, letting her own hurt show. "Did I say that? Did I imply it? What have I paid you, that gives you the right to accuse me like that? I'm only acting on what I saw in you. When you look at me, you see something you wish you could be: a person who doesn't care what's proper, who does what she likes and smiles at it all, a person without any chains. And it attracts you. But you're too scared, too worried about what

Lune thinks, and your father, and everyone else, to do what *you* want, and so I did it for you. How is that wrong?"

All the anger had gone out of him while she worked herself up to a shout. He wasn't really mad, she realized—not at her. At himself, yes, for letting his father sell him in marriage, and for wanting what he thought he shouldn't. Irrith had listened to farmers in Berkshire complain about the bad behavior of the so-called polite folk, keeping mistresses under the same roof as their wives, and had thought it common; and maybe it was, but not with Galen.

At least, he didn't *want* it to be.

He'd retreated behind his chair; now she followed him, standing so close their buttons touched. "I'll go away when you marry," Irrith whispered, realizing only after it came out that for the first time in her timeless life, she was willing to let go of a mortal before she tired of him, for *his* sake. Because otherwise it would hurt him too much. "Let me enjoy this now, Galen. You love the Queen, and you want to hold faith with Miss Northwood, and you want to honor your father and help your sisters and learn great things and save the Onyx Hall—you want *so much*, and so intensely, and there's nothing like that for us, don't you understand? Nothing except you."

By the end she wasn't even sure she was making sense. It didn't matter, though, because this time Galen was the one to move; his arms lifted her onto her toes so he could more easily reach her mouth, and for a few moments Irrith forgot to think about the listening Edward Thorne at all.

But the servant must have been waiting, for when Irrith lost her balance and staggered, breaking Galen's embrace, he coughed politely from the doorway. "Lord Galen," Thorne said, for all the world as if he'd seen nothing at all, "you asked me to remind you of Dr. Andrews."

He might have been speaking Greek. "Yes, thank you," Galen said distractedly, then came to himself with a jump. "Oh, yes. Irrith, I'm sorry—I'm to meet with Dr. Andrews, now that we've made a place for him in the Onyx Hall, and to introduce him to a few scholars who have volunteered their assistance. We must get him started on his work."

She could hardly begrudge it. If they didn't save the palace, there would be no more Galens for her to play with. "May I come?"

"If you wish to—though I fear it will be terribly boring. We cannot expect to solve our problems on the first day." Galen accepted Thorne's ministrations, straightening what Irrith had disarranged.

"If I grow bored, I'll leave." Andrews was a consumptive, after all. She wasn't hoping for him to drop dead in front of her—that wouldn't help Galen at all—but it was interesting to watch a man die by degrees. "Until then, I should like to hear what he has to say."

Following on his Midsummer thought, Galen had assembled a small group of faerie scholars to work with Dr. Andrews. Lady Feidelm; a lesser courtier named Savennis; Wrain, a sticklike sprite who looked to be half again Irrith's height but no more than her slight weight. The von das Tickens said they would look in from time to time, or rather Wilhas did; Niklas, being his usual unsociable self, declined. Ktistes would follow their efforts from his garden pavilion.

They met in the chamber Galen had arranged for Dr. Andrews's use, and settled into chairs near the hearth. "How do you like your laboratory?" he asked, gesturing toward the other end of the room. Servants had brought in suitable furniture, and he'd tried to equip the place with things he thought Dr. Andrews might need: bookshelves, a writing desk, a large table for experimentation. Proper equipment would have to wait until the doctor made more specific requests.

"This place is incredible," Dr. Andrews admitted. "The palace, that is—though I do appreciate the laboratory. To think that all this lies beneath the feet of unsuspecting Londoners . . ." He shook his head, lost for anything else to say.

"And they will *stay* unsuspecting, won't they?"

Galen glared at Irrith. Andrews might not hear the threat shading that question, but he did. Fortunately, Andrews hastened to reassure her. "Oh, yes, my dear. I've been given a miraculous opportunity here; I would not squander it so easily."

She bristled at the condescending address. Andrews had lost his fear of Irrith on Midsummer's Eve, but it seemed Galen had not made it sufficiently clear that for all her youthful appearance, Irrith was both a lady knight of the court, and a hundred times older than Andrews could ever hope to be. An old man's tendency to call every young woman "my dear" would not please her.

Hurrying to smooth over that ripple, Galen said, "I imagine you have a great many questions—indeed, I *know* you have them, as you've already shared several with me."

Andrews began to count them off on his fingers. "Why are certain aspects of religion disquieting to the fae? Why can I say 'Heaven' without troubling anyone, but not other words? Why is iron anathema? How are glamours created? What are they composed of? Why can the mad see through them? Why does tithed food protect, and what would happen if someone were to tithe stuffs other than bread or milk—ale, perhaps, or meat? How was this palace created, and how is it both here and not here in the space below London?" Having run out of fingers somewhere in his count, he stopped and, with a shrug both sheepish and helpless, he said, "What *is* a faerie in the first place?"

Irrith gaped at him. "I thought you were a doctor, not some windy old philosopher."

"Philosophy is the root of knowledge," Wrain told her, having listened quietly to Andrews's litany. "And the mortal belief is that one cannot truly answer final questions without first understanding the foundational ones."

"*Mortal* belief?" Andrews repeated.

Lady Feidelm smiled at him. She was an imposing creature, as tall as Andrews himself, but friendly in her way. "We do not work by reason, as you do, Dr. Andrews. Though from time to time we craft some new design, as Dame Irrith is doing to conceal our land from the comet, we do not experiment for the improvement of our charms. What you see as a craft is not so to us; it is instinct, and our very being."

He had a notebook out, and was bracing it against the arm of his chair as he scribbled notes with a small pencil. "Yes—but so, too, is gravity a kind of instinct; objects do not reason how they fall to earth. Yet it can be investigated by determined minds. Mr. St. Clair, I believe I will need to work both here and at my house; though you have been very generous in providing this chamber, there are some experiments I will have to conduct elsewhere, lest I make myself very unwelcome here."

The astonishment was near universal. Galen said, "Surely you don't mean to experiment with iron, or the divine name."

Andrews looked up from his notes. He took in the various reactions, ranging from Irrith's appalled gape to the wary consideration of the scholars. "Mr. St. Clair," the doctor said, laying his pencil down, "you've asked my assistance in defeating a faerie creature. To do so, I will need to understand the weaknesses of the fae—what their effect is, and on what basis they operate. I will be glad to hear the opinions of these gentlemen, and this lady, but without judicious experimentation, I fear I will not be able to add much to what they already know." He paused, then added, "I assure you, I mean no harm."

"I will work with the doctor." That was Savennis, who had said nothing since his introduction to Dr. Andrews. The quiet courtier grimaced. "It may not be pleasant, but I believe he's right: it *is* necessary."

Galen had seen what happened when unprepared fae were struck with holy force. And even now, the wound in Lune's shoulder pained her, legacy of an iron knife a century before. Savennis's courage in even facing that bane awed him. "Her Grace and I will reward you for your service," he promised the pale, bookish faerie. "And Dr. Andrews, you will inform me of everything you intend to do with Savennis, *before* you attempt it. If I say something goes too far, you *will* heed me."

"Of course," Andrews murmured, and relief shone in Savennis's eyes.

The exchange cast a nervous pall over the room, which Galen did his best to lighten. "I've arranged for a servant, a hob named Podder, to see to your needs here, and to bring your reports to me and the Queen. Beyond that, I think I've done what I can for now; I will leave the rest of you to your philosophizing. Dame Irrith, do you wish to stay?"

The sprite was perched on the edge of her chair, toes turned inward like a young girl's, but a pensive look on her face that no young girl had ever worn. She shook her head slowly, then brightened as a thought came to her. "You, Lord Galen, have business elsewhere, I think—telling the Queen your happy news."

He cursed her even as Andrews said, "Happy news? Are you perhaps betrothed, Mr. St. Clair?"

"I am," he said, masking his dread with a smile. *She's right, and you know it. You must tell Lune.* "To Miss Northwood, whom I have told you of. We're to be married in the spring."

Andrews shook his hand vigorously, pouring out good wishes for them both, which the fae echoed as if speaking phrases in a foreign language. Irrith watched all of this with good-natured malice. "I will return when I can," Galen said, retrieving his hand from the doctor. "In the meantime, may all the powers of Heaven and Faerie both speed you in your work."

Galen sank to his knee on the carpet before Lune and said, "Your Grace, I have come to inform you that I am betrothed."

Silence answered him. She couldn't have been taken entirely by surprise; she knew he was seeking a wife, and the formality of his posture made this more than an ordinary visit. But Lune said nothing.

At first. Just as Galen bit his lip, though, Lune spoke. "My congratulations, Lord Galen. Is your future bride the Miss Northwood I've been hearing of?"

"Yes, madam." She'd probably sent her spies to examine the lady more directly; Lune liked to be well informed.

He hesitated, then lifted his head, away from contemplation of the carpet's plush surface. Lune's thoughts were impossible to read. "Madam," he said, distress roughening it, "please, believe me when I say this will change nothing. The Onyx Court is and shall remain the priority of my life." *You will remain the priority of my life.*

Every movement she made was flawlessly graceful. Lune extended one hand, drew him to his feet. Even through the layers of his coat and shirt, the touch made him shiver. Her shoes brought her very near to his height; Lune was a tall woman, and he was not a tall man. It seemed fitting. He would not have felt right, looking down upon her.

I love you.

Words he could never say.

Lune smiled, her hand rising to his shoulder. "You needn't worry, Galen. No one doubts your dedication to this court, least of all myself. Nor should you doubt your contributions; you have brought us Dr. Andrews, who I'm very sure will be a great help to us in our struggle. I do not thank you often enough, except as rote courtesy, so let me say it now: you have my gratitude, for all you have done, and all you will do. And that will not change when you wed."

Nobility came so easily to her. He fancied it a relic of the past, preserved in this world out of time; in this fallen age, when even the highest descended to the riots of the theater and tavern, debauching themselves with drinking and smoking, whoring and fisticuffs, Lune seemed the living memory of true noble grace. Or perhaps only fae ever attained that ideal, and mortals merely aspired to it, falling short of the true glory.

"So thoughtful." Lune put one finger under his chin and tilted it up. His breath stopped. "There is always so much behind your eyes, Galen. Most of it melancholy, I think. I'm sorry you came to this court in such a troubled time. I fear you've seen little of its gaiety, and much of its tragedy."

He wanted so badly to catch her hand in his. "Your tragedy," he managed to say, "is more precious to me than the best the mortal world has to offer."

Lune stilled. More soberly, she said, "Be cautious of that feeling, Galen. You've drunk a cup of faerie wine; your body and soul will always crave more. But if you discard your world to live wholly in mine, it will break you. You'll become a shadow of yourself, desperate and mad, destroyed by the very thing you desire, and what's more—cruel as it is—you will no longer serve this court. I need you mortal, Galen. Even though I know the price it bears."

Death. But how could he say to her that it wasn't faerie

wine he craved, it was *her*? They had kissed once, when she raised him to the rank of Prince, sealing the bond between them. He still dreamt of that kiss. And now she stood so close, mere inches away, so that all he would have to do was lean forward . . .

Galen stepped back. Unsteadily, he said, "I would die a hundred times for you. And for this court. I know you will live forever, and another man might envy it; but I will be what you need, *do* what you need, and count my life well spent when it ends."

"I know," Lune whispered, and sorrow filled her eyes. No doubt he wasn't the first man to say that to her. The obelisk in the garden bore the names of those who had gone before. And she bore enough of a human touch to mourn them.

He swallowed the lump in his throat and made himself lighten his tone. "The wedding will be in the spring. By then, I'm sure, we'll have disposed of this threat, and I can enjoy the gaiety you spoke of with a free heart."

Lune accepted his diversion, crossing the carpet to study the small orrery the von das Tickens had put in this, her private closet. "I shall have to consider what gift to give you, and your bride. Not faerie gold, I promise you: something that will last."

"I treasure it already," Galen said. He meant the response to be light, but did not quite succeed. Bowing, he added, "I should go. Lady Feidelm and the others are with Dr. Andrews, to answer his questions about faerie matters, but I would like to aid them."

She nodded, not turning to face him. "Let me know what comes of it."

"I will." Hand over his heart, Galen bowed again, and retreated from her chamber.

Once well away, he collapsed against the cool stone, breathing fast. "You're mad," he whispered to himself, hearing it echo into the darkness. "Desperate and mad, and you know she does not love you."

But if he saved the Onyx Hall, then he might at least be worthy of her.

Even a fancy as strong as his could not sustain the image of himself in armor, riding a brave steed, facing down the Dragon like a knight of old. He would find a way, though. He would save the palace, and the Queen, and then, perhaps . . .

A hopeless dream. But he could not let it go.

The Onyx Hall, London: August 3, 1758

Lune stopped her pacing when the usher entered and bowed. "The Lord Keeper is here as you requested, madam."

She waved for him to be escorted in, and made herself breathe slowly, however much frustration tried to speed it. Once Aspell had made his greetings and the usher departed, she said, "Hairy How reported to me this morning that another delivery of tithed bread has been stolen."

"That will disturb your subjects, your Grace."

"I don't need you to tell me that," she snapped, and he promptly bowed an apology. Lune made herself moderate her voice. "I have no intention of letting this become common knowledge, Valentin. The Hall has enough troubles already. But it does mean I'll have to reduce the allowance to your spies."

He frowned. "Madam, they'll be less effective—"

Another thing she didn't need him to tell her. "I'm afraid it's necessary, at least in the short term. The treaty I've arranged with the Greeks—presuming I can get their final agreement—requires some work above, and the fae who carry it out will need protection."

"As you wish, madam."

Lune almost dismissed him, but paused before saying the words. There were many causes that could explain the disappearance of the tithe; indeed, it was a pattern that fed on itself. Less bread coming into the Onyx Hall meant less available to her subjects, which caused them to hoard it, which caused its value to rise; some fae were in debt to a staggering degree. Which could, in turn, cause a few clever souls to think of waylaying her messengers.

That was one of the less sinister explanations. Others were not so innocent. "Valentin . . . give me your opinion. Could this be a Sanist plot?"

His sinuous body stiffened. "Sanists? What benefit could they gain from intercepting the tithe?"

"Aside from making me look like a poor Queen?"

Her dry answer seemed to miss him entirely, for he was frowning. "Or another possibility. Madam, I've had no luck in discovering any meeting of the leading cabal. It occurred to me they might be meeting above—but the great difficulty in that was explaining how they could afford to do so. I thought they kept mortals on hand to provide them with bread; my spies have been following that possibility. If they are the ones ambushing your messengers, though . . ."

Sun and Moon. If they *were* meeting above, Aspell would never find them; the city had grown too big, with a thousand mortals for every faerie below. It would be simplicity itself for conspirators to blend in among them and vanish.

He bowed anyway and said, "I will pursue this possibility, madam."

"I may have to keep funding your spies," she said grimly. "One to accompany every delivery as it comes in. Catching the thieves may be our only hope of finding their masters."

"An excellent idea, your Grace," Valentin Aspell said. "Whether Sanists are involved or not, we must keep the tithe coming. I will put my people to the task at once."

The Onyx Hall, London: August 15, 1758

Magrat was in the same position as always, hunched in her corner of the Crow's Head, gin cup in hand. Her lipless mouth quirked when Irrith approached. "Let me guess. You've come to call in your favor."

Irrith dropped onto the stool across from her. "Something small, like I promised. Just the recommendation of a few names. I need stealthy sorts, goblins or pucks, to help me break into a mortal place."

"The house of that fellow the Prince has brought among us? I hear things about him, you know."

Almost every conversation with Magrat went this way, the church grim trying to tempt her listener with vague promises of information for sale. Sometimes the information was real; sometimes it wasn't. "Not him," Irrith said. "But I won't tell you where, so don't bother asking. We'll be stealing something for the Onyx Hall, and I need hands to help carry it. Who do you recommend?"

Disappointed by the failure of her bait, Magrat set her gin down and began to count possibilities off on her fingers. "Scadd. Greymalkin, or Beggabow. Your old friend Angrisla—"

"She's here?" Irrith asked, surprised. "I thought she went north."

"And you went to Berkshire. People come back, sometimes." Magrat tilted her head sideways, thinking. "Dead Rick, if you want someone to listen or sniff for guards. Lacca. Charcoal Eddie, assuming you can put up with his sense of humor. Something for the Onyx Hall, you said—is this for the Queen?"

Irrith wasn't a good enough liar to say *no* and be believed, and her hesitation was answer enough. "Careful," Magrat warned her. "Some folk in this place are Sanists."

The word still made Irrith twitch, despite what Aspell had said. "So?" she said, a little too loudly. "What's going on with her and the Hall doesn't change the fact that we're in danger—*all* of us. If we don't do something about that, there won't be any palace *or* Queen to fight over anymore."

"Watch what you say, little sprite." The low, rumbling voice came from the next table over, where a thrumpin with a face to shame a demon sat. "You haven't been here but a bare year—less—and you don't know much. She may say it's all to defend this place, but some of the things the Queen does are making it even weaker."

"Like what?" Irrith demanded.

"Like that Calendar Room," the thrumpin's drinking companion said. "Why do you think she kept it secret? Because it's feeding off the future of the Onyx Hall, every time some-one goes inside, draining tomorrow away so we'll have noth-ing left!"

They'd drawn a great deal of attention now, of all different kinds. A knocker with a thick Cornish accent laughed. "Aye, sure—and that's why she told us all about it, I suppose? Fool. If it were destroying the Hall, we'd never have heard a whis-per of its existence."

"What about the earthquakes, then?" the thrumpin said, standing up. He wasn't much taller than the knocker, but much thicker bodied, so he seemed to loom over the goblin. "Cannon, they said—like hell. Cannon don't shake the whole of London. Mark me well, that was the Hall almost falling apart. And it killed Lord Hamilton, too!"

"He died *six years later*!" someone yelled.

In the corner, gin cup once more in her hands, Magrat was cackling to herself. "You've done it now, Berkshire. Want to make any wagers?"

"Wagers? On what?"

Irrith got her answer a moment later when the first tin cup flew. Who its original target was, she didn't know, but it caught the thrumpin in the ear and he bellowed in rage. He tried to shove through the crowd, the knocker shoved him back, and then the skinny mine spirit went down—tripped by either a stool or someone's foot, and no chance of telling which. Then the brawl was on, Sanists against loyalists, except the two sides seemed to fall apart early on, with various goblins and pucks gleefully provoking chaos wherever they could.

Rather than be a part of that chaos, Irrith dove under the table and watched the legs stagger by. Magrat poked her with a foot. "For this entertainment," the church grim said, lean-ing down to speak under the table's edge, "I'll give you a bit more for free. Don't take Lacca."

"Why not?" Irrith asked, wincing as someone howled in pain.

"Because she's over there chewing on that knocker's arm," Magrat said, grinning toothily. "Most Sanists don't have any-thing personal against the Queen. She's different."

A sour taste filled Irrith's mouth. *Too far. Aspell's one thing; Lacca's another.* "Thanks for the warning," she said, and settled against the wall to wait for the brawl to end.

Memory: February 8, 1750

The hour being a little after midday, many people were awake and about their business in London when the earth beneath their feet suddenly bucked as if to throw them off.

The shock was felt in all the neighboring towns, and even so far as Gravesend, and caused much distress. But nowhere was any person so angered as in the subterranean chambers of the Queen of the Onyx Court.

"You told me this would be safe!" Lune raged.

Gertrude had tried and failed to make her Grace lie down. Lord Hamilton was more tractable; he at least sat in a chair, sipping occasionally from the medicinal mead the brownie had given him. Lune insisted on pacing, her skirts whipping into a small vortex every time she turned.

If Ktistes could have fit in her chamber, she would have had the centaur there; as it was, the von das Tickens stood alone against her anger. "It *vas* safe," Niklas growled, unimpressed by the royal anger. "Nobody vas hurt. Even that horse-man says the charms are not damaged. Just a little shaking of the ground, is all."

She glared silver murder at him. "You caused an earthquake. I should have heeded my instincts and my common sense, when you first suggested using *explosives*."

"We don't have much choice, Lune." Hamilton had recovered enough to argue with her. The sudden jolt had dropped them both where they stood. Which they had expected—such an alteration to their realm could not help but affect them—it was the echo into the world above that came as an unpleasant surprise. The Onyx Hall both did and did not exist in the earth beneath the City, and apparently the blast had crossed that boundary. "We need a high-ceilinged chamber in which to construct the clock. Nothing suitable exists in the Hall, not that can be made secure. And unless we find some better way to hang the pendulum than off a moonbeam, we'll need some way to draw the light down, of which the Monument is our best option. We're lucky to have even *one* zenith telescope inside the City walls."

Inside the walls. That was a goodly portion of the problem. "The Sanists will find all the fodder they need in this," Lune said. Her angry stride weakened, and she put one hand out for support, catching the black wall. "If I admit we've been blasting a new chamber, changing the fabric of the palace . . ."

"Then lie," Gertrude suggested, cheerful as always.

The Queen nodded, anger giving way to thoughtful calculation. "We can't hide it, that's for certain. But another story . . ." Inspiration straightened her back once more. "We need Peregrin. A cannon blast could explain it—development of a weapon against the Dragon. That's the best we can hope to make of it, I think."

"Von moment," Wilhas said delicately, as Gertrude went to the door. "There is a small complication."

Lune's expression chilled once more. "What?"

"Ve need to do it again," Niklas said bluntly.

Hamilton groaned and reached for the mead again. "You didn't blast far enough?"

The dwarves shook their heads, mirror images of each other in red and blond. "Not even halfvay," Niklas said. "Ve need a bigger charge. Not yet—it vill take a little vile to prepare—but next month, I think."

Lune said, without much hope, "Is there any way to prevent it from disturbing the Hall and the City again?" More shaking of heads. She finally sank into a chair, head rolling back. Her exhaustion was as much of the will as of the body. "Then I will definitely need to speak to Peregrin. When will you do it?"

"March eighth," Wilhas said. "The new moon is good for these things. Ve just missed it this time, and that I think did not help."

One month later, to the day. Lune rubbed at her eyes, then

said, "Get it right the second time, gentlemen. A third earth-quake in as many months, and Londoners will be convinced the end is at hand."

Montagu House, Bloomsbury: August 18, 1758

The blank front wall of Montagu House was well lit by moonlight as five fae came strolling up Great Russell Street. Irrith would have preferred to wait for the new moon; faerie charms were always helped along by details like that. But they needed to steal their target in time for Lune to trade it to the Greeks in time for them to provide help creating clouds in time to hide from the comet, and no one felt comfortable wasting two perfectly good weeks just to make the thieves' lives easier.

They paused at the corner of Bloomsbury Square. Five simple fellows out for a walk, never mind the late hour; Irrith hoped no constables would pass by, keeping the houses of the wealthy safe. She squinted down the street, then nodded to the sharp-faced fellow that was the disguise of Charcoal Eddie. "See those rooms above the gate? That's where the porter lives. But don't have him open the main gate; it'll be much too noisy. Use the eastern door instead—"

"I remember," the puck said, annoyed. "I flew over it this morning. Eastern door in the little courtyard. Give me three minutes." Without bothering to make sure they were still alone, he hopped into the air, and flashed off down Great Russell Street in the form of a shabby-feathered raven.

"Do you know where to find the stand?" Angrisla murmured into her ear. Unlike Eddie, the mara was keeping very careful watch indeed over the square and the surrounding streets.

Irrith shook her head. "Lord Galen said they've brought everything into Montagu House for sorting, but things are still being moved around. It's big, though. We shouldn't have much trouble." Assuming the Greeks were right, that it was even there to begin with. One piece of old bronze looked much like another, to Irrith; how could they be certain?

In the quiet street, the sound of a bolt being shot back echoed like a gun. Irrith jumped, and got a disgusted look from Dead Rick. "Come on," she muttered, and under the cover of cloaking charms, they all went forward.

The warm weather meant the porter had been sleeping with his window open; it also meant he was standing in the court-yard stark naked, with his eyes shut and gentle snores issuing forth. Eddie was lounging against the stable wall, smirking. "Do we keep him with us?"

"We'll get the front door open, then send him back to bed," Irrith said. "If anyone does come upon us while we're search-ing, it'll be easier to hide without a naked sleeping mortal wandering around."

The puck pouted, but he was being well rewarded for his help; he made no more protest. "This way, ladies and gents," he said, and gestured toward a nearby arch.

Even with charms, Irrith felt terribly exposed in the great open courtyard of Montagu House. Windows lined the house's front and the two wings, which any sleepless servant could glance out of, and she kept thinking she saw movement in the shadows of the front colonnade. Greymalkin, the last of their party, regarded her with pitying contempt. "Missing the trees, Berkshire?"

She was, but not for a whole loaf of bread would she have admitted it. "Just keep watching," Irrith hissed, and stood nervously as the porter unlocked the front door.

Once they were inside the darkened house, it was better. She sent Eddie to escort the porter back to bed and then keep watch, while she and the others followed the directions Galen had given, up the staircase on the left and into the collection rooms of the British Museum above.

"Ash and Thorn," Dead Rick muttered when Irrith threw the curtains open. She flinched, thinking of the Sanist news-paper that had taken that name. He was a skriker; had he been the dog who attacked her at Tyburn? But he seemed to mean the words only as an oath. "What is all of this *for*?"

Curiosity, Irrith thought. It was like her cabinet, ten times over—no, a hundred times. The walls were lined with cases the height of a giant. Their top shelves were enclosed in glass, held shut by prominent locks; their drawers, when Greymalkin slid one out, proved to be covered over with wires, their openings too small even for her slender fingers. And all of it, shelves and drawers and opened crates on the floor, was crammed with objects of a thousand kinds. In the moonlight from the windows, she saw coins and masks, dried plants and dead butterflies, an astrolabe and a polished round crystal the size of her fist.

She wanted nothing more than to spend the whole night looking through it all—well, not the dead plants and insects. Those served no purpose she could see. But the things made by men . . . those could occupy her for days.

Especially since there was more than one room. "Let's move on," Irrith said reluctantly. "The stand must be somewhere else."

The antiquities, unfortunately, were scattered through many rooms. The fae went through them quickly, passing statue after statue, baskets, drums—and even the goblins, accustomed to moving in darkness, seemed skittish. Irrith kept thinking she heard voices, just beyond the edge of understanding. Or *things,* moving in the shadows. Some of these objects came from far-off lands, and she wondered what they'd brought with them.

"Damn it," she muttered, almost for reassurance. The stand had to be here *somewhere.* Up in the attics, perhaps? Galen hadn't been able to tell them where the unsorted items were. The new museum had been given so many collections from other folk, they were still struggling to put it all in some kind of order.

"Hsst!" Angrisla stood at the far side of the room. "What's through here?"

"Manuscripts," Irrith said; the mara was already gone, vanished through the door. The room beyond was pitch-black, but that hardly bothered a nightmare. After a moment, her hideous face appeared in the doorway. "Bronze, about your height?"

Irrith's heart leapt. "Three legs?"

Angrisla nodded, and they all hurried to see.

It stood in a corner of the manuscript room, with—Irrith snorted—a Chinese vase sitting on it. "Doesn't look like much," Greymalkin said.

She was right. Ktistes had shown so much reverence when speaking of this, Irrith had expected . . . she didn't know what, but something much grander than what they found. The stand was nothing more than a plain bronze tripod, with only a little decoration down its legs, and a shallow bowl at the top.

Dead Rick sniffed it, as if his nose could somehow find its value. "What do the Greeks want it for, anyway? If it's so useful, why would the Queen give it up?"

"For something we can't do ourselves," Irrith said. "Ktistes said some old Greek woman used to sit in that bowl and give prophecies. But it won't work for us." She moved the Chinese vase onto the floor and beckoned for the others to help. "Come on; I can't carry this on my own."

Angrisla took the bowl, and Dead Rick ended up with the tripod itself. Irrith left the vase precisely where the stand had been and closed the drapes and doors behind them. The theft would be obvious, but no sense leaving more signs than they had to.

Out in the courtyard, she became aware of noises coming from the gatehouse chambers. Muffled cries, like a man having a bad dream, interspersed with Charcoal Eddie's cawing laughter. "Blood and Bone," Irrith swore. Greymalkin was grinning. "Go on—get the tripod out of here. I'll follow in a minute, with Eddie." She ran for the gate.

Upstairs, the puck was perched at the foot of the porter's bed, his glamour discarded. The porter and his wife both twitched and moaned, the sheets tangled around their feet. "What are you doing?" Irrith demanded in a strangled whisper.

He sneered at her. "Getting my reward. The Queen said I could play with the porter afterward."

"*Later,*" Irrith said, and grabbed his arm. Eddie fell off the bed with a yelp. "After we're gone with the tripod, and they've stopped worrying about the theft. Then you can come play with him all you like." Ignoring the puck's protests, she dragged him back down to the courtyard and out onto Great Russell Street.

Angrisla was waiting with the bowl at the far side of Bloomsbury Square. Irrith's heart missed a beat. "Where's Dead Rick? And Greymalkin?"

"Gone on ahead." The mara's black eyes missed nothing. She said, "He'll deliver it safely, Irrith—don't worry. He's loyal."

How could Angrisla be sure, if she'd been gone from the Onyx Hall? But it reassured Irrith anyway. "Let's get home, then, and collect our rewards from the Queen."

Red Lion Square, Holborn: August 23, 1758

When the maid knocked on the door to Dr. Andrews's bed-chamber, the voice from the other side was reassuringly strong. "Come in."

She opened it, curtsied, and announced, "Mr. St. Clair to see you, sir," then stood aside to let Galen pass. Entering, he saw the cause of Dr. Andrews's vigor: Gertrude Goodemeade, half again as tall as she should be, but still recognizably her-self. The empty cup in her hands said she'd already fed the ailing man another dose of her restorative draught, the best medicine the fae could offer. What was in it, Galen had no idea—beyond a base of the Goodemeades' namesake brew—but Andrews had agreed to drink it. Though the draught was no cure for consumption, it did help him regain his strength, and the doctor's recent collapse made him desperate enough that he would accept anything that offered him a chance.

The disguised brownie curtsied to Galen, though she re-frained from addressing him by title. Andrews said, "Mr. St. Clair. As you can see, I am not yet dead."

"You're looking much better," Galen replied honestly. "Much more improvement, sir, and you'll be in better health than you were when first I met you."

That last was an exaggeration, made to bolster the man's spirits. Andrews still lay propped up against pillows, and his color was far from good. "As much as I would welcome that," the doctor said, "I will settle for sufficient strength to rise from this bed. I'm eager to return to work."

Gertrude clucked her tongue. "Now, Dr. Andrews—I might be no physician, but I think you'll agree I've seen my share of sick men. You know full well that too much eagerness might land you right back where you are right now. And the air in that place is too cool; it wouldn't be good for your lungs."

"It's also dry, though," Galen said. "Isn't that supposed to help? We could always bring in something to warm the space. And perhaps some of its . . . *subtler* qualities might help."

His attempt to hint at his sudden inspiration failed; the other two looked baffled. Galen cast a wary eye upon the bed-chamber door. Andrews insisted his servants were the model of discretion, and Galen admittedly had seen nothing to disprove it. Still, he lowered his voice before he went on. "The passage of time—or lack thereof. Men grow no older while in that place, do they? Might that not also pause the progress of his disease?"

It had seemed like a brilliant idea; he was therefore crushed when Gertrude shook her head. "Folk have died of disease there, Galen. One of your predecessors used to keep patients in the Billingsgate warren, because the space was clean and quiet. Some got better, it's true, but not all."

He should not have said it in front of Dr. Andrews. The man's expression showed the broken pieces of hope, and the powerful desire to cling to what remained of them. "Still—" He paused as if he was going to cough, but drew a clear breath and forged on. "Part of my difficulty is the encroachment of weakness, and some of that *is* age. Even if it offered me only small help . . ."

"It would be better than nothing," Galen agreed. "Come, Gertrude—is it not worth a try?"

"You know the risks," Gertrude said in an urgent whisper. "Dr. Andrews, surely they warned you; to stay too long below brings its own kind of weakness."

If she thought that would dissuade anyone, she was wrong. Andrews merely said, "I would trade that risk for the one I face now."

The brownie bit her lip uncertainly, turning the empty cup around in her hands. Galen willed her to see the man lying in his nightshirt, pale and burnt thin by disease, the man in whom he had placed his hopes of a solution against the Dragon. The fae were Andrews's one hope of survival, and at the moment, he was theirs. If this had the smallest chance of extending his life, and therefore the time in which they might find solutions to their problems . . .

"Isn't for me to decide," she said at last, taking refuge in lack of authority. "It's yours, Lord Galen, and the Queen's. If you think it worth trying, and she agrees, then so be it."

"I will consult with her immediately," Galen said, before Andrews could even ask. The pieces of hope were beginning to knit themselves back together. Fear of them breaking again, however, made him add, "The Queen has more experience of this than I. If she says it would do more harm than good, I'll have to heed her."

Andrews sagged back against his pillows. "I understand."

They left him then, for whatever good the draught had done him, he still needed rest. No servants scurried guiltily away when Galen opened the door, so it seemed their imprudently direct words had not been overheard. Gertrude waited until they reached the square, though, before she took him by the sleeve.

"I have experience of this, too, Lord Galen," she said. Her face was suited for merriment, not somberness, but her eyes made up all the difference. "If you do bring him below—not just for an afternoon here, a day there, but for days on end—you must watch him carefully. Mortal minds don't fare well among us, and it is his mind, as much as his body, that you need."

Once it had felt peculiar, addressing a woman who scarcely came up past his waist; now it felt even more peculiar, seeing Gertrude under a glamour of height. Though it should not have, the difference lent weight to her warning. "I won't forget it, Gertrude. I'll watch him myself; he's my responsibility, after all, and my friend beyond that."

It didn't erase her worry, but she nodded. "That's the best anyone can ask for, then."

The Onyx Hall, London: August 29, 1758

With the theft of the tripod from the British Museum's collections, few barriers remained between the fae and the creation of a veil to conceal England from the comet. Galen, considering that business all but done, had almost forgotten the debt he owed—until Edward brought him a letter written in a flowing, foreign hand.

The genie.

Galen cursed. Mrs. Carter had confirmed the inscription on the bowl; it was an adaptation of some Arabic invocation, summoning clouds and rain. Lune had given Irrith permission to use it, which meant Abd ar-Rashid had done them a genuine service. Now Galen must do him one in turn.

At least he had an easy means of discharging his duty. Galen wrote to Dr. Andrews, whose health had improved distinctly since his removal to the Onyx Hall. The man was sleeping below more nights than not, with Podder to see to his needs; it was simple enough to arrange a meeting between him and Abd ar-Rashid.

The genie was too polite to complain of the delay, beyond the gentle nudge of that one letter. Galen was rather more worried about Dr. Andrews. Given the man's new familiarity with the fae, it seemed silly to disguise Abd ar-Rashid as anything other than what he was; but how would the doctor respond to an Arab? Would that strangeness be just one more drop in the sea that was the Onyx Hall, or would it be one too many?

Andrews seemed composed enough, and even friendly, when Podder showed them in. He was sitting up in a chair, dressed properly once more, and if he didn't rise to greet them, that was easily explained by his health. "You will forgive me, I hope, Mr. Abd ar-Rashid," the doctor said, indicating his seated position, and the genie hastened to assure him of it. "Mr. St. Clair tells me you come here for learning."

"It is so," the genie said, settling into his own chair. "Heard I of your Royal Society, and wish to converse with its Fellows upon many topics. A physician, you are?"

Andrews smiled ruefully. "I was, until my illness forced me

to retire from such work. But I daresay I could spare the effort for a bit of tutoring; indeed, with instruction, I expect you could assist me in basic tasks, which would be a great boon to the work Mr. St. Clair has asked me to do."

All Galen's happy satisfaction drained down to his stomach and congealed into something more like embarrassed horror. *Oh, God. He misunderstood me completely.*

Abd ar-Rashid's excellent manners kept him from saying anything immediately offensive, but his back stiffened. Choosing his words with care Galen suspected had nothing to do with his imperfect English, the genie said, "I fear there is a . . . confusion? A physician I am already, studying the medical arts since the days of Ibn Sina."

"Yes, well, we've come on a bit since Avicenna," Andrews said with a dismissive wave. "He was good enough for his time, I suppose, but after seven hundred years anyone would be a trifle . . . hmm . . . outdated?"

"O doctor," the genie replied in that same, even tone, "wrote Ibn Sina, seven hundred years ago, in the *Al-Qanun fi al-Tibb,* that the disease afflicting you can go to others—but maybe the physicians of England forget, as I see you do not keep away from the healthy."

Andrews went from patronizing to affronted with remarkable speed. "Contagion? Balderdash; that's as great a piece of nonsense as the innkeeper who thought it was caused by faeries. They have assured me it is not so."

Once Galen belatedly found his tongue, the words poured out. "My apologies to you both; I fear the misunderstanding here is entirely of my doing. Dr. Andrews, Lord Abd ar-Rashid is a traveling scholar, who spent the last several years among the academies of Paris. He asked me to provide him with an introduction to the scholars of the Royal Society, and given his . . . nature, I thought it best to begin with you. I do beg your pardon for giving the wrong impression, but he wishes to *exchange* ideas. I have no doubt that English and Arabic physicians both have learned many useful things over the years, which each of you could benefit from—and surely, gentlemen, you share more than you differ. The four humors, for example—"

They shared something indeed, turning on him. "We physicians of learning are finished with that idea," Abd ar-Rashid said, his accented reply interweaving with Andrews's heated, "Only quacks and unlettered country doctors still follow that notion." Then they both stopped, each eyeing the other like a pair of wary tomcats.

"Paracelsus," Dr. Andrews said, as if testing something.

The genie nodded. "*Iatrochimie*—I do not know it in English—though little was the understanding of chemistry to guide him, and he went wrong often."

Which was perfectly incomprehensible to Galen, but Andrews nodded grudgingly in return. Though the two embracing each other as brothers in medicine seemed unlikely, at least Andrews was no longer regarding the Arab as he might a precocious child. "A different perspective might be refreshing, I suppose," the doctor allowed. "I would be interested to hear what you learned in Paris, sir. My correspondence with gentlemen there has fallen sadly by the wayside during my illness."

Which left the genie, who had recovered a kind of blankness that Galen suspected meant his thoughts were not fit to be shared. "Lord Abd ar-Rashid," Galen said, "if you would consent to work with Dr. Andrews, addressing a certain philosophical problem we face, then her Grace and I would be most grateful. We could offer you lodgings within the Onyx Hall, and the protection of mortal bread, should you need it."

The genie thawed a bit at the offer of hospitality—or perhaps it was the philosophical problem. If he was half so curious as reports made him out to be, then that would be like the scent of game to a bloodhound. And he'd made some acquaintances among the fae of the Onyx Hall; if he didn't already know of the comet, he would soon. Galen had judged, and Lune agreed, that there wasn't much to be gained in trying to keep that secret from the foreigner. Much better to offer him honesty, and see if they could gain his help.

"O Prince," Abd ar-Rashid said at last, "the lodgings and the bread I need not. But I appreciate the offer. If Dr. Andrews agrees, so, too, do I."

It was the best he was likely to get. Galen could only hope

this partnership would grow less thorny over time. Abd ar-Rashid might make a valuable addition to their scholarly circle. He had, after all, studied in foreign lands, where many strange things were known.

"Good," Galen said, with heartier cheer than he felt. "Then I shall leave you to your conversation, gentlemen, and see about fetching you a salamander."

The Onyx Hall, London: September 1, 1758

Irrith held the pole at arm's length, walking with slow care to ensure the brass box swinging from the wood didn't accidentally brush into her. Even with that precaution, she could feel the heat radiating from the metal. The salamander had been *most* unhappy when she slammed the lid shut on its head.

She had to bang the end of the pole into the door in lieu of a knock. Podder opened it, and shied back when he saw her burden. Edging past the nervous hob, Irrith came into Dr. Andrews's laboratory.

The mortal man was waiting for her, along with Galen and a dark foreigner she'd seen around the Onyx Hall. He must be the Arabic genie Segraine had mentioned, Abdar-something. "Ah, my dear, very good," the doctor said, waving her forward, toward a contraption Irrith recognized as being one of Niklas von das Ticken's discarded Dragon-cages. It stood well above the bare floor, on a slab of stone, with a bucket of water waiting at each corner. "In here, if you would."

She dropped the brass box inside and slid the pole free. "He's burning since I grabbed him," she said by way of explanation. "Can't touch the latch, but if you have something long enough to reach through . . ."

Their servant Podder fetched a thin-bladed knife and handed it to Galen, who approached the cage warily. After some fumbling, he succeeded in lifting the latch, and the salamander immediately poured free of its prison. The creature hissed and spat sparks when it discovered the new confinement of the cage.

"Take good care of that one," Irrith said, leaning on her pole. "It was a right bastard to catch; I don't fancy going after another."

Dr. Andrews was peering through the bars, drawing closer and closer; he leapt back when a lick of flame almost singed his nose. Rubbing his hands with undisguised eagerness, he said, "I fear we may need several, my dear. The chances of our correctly extracting pure phlogiston on the first attempt are dubious at best."

"Pure *what*?"

"Phlogiston." Galen smiled at her. He looked happy, she realized; he truly enjoyed this sort of thing, poking and prodding at creatures to learn what made them go. Far more than he enjoyed politics, and she could understand that very well. "Fire—in its pure form."

Irrith grinned back. "I can spare you the effort, then. Here's your flodgy-thing." She prodded the salamander with the end of her pole. It attacked the wood with astonishing speed; fast as she drew back, she didn't save the tip from catching fire. "See?"

With two delicate fingers, Galen guided the burning end down into a bucket, where it died in a hiss of steam. "We know the nature of the salamander, Irrith; that's why we asked you to catch one. But we need to separate the fire from the creature."

"But the fire *is* the creature," Irrith told him. Clearly he did *not* understand, whatever he claimed. "That's what a salamander *is*: elemental fire."

"That is an outdated theory, my dear," Andrews said. She was beginning to grit her teeth every time he called her that. Irrith didn't need her title, but she would have appreciated the simple courtesy of her name—especially coming from someone whose entire span, cradle to grave, was scarcely a flicker of her own. "Robert Boyle showed the insufficiency of the classical elements as a means of describing the world, so that now we think there are many more elements, though so far the definition of them has proved beyond us. Phlogiston may be one of them, but it is not elemental fire, and this creature cannot be composed of it."

Irrith had forgotten the Arab, standing silent watch over this exchange; she jumped when he spoke. "The lady is correct. Created were my kind out of smokeless fire. This salamander is the same, perhaps."

Andrews's mouth took on a sour cast, and Irrith smirked at him. "See? Faeries are different."

The mortals against the immortals. Galen was even standing next to Dr. Andrews, though the genie was a little distance away, half-aloof. In mollifying tones, the Prince said, "It doesn't work that way, Irrith. The whole object of natural philosophy is to discover the laws of the world—laws that must and do apply in all places equally."

"*The* world! But we're in a different one, aren't we? Or halfway between two, I suppose." She gestured with the charred pole, skimming it over the cage in a shallow arc just for the pleasure of watching Dr. Andrews twitch apprehensively. "I bet you have a law saying time has to pass at the same speed everywhere, but faerie realms don't obey that one, either."

Galen hesitated, but Dr. Andrews did not. "Let me demonstrate something to you, my dear. I haven't yet devised an experiment to investigate the illusions spoken of at Midsummer, but I can show you something simpler."

He went to one corner of the room, where various prisms, lenses, mirrors, cards, and other items were piled on a table. "Mr. St. Clair, are you familiar with the basics of optics? Excellent. Then if you would aid me—I intend to conduct Newton's *experimentum crucis*. That should be enough to begin with."

Together the men set up a pair of prisms and two cards, one with a small hole pierced in it. "Now," Andrews said, holding up a small box, "this contains a faerie light, which we may use as our source. In Newton's time, there were two competing theories of light: one being that a prism creates its rainbow effect by 'tinging' the light as it passes through, and the other being that it merely bends the light, separating its different components by the different angles of their passage. That latter is the true theory, as I will now show. If we pass our source through the first prism—" Lifting the box's hinged flap, he created a rainbow against the first card. Podder whispered to the faerie lights around the room, so that they dimmed and the rainbow appeared more clearly. "Thank you, Podder. Now, if we position this card so that the hole permits the violet light through, we may send that portion through a second prism, and when it strikes the second card—Mr. St. Clair, if you would—"

Galen moved the pieces into position. A moment later, the card fluttered from his hand, whispering to a halt on the stone.

But not before everyone had seen a second, stranger rainbow cast across its white face.

In the near darkness, Dr. Andrews stuttered, "I—it should have—"

"Been violet." The genie's accented voice lent a touch of strangeness to an already strange scene. "As in Newton's essay 'Of Colours.' But he used sunlight."

Not a faerie light. Irrith heard a creak: Andrews collapsing into a chair, like a puppet whose strings had been cut. Podder hastily brightened the room again, revealing the doctor white as a sheet, and hardly breathing.

"Our world is different," Irrith said, and thought it very virtuous of herself that she let only a little of her smugness show through.

The urge to gloat faded, however, when she saw Galen. He was still on his feet, but he looked almost as appalled as Dr. Andrews, as if someone had come along and told him Heaven was empty, with no one watching over him. "What?" Irrith said, uncertain now. "Isn't this good? You have what you were after."

Galen's head moved side to side, blindly; it might have been stirred by the wind. "No. It isn't good. Because if nature as we understand it does not operate the same here . . ."

Dr. Andrews's whisper would have been inaudible in a less-silent room. "Then nothing we know is of any use."

"I do not think so."

That came from the genie. Abd ar-Rashid, that was his name. He looked from Andrews to Galen to Irrith, then went on in a more judicious manner. "It is only my idea, uncertain in truth. But I am wondering, for some time . . ." His sharp-tipped fingers played against each other, a nervous gesture that made him seem much more familiar than foreign. "That which is right in your world, appears to be wrong in ours. Perhaps that which is wrong in your world becomes right, in places such as this."

"Earth, water, air, and fire," Irrith said. She pursed her lips in doubt. "For salamanders and sylphs and the like, maybe—but we aren't all elemental creatures."

"No. But mixtures of those four, perhaps, as not true of mortal substances."

Andrews was still white and unreassured. "But there have been many wrong ideas—more wrong ideas than right. How are we to know which ones apply?"

Galen exhaled sharply; it might have been a laugh. Certainly a faint, mad light was growing in his eyes. "Even as Boyle did, and Newton, and all the others. We experiment. At great speed, I should think; though once the Dragon is disposed of, we'll have greater leisure to explore the laws of faerie science."

Those two words formed such an incongruous pair that Irrith stifled her own laugh. She didn't want to mock the Prince. On the other hand, she knew enough of what he meant by experimentation to doubt whether it would work; surely her world and the people who inhabited were not some kind of clockwork device, predictable once one found the gears. But he seemed to think it worth pursuing, and he knew enough of faerie things that she trusted he would get something of use out of it.

Abd ar-Rashid said, "Speaks alchemy of four elements, and three principles, and such. These ideas from Arabia, and I know something of them; perhaps they are of some use here."

It brought Andrews upright in his chair, and then onto his feet once more. "Yes. It failed the mortals who tried it, but it should be easy enough to determine whether we find different results in this place." The hand-rubbing was back, this time with blazing eagerness that made him look almost healthy for a moment. "Come, gentlemen. Mr. St. Clair is right. We haven't a moment to waste."

The Onyx Hall, London: September 15, 1758

Lune came to Galen in his own chambers—a startling reversal of their usual habit. Once they were settled in the parlor, she dismissed Edward Thorne and her own attendants, with Sir Peregrin to guard the door and make certain no one listened in.

"The Delphic tripod has been delivered to the Greeks," she said, without preamble. "We have their agreement, and their aid. In three days' time, we shall take action to hide this island from the comet. The effect will not be complete until a fortnight has passed; Savennis has advised Irrith that it would be more effective to link it to the waning of the moon, rather than the new moon itself. But when it is done, we should— I hope—have some protection."

Galen's muscles kept drawing themselves tight, despite efforts to release them. "For how long?"

The Queen shook her silver head. "No one can say for sure. This has never been done before."

She didn't ask what progress he made, with Dr. Andrews and his scholarly coterie. Their reports to her were quite thorough. So far it was more theory than experiment, but they had done enough to confirm the genie's suggestion, that the old model of matter, discredited for the natural world, was yet applicable to the supernatural. It felt like a step backward: symbolic laws in place of mechanical ones, effects governed more by poetry than physics. The Royal Society would weep if it knew. So long as their circle could manipulate it to their benefit, though, Galen did not care what basis faerie science operated on.

Lune broke his distracted reverie. "There is one other change you should be aware of."

Something in her tone warned him. Gut tightening again, Galen waited for her to go on.

"I will not be there with you."

It struck like a blow. "At Greenwich?" She nodded. "But— why?"

By way of answer, she handed him a folded piece of paper, that he soon recognized as one of the Onyx Hall's news-sheets.

The Ash and Thorn, of course, and when he unfolded it he saw immediately what provoked her declaration. The article was unsigned, but it might as well have borne the identification *A Sanist.*

> As all are aware, these past few months have seen the fading of the Square Gallery, which many fae had recently been accustomed to using as a cricket pitch. It can be no coincidence that this fading follows hard upon Midsummer, when her Majesty the Queen was pleased to attend the celebrations in the Moor Fields. A sovereign is her realm, and this sovereign and realm alike are wounded; the departure of one from the other can only further weaken that which is already frayed. The well-being of the Onyx Hall depends on the uninterrupted presence of the Queen, which alone can slow the decay.

Galen's exclamation was a poor outlet for his fury. "If they paid an ounce of attention, they would know another portion of wall was taken down just after Midsummer! This has nothing to do with a few hours' absence on your part."

"I'm sure they know of the destruction," Lune said, with a sigh of profound weariness. "But to their logic, the two are not separable. Had I stayed below, perhaps the wall would have stayed up, or its loss would have had no effect. And the logic is less important than the theme, which is that I am failing to do my duty by the Onyx Hall. My reckless visit to the Moor Fields is simply the miniature of my insistence upon remaining Queen."

He handed back the paper before he could fling it into the fire. The Sanists he could not dispose of, however much he wished to; instead he concentrated on the more immediate matter. "So you will not be at Greenwich."

Lune's mouth curved into a sly smile. "That isn't what I said. I will not be *with* you; as far as anyone other than yourself, Peregrin, and Lady Ailis are concerned, I will be in my chamber, like a good and virtuous Queen. But true virtue—not the sham they demand of me—means I will be at Greenwich, disguised. Thus will both our need and the Sanists' concerns be addressed."

This did not seem the wisest of ideas. Fae could detect a glamour, after all, though seeing through it took effort they rarely bothered to expend. Then Galen remembered the dancers: twelve of Lune's ladies and attendants, robed and masked, who would take part in the ceremony to conceal Britain. Ailis was close enough to Lune in height that no one would notice the difference.

"I will not leave you to do this alone," Lune said. "Not because I do not trust you, but because I do not wish to discover, too late, that my absence produced a fatal weakness in our concealment. Though I fear you'll have to bear the final burden alone."

"The Sanists, though." Galen clenched his fists until his knuckles ached. "Bowing to their demands, or even giving the appearance of it—do you not fear the precedent that sets?"

The smile had lost some of its vigor when she spoke of the possibility of weakness; now it faded entirely from view. "I do. But I must choose my battles, mustn't I? A faerie has the same number of hours in her day as a man does—unless she goes to a place outside of time, and I cannot mend the rift with the Sanists while cloistered away in the Calendar Room, or self-exiled to Faerie. That I must address the problem they pose is beyond question. If I can postpone it until after the Dragon, however, then I will do so."

Galen couldn't fault her desire. Nor did he have to remind her of the *if* in that sentence. "We certainly don't need the distraction. Very well, madam; I will *not* see you at Greenwich. And may our efforts prove sufficient for our need."

Royal Observatory, Greenwich: September 18, 1758

For the second time in a century, the fae of London invaded and occupied the Royal Observatory.

Performing so large an endeavor in so open a space made

Irrith deeply nervous. This was not Moor Fields, protected by centuries of tradition, where the only folk awake at late hours had no good purpose anyway; this was a royal establishment, with men who often worked at night, and a hospital full of naval men just beyond the base of the hill. She tried to reassure herself that at least poor sickly Bradley was getting a good night's sleep for once, but it didn't go far. The observatory swarmed with faeries, and she couldn't help but wonder what would happen if someone chanced to wander up the hill with a message for the Astronomer Royal.

To Segraine, who waited at her side, Irrith said, "How exactly did it come to this?"

"To what?" the lady knight asked.

Irrith gestured at the fae busily clearing the courtyard of the observatory. "My plan. It started so simply: hide from the comet. Somehow it's come to involve two faerie tricks, one mortal proverb, a deal with Greek wind spirits, a magic Arab bowl, and an entire observatory."

"And a German story," Wilhas von das Ticken reminded her, from the other side. "Although, in fairness, you had the flute idea before ve told you about the Pied Piper."

"Together with assorted nymphs, masks, pitchers, and enough will-o'-the-wisps to light up the length of the Thames," Irrith said, with resigned amusement. "I suppose we're trying to hide all of Britain, and I should have known that would mean something large, but—Blood and Bone, I didn't expect something so *motley*."

Segraine shrugged. "It's the Onyx Hall. I doubt you'll find a more motley faerie court in all of Britain."

Looking past Wilhas and Niklas to Ktistes and the Irish Lady Feidelm, Irrith had to agree. All that was missing was Abd ar-Rashid. But no one seemed to be certain just how much they were trusting the heathen, and so he had not been invited to this night's effort—even though he'd provided the mirrored bowl that would be the centerpiece of their ceremony. A bowl that, rumor had it, was crafted on their behalf by a Dutch Jew: another patch in the ragged cloak that would conceal Britain.

No genie—and no Queen. Irrith went to stand by Galen,

who kept his hands locked behind his back as if afraid of
what they would do. "I'll go to the Onyx Hall this minute
and fetch her, if you like," Irrith muttered to him. "She should
be here." Whatever the Sanists said. Irrith wasn't certain
whether the loss of more wall, and more Hall with it, had
anything to do with Lune's visit to the Moor Fields, but even
if it did, the Queen should still be here. That was the whole
idea of the Onyx Court, to have faerie Queen and mortal
Prince working together.

Galen's answering smile showed a strange mixture of serenity and nerves. "No, Irrith—it won't be necessary. We have
everything we need."

"I hope so," she murmured, waving everyone into position.
The pucks' hands glowed with will-o'-the-wisps, casting an
eerie light over the space. "Because I don't want to do this a
second time."

Then she hushed the crowd, because the dancers were entering.

They'd climbed up the hill from the bank of the Thames,
right past Greenwich Hospital, with their faerie faces in
plain sight. Or rather, faces not their own: they wore masks
of shimmering water, that covered even their eyes. How they
could see to walk, Irrith didn't know. Their robes were softly
shifting fog, and they bore pitchers of river water in their
hands, for they were representing the nephelae, the Greek
nymphs of clouds and rains.

Il Veloce, one of the Onyx Hall's Italian fauns, began to play
a meandering tune on a syrinx, guiding the masked nymphs
into a circle around the mirrored bowl that rested in the center
of the courtyard. Their dance was a simple thing—they could
hardly manage more, burdened as they were—but its movement swirled in gentle, liquid arcs, bringing them gradually
inward. One by one, the nephelae poured the contents of their
pitchers into the bowl.

It would have been prettier if it were clean, Irrith thought
with grumpy distaste. But prettiness wasn't to the purpose.
For the making of clouds, the Thames's cloudy water was very
good indeed.

The hairs on her arms and neck were rising, in response to

the presence gathering above. The night was clear—for the moment—but something waited in the sky, a power both foreign and familiar. Lune's negotiations through Ktistes had spoken of the winds by their Greek names, because the Greeks knew how to form deals with them, but surely these were the same winds that had blown across England since the beginning of time. *Call them Boreas, Euros, Notos, and Zephyros, or simply North, East, South, and West; it makes no difference.* Some fragment of their power had agreed to serve as temporary shepherds for what the earth-dwelling fae would create tonight.

The time for that creation had come. Galen walked alone across the courtyard to the mirrored bowl. He turned a little as he searched for a good grip on the Arabic-inscribed rim, and so she saw the strain on his face as he heaved the thing upward; it had not been light when empty, and now it contained twelve pitchers' worth of water. Lune should have been there to help him, Irrith fumed. Instead the Prince had to set his feet and force it above his head without aid. *Hurry,* Irrith whispered silently. *Before he drops it.*

As if they heard her, the nephelae drew close, lifting their fog-robed arms toward the bowl's rim.

The water within began to stir.

At first it was just a wisp, too faint to be certain it had been there at all. Then a mist arose, clearly visible above the rim, glowing faintly in the night. The mist thickened, and grew, and billowed slowly upward, into the empty and waiting sky.

Mortals said that clouds, however dark, contained silver linings. If clouds were the clothes of Britain, then to turn those linings outward required something of silver: a bowl, whose mirrored interior showed the world upside down, reflecting skyward the clouds that were born in its heart. Up they floated, to be met by their guides; will-o'-the-wisps leapt free of their holders' hands and, to the tune of Il Veloce's continued piping, danced away from the hilltop, toward the island's far-distant edges. Errant breezes stirred Irrith's hair against her cheeks, little brushes this way and that, as the winds above coaxed the nebulous masses of the clouds toward their new homes.

Still the clouds issued from the bowl. One of the dancers

was the sylph Yfaen, and another was a river nymph, both with some touch on the weather; Irrith had never seen such a large effort from either. How much water could be left inside, with so much fog already streaming outward from Greenwich? It wasn't nearly enough to cover the entire island, but that was the purpose of the next two weeks: to grow from this seed, until all of Britain was protected.

Surely they had enough for that now. Yet Galen still stood, arms trembling, head thrown back, teeth clenched with the effort of keeping the bowl aloft. His body arched like a bow beneath the weight. Irrith almost ran to support him, but her hands would not reach so high, and she couldn't disrupt the ceremony. *Lune should have been here. He can't do this alone.*

At least one nephele seemed to think the same. Her hand twitched foward, as if to take some of the burden. But whether that broke the ceremony, or she was simply too late, it did no good; with a cry, Galen dropped the bowl. It clanged off his left shoulder as he tried to wrench clear, its remaining water leaping outward, and then the metal rim struck the ground, denting and sending the whole thing rolling away.

Irrith hurried forward, cursing under her breath. The nephele was supporting Galen on his good side, while he let out a flood of his own foul language. Even in pain, though, he remained aware of those around him; not a single word belonging to Heaven slipped out.

"You did well," Irrith said, knowing he wouldn't believe her. "We have enough to protect us."

"Yes," the nephele murmured, too quietly for anyone beyond Irrith and Galen to hear. "You did very well indeed." And then her eyes flicked upward, toward Irrith, and even through the shimmering uncertainty of her mask, they gleamed silver.

The sprite had enough sense not to blurt out the realization that came into her head. She waited until she could say something safe, then offered, "He should sit down. Once he's feeling better, I'll take him back to the Onyx Hall. I'm sure the Queen will want his report."

"I'm sure she will." The nephele rose with fluid grace and backed away. "Thank you, Dame Irrith."

You're welcome, madam. Irrith glanced around at the hovering fae, then at Galen. He was standing on his own now, with his right hand clasped to his injured shoulder, and his face beaded with sweat. Even with his brow knitted in pain, though, he watched the disguised Queen go, and joy brightened his eyes.

Sighing, Irrith tugged him away from the fallen bowl. "Come on, Lord Galen. You've taken care of Britain; now let others take care of you."

PART FIVE

Separatio

Autumn 1758

Trust not yourself; but your defects to know,
Make use of ev'ry friend—and ev'ry foe.

—Alexander Pope,
"An Essay on Criticism," II.213–4

The beast hungers. It starves. There is too little sustenance in this stone, this dust and frozen matter; it needs more. There was wood once; there was plaster and straw, pitch and oil and tar. A feast for the flames. More than any creature could ever eat, but the more it consumed, the more its appetite grew, until all the world was not enough to sate it.

It remembers that. And it remembers something else, too: fuel of a different kind. There was a place, a city, a shadow beneath; there was power there, of a kind like the beast itself. Not kin like the sun, bright fire—this was cool and dark. Born of the sun's eclipse, but shaped by creatures who, like the beast, were made of something other than matter.

They named it Dragon. They fought it, and trapped it, and bound it to this frozen prison, exiling it to the farthest reaches of the sun's realm.

The Dragon remembers. And it hungers for vengeance.

Mayfair, Westminster: September 23, 1758

> *Dear Mr. St. Clair,*
> *I was very sorry to hear of the injury to your shoulder. The daisy chain of gossip from your mother to Mrs. Northwood to Mrs. Montagu to me says you were kicked by a rearing horse in Fleet Street, from which I conclude there is a much more interesting story I have not heard. I implore you to call upon me at your earliest convenience so we can discuss it further over tea. I have something here that I believe you will be interested in, as well.*
>
> > *Your affectionate Sylph,*
> > *Elizabeth Vesey*

No one would believe the story of the horse; that was why Galen had not tried it. Instead he'd taken advantage of his father's bad opinion of him. That his only son might be set upon by footpads while heading toward a Covent Garden brothel was easy enough for Charles St. Clair to believe—especially when there was a witness. At Lune's suggestion, he'd dulled the pain with wine, then dug Laurence Byrd out of his customary midnight carouse. Not ten feet out the door, a pair of disguised goblins had set upon them, one feigning the strike to Galen's shoulder, before both fled Byrd's enthusiastic fists. It left Galen's father in a profoundly foul mood, but not a curious one, which might have led him to inquire where his son had been so late at night.

But his mother, eager to maintain the forms of gentility, had invented the tale of the horse. It served Galen's purposes;

that would make the respectable rounds, lending credibility to the Covent Garden tale. The subterfuge gave him something to think about other than the massive bruise that was painting his shoulder spectacular colors.

He looked a shabby thing indeed as he went to Mrs. Vesey's house; the tight fit of his own coats was unendurable, and so he was wearing a castoff of his father's. But to her he could tell the truth, and so he looked forward to the visit.

Until the footman escorted him into the parlor, where Galen almost dropped his hat in surprise.

Delphia Northwood rose from her chair and curtsied. Next to her, an insufferably smug Mrs. Vesey did the same. After a moment, Galen remembered himself and bowed. "Good morning, Mrs. Vesey. Miss Northwood—I thought your family had gone into the country, now that the Season is over."

"They have, Mr. St. Clair," she admitted. "But Mrs. Vesey invited me to stay here with her for a time."

"Her mother was suffering vapors over her upcoming marriage," Mrs. Vesey confided. "And speaking of which—come, Mr. St. Clair, the two of you are to be married. Surely it isn't too much for you to address your intended by her Christian name? You wouldn't mind, would you, my dear?"

Miss Northwood colored and looked as if she wished she hadn't left her fan on the table by her chair. "Only if he insists on calling me Philadelphia."

"I have nothing against Greek names," Galen said, smiling. Jonathan Hurst had teased him upon that point, speculating as to other Greek-named fellows that might make husbands for Galen's sisters. Which had plunged Mayhew into a melancholy over Daphne, of course. But perhaps, once the Northwood money was securely invested, Galen might persuade his father to let at least one sister follow her heart.

Mrs. Vesey was looking expectantly at him. "Then let it be Delphia," Galen said, stepping into this brave new territory of intimacy. She shifted slightly, as if she, too, felt the thrill the word brought.

Their hostess beamed in satisfaction and said, "Come, let us have tea. And you, Mr. St. Clair, can tell us of your poor shoulder. Does it hurt you terribly?"

"No, I am quite well," he said—a polite little lie.

The tea things were already set out on a table, except for the hot water; Mrs. Vesey rang a bell for it as they settled themselves once more. She then bent her attention to unlocking the tea box, but spared enough to go on questioning him. "Now, it is clearly utter nonsense that you were struck by a horse, for I know you would not be on foot in the middle of Fleet Street. I am no gossip, of course, and neither is Miss Northwood; you can trust us with the truth. What really happened?"

Too late, he saw the trap she'd so neatly laid. He'd come here anticipating the opportunity to speak freely; she, perhaps guessing that his injury had something to do with the fae, had deliberately surprised him with Miss Northwood. She could just as easily have asked Yfaen, but it seemed Mrs. Vesey had not given up on her mad notion that Galen should reveal the Onyx Court to his intended bride.

As if Mrs. Vesey did not know exactly what she was doing, Galen said repressively, "The tale is not fit for this company."

It did precisely as little good as he expected. Delphia came unwittingly to his rescue, though, once the maid had brought in the hot water. "I believe it's customary for young men approaching their weddings to enjoy one last bout of foolishness. I promise you, Mr. St. Clair, I will not hold it against you."

Which gave him license to recount an expurgated version of the Covent Garden story. Galen kept it to the footpads' attack, declining to go into detail about what either he or Byrd had been doing there. Mrs. Vesey did not bother to hide her disbelief, and so once Miss Northwood had made appropriate noises of sympathy for his pain and approval for his valor, he fled to a safer topic. "Will you be in London long, Miss—ah, Delphia?"

She glanced sidelong at their hostess, who smiled into her tea. "Yes—ostensibly to ready myself for the wedding," his bride-to-be said. "But Mrs. Vesey, as she hinted before, was rescuing me from my mother."

"And there is a great deal of London Miss Northwood has

not experienced," Mrs. Vesey added serenely. "For one who has grown up here, she has seen shockingly little of the city. Perhaps we could arrange some excursions, Mr. St. Clair—what do you think?"

I think you are a meddling old woman. But he couldn't put any real venom behind it. His proposal to Miss Northwood had been shaped by the desire for honesty; Mrs. Vesey's suggestion offered him a way to remove yet more barriers of deception. For that, he could not fault her.

Still, it was out of the question. Telling the truth would mean telling Miss Northwood about Lune, and he feared the consequences if the mask that covered his adoration slipped in his future wife's presence. Besides, Galen had enough to concern him already. "Well, if the purpose of your visit is to escape your mother's watchful eye, M— Delphia, then perhaps I can arrange an evening at the theater. Or have you ever been to the opera?"

By means of such diversions did he shift them to safer topics. Mrs. Vesey, however, let pass no opportunity to refer in cryptic fashion to the fae, until surely a girl as intelligent as Delphia had to wonder what second conversation was being conducted under her nose. Galen could do nothing about that, short of contriving to chide Mrs. Vesey in private, so he endured the awkwardness as best he could, and escaped as soon as it would not be abominably rude.

But as the sedan chair carried him home from Clarges Street, his mind kept drifting away from Dragons and faerie science in favor of imaginary conversations with Miss Delphia Northwood. His experience with Dr. Andrews had taught him valuable lessons, ones he could make use of . . .

Ridiculous, he told himself firmly. Dr. Andrews was making valuable contributions to their planned defense. This was a matter of sentimentality, nothing more, and not justifiable in its risk.

Still, he could not stop thinking of it.

You are a fool, Galen St. Clair. And that was one statement even his divided and disputatious mind could not argue with.

Covent Garden, Westminster: October 3, 1758

Three hundred sixty-four nights out of the year, Edward Thorne was a loyal protector of his master's secrets.

On the three hundred sixty-fifth, he told Irrith, without prompting, where Galen could be found.

Or at least his general location. She unearthed the Prince in the third tavern she tried, spotting him with ease, even though he'd obviously made some effort to dress as less than a gentleman. After all, not every footpad here was a disguised faerie playing a trick. Galen wore a baggy, shabby coat over equally shabby clothes, but his wig was too neatly groomed. Irrith spotted it from clear across the tavern. Someone would steal it if he wasn't careful.

He was staring moodily into a cup she hoped didn't hold gin. Magrat had warned her that the poor of nearby Seven Dials still adulterated their spirits with turpentine or acid, and Irrith feared Galen was too sheltered a soul to know that.

When she dragged a stool closer, Galen glanced up only long enough to see her. "I'm too tired for guessing games," he said, slurring the words.

"Irrith," she said. "I thought you might like company."

He went back to his contemplation of the cup. "I don't need a nursemaid."

"Never said you did." Irrith leaned forward and sniffed. The familiar burn of gin reached her nostrils, but she didn't smell anything wrong in it. *Good; he bought the legal kind.* "One question, though, and then I'll hush up and help you drink yourself under the table. Edward says you go drinking every year on this night, but usually someplace nicer than Covent Garden. Why so grim this time?"

She had observed of him before that he often tried to discipline his expression, and also that he was very bad at it. On this occasion, he didn't even try. Irrith saw the full play of his shame, despair, and hopeless love. Galen choked down a sip of the bitter gin, then said, "Because this year, I am betrothed."

Since it was Galen, Irrith tried hard to understand why that should matter. True, it was the Queen's mourning night. Until dawn, Lune would keep solitary vigil in the night garden, grieving for her first Prince, who lay buried in the Onyx Hall. She did so every year on the anniversary of his death. It was a painful reminder to Galen that her love was not for him—but why should his own step toward marriage drive him to cheap gin in a filthy tavern? It didn't put Lune's heart any further out of his reach than it already was.

She tried to understand, and failed. Instead she said, "I think you need distraction. But finish your drink first."

He lifted the cup, paused, and said, "Please, for the love of all that's unholy—change your glamour before I go anywhere with you."

Irrith grinned. She'd forgotten she was disguised as a rough young man. While Galen downed the remainder of his gin, she went outside and found an unoccupied shadowed corner; by the time she came back, this time as a woman, he'd given the tavern's owner a shilling for the best room in the house. It wasn't a *good* room, especially for that price, but it was preferable to the Onyx Hall on this night—or Leicester Fields on any night—and if the mattress was home to a troop of bugs, neither of them was in a mood to care.

Afterward, they lay curled together against the chill of the October night. Irrith ran one hand over Galen's short hair, soft against her fingers. Without his wig and coat and walking stick, she reflected, he was not Lord Galen, Prince of the Stone, nor the gentleman Mr. St. Clair. Only Galen, a tumultuous human heart wrapped up in a body that seemed scarcely able to contain it.

Those absences made him vulnerable; the darkness made him brave. "I sometimes think," Galen whispered, "that it would be better if she knew."

"Which one?"

An injudicious question. He curled tighter, like a snail pulling into its shell. But his shell was draped over the rail at the foot of the bed, or dropped carelessly on the floor. After a moment, he said, "Both, I suppose."

Irrith didn't know Delphia Northwood. She did know Lune. Before she could doubt her own impulse, Irrith said, "The Queen does know."

That sent him flying away from her as if propelled by a

bow, almost falling off the narrow bed before fetching up against the rail. He said, helplessly, "Oh God, no."

The word glanced off the protection of the tithe, but Irrith flinched nonetheless. Then she pushed herself upright, studying him. The light coming through the room's one narrow window was scant indeed, only what filtered in from the inadequate lanterns on Covent Garden square; it was just enough to trace the wing of his collarbone, the line of his uninjured arm clutching the rail, the right-hand side of his face. Not enough to see his eyes.

No way out but through the truth. Some of it, anyway. Galen didn't need to hear that the rest of the Onyx Court knew it, too. "She's known for a while."

He stayed motionless for three heartbeats, then buried his face in his hands.

"You said it might be better," Irrith reminded him. "Think about it, Galen—if it bothered her, you would know."

His reply was muffled by his palms. "Except now I must face her. Knowing that she knows. Damn it all, Irrith—why did you have to tell me?"

Because I thought it would help. Because I still can't tell how your heart works, what will make you happy, what will send you off in despair.

This time, she'd clearly done the latter. Galen dropped his hands and said, "She never should have chosen me."

The dark hid her second flinch. Irrith hadn't forgotten what the Goodemeades told her. *Would this man have been Prince, if Lune had another choice?*

It didn't matter. He *was* Prince, and was striving with everything he had to be a good one. This doubt was his greatest enemy. "Lune isn't stupid," Irrith said forcefully. "You love her; don't you trust her? She wouldn't have chosen you if she thought you weren't suitable." No matter what her courtiers said. Lune had ignored them before, when she had to; she would have done the same here.

Irrith wasn't sure he'd even listened to her. After a moment, though, Galen spoke. "Do *you* think I'm a good Prince?"

She was as bad a liar as he was. A simple *yes* would be obviously trite; a longer assurance would give away her own doubts. And she'd always preferred honesty, anyway. "I think you've been dealt the worst hand of cards of any Prince I've ever known. Comet, Sanists, your own family interfering with your life . . . and then there's Lune. The old Princes all had problems of their own, but you had yours from the start."

"So you think I'm a failure."

"No. You didn't let me finish." Irrith tucked her feet up, leaning forward to seek out his eyes in the shadows. "The Princes have all been different sorts of men, who bring different kinds of strength to the Onyx Court. They've all shared one thing, though: they care too much to give up. Whatever trouble the court faces—and believe me, there's been a lot— they keep fighting. If the day ever comes that you run away, *then* I'll call you a failure. But not before."

His back had stiffened at the thought of running away, proving her very point. Galen seemed to realize it, too. He swung his legs over the edge of the bed, then sat thinking. One hand scratched absently at his ribs, and Irrith thought she felt something crawling up her own leg. They might be ignoring the bugs, but the bugs weren't ignoring them.

"If she knows," he said at last, "then I cannot possibly tell Miss Northwood."

"About the Onyx Court?"

He nodded. "I had considered it, but—no. Mere foolishness."

"Why? There's always the risk that a mortal will attack us, or tell everyone we're here, but we risk it just the same. What are you afraid will happen—that she'll cry off once she knows what you do with the other half of your life?"

His drifting hand stilled, then lowered to his thigh. "I had thought—" Galen began, but stopped.

Irrith waited patiently. This time, she was fairly certain that anything she might say would frighten him off.

Galen sighed, with less of a melancholy sound than she expected. "I'd considered the possibility of telling her *after* our marriage. But you are right; if I did it before, she might cry off."

Which he would consider a good thing. He wasn't thinking of his family right now, Irrith could tell. Only of Lune, and of the voice in his head that told him it wasn't right to serve two mistresses at once.

On the other hand, this would give *her* a chance to observe Miss Delphia Northwood for herself. Irrith had of course spied on the young woman a little, because she was curious, but turned up nothing worthy of remark. Seeing her with Galen would be much more interesting.

"I think you should," Irrith said. "It's only fair."

He made a wordless, frustrated noise. "But I'll have to ask the Queen first. And that will be . . ."

Uncomfortable. To put it mildly. Oh, how Irrith wished she could be a fly on the wall for that conversation.

Another, heavier sigh. "I'll consider it," Galen said.

Irrith crawled over to where he sat and put her hands on his shoulders. "Tomorrow. I think you've done enough thinking for tonight."

The Onyx Hall, London: October 13, 1758

Since establishing his residence in the Onyx Hall, Dr. Andrews had thrown himself into the work the fae set for him. Podder had unearthed notebooks belonging to Jack Ellin, a previous Prince, which indicated that he suspected the refraction of a prism might have an unknown effect upon the Dragon's spirit; that was why they'd used a modification of Newton's reflecting telescope for its exile. Andrews, remembering their startling results with the *experimentum crucis*, had decided to conduct further optical experiments with the salamander.

Galen was delayed by Mrs. Vesey's insistence upon him dining with her and Miss Northwood, but he hurried to Billingsgate as soon as he could and descended into the warren that held Andrews's chambers. Upon entering the laboratory, he found Andrews pacing in agitation. The man's face was pale and dewed with sweat, and the rims of his eyes were red. "What result?" Galen asked.

The doctor gestured to the other end of the room. "See for yourself. The light faded too fast for me to try."

The apparatus stood facing a sheet tacked to the wall, a prism on a stand. The stand's platform held a blackened pair of tongs and—

Galen poked at the shriveled thing with one fingertip. "What is this? It doesn't look like a salamander."

"It's the heart of one."

He shot upright. On the table nearby lay an empty cage and an unmoving form: the corpse of the captured salamander. Its belly gaped open, revealing a charred cavity where the heart had been.

"A curious thing," Andrews said, still pacing. "I would swear the creature had nothing *but* a heart. No lungs, no intestines. I can't be sure; even making the incision without being burnt was difficult. And everything seemed to alter subtly when it died."

Horrified, Galen spun to face him. "You cut this creature open while it lived?"

That finally halted the doctor. Andrews, much taken aback, said, "How else am I to understand how it functions?"

"But—you—" Galen flung one hand toward the prism. "I thought this was an experiment with *light*!"

"It was." Andrews came forward and collected the leather gloves he'd evidently dropped on the floor. "And how was I to get that light? Oh, certainly the creature spat fire while it lived—but it was only fire. I could detect nothing strange about it at all. It is the *essence* of the creature we wished to pass through the prism, and I'm told it was the Dragon's heart they used before. Unfortunately, this one burnt out too quickly." He paused, gloves in hand. "Animal vivisection is a common practice in medicine, Mr. St. Clair. We must know how the body works before we can heal it."

Galen could not stop looking at the salamander's corpse. He knew well enough that their research sometimes involved uncomfortable things; he had, with reluctance, authorized Andrews's work with Savennis, observing the effects of prayers and church bells both with and without the protection of bread, and the faerie's sensitivity to the proximity of iron. This went further, though—and Galen had not thought to include the salamander under his authority. It wasn't an intelligent creature, of course, not like Savennis. Still. He, as Prince, had brought into the Onyx Hall a mortal who killed a faerie.

"You should have consulted me before you did this," he said quietly.

Andrews, tidying up his equipment, paused again. "Ah. I didn't realize. Will this anger the Queen?"

"I don't know. And that is why you must consult me." Galen yanked his hat off, then made himself stop before he could fling it across the room. *Is this not what you brought him here for? To apply mortal methods of learning to your faerie problem?*

The doctor nodded with good grace. "I see. My apologies, Mr. St. Clair. I did not mean to cause trouble." Then his expression brightened. "Oh—but my experience with the salamander gave me an interesting thought. Come, let's sit down, and I will tell you about it."

Sitting down meant going to the other end of the room from the corpse and its shriveled coal of a heart. Galen doubted that was coincidence. He went willingly, but waved away Andrews's offer of coffee.

"It had to do with what that Arab fellow said," Andrews began, "concerning alchemy. Now, most alchemists were mountebanks or poor deluded fools, and I very much doubt if any of them ever made an ounce of gold out of anything else, unless it was the hopes of their credulous clients. But what if it works here? Among the faeries?"

Galen frowned. "Dr. Andrews—I love a good conjecture as much as the next man, but how does this help us against the Dragon?"

"It doesn't," the doctor said, with far more excitement than those words merited. "But it may provide a way to make the Dragon help *us*."

Which explained the excitement, but not its cause. "I don't follow you."

"Do you know anything of alchemy?" Galen shook his head. "It wasn't just about turning dross into gold. That transformation, as they conceived it, consisted of purging a metal of its flaws and impurities, bringing it into a more perfected state. And the same thing, Mr. St. Clair, could be done to the human body."

Galen shook his head a second time, still not following.

"I am talking," Dr. Andrews said, "of the philosopher's stone."

He'd heard the phrase, in much the same way he'd heard of faeries before he saw Lune in the night sky. A foolish fable, indicating something dreamt of but unreal. In this case, the means of achieving mankind's dearest dream.

Immortality.

But what could the Dragon have to do with that? Dr. Andrews said, "The details are complicated—indeed, over the centuries men devised a hundred variants upon the theme, and as I said, I doubt very much if any of them worked. Much of it, however, comes down to two substances: philosophic sulphur, and philosophic mercury.

"These are not to be confused with the substances we know, brimstone and quicksilver. They represent principles, an opposing pair. Sulphur is hot, dry, and active; it is fire and air, the red or sun king, brightly burning."

"In other words," Galen said, his mouth drying out, "the Dragon."

Andrews nodded. "It seems very likely that this beast is the embodiment of the sulphuric principle. Mr. St. Clair, if the alchemist can conjoin and reconcile those two opposing principles . . . he creates the philosopher's stone."

Had they been sitting in Andrews's house on Red Lion Square, it would have seemed absurd. The philosopher's stone? Immortality? But they were in the Onyx Hall, where even the mundane trappings of chairs and carpets and tables could not disguise the fey quality of the place, the hushed mystery of London's shadow.

Here, perhaps, it might be possible.

Andrews might as well have reached inside Galen's head and turned his brain upside down. Not to fight or imprison or banish the Dragon, but to *use* it. Transform a threat into a tool, and once they had done so . . .

Galen's fancy immediately slipped its leash, imagining not just the defeat of the Dragon, but the consequences of that success. Fame, fortune—the King was almost seventy-five. What might he give to the men who could restore his youth?

A dose of common sense helped. "As I understand it, alchemists worked with laboratory equipment, boiling and distilling things. How in Heaven's name are we to wrestle your philosophic sulphur into any kind of conjunction, when it will be trying to burn us all alive?"

"I haven't the first notion," Andrews said. The gleam in his eyes chilled Galen, even as the possibility that sparked it quickened his breath. "That, Mr. St. Clair, is what we must devise."

The Grecian, London: October 14, 1758

Under most circumstances, Irrith would have enjoyed the chance to go into the city on someone else's bread. After all, every bite she got from another was a bite that didn't come out of her own meager store, and then she had a whole day of safety in the world above.

Most circumstances did not involve Valentin Aspell, and a meeting she wasn't at all sure she wanted to attend.

They shared a hackney, which put her much closer to him than she wanted to be. The uncomfortable silence lasted for a few minutes before Irrith said, "Aren't you going to make me swear an oath?"

His whisper-thin eyebrows rose. "An oath?"

"Not to tell anyone about this."

Aspell glanced out the window of the carriage, at the crowded streets creeping by. "Dame Irrith, do not insult my intelligence. At the first hint of such a demand, you would run as far from me as you could—and with good cause. Oaths are for conspirators with something to hide. The people you will see today practice a degree of secrecy, yes, because it would be easy for someone to use our words against us. But I assure you: those you will meet are no different than you."

She squirmed uncomfortably on the stained bench. *If they're no different from me . . . then I'm no different from them.*

But Aspell had assured her the purpose of this meeting was to discuss a means of preserving the Onyx Hall, against both its fraying and the Dragon. True, clouds blanketed the sky above them; the ritual had done its work. That didn't get rid of the beast, though. And it did nothing to reverse the Hall's decay.

Hence today's meeting. Irrith wasn't surprised to find it taking place above. Lune kept a good eye on both worlds, but there was no way she could watch London as closely as the Onyx Hall. If fae wanted to do something secret, their chances were better among the humans, whose teeming masses would take little notice of anything they did. Still, the choice made Irrith frown. Aspell had handed her a piece of bread without so much as a blink—not that he blinked often anyway. That kind of generosity wasn't normal, especially nowadays.

She thought again about the black dog that ambushed her on her way into the city. Had there been other such attacks? If so, Lune had kept them quiet. *But she would, wouldn't she? Doesn't want anyone to know if she can't keep the tithe safe.*

Her stomach was doing a queasy dance even before they arrived at their destination and she discovered it to be another damnable coffeehouse, under the sign of the Grecian. Foul drink; just what her nerves needed. If Aspell insisted she have some, she *would* run away.

They didn't sit at the tables, though. Aspell spoke briefly to the owner, then led Irrith into an upstairs room, where a coal fire tried to warm the air and mostly just stained it with smoke. Several people already waited there. Fae, obviously, concealed under glamours, just as she and the Lord Keeper were. It had the feel of conspiracy, however much Aspell insisted on their good intentions.

He counted them swiftly and nodded. "We are all here. Let us begin."

This was all? Irrith made it only eight in the room, not counting the two of them. Then again, it would be too suspicious if a lot of fae all vanished at once. No doubt some of these would report back to friends of theirs. And Aspell must have some means of identifying those who came, or a spy could join them without anyone knowing. He was too clever for that.

She wished the word *spy* hadn't crossed her mind.

"We have a newcomer among us today," Aspell said, gesturing to her. Irrith was glad of her habit of masculine glamours—then she wondered. Everyone in the Onyx Hall knew of that habit. Should she have looked female today? At least Aspell had the wit to use the right pronoun when he said, "I have asked him here to tell us what he's seen of the Queen."

Blood and Bone—she hadn't expected to be shoved into this so quickly. Rising, Irrith made an awkward little bow, and tried to figure out how to begin. "Er—the Queen. She's . . . at first I thought it was that she's tired. And, you know, that could be from a lot of things. We don't have to sleep like mortals do, but working all the time the way she does—that would tire even a hob.

"But I don't think it's that. She's tired, but there's something else, too."

Irrith swallowed hard. *Hob* was another word she shouldn't have thought; it summoned up an image of the Goodemeades. What would they say, if they knew she'd come here today?

She'd come for a reason. Not for Aspell's sake, or out of disaffection with Lune and the Onyx Court. No, she was here because she didn't want to see those things lost.

Irrith said, "I think her Majesty's fading."

With those words out, it was easier to go on. "My best guess is that the Hall is calling on her strength to hold itself together. Only a little; it's hard to see the effect. I wouldn't have noticed it except I—" She caught herself before she could say anything that would betray her identity. "It's slow. But if Ktistes can't find a way to mend it, and especially if the mortals tear down more bits . . ." Irrith gestured helplessly. "It will only get worse."

"Like two cripples holding each other up," one of the fae said. "Keeps either one from falling over, at least for a while. But it doesn't make either one whole."

"The Queen isn't crippled," Irrith said sharply, forgetting Lune's hand for a moment. *That's only a hand, though.* "And

Ktistes already made the entrances work again, after they burnt in the Fire. He's clever; he'll probably find a way to repair this, too."

Aspell made a placating gesture. He'd disguised himself as a pale-faced clerk, though he'd forgotten to put inkstains on his fingers. "All of us are here because we share a common goal, and that is the preservation of the Onyx Hall. If the centaur could restore our home to health, we would all be satisfied.

"But he cannot, because the foundation is too badly cracked. The sovereign is her realm. It cannot be whole unless its ruler is."

"Has anyone tried healing Lune?" Irrith asked.

It produced grumblings around the table. No doubt they'd been through all of this before, maybe years ago. And she'd just made it obvious that whoever she was, she'd only recently come to the Onyx Hall—if they hadn't guessed that already. "Well, *have* they?"

The man at the far end of the table said, "There was talk of getting her a silver hand, like that Irish king. But silver doesn't make you whole."

"And besides," another added, "there's the iron wound. You can talk all you like about healing her hand, but nothing heals what iron does to you."

Nothing *they* knew of. Irrith wondered if Abd ar-Rashid could do it. Apparently iron didn't bother his kind, and he said he knew a lot about medicine. If he could heal the Queen, this whole problem would go away.

Or would it? Irrith honestly didn't know whether making Lune whole would do anything to help the Onyx Hall. It might rob the Sanists of their best argument against her, and that would be something—but the real malcontents would still say that Lune had failed as Queen, because her first duty was to hold her realm together.

Aspell said quietly, "There is another issue."

The grumbling and argumentation quieted. The Lord Keeper waited until he had perfect silence, apart from the noise of the coffeehouse downstairs, before he spoke again. "The Dragon."

"We're hidden from it," someone said immediately. "Aren't we?"

Irrith bit back her answer; that really *would* betray her identity. Aspell gave a sinuous shrug. "We're hidden, yes. And the Dragon was imprisoned; and the Dragon was exiled."

And all of it, ultimately, had failed. Irrith wished she could argue, but the concealment had been her own idea in the first place. She, of all people, was aware that it might not last.

She asked, "What does that have to do with the Queen?"

He placed his hands carefully on the table, bowing his head. The tallow dips around the room didn't give off much better light than the smoky fire, but despite the gloom, he looked more weary than sinister. Irrith just wished she could tell whether that was a pose. "An unwelcome thought has come to me," Aspell said. "One I have labored mightily to dismiss, but it will not go. It is my great hope that we find some other defense against this threat; I want no one here to doubt that. If, however, we do not find another answer, then we must consider this, our last, most desperate resort."

Irrith's heart sped up with every word out of his mouth. Whether he meant malice or not, his need for such a preface could not bode well.

The Lord Keeper sighed heavily and went on. "While the Queen hunts answers in the world above, we cannot afford to lose sight of our own world, and the lessons it teaches us. She spent a great deal of time some years ago soliciting advice from other lands, asking after great dragons in their past, and what had been done to address them. In this, I believe, is an answer we must consider."

"Just say it already," Irrith snapped, unable to bear the delay any longer.

He lifted his head and met her gaze. "The sacrifice of a woman to the dragon."

No one said anything. A fellow somewhere beneath Irrith's feet shouted merrily to one of his companions, until she wanted to run downstairs and bid him be silent. *A strange day, this is, with faeries above and mortals below.*

And a far stranger day, Irrith of the Vale, when you stand here and listen to Valentin Aspell propose feeding Lune to the Dragon.

Because that had to be what he meant. "You cannot be serious," Irrith said, through numb lips.

"She'll take the whole damn Hall with her!" someone else exclaimed.

The Lord Keeper straightened swiftly, hands raised. "Hear me out. First and foremost, I tell you this: *I intend nothing against the Queen's will.*"

It broke through the shell of horror that had encased Irrith's body. Her heart, which seemed to have stopped, leapt back into action with a bone-jarring thud. "I am not advocating regicide," Aspell went on, distinctly enough that Irrith spared a moment to hope someone had done something to keep their voices from escaping the room. *Regicide* was not a word to toss around lightly in *either* world. "But let me explain my reasoning to you, and the course of action I see before us."

Again he waited for his audience to quiet. When they had done so, he spoke in a softer tone. "The Dragon has had a taste of her Majesty. It knows her scent, if you will."

Irrith shook her head. "It knows the scent of the Onyx Hall."

"Both, then—but in such circumstances, as I understand it, as to make the Dragon connect the two. And certainly, as matters stand now, they *are* connected. The loss of her Grace would almost certainly mean the loss of the Hall."

Loss. A delicate word, much less ugly than the two it replaced. *Death. Destruction.*

"However," Aspell went on, "were the Queen to be separated from her realm—to be no longer the Queen—then I believe she would still attract the Dragon's interest, without endangering the palace. And in that manner, we might divert the beast from its purpose."

Some of the gathered eight were shifting uncomfortably in their seats. Others had an avid gleam Irrith did not like at all. One of the shifters said, "What's to stop it from devouring her, then moving on to the rest of us?"

The man next to him nodded. "I've heard those stories,

too. A maiden a year, or some such. Appeasement isn't safety; it's just a bit of breathing space."

"We could use it to bind the Dragon, though," another said. "Not just one year, but seventy-five years of safety—or seventy-six, or however long it is."

"And how much good has more time done us? The Queen's got that Calendar Room of hers, but it hasn't given her an answer, has it?"

More voices rose, the entire thing degenerating into just the kind of squabbling that Irrith most hated. But arguments aside, she realized, this was the closest thing to an actual plan she'd heard anyone offer. It was already autumn. The comet would reach its closest point to the sun in March. That meant that even now it drew near, and only a thin veil of clouds protected them. It was all well and good to say that natural philosophy would save them, but so far it didn't seem to have provided any real proposal for how to do that.

The sacrifice of the Queen might be the only option.

And Lune would do it, too, Irrith thought. The Sanists' ordinary arguments might fall on deaf royal ears, but the Dragon could well be a different matter. Aspell didn't have to intend anything against the Queen's will: if the beast stood before them, and no other option presented itself, then Lune might sacrifice herself freely, for the sake of her people.

Which was the thing Carline had never understood. Whatever mistakes Lune had made, she always put the interests of her court ahead of her own. That was a rare thing in a ruler, faerie or mortal. Who else could be trusted to do the same?

"We will decide nothing here today," Aspell said at last, cutting through the general clamor. "As I said, this is a matter of final resort. But we must bear in mind the possibility."

He looked at each of them in turn as he said it, and last of all at Irrith. She nodded, awkwardly, as if her head were on a string held by some careless puppeteer. A strong part of her wished she had never come to this place, to hear the possibility that Lune's death was the only thing that could save them.

The rest of her was glad she had. Because if it came to that desperate pass, Irrith would throw herself at the Queen's feet and beg. If Lune *could* save them, then she must.

The Onyx Hall, London: October 15, 1758

For mortals, Sunday was a day of rest—or at least it was supposed to be. Lune knew quite well that many of them nowadays went walking outside of London, or enjoyed less respectable diversions. Galen was required to attend church with his family more often than not, though, as many Princes before him had done, and so she'd formed the habit of spending her Sundays on work that did not involve the mortal world.

This week, that meant efforts to keep her court from disintegrating. Only a few had left so far, but many more were planning to do so; Lune didn't need spies to learn that. The prudent ones had chosen dates for their departure, based on their assumptions of when the Dragon would appear. The more reckless—which was most of them—thought they could run when it did.

She intended to consult Rosamund and Gertrude, possibly even to slip away in secret and go to Rose House. Keeping below, for the comfort of her court, was threatening to drive her mad. Before she could make plans, though, a knock sounded at the door. "Come in," Lune called.

It proved to be her attendant Nemette, who curtsied. "Your Grace, my apologies. Lord Valentin wishes to speak with you."

Good news, or bad? Nemette could not answer that question for her. "Send him in."

The Lord Keeper's expression told her no more than her attendant had. "I am sorry to disturb you with what may just be an idle rumor, your Majesty, but—"

She waved him past the rest of the courtesies. If it was important enough for him to call on her, rather than waiting for one of their ordinary meetings, then she would listen. "It may be," he said, "that the Sanists are considering a more . . . political solution to their concerns than we thought."

Now she understood his ambivalence. A "political" solution could be good news, or not. "Of what sort?"

"They seek a successor to your throne."

His choice of term gave her pause. Those who took power

without leave were more commonly called "usurpers"; his phrasing implied something more legal. Inasmuch as such a word could be used for a faerie realm, where laws were haphazard things, when they existed at all.

But her realm had more laws than most. And while faerie monarchs rarely designated heirs as mortals did—after all, they could in theory rule forever—it wasn't an absurd thought here.

"How did you learn of this?"

Aspell spread his hands. "Fourth-hand rumor, I'm afraid; it may be entirely false. But I believe there was a meeting yesterday, of the Sanist cabal. Somewhere above."

Lune laid aside the pen she was still holding and frowned at the stain where it had dripped. "Where do they expect to find this successor?"

"Not Lady Carline—I beg your pardon, the former lady—if that is what you were thinking, madam. Possibly elsewhere in England. Some faerie monarch with whom you could be persuaded to form an alliance, perhaps, and who in time would rule here."

As if she were a mortal Queen, to wed and pass power to her husband. Lune cleaned her pen, to give her hands something to do while she thought.

Aspell waited, then said delicately, "Madam, without meaning to give any sanction to the Sanists . . . might it not be a wise choice, to make some kind of provision for your court? If it should come to pass that—"

He didn't finish the sentence, for she stopped him with a glare. "Do you recall Elizabeth Tudor? She, too, had councillors who pressed her to name an heir, and she, too, resisted. Because she knew the moment she declared the succession, her own position would weaken; others would begin to look to the next monarch, and she would become . . ." Lune's lip curled. "Dispensable."

She heard him draw slow breath. Were it someone other than Valentin Aspell, she would have said it was to steady his temper. "I do recall her," the Lord Keeper said. "And I also recall the uncertainty her people suffered, wondering what would become of them when she was gone, and the intrigues that resulted."

"Yes, well, unlike Elizabeth Tudor, I have the option of living forever." Lune stacked her papers and stood. "If any of my fellow monarchs are approached, I'll hear of it. In the meantime, continue with your own work, and trouble me no more with talk of a successor."

Leicester Fields, Westminster: October 24, 1758

Galen expected a lecture when he came in the front door of his house. Or at the very least a summons to his father's study; he could hardly expect the man to wait around on the staircase in anticipation of his feckless son's return. Especially when that return had become so unpredictable of late. But the footman took his cloak and hat without comment, leaving him free to follow his valet up the stairs. "Just turn down the sheets, Edward," he said through a yawn. "I need sleep more than food." And if it was scarcely sunset, he didn't care. Galen could not remember the last time he'd slept properly.

With his thoughts full of soft pillows and warm blankets, and the anticipated threat of his father escaped, Galen thought himself out of danger. He was entirely unprepared when the door beyond his own flew open and Cynthia emerged, dressed only in her shift and stays and trailing a scandalized Jenny.

"*There* you are," his sister said, and seized his arm. "We need to talk."

She hauled him into his own room before he had a chance to say anything. "Out," she commanded Edward, who, to his credit, stood his ground long enough to receive Galen's nod. Then he shooed the wide-eyed maid out and closed the door behind them both.

Cynthia let go, leaving Galen adrift in the middle of his floor. "Cyn, what's wrong?"

"You can tell me that better than I can," she replied. "Where have you *been*?"

His father wasn't the only one capable of noticing his absence. Up until now, however, Charles St. Clair had been the only one who made noise about it.

Galen sank wearily into a chair. It was true; he hadn't been home much of late. Too much time in the Onyx Hall—maybe more than was good for him—but what else could he do, with their time running out? If it weren't for the eleven days that would elapse, he would have long since taken his chances with the Calendar Room. Abd ar-Rashid was in there right now. It should be Dr. Andrews, who had proposed this matter of the philosopher's stone in the first place, but his health wouldn't permit it. When the genie emerged, Galen hoped, they would have a way to translate Andrews's mad alchemical dream into reality.

None of which he could tell Cynthia. "Your friends came by yesterday," she said. "Mr. Hurst, Mr. Byrd, and Mr. Mayhew. They said you haven't been to your club in weeks—nor have you answered their letters." She nodded at his writing desk, which held an entire pile of unopened envelopes he hadn't noticed. "I'd thought you might be carousing with them, one last bit of bachelor wildness before you settle down with Miss Northwood . . . it wouldn't be like you, no matter what Father thinks, but perhaps you decided to try. Apparently not, though. Galen, where have you been?"

That was twice she'd asked. *A third time, and I'll have to answer,* he thought vaguely. *Like a faerie.* Not that it was true for faeries, not that he'd noticed. But perhaps some of them were bound in that way. Stranger things had happened.

"God," he moaned, and buried his face in his hands. "I can't even think straight. Cynthia, my dear . . . I'm sorry."

She sank to her knees on the carpet in front of him and took him by the wrists, in a gentler grip than she'd used before. "You don't have to apologize! Mother all but jumped over the moon after you offered for Delphia; you could light her boudoir on fire and she'd forgive you. Even Father hardly cares what you do, so long as you march down the aisle and collect a bank note from Mr. Northwood at the other end. But I'm *worried* for you. When was the last time you slept?"

He couldn't have answered that if he wanted to; it was in the Onyx Hall, and he didn't often check his pocket-watch while there. "I was intending to go to bed now," he said, lifting his head so he could nod toward his pillow. Edward had gotten halfway through the task of turning down the sheets, and a pan of coals was warming for him in the hearth.

"I won't keep you long," Cynthia promised. "But don't think I haven't noticed you avoiding my question."

Fortunately, she didn't ask it a third time. Faerie weakness or no, he wasn't sure he'd have the wit to give her a safe answer. "Attending to affairs," Galen said after a moment.

"Gaming debts?"

"No!" He stared at her, appalled, and she smiled an apology, stroking his arm. Galen wished she'd chosen the other arm; his still-healing bruise ached under her hand. He controlled his wince, though, lest he get her thinking about his supposed encounter in Covent Garden, and whether that might have something to do with his "affairs."

Taking her hands in his own, Galen said, "Cyn . . . I'll be like this a while longer, I fear. It's all right, though. I need to get more sleep—you're right about that—and I promise I will try." His stomach rumbled embarrassingly, and he laughed. "Also more food. I forget to eat, sometimes."

"By the time you wed, you'll be a stick," she said chidingly. "You'll be half the man Delphia said she would marry."

Delphia. Galen's grin slipped. "I'll fatten up for the wedding. Fat and gouty, just like Father." She smacked him on the knee. "In all seriousness . . . thank you."

"For what?"

"For caring." Lack of sleep made him too easily tearful; he fought the urge back, though his vision swam a little. "As you said, all Father cares about is Delphia's dowry. And Mother isn't here, making sure I eat and rest. You are. And I cherish that."

Cyn rose up on her knees so she could hug him more easily. Galen laid his cheek against her hair. She was and always had been his favorite among his sisters, and the one thing he would miss when he and Delphia established their own household.

"You had better take care of yourself," she said into his shoulder. "Or I'll follow you with a plate in one hand and a pillow in the other."

More laughter bubbled up. "I will."

And thank you, dear sister, for the favor you did unawares.

This ambush, Cynthia concerned for his well-being, curious about his absences—it settled the question that had plagued his heart since May.

He did not want Delphia to suffer such doubts.

By his prerogative as Prince, he would tell Miss Philadelphia Northwood of the Onyx Hall.

Memory: November 9, 1756

The library of the fae was a marvel. Galen laughed at the thought; *everything* in this place was a marvel. More than a year since he'd gained entrance to the Onyx Hall, and he still gaped like a country squire come to London for the first time, stunned afresh by each new wonder.

No one could blame him in this instance, though. The shelves rose in three levels around him, rimmed with silver balconies and ladders of ivory, a temple to the written word. Surely even the great library of Alexandria had not been this grand. He saw works in Greek and Latin, French and stranger tongues—and then, as if to bring him back to earth before his thoughts grew *too* lofty, shelf after shelf of common novels, including all twenty-three volumes of La Calprenède's *Cléopâtre* and what looked like the complete works of Mademoiselle de Scudéry.

"Novels are very popular among the fae."

He would have recognized that clear, musical voice blindfolded. Galen turned and bowed deeply to the Queen of the Onyx Court. "Your Grace. I did not hear you come in."

She moved like a ghost, to approach unheard in the hush of the library. There had been others in here when he entered—an Irish lady he'd seen before, a mortal man who seemed to be the place's caretaker—but they had vanished, leaving him alone with the Queen.

Who looked ghostlike indeed in her white gown. She wore it for mourning, he knew; black was too common a color in this dark realm for it to carry the significance mortals gave it. Court rumor said she would wear it until she chose a Prince to replace the one who had recently died. Galen didn't know what had befallen Lord Hamilton; rumor had plenty to say about that, but none of it agreed with any of the rest. The man hadn't been seen in months, except by Lune's closest advisers, and then one day she told the court he was gone.

The Queen beckoned for him to follow, and led him away from the novels to one of the tables at the center of the library. Someone had moved a chair away so that it faced the open carpet, and here Lune settled herself, white skirts floating down like a cloud. There was no chair for Galen, but he wouldn't have felt comfortable taking one anyway. *She came here seeking me. Why?*

When he first came to the Onyx Hall, he'd counted himself lucky to glimpse the Queen from afar. He attended her court audiences as often as he could purely because they afforded him a chance to watch her, regal as sovereignty itself, seated upon her great silver throne. In the last few months, though, his luck had grown beyond measure: he'd been invited to attend upon her in the lesser presence chamber, or to escort her during an idle walk in the night garden. Thus he'd found that her mind was as great as her beauty, and turned often to varied subjects, from Britain's strife with France to the reception of the latest opera. Indeed, that was how he'd discovered the library; the Prince's valet, Edward Thorne, had told him that many newspapers and magazines could be found there. If Galen was to keep the Queen's interest, he needed to read more widely than his restricted allowance would permit.

Now this—a private audience . . .

She said, without preamble, "Mr. St. Clair, I have come here today to say something that may seem like a generous offer. I assure you it is not. Rather call it a favor—one I must beg of you, for the good of my court."

He had to be dreaming. God knew he'd dreamt this many times: Lune coming to him, some deed only he could accomplish, and then her gratitude . . . embarrassment and surprise made him fumble his reply. "Anything for I— that is, anything I can do for you, madam, I'll do without hesitation."

Her silver eyes were grave. "No, Mr. St. Clair. I want you to hesitate, for I want you to consider this with all due care. But I have come to offer you the title and office of Prince of the Stone."

It *was* a dream. Galen would have pinched himself, only he didn't want to wake up.

"You know the danger that threatens this realm," the Queen went on. "Whatever Prince stands at my side will be in peril; he cannot escape it. But without a Prince, I am weakened. The Onyx Hall needs both a mistress and a master. I have chosen you to replace Lord Hamilton, but the ultimate choice is yours. If the burden I would place on you is too great, you are free to refuse."

With every word she spoke, reality struck more strongly home. This was not a dream. She was truly here, and so was he, and she wanted him to be Prince of the Stone.

I'm not qualified.

He'd seen Lord Hamilton. A gentleman of about forty, with a sharp mind and connections throughout society; *that* was what a Prince should be. Not the twenty-year-old scion of an impoverished family, who had been in the Onyx Hall for scarcely a year.

Some fragment of that last thought must have escaped his lips, for Lune smiled. It was the first bright expression he'd seen on her face since Lord Hamilton's death. "You might be surprised to hear that you're far from the rawest newcomer to be elevated in this fashion. Other Princes have had less time. And they've done perfectly well."

But surely they were more prepared! He managed to keep that reply behind his teeth. Under no circumstances could the Queen be permitted to know his doubts.

If he was concerned about that . . . then he had already made up his mind.

Prepared or not, qualified or not, Lune had come to beg a favor of him. He would have cut off his left arm and given it to her if she asked; he could do this, too.

Belatedly, Galen sank to one knee. The sapphire toe of her shoe extended past the hem of her skirts, and upon this he fixed his gaze. "Your Grace, everything I am, everything I have, and everything I can do is at your disposal, now and forever. If you want me as your Prince, then I can do nothing but accept."

And pray I don't disappoint you.

The Onyx Hall, London: October 30, 1758

The sixteenth draft of Galen's intended speech to Delphia went into the fire along with its fifteen predecessors. How did one go about telling his wife-to-be that he consorted with faeries?

He was glad to be rescued by Edward Thorne, knocking at his study door. "The genie is here to see you," his valet said.

He shot to his feet. "Bring him in." As Abd ar-Rashid passed Edward, carrying a sheaf of papers, Galen added, "Oh, and summon Dr. Andrews—"

The genie held up a hand to forestall him. "If you please, O Prince, I would like first to speak to you. Alone."

The valet paused, looking to his master. Galen, though puzzled, nodded agreement. "Very well. Coffee, then, Edward. My lord, please, be seated."

He didn't ask how long the genie had been inside the Calendar Room. Few wanted to talk about it after the fact, whether it had been a month or ten years. Galen simply asked, "Can it be done?"

"That cannot be known, Lord Galen, without attempting the work directly. But yes—I believe it to be possible."

The philosopher's stone. Galen's heart skipped a beat. "How?"

Abd ar-Rashid rose and went to a nearby table, looking to Galen for permission. At his nod, the genie carried the table over to their chairs, so he could lay his papers out where they both could see. Diagrams and notes in multiple languages covered them, ranging from English to Latin and Greek and the incomprehensible scribble of Arabic. "The ultimate intention," Abd ar-Rashid said, "is what your alchemists have called the 'chemical wedding.' This, according to the writings of Jabir ibn Hayyan, is the joining of philosophic sulphur to philosophic mercury: two purified opposites, reconciled to one another, producing perfection."

His English had improved. Had the Arab really spared the time and attention within that room to better his command of the language? It made no difference for those waiting on the outside, and certainly there were days enough to spare, but it spoke volumes about the genie's dedication to his purpose. "And that perfection is the philosopher's stone," Galen said.

"Yes. Ordinarily the alchemist begins with some base substance, the *prima materia,* and this he subjects to many processes in his laboratory—from calcination to congelation." The genie pointed to a list on the second page. "He does this in order to obtain sophic sulphur and sophic mercury in their pure forms. Purity is necessary: without it, you have the same corrupt matter that all metals are made of, instead of the philosopher's stone."

"But we aren't working with metals."

"No. And that is why I wished to speak with you privately." Abd ar-Rashid settled back in his chair, folding his hands together like one at prayer. Like a Christian, at least; the genie regularly went above to carry out his scheduled prayers, five times a day, but Galen had never watched him at it. He had a difficult enough time understanding that this creature could be both a faerie and a worshipper of God—even the Mohammedan God.

Despite the detailed notes in front of him, Abd ar-Rashid seemed to have difficulty articulating his concern. "The notion of Dr. Andrews is that the Dragon is sophic sulphur. I think he may be correct. This allows you to escape the labor of purification—for one substance, at least. But you also need sophic mercury."

His reluctance was clear; the cause of it was not. "That is a challenge," Galen conceded, "but with the Calendar Room at our disposal, I'm sure we have the time to think of a suitable source—"

The Arab frowned more deeply. "I have already done so, Lord Galen. But I fear the answer is not one you wish to hear."

Galen stilled. After a moment, he said, "You needn't fear

any retribution from me, Lord Abd ar-Rashid, for anything you say. Tell me what you know, and we will continue from there."

The genie said, "Your Queen."

It was more unexpected than offensive. Galen had been thinking of the Thames; they said it was home to an old god, that fought the Dragon back in the days of the Great Fire. But no one had spoken with Father Thames since then, except perhaps the river fae, and maybe not even them. "Don't you need a spirit of water?"

"Water and earth are the elements associated with sophic mercury, yes. But it is also other things: feminine, for one. And also this." Abd ar-Rashid handed another paper to him with a bow. It held a sketch, copied with painstaking care from some old woodcut, showing a richly dressed man and woman joining hands. The symbolism of both figures was clear. "As philosophic sulphur is the sun king, so is mercury the moon queen."

Lune. They called her a daughter of the moon; for all Galen knew, it was literally true. She certainly looked the part. Abd ar-Rashid was right; that wasn't an answer Galen wished to hear. "She's already fought the Dragon once, sir, and been wounded badly for it. But no—we aren't talking of fighting, are we? So you would want to—"

It died in his throat. Abd ar-Rashid said, "As I understand it, sophic sulphur was obtained by cutting the heart of the Dragon from its body. The obvious answer would be to obtain sophic mercury the same way."

Galen set the paper down with excessive care. "Obvious, perhaps—but not acceptable." He'd promised not to punish the genie for speaking; he had to hold to that. Whatever he felt inside.

Abd ar-Rashid held up a mollifying hand. "And this is why I asked to speak in private, Lord Galen. Others will think of this. The image of the moon queen is widespread in European alchemy; no one can look into the matter without encountering it. And the connection to her Grace is clear. If it is not too presumptuous of me to say—be very cautious with whom you share this plan."

The door opened, and Galen almost jumped out of his skin. But it was only Edward, bringing in the tray with its coffee and bowls. Galen dismissed the valet and poured for himself and the genie both, needing the coffee to steady his own hands. "Thank you," he murmured, out of sheer habit. "I will. Be cautious, that is. You said this is a thing of European alchemy—does Arabic practice offer an alternative?"

"If it did, I would have presented it to you already," the genie said, with obvious regret.

Then they would have to find their own alternative. Some other source for the mercury, or a way to obtain it without harming Lune. Surely there would be something.

Galen burnt his tongue on the coffee, hissed in pain, and set it down. "May I see those papers?" Abd ar-Rashid handed them over with a bow. A quick perusal told him very little; his Latin and Greek were even rustier than his French, and the Arabic escaped him entirely. "Translate these for me, if you will. The original we will keep in strictest security; my copy will be shown only to a very few."

"Dr. Andrews?"

The man had such hopes for this plan. Galen could not blame him; the philosopher's stone was said to cure all ills. Including, perhaps, consumption. But under no circumstances would Galen allow Lune to come to harm. "I'll tell him myself. The Queen will decide what to say to the court as a whole."

The genie bowed again, accepting the papers back. "I trust to your wisdom, Lord Galen."

The Onyx Hall, London: October 31, 1758

After her visit to the Grecian, Irrith was ashamed to be offered a position among the Queen's ladies when they rode out on All Hallows' Eve.

It was an ancient tradition; not even the concerns of the Sanists, that it wasn't safe for Lune to absent herself from the Onyx Hall, could put a halt to it. All Hallows' Eve was one of the great nights of their year, and Lune had duties she must maintain. Tasking them to another would only create more fear than her departure from the palace ever could.

Riding with the Queen was the sacred part of the tradition, if that word could be used for a faerie activity. Others in the Onyx Court would find their own, coarser amusements. This was the dark mirror to Midsummer's gentle diversion. Black things would happen tonight, frights and horrors and hauntings, with the court's goblins leading the way. But while they entertained themselves in the streets, Lune and her companions would ride above, collecting the ghosts of the dead.

Hairy How, the Lord Treasurer, distributed bread to them all. Irrith ate hers slowly, feeling the mortal weight upon her tongue. Such labor went into it: the farmer in his field, planting and reaping the grain; the miller grinding it to flour; the country housewife mixing and kneading and baking it into bread. Or perhaps this was one of Dr. Andrews's tithed loaves, bought in a London marketplace, or carried from house to house by a street-seller. So many humans, doing so much work—and how many of them knew of the fae who ate the result?

A few more, if they looked up at the right moment tonight. But grand faerie spectacle had gone out of fashion with the Puritans; even now, when folk went rambling in the countryside on Sundays instead of attending church, it wasn't wise to draw too much attention. They would ride because the fae owed a duty to the dead, not because they wished to announce their presence to London.

"You'll have new chance to mock my riding skills tonight."

Irrith jumped. When the Queen rarely went anywhere without a host of attendants, it was easy to forget that she could move very quietly indeed. Lune stood behind Irrith, wearing a riding habit of black. She only wore the color on All Hallows' Eve. It cast a grim pall over her usual serenity.

A pall that was somewhat countered by the dog frolicking at her side. Teyrngar, a cream-coated faerie hound, knew full well what night it was, but the solemnity mattered less to him than the chance to run free. Smiling, Lune scratched behind his red ears.

With her good hand, of course. The left, as always, hung in

a stiffened claw. Irrith wondered if it hurt her, as the iron wound surely did.

Belatedly she remembered her manners and dropped into a curtsy. "I would never mock you, your Majesty."

Lune's smile turned wistful. "You used to. I confess a part of me misses it."

It was true that the Queen was a terrible rider. Living in the Onyx Hall, she rarely had cause to sit a horse. But the terrible weight of knowledge and doubt inside Irrith's head made her reluctant to open her mouth, for fear something might slip out that shouldn't.

"Ride alongside me," Lune said, taking Irrith's arm with her good hand. "Then you can catch me if I fall."

If she fell, it would be the fault of her mount. The tatterfoals and brags changed before they passed through the Old Fish Street arch into London, dropping to all fours and growing into horse shape. But the arch was too low to admit a rider, and so they went in pairs into the small courtyard outside, where the riders climbed astride and rode out onto the larger street. When their company had formed up, all thirteen riders and the hound, well masked by charms, Lune gave the command—and they leapt into the sky.

The surge took Irrith's breath away with delight. *It's been too long since I rode beneath the moon.* Not that there was any moon now; it was in its dark phase, and the ever-present clouds veiled the stars. The only real light came from London below, lanterns marking the better streets, candles burning late into the night. *Still. Free air—above the coal smoke for once—and a horse beneath me, and no politics to concern us.*

Old Fish Street was the easiest passage for horse-shaped beings, but they had to ride east to begin the night's work. Irrith marveled as she saw how far the city stretched: past the Tower, past the docks, houses stringing out along the river, the water clogged with ships at anchor. "Wapping," Lune said at one point, nodding downward; that was where Abd ar-Rashid lived. Though he was more in the Onyx Hall than not, lately—him and the mortal doctor both.

When they'd reached Lune's chosen point, she gave the command, and they turned westward once more. Irrith's gaze swept the ground below, seeking the telltale flickers that would indicate a ghost. A goblin in the Vale had said once this ritual was like a housewife sweeping her floor: it didn't get all the dirt, but without the effort, filth—or ghosts—would pile up until there was no living among them. With the number of people London held, she imagined they had more shades than most.

Cries rose from three throats at once, but Irrith was the first to move. Her horse swooped downward, carrying her with terrifying speed toward a dingy house. Irrith leaned sideways in her saddle, hand out, and concentrated as she skimmed over the battered roof tiles. Goblins were better at this than sprites, but she was here first, and she was determined not to miss.

A feeling snagged her fingers, like fog. She seized hold and wrenched upright, and when her mount leapt upward once more, a tattered wisp of white trailed from her fist. It moaned as she rejoined the company above, bearing their first catch of the night. "My child," the dead woman sobbed, face rippling in the wind. "Oh, my poor child, lost, lost . . ."

"What happened to your child?" Irrith asked, but the ghost showed no sign of hearing her.

"Few of them will converse," Lune said. The Queen made a regal figure on her white tatterfoal—so long as you ignored her good hand's desperate clutch on the reins. "The ones with that awareness often resist joining us, because they know they must go on at the end of the night."

Teyrngar dove to retrieve a second ghost. "What makes them stay?" Irrith asked, studying the ground once more. "Any of them—the ones we clear away each year, or the ones that go on haunting. These aren't *all* the dead mortals; we'd have to sweep the city every week for that." The children alone would form a train to the far horizon.

Lune shook her head, gazing out over the city with a melancholy air. "Any number of things. Love for kin who still remain—that seems the most common. Sometimes it's hatred instead, especially among those who were murdered. Or attachment to material things, their wealth or their home . . ."

anything a human cares passionately about can tie them to this world."

Riders flew up and down, harvesting the night's crop. Already they'd gathered enough ghosts that Irrith couldn't get an accurate count, and they were only now passing the Tower again, heading west. The eastern end of London had contained a great many specters. "Or interaction with faeries," Irrith said.

"Yes," Lune said softly. "Sometimes."

Thinking of her dead lover, no doubt. Irrith wished he'd had the consideration to die in the spring, further from All Hallows' Eve. Or to leave a ghost, so Lune would have him in some form.

She went down several times more, but the goblins, annoyed by her early victory, outraced her to most of the ghosts. Irrith ended up mostly riding by the Queen, sighting the shades for others to catch. After calling out three in quick succession, she said, "I've often wondered what it must be like, knowing there's something after death. Hell wouldn't be so pleasant, of course, but there's always the chance of Heaven—and maybe something, however bad, is better than nothing at all."

A howl snapped her attention downward. The fetch Nithen rode toward them, cackling, one hand dragging a struggling ghost by the scruff of his neck. That one, it seemed, was not happy to leave. Perhaps he knew he was destined for Hell.

She almost missed Lune's response in all the noise. "They say, you know—some scholars do—that not all faerie souls come to an end when their life does. That some go onward, though where, they do not know: perhaps Heaven or Hell, or the deep reaches of Faerie, or somewhere else entirely."

Curious, Irrith asked, "Do you believe it?"

"I do."

They were no longer riding in a straight line along the river; with London stretching so far north, they had to make gentle bends, sweeping the city and even crossing into Southwark. Their ghostly horde grew ever larger. Lune tried turning to survey their ranks, but quit when she slipped in her saddle. "I've seen it happen—at least, I think so. The faerie in question vanished, so who can say what happened to her. But I believe her spirit continued on."

Irrith had heard the stories, but dismissed them as—well, as mortals dismissed stories of faeries. Charming fictions. Then again, faeries were not fictions, so perhaps their continuance wasn't, either. But this wasn't the certainty mortals had, one of two choices, or maybe Purgatory if the Catholics were right. It was a true mystery, with nothing but guesses to light the path, and all of those guesses possibly wrong. Maybe there was nothing for the fae but black void, the end of all existence.

"Which would you choose?" Irrith asked. They were crossing above the western city now, from the hovels of Seven Dials to the townhouses of Grosvenor Square. She wondered who left more ghosts, the poor or the wealthy. The poor died in greater numbers, certainly, but who clung harder to this world?

The Queen bent her head until her chin almost touched the black shadow of her riding jacket. "Sometimes I envy the mortals their assurance of continuation. But when I am weary, then I think it preferable to end as we do—a true end, with nothing after. Rest at last."

Valentin Aspell's voice whispered in memory, saying, *a sacrifice*.

Weariness. Had it worn on Lune so much she would welcome that end? Especially if it would save her people?

Irrith suddenly wished she'd never come out this night, never accepted Lune's invitation to ride at her side. And she spared an additional wish that they'd been riding sticks of transformed straw instead, rather than two faeries who had no doubt been eavesdropping on this entire conversation.

Fortunately, they were almost done. Lune had timed their ride well, no doubt from centuries of experience: as they flew above Hyde Park, leaving the habitations of London behind, distant church bells began to toll. Twelve strokes for midnight, and Irrith twisted in her saddle to watch as behind them, the ghosts began to fade away. Their mighty host, a thick veil of white, thinned and fluttered apart, voices whispering their last. *He'll regret. Remember me. My child . . .*

Then the thirteen fae and their mounts were alone in the night sky, with Teyrngar loping a circle around them, and it was All Saints' Day.

"What would you choose, Irrith?" The Queen patted her mount's neck with her crippled hand, and he turned homeward. "I doubt He would permit us into Heaven, but if you had a choice between the torments of Hell, or nothing whatsoever."

Irrith didn't even have to think about it. "Hell. Anything's more interesting than just *stopping*."

Lune's smile shone briefly in the night. "I am not surprised. Well, fate willing, you will not face that choice soon."

The Onyx Hall, London: November 3, 1758

Despite the press of time, Galen hesitated to tell anyone what Abd ar-Rashid had said. He had James Cole, the mortal keeper of the Onyx Court's library, dig out what old alchemical manuscripts they possessed, and lost himself in a welter of incomprehensible symbolism: green lions and dragon's teeth, playing children and mating dogs, severed heads and homunculi and strange hermaphrodites. He could make little sense of it, but the genie was right on one count; the image of the moon queen appeared again and again.

In the end, there was nothing he could do but tell Lune. She listened in silence, and when he was done, merely said, "We should discuss this with Dr. Andrews."

Summoning him would invite an audience of courtiers, or else avid whispers when Lune sent them away; instead, the Queen and Prince went to his laboratory. Since their conversation a few weeks before, the doctor had set up an entire table full of pendulums, whose purpose Galen could not begin to guess.

Andrews himself looked like a corpse that had not slept in a week, but febrile vitality shone in his eyes as he came forward to greet them. "You've come at a happy time—I have something to show you."

Heedless of Galen's half-voiced protest, the doctor hurried over to the table. "I've weighted these bobs differently, with different substances," Andrews said, "and timed them against that clock." He nodded at a regulator positioned on the wall behind. "It's a repetition of an experiment Newton performed in the early 1680s, which caused him to discard his notion of aether. Let me show you—"

It was clear he wouldn't be easily diverted, but he could be sped along. "You needn't repeat the experiment again," Galen said. "We trust your work. Just tell us your conclusion."

"Aether *does* exist."

Lune stood a short distance away, hands gently clasped against her skirts. "I fear I haven't Lord Galen's education, Dr. Andrews. What does that mean?"

"Aether," he repeated, pronouncing the word clearly. "Said by Aristotle to be the fifth element, the *quintessence*. At the time that Newton performed this experiment, the thought was that aether existed everywhere, penetrating all solid things. His pendulums showed that it did not. *My* pendulums show that it does."

Galen understood his point—to an extent. "Another facet of reality that's different in faerie spaces. But what is the significance?"

"Faerie spaces! Exactly, Mr. St. Clair. I propose—though I've had little time to think it through; I've only just finished the calculations for the pendulums—that it is the presence of aether which *defines* faerie spaces, and differentiates them from ordinary ones. And furthermore, it may resolve a conundrum I've been pondering for some time now."

His voice, Galen noticed, was lighter than it had been, as if Andrews were speaking using only his throat, not the resonance of his chest. A sign of the man's agitated excitement? Or a symptom of his worsening illness? *I fear we'll lose him before we're done. I would fear to lose him at all, but I'm not sure it can be avoided—not by any means short of the philosopher's stone.*

"The Dragon," Andrews said, recalling Galen to himself, "is a spirit of fire. So people have told me on many occasions. And I've heard the tale of its exile, the light of its heart being projected onto the comet. But what of its body? Is it a spirit, or a creature?"

Lune, the only one of them who had seen it with her own eyes, said, "It had a body. What we placed in the prison was its heart."

"Then what was its body composed of?" Andrews asked. "If the spirit is fire, and if those elements obtain in this world—"

"Aether." Now Galen saw what he aimed at. "You think faerie bodies are aethereal."

"They could be. The transmission of your Dragon to the comet could, I think, have given it an airy component, which is why I judge it to be sophic sulphur, which shares the qualities of fire and air. And at present—if I am right—it is fire and air *without* aether, for it is without a body." Andrews's vitality seemed to drain away all at once. His hand groped vaguely in the air; then he turned, searched, and found a chair next to his main working table, into which he sank with a sigh. "But we have only one half of the equation. We still need sophic mercury."

Galen wished—rather childishly—that Lune would be the one to tell him about their concerns. But no; this was his responsibility, and he knew it. "That is what we came for, Dr. Andrews. There is . . . a difficulty."

He paced a few steps, made himself stop, and clasped his hands behind his back. "If what you say is correct, then we must separate the principle from its aethereal component— yes? But the only established method for doing so would kill the source. And that isn't acceptable."

"The source . . ." Andrews's fingers curled into the stained handkerchief they held. "Mr. St. Clair—have you found one?"

"Abd ar-Rashid believes he has," Galen answered, each word coming out leaden with reluctance.

"Where?"

He couldn't say it. Tension rendered him mute. Lune, motionless where she stood, did it for him. "In me."

Andrews shot to his feet and staggered, off balance, before catching himself against the table. "You— Ah, yes, it *would* be feminine, I suppose—"

"It is the moon queen," she said, and her hair seemed to

shine brighter with the words, as if to make her point. "Matched with the sun king. I know a little of alchemy, from old experience, and I believe the genie is right."

"But we can't do it," Galen said, finding his tongue once more. "At least, not in the same manner as the Dragon. There are two things you must understand, Dr. Andrews. The first is that no one—*no one*—can be permitted to hear of this. We three know, and Abd ar-Rashid, but even the rest of the scholars must be kept in the dark. Our problems are not merely intellectual, but also political; the danger of this news is very great."

The doctor nodded, clearly only half-attending to Galen's words. "The second," Galen went on, more forcefully still, "is that we will *not* proceed with any attempt to create the philosopher's stone unless we have devised a way to extract this principle without harming her Grace. Or for that matter, any other faerie, should a substitute be found. Do you understand?"

Andrews's eyes cleared of their fog, and this time his nod was more sincere—but also hesitant. "I do, Mr. St. Clair. Your Majesty. If I may, ah, present a certain argument, though . . ."

"You may always speak," Lune assured him. "We brought you here for your thoughts; they are of no use to anyone if not shared."

He twisted his bony hands around one another and began to wander, stepping on his fallen handkerchief as he went. "The philosopher's stone is more than a means of creating gold. It is perfection, and it *creates* perfection. It has the potential to heal every gouty gentleman in Westminster, every fever-stricken child in Seven Dials—to transform our society into a veritable paradise on earth.

"At the present moment, we have, or believe we have, one half of what is needed, which—if true—is further than any alchemist has likely got since the world began. Nor is it some tiny spark of a salamander's heart, either: it is a *Dragon*. One stripped of its body, which has voyaged through space itself. A purity and power unmatched by any other."

He paused for breath, and Galen spoke into the gap. "You

believe this to be, not just a chance to make the philosopher's stone, but our *only* chance."

Andrews managed a faint laugh. "As much as I can be sure of anything, which is not much. But yes—if it can be done at all, I think it can be done now. And perhaps not ever again. And madam . . ." The beseeching in his face was painful to see. "Is that not an achievement worthy of sacrifice?"

For the briefest instant, Galen thought he saw a glitter in Andrews's eyes. A strange light, that saw beyond reality—even the reality of a faerie palace—into visions of that which was not. Only a touch, the merest whisper of madness . . . but it was there.

Or perhaps Galen imagined it, because the alternative was too dreadful to contemplate. That a man, in full possession of his sanity, might suggest that Lune sacrifice her life.

He could not bear to look at Lune, and therefore heard only her voice, as cool and unruffled as ever. "Dr. Andrews—this is still no more than speculation. You can craft a pretty argument that alchemy works in this realm, and that the Dragon is your sulphur; but we have no certainty that it's true."

To Galen's relief, Andrews nodded, with no sign of mad delusion. "This was the flaw of Aristotle; he and his brethren thought the world could be understood by reasoning alone, without need of experimental testing. Our situation is unfortunately complicated by the impossibility of proper tests; when the Dragon comes, we will have only a single chance to transform it. I'm aware of the uncertainty, madam, and will do everything I can to reduce it. But I beg you—as abominable as it is of me to say this—please consider what we stand to gain."

Galen's mouth had gone dry. It wasn't madness, as much as he wished it were. If their reasoning proved correct, then the benefit would be incalculable.

But so would the cost.

Hating himself for that thought, Galen finally turned to Lune. Speaking as much to her as to the doctor, he said, "But we *will* find another way. That, Dr. Andrews, is what the experimentation is for. Like miners, we will draw the metal from the ore." He cursed his choice of metaphor the instant it left his mouth, as his imagination supplied him with reminders of smelting. The ore did not survive the process unharmed.

Still, Andrews nodded. His expression had gone thoughtful again. "It will be difficult, Mr. St. Clair, to work on that matter without the assistance of your scholars. Two mortal men and one heathen faerie—we aren't likely to get far on our own."

Lady Feidelm, Wrain, Savennis. More distantly, the von das Tickens and Ktistes. Lune moved for the first time since she had entered, studying the room; not the furnishings, but the walls and fittings. "We can ensure that nothing said in here will be overheard. I would keep the number to a minimum— only those that work with you here. That, I think, will be safe enough."

So not the dwarves or the centaur. Galen wondered it if was mere accident that excluded the foreigners. *Well, Lady Feidelm is Irish. She has been here longer, though, and proved her loyalty to this court.* And Abd ar-Rashid—but they could hardly leave him out, when he was the one who pointed to the moon queen in the first place.

"Be careful," Galen said, bowing to necessity. "And work fast. The sooner we have an alternative, the safer we will all be."

And not only against the Dragon.

The Onyx Hall, London: November 14, 1758

Irrith only rarely attended court. The pageantry could be amusing at times, but the business Lune conducted during that time interested her very little. It was, however, the one place she could be sure of finding Valentin Aspell—aside from his chambers, and visiting him there would draw far too much attention.

The greater presence chamber, when she arrived, seemed much emptier than she recalled. Even a full court, summoning everyone in the Onyx Hall, didn't really fill the enormous

space, but the assembled lords and ladies seemed like a handful of dice rattling around in an oversized box. Leaning over
to Segraine, who was not on duty today, Irrith whispered,
"Where is everyone?"

The lady knight shook her head almost imperceptibly.
"Fewer every time. Some are still in the city, but drawing back;
others have gone entirely."

As Carline had predicted they would. And the comet hadn't
even been sighted yet.

Lune called forward Sir Peregrin, the Captain of the Onyx
Guard. Four knights followed him, carrying a long, narrow
box, which they placed on the floor when they knelt. The
captain said, "Your Majesty, the yarthkin Hempry has hafted
a piece of the jotun ice to length of ash." He gestured, and the
knights uncovered the box, revealing an enormously long pike,
its end glinting with the same near-invisible material Irrith had
seen them wrestling with a year ago. "I have selected these
four to be your spear-knights: Sir Adenant, Sir Thrandin, Sir
Emaus, and my lieutenant Sir Cerenel. They will stand ready
to do battle with the Dragon, and to stab it through its fiery
heart, for the defense of the Onyx Hall."

The Dragon might or might not have a body when it returned, but it *would* have a heart; that much, they were certain of. Lune thanked the spear-knights and made a speech
Irrith didn't bother listening to. She waited impatiently until
court was adjourned, then drifted in Aspell's direction, knowing better than to run straight for him. Still, the Lord Keeper
glared when she drew near. "I am quite busy, Dame Irrith."

"I have something to tell you," she whispered. He was the
one who brought her into this; if her inability to skulk well
bothered him, it was his own damned fault.

His thin-lipped mouth barely moved in response. "Crow's
Head. Two hours."

For a meeting like this, it was probably the safest place in
the Onyx Hall, given the copies of *The Ash and Thorn* scattered around. And it wouldn't be easy to slip spies past
Hafdean, the surly hob who kept the place. Irrith, lacking a
pocket-watch, went early, and sat beneath the preserved human head mounted prominently on the wall. Magrat wasn't

in her usual place. Perhaps the church grim was off haunting some religious folk.

Eventually Hafdean nudged her in passing. Irrith hadn't seen Aspell come in, nor anyone under a glamour, but she wasn't surprised; she went through a door at the back of the main room and found herself in a small chamber that undoubtedly had another, hidden exit. Aspell was there, pacing. "You had best not make a habit of this, Dame Irrith. What do you want?"

"To tell you something Lune isn't making public," Irrith said, ignoring the insult in his tone. "I think only she and the Prince know about this." Galen had brought it up while they lay in bed together, not so much conversing with Irrith as talking at her, voicing his fears like that would exorcise them. "Do you know what Dr. Andrews has been up to?"

The Lord Keeper waved dismissively. "Some mortal thing, involving experiments and calculations. Savennis and those other bookish sorts are helping him."

As she'd suspected. The Queen was keeping this very quiet indeed. But Aspell needed to know, so he wouldn't do anything rash.

Irrith explained to him about the philosopher's stone, as well as she understood it. "It isn't ready yet; they need the other half, this mercury, and apparently that will be difficult to create. Still, it's different from anything anybody's thought of in the last fifty years, and I think it's more likely to work than those bloody spear-knights."

Aspell's pacing had halted while she spoke; now he leaned against the dirty wall and crossed his arms. "And you are telling me this because . . ."

"Because you need to know they *do* have a plan. Not to trap or kill the Dragon, but to *change* it. That's better than— than what you were talking about. Before." Even in the Crow's Head—perhaps especially in the Crow's Head—she didn't feel comfortable naming it directly.

He seemed amused. "So you've brought me this confidence in order that I might know we have other hopes. And therefore not pursue this one too far?"

"Yes!" she said angrily, hands tightening into fists. "You

said it was a last resort; I'm telling you we have others that can come before it."

His thin mouth hardened into a stone line. "Dame Irrith, I think you fail to understand something very important: if it *does* come to that extremity, we shall have little or no time in which to act. A last resort is, by its nature, the thing one does when the alternative is immediate disaster. We cannot abandon our preparations unless there is a *surety* of success with some other plan—and in truth, not even then, for this is too great a threat to admit of complacency."

For all the soundness of his argument, it still produced a queasy feeling in Irrith's stomach. "What preparations, though? You said you would do nothing against the Queen's will."

"Indeed." He drew close, much closer than she liked, and dropped his voice so not even the sharpest-eared goblin at the keyhole could have overheard what he said next. "You already know what I mean, Dame Irrith. The Queen must agree to sacrifice herself. And if she is to do that in time to save London, then it must not come as a surprise; her mind must be prepared for the idea. When the choice comes, there will be no time for explanations or arguments."

Cold ran down Irrith's back as if someone had poured the deepest, blackest waters of the Thames over her head. He was right—and right that she already knew. After all, what had that conversation with Lune on All Hallows' Eve been, if not an attempt to raise the specter of death in Lune's mind?

She whispered, "Galen would never let her. He loves Lune too much. He'd die before he let harm come to her."

"Can he be prepared?"

To give up Lune? Not a chance. So she might lose them both: Lune, in trying to save the city, and Galen, in trying to save *her*.

It felt like someone had placed iron bands around her heart. She didn't want to lose either one. Even wounded, Lune still commanded Irrith's respect and admiration; were it not for those two physical flaws, Irrith would have no desire to see her replaced. Who else could balance out this lunatic court, faeries and mortals and ambassadors from distant lands?

But it did little good to save the Queen and lose her court.

"So you want me to make certain she's thought about this. Before the Dragon comes."

"You are close to her," Aspell said, still in that all-but-silent murmur. "And she respects your honesty. If you say it to her, she will listen. She may not agree—not immediately—but the idea will stay in her mind."

Irrith thought he held her influence in much too high esteem; she wouldn't call herself "close" to Lune. But it couldn't hurt to try. If they found some better way, then Lune would never have to face that choice at all.

"Very well," she muttered, staring blindly at her toes. "I'll do what I can." *Let him think I mean only what he asked for.*

She would speak to Lune, yes. The rest of her time, she would spend in the Temple of Arms, training to battle the Dragon. If it came to Lune sacrificing herself, it would only be after Irrith had done everything possible to prevent it.

I don't know that I'm willing to die to protect her. But by Ash and Thorn, I'm willing to fight.

The Onyx Hall, London: November 21, 1758

Abd ar-Rashid had gone into the Calendar Room again, to contemplate ways of obtaining sophic mercury without danger to Lune; he would not emerge for eleven days. Lune herself spent half her waking hours with the Goodemeades, using their countless connections of friendship to persuade undecided faeries to stay. Neither of these were matters Galen could help with, and Dr. Andrews had gone back to Red Lion Square for a much needed respite.

In that brief lull, Galen decided that he had put a certain matter off for much too long, and went in search of Irrith.

He found her at last in the Temple of Arms, where he was not looking for her; the sprite was friends with Dame Segraine, and he thought the lady knight might know where to find her. He was startled instead to discover Irrith practicing against the musket targets, with her mouth set in a fierce grimace.

The masters of the Temple had long since taken the stance that the clever folk of the court could prepare all the tricks and traps they liked; *they* would stand ready for battle, and would train anyone else who wished to do the same. If all else failed, the Onyx Court would have this last line of defense, the bodies and sword arms of its bravest subjects.

Or musket hands, as the case might be. Elfshot, their usual ammunition, would do no good against the Dragon; they used it for practice, but when the time came it would be iron balls they sent into their enemy's flesh. No one held out much hope that it would do more than annoy the creature that had once destroyed its iron prison. Still, that annoyance might be used to create openings for the spear-knights and their icy blade.

The black powder reek clogged his throat, but he waited until Irrith had finished her current shot. The sprite bit the end off a cartridge, poured some powder into the pan of her musket, dropped the rest of the cartridge down the barrel, rammed it home, then cocked and lifted her weapon. Galen timed her surreptitiously through this operation: nearly thirty seconds. Not nearly up to the standards of a soldier. And, judging by her deepening scowl as she lowered the gun, she knew it.

He laid one hand on her shoulder; with all the musket fire from herself and those around her, she would be half-deaf. Irrith jumped far enough to make him glad he'd waited until her gun was empty, then saw him and followed his beckoning hand, out of the practice ground.

"Didn't you once say to me that you had no intention of fighting?" he asked, once they were in the quieter space of the armory.

A curious mixture of determination and guilt answered him. "I'm no good with your alchemy," Irrith said, and laid aside her musket for cleaning. "This at least gives me something to do."

Galen smiled. "In that case, I have something that might be more suited to your talents."

The hope that blazed up in her eyes dimmed when he continued, "It has nothing to do with the comet. But if I don't follow through on this now, I fear I'll lose my courage; and I will need help to do it the way I would like to."

Irrith eyed him suspiciously. "To do what?"

"To tell Miss Philadelphia Northwood," Galen said, "about the Onyx Court."

Hyde Park, Westminster: December 1, 1758

Not even the first nibblings of winter's wind could keep the fashionable away from Hyde Park, one of their preferred stages for displaying themselves to the admiration of their rivals and lessers. From her perch in a tree, Irrith could hear the distant clatter of carriages, most of them circling the Ring in the center of the park. Try though she might, she could not see the appeal of that pastime; they went 'round and 'round like spinning tops, for no other purpose than to show off their conveyances and horses and footmen. In weather such as this, there would be no fashion of dress to see, and little conversation. Why waste the time?

I suppose that *is the point—to waste time, because one has it to spare.* Irrith sneered at that extravagance even as she envied it. The creeping tension of the Onyx Hall had infected her so thoroughly she chafed at anything that seemed a diversion from their task. Like playing games with the Prince's future wife.

Which was the thought that made her agree to help. If playing games with a mortal seemed like a waste of time, then Irrith had fallen far indeed.

So she sat in a tree just north of the Serpentine's cold waters on this bleak December day, waiting for the approach of a particular carriage.

Blast Galen anyway. The plan he'd described to her was a farce, one she was embarrased to take part in. Irrith dangled her legs off the branch, careless of the icy air, and decided she would do this her own way. And if that frightened off Delphia Northwood . . . well, then the woman wouldn't last long in the Onyx Hall anyway.

The Hyde Park setting gave her a good idea, too.

The rattle of wheels stopped the swing of her legs. Peeking through the leaves, Irrith saw a carriage approaching along the rough path that followed the north bank of the Serpentine. Already it was quite close; she had to hurry, throwing on a suitable glamour before dropping light as a leaf onto the ground below. Then she ran out in front of the carriage and flung one hand up in imperious command.

The horses shied very satisfyingly. The man holding their reins swore, then flinched at his own ill manners, which would not be appreciated by the ladies inside. Irrith grinned at him. By all appearances the driver was a servant of Mrs. Vesey's, but that was as much a lie as her own seeming; beneath the illusion, it was Edward Thorne. Galen thought it better to keep this entire affair in the hands of those who knew what it was about. The only one here today who did *not* know was Miss Northwood.

Who might or might not be the future Mrs. St. Clair. Right now, that was in Irrith's hands.

"You, out of the road," Edward called in a loud voice, and shook the reins. He did a remarkably good job of making it sound like he was trying to goad the horses onward, but it was a great deal of noise for very little effect, and the animals weren't going anywhere until Irrith told them to. He gave her an uncertain frown, though. Galen had given very specific instructions, and one of those had been that the stranger who stopped them in Hyde Park would be a woman.

Irrith flicked her long coat as she dropped into a grand bow, hat over her heart. Then she stuck her tongue out at Edward, in case he hadn't yet guessed that she hid under the masculine glamour. But she had to straighten her expression hastily when Miss Northwood's wide-hooded head poked out one carriage window, looking to see what the problem was.

Her eyes went very wide when she saw Irrith.

The sprite paced with deliberate strides past Edward, who by then had assumed a posture of blank, unseeing trance, as per the Prince's instructions. Miss Northwood drew back in fear, and murmured something half-audible to her companion in the carriage. A moment later Irrith drew level, and opened the door to find Mrs. Vesey prepared to play her part.

"Ladies," Irrith said, with a courteous bow, "I apologize for troubling you. But at noon today I am bound to appear in a meadow of this park and face my mortal enemy in a duel, and if I am to have any hope of defeating him, I must bear the good luck of a maiden's kiss."

She wished she had a mirror in which to see her own glamour. For this, she had added every detail she could think of: a man's suit all of green; hair as silver as Lune's; a fresh hawthorn blossom growing out of her buttonhole, ignoring the December chill.

And a face that, while not her own, was as faerie a face as any in the Onyx Hall.

Miss Northwood appeared to be staring at the exaggerated point of her ear. Mrs. Vesey said, in a tone of artful regret, "Oh, good sir, I would—but I was wed many years ago. Delphia, my dear—"

The young woman startled like a cat, and stared wildly at Mrs. Vesey. "What?"

"A kiss for the gentleman," her friend reminded her. "So he may win his duel."

She was supposed to be a woman, begging a pin to keep her tiny faerie cows from straying. This was Hyde Park, though, where men held their illegal duels, and that was far more interesting of a story. Fortunately, Mrs. Vesey adapted quickly. Miss Northwood, on the other hand . . .

The brief flash of her tongue over her lips betrayed the young woman's uncertainty. Still, Irrith had to grant the strength of her nerves when she said, "Sir, I fear you are not human."

"No, I'm not," Irrith agreed cheerfully.

Even though it was obvious to see, the admission made Miss Northwood's eyes widen. "How—how am I to know that you deserve to win your duel?"

Delight began to tickle Irrith's heart. Let Carline collect the beautiful people; Irrith preferred the ones with spirit. "Does it matter?" she asked. "I'll grant you good luck in return for for your kiss, and the outcome of the duel is hardly any concern of yours."

"It *does* matter," Miss Northwood insisted, eyes darting to Mrs. Vesey in a desperate plea for either confirmation or assistance, possibly both. "I should not want to help you win if you don't deserve to. And to ask a *kiss*," she added, warming to her topic. "It's very inappropriate, sir; I do not know you."

Perhaps the pin would have been the better course after all. Irrith floundered for a reply. She'd done all she needed to, really; the notion was to have Miss Northwood encounter faeries, and then for Mrs. Vesey to admit calmly to their existence, whereupon the young woman would be advised to speak with Galen, as if he hadn't arranged it all himself. Far too complicated, in Irrith's opinion, but he'd learned his lesson too firmly after Dr. Andrews: faeries first, explanations later.

But she refused to give up so easily. She'd asked for a kiss, and she would get one. "It need only be on the cheek," Irrith said. "I am a gentleman, I assure you. As for your doubts about my honor . . ."

Well, she'd eaten bread. That wouldn't make this enjoyable, but at least it wouldn't hurt her. "If either of you ladies has a cross about you?"

Mrs. Vesey's eyes widened. She looked to Miss Northwood, and Miss Northwood looked to her; both of them shook their heads. *This modern age,* Irrith thought, caught between annoyance and amusement. *Time was, you couldn't throw a rock without hitting someone with a cross.* Resigned, she said, "I was *going* to swear on a cross that I intend no harm this day to anyone who doesn't deserve it. But you've spoiled my plan—and, I might add, quite spoiled this meeting, which was supposed to be a brief and mysterious encounter. Look, a magical stranger in Hyde Park! But no, you had to *argue.*"

She glanced up to find the most extraordinary expression on Miss Northwood's face. It turned out to be laughter, bubbling up out of the young woman's throat and lighting her eyes. Even Mrs. Vesey began to chuckle. Edward Thorne sat very still, but Irrith could tell he was dying to turn and say something.

"Here." Miss Northwood leaned forward and planted a brief kiss on Irrith's cheek. "For your luck, and I am sorry that I don't know how to behave properly when accosted by a faerie."

Irrith mock-frowned at her. "Serve you right if I gave you no reward. But you've amused me, and for that I'll give you two things. One, when you return home, you'll find your favorite rosebush in bloom. Second, I will bless your dreams, miss, that you may find happiness in them." And she swept Miss Northwood a grand bow.

"Thank you," the young woman said gravely.

Not anything like Lune. Nor, for that matter, like me. But Irrith could see why Galen had chosen her—and, though it made her teeth hurt to admit it, she couldn't fault the choice.

In which case, this encounter deserved to end properly, even if the middle had gone awry. Irrith vanished herself before their eyes, then patted Edward Thorne's leg in passing as she stole away, behind the tree in which she'd hidden before. She listened as he came out of his "trance" and called out to the ladies; Mrs. Vesey reassured him, and then they drove onward, leaving Irrith to guess at the conversation that ensued.

Not at all what Galen had intended. But it would do the work.

And I have to get to Rose House, or that bush will be a sore disappointment when Miss Northwood goes looking.

Leicester Fields, Westminster: December 2, 1758

"Oh, thank *goodness* you're home this morning." Cynthia hurried across Galen's bedroom, with free disregard for her brother's half-dressed state and Edward's meaningful cough. "You're needed downstairs. Delphia has called upon me, but you're the one she wants to speak to, only she can't call upon you and have it be proper. Mama, thank Heaven, is out with Daphne, and I can make Irene be silent; so long as you are quick, Papa will never know. But you must come downstairs *now*." Edward coughed again. "After you've put some clothes on, of course."

Galen sat blear-eyed and staring at the carpet through her entire speech. *Damnation. Too soon!* The plan was for Mrs. Vesey to arrange a visit at her house, where they could speak in greater safety—and even that had worried him enough that he'd scarcely slept last night. But Miss Northwood, it seemed, was too impatient to wait.

Unless she didn't intend conversation. Perhaps she'd come to Leicester Fields to cry off their betrothal.

That thought jolted him to unpleasant wakefulness. Edward was already there, with a shirt and breeches and everything else he needed; Galen was at present wearing only a set of drawers. Cynthia, blushing a little, retired to let him dress. Galen hurried everything on, with such speed that he almost went out without his wig; fortunately, his valet was more alert than he.

At the door to the parlor, he stopped and tried to slow his heartbeat. But the pounding refused to answer to the commands of his will, and so it still shook his ribs when he walked in and found Delphia Northwood waiting on the settee with his sister.

"I'll see to Irene," Cynthia said with a mischievous giggle, and slipped past Galen. What she thought they intended, he could only imagine; surely it fell far short of the truth. Whichever truth that might be.

What did a woman look like when she had made up her mind to cry off? He had no idea. Miss Northwood was letting nothing slip; the firm clasp of her gloved hands upon each other could have indicated anything at all. He stood in awkward silence, not knowing what he could possibly say.

Seen any faeries lately?

Are we still betrothed?

Chilly morning, isn't it?

Miss Northwood said, "Did you arrange that incident now so I would have time to find a way out of this marriage?"

Galen's heart attempted to leap straight out of his mouth. It took him three tries to swallow it back down. Then he said, unsteadily, "I suppose it would be foolish of me to pretend I did *not* arrange it."

"Yes. It would." She rose, hands still clasped tight, and then stopped as if she did not know where to go. "Why did you do it?"

He looked down. There was a small muddy scuff in the carpet just ahead of his left foot, not fresh; the maid should have cleaned that away. "I wanted you to know because it seemed unfair to leave you in ignorance of the greater part of my life. It happened now because yes, I thought you should have the opportunity to escape if you wished to. And I arranged it in such roundabout fashion because . . ." The words clogged in his throat. "Because I could not imagine sitting in Mrs. Vesey's parlor and explaining it all to you, as if I were lecturing on some foreign land. I wanted you to see. And I thought that would be a safe way to do it, for if you were terrified by the experience, then Mrs. Vesey would tell you nothing, and I would know this is not something I could ever share with you."

But Mrs. Vesey *had* told her, clearly. That gave him a tiny bit of hope.

Her sudden exhalation made him realize she had been holding her breath. "How very characteristic," Miss Northwood said, and sat down hard precisely where she had been before.

"Characteristic?" Galen said, daring to lift his gaze.

She met it with a rueful smile. "Of you. At Sothings Park you said you were a romantic, and I see that it's true. A gentleman all in green, a duel in Hyde Park . . . much more interesting, I suppose, than a lecture in Mrs. Vesey's parlor. Though that came later, once we had driven back."

Gentleman? Duel? What in Mab's name did Irrith do? Galen hadn't gone to the Onyx Hall last night, too nervous to hear the tale. Well, whatever the disobedient sprite had done, it achieved this much; it showed Delphia what she must see, and Mrs. Vesey had told her what she must know.

Now the decision was hers.

He came forward to kneel at her feet, but not too close. "This is the business that occupies me, Delphia. It will occupy me until the day I die. There is a great deal that even Mrs. Vesey doesn't know, which I'll tell you about, if you want to hear; some of it is not so pleasant. But all the secrets in my life arise from this one. If you want no part of it—if you prefer a husband whose secrets are of a more ordinary kind—then say so now, and we will end our betrothal. I will help you find a way to avoid Mr. Beckford's son."

Miss Northwood's fingers curled in at the name. Then they relaxed, one slow degree at a time.

"No, Mr. St Clair. I will marry you still—on one condition."

"Name it," Galen breathed.

She caught and held his gaze, and in her eyes he saw both steely determination and a hint of joyous curiosity. "That the secret belong to me as well as you. Take me to the Onyx Hall."

The Onyx Hall, London: December 8, 1759

Ever since ascending to the rank of Prince, Galen had rarely spared the time to really look at the faerie palace that consumed so much of his life. Though he spent long hours there, he almost never took notice of the place itself; he was too busy debating theories with the scholars, reporting to Lune, occasionally dallying with Irrith. His surroundings were of little import, compared with his concerns.

Delphia made him see it through new eyes.

Everything was a wonder to her, from the swift but gentle drop of the Newgate entrance to the grandeur of the greater presence chamber. She marveled at the sleek elegance of the black stone, that never seemed to show any wear; she delighted in the faerie lights that followed in her wake. Even the most grotesque of the court's goblins failed to discompose her. Of course, those she encountered were on their best behavior; Lune had seen to that. But their faces alone would have been enough to frighten any young woman with less steel at her core.

He presented her to the Queen, in the more intimate environment of Lune's privy chamber. Lune received her kindly,

showing no hint of impatience at her Prince's decision to
spend time on this matter. Galen himself said little. Some
cruel bit of wit on Fate's part—or perhaps Irrith's—had put
the sprite in attendance upon the royal person that day. *The
woman I love, the woman I am promised to, and the woman
I am bedding, all in one chamber. I suppose I have no one to
blame but myself.*

He declined Irrith's offer to accompany them on their tour
of the Hall. What mischief she had in mind, he didn't know,
and didn't want to discover. Instead he and Delphia walked
alone—truly alone, without even Edward to attend them.
"Your valet comes here with you?" she asked, surprised, and
he explained about the man's faerie father.

"It makes matters easier," he said, as they approached the
Hall of Figures, where the gems of the Onyx Hall's statuary
were kept. "I have chambers here in the palace, and often stay
in them; if you've heard Cynthia complain of my absences,
that is why. Having one valet who can attend me in both
worlds is simpler than managing two. The servants who maintain my quarters are faeries, though."

"Perhaps I—" Delphia began, then lost the rest of it in a
gasp. They stood at the top of a half flight of stairs, which
gave a splendid view of the long gallery, lined on both sides
with statues. Some, in imitation of mortal habit, had been pil-
laged from Italy and Greece. Others were older and cruder, or
simply stranger, taken from no land or time Galen knew of.
He'd never liked this place; the frozen ranks of figures un-
nerved him too much. But Delphia, seeing them for the first
time, was entranced.

Then he realized her eyes were fixed on the far end of the
gallery, where stairs led up again to a dais and the far doors,
and a single statue stood in glory.

They made their way toward it slowly, for there were other
things in the chamber worth seeing. On this side, an enormous head, so lifelike it might have been taken from a noble-
faced giant; across the way, a strange tangle of honey-veined
marble, a figure half-emerging from the trunk of a tree. But
mere stone was by comparison a weak thing, so before long

they climbed the stairs and stood before the sculpture Galen liked least in all the Onyx Hall.

The flames spiraling around the central form gave off enough heat to prove their reality, not enough to drive the viewer back. They moved, though, writhing and twisting, and created the illusion that the figure trapped within them was moving, too. He towered above Galen's and Delphia's heads, hands clenched around semisolid flames, massive shoulders hunched as if to tear his enemy apart, and such was the skill of the artisan that it was impossible to tell which was winning, giant or flames.

Delphia held one hand up, fingers glowing against the ruddy light, and breathed, "What is this one?"

"A memorial." Galen wrapped his arms around his body, though it was impossible to be cold while standing upon the dais. "This realm's answer to the Monument to the Great Fire. Have you ever been there?"

She nodded. "The view from its gallery is splendid."

"There are folk here who remember that fire—who saw it with their own eyes. Who fought it." The curling flames, twining serpentlike around the statue, trapped his gaze and would not let him go. "I told you there were less pleasant things, ones Mrs. Vesey does not know about. This is one of them."

Delphia turned away from her contemplation, hand dropping to her side. "What do you mean?"

He gestured at the statue. "That's meant to represent a giant in battle with the Dragon. The Fire was more than flames, Delphia; it was a great beast, that tried to devour all of London—and succeeded in devouring a great deal of it. While the mortals fought the blaze, the fae battled its spirit. And in the end they imprisoned it."

With the light behind her, Delphia's expression was hard to read, but he thought he saw her brow furrow. "A grand and terrible bit of history . . . but you look as if it troubles you even now."

"It troubles us all," he whispered. "Because it's coming back, Delphia. The comet everyone is waiting for—that is the Dragon's prison. If I have been tired and distracted and absent these past months, it's because the day is not far off when we will be back to this." And he gestured at the statue, the faerie locked in combat with the beast.

She cast a glance over her shoulder, then back at him. "You mean—some kind of battle?"

"We hope not. But I fear—" He shivered, and pressed his elbows into his ribs, as if that would stop it. "I fear that all our clever plans will come to nothing, and it *will* be this. Battle against an immortal beast, in order to save London. And people will die. Fae, and perhaps mortals, too."

Perhaps myself. The thought terrified him, and yet he clung to it, as if familiarity could wear down the sharp edges, rendering the fear incapable of wounding him. Galen did not want to die, but he wanted even less to live a coward. If it came to battle . . .

Here in the Onyx Hall, he could not speak God's name, but he could cry out in his thoughts. *Please, O Lord, give me the courage to face that prospect like a man.*

Delphia came forward, hands rising and then hesitating. But there was no one in the Hall of Figures save they two, and so she went on as she had begun, wrapping her arms around his stiff body and laying her cheek along his. After a moment Galen uncrossed his own arms and laid his hands on her waist, feeling the rigid armor of her stays. Irrith rarely wore any—a comparison he should not be making, not when Delphia would be his wife.

"I don't understand everything you've said," she murmured. "Comets and Dragons and all of that. But I'm sure it will be all right."

Meaningless words. As she admitted, she had no understanding of the circumstances—the Dragon's power, the details of their plan, any of it. Still, he needed to hear that assurance, empty though it was.

I'm sure it will be all right.

Galen disengaged from her embrace, forcing himself to concentrate upon her face, and not the fiery memorial behind. "Thank you. Now come; there are more—and more pleasant—parts of the Onyx Hall to see."

The Onyx Hall, London: December 25, 1758

On certain days—May Day, Midsummer, All Hallows' Eve—the fae went out into the mortal world to uphold their ancient traditions.

During the Christmas season, they stayed below.

Deprived of Galen's company, and bored as a result, Irrith went to the night garden. There she passed the day playing increasingly absurd dice games with Ktistes, sprite and centaur taking turns to add a new rule with every new round. They threw the dice upon the polished boards of his pavilion, chatting upon inconsequential subjects with determined carelessness, until Irrith, rising to stretch, caught sight of something outside.

A holly nymph, spirit of one of the garden's trees, stood on the dewed grass with her head tilted back, staring upward.

"What is it?" Ktistes asked. Irrith didn't answer; by then, her feet were already carrying her down the ramp and onto the grass, into open space where she could see the ceiling above.

A comet blazed across the night garden.

The faerie lights that formed its sky had drawn inward, leaving most of the ceiling black and empty. The tail of the comet pierced that blackness like a sword, trailing back from a core of brightness too painful to look at directly. It stretched nearly from one side of the garden to the other, a radiant omen of doom.

The knocking of Ktistes's hooves against the wood sounded hollow as death behind Irrith. Then the centaur was there, and she put one hand against his flank, needing the support.

"Someone has seen it," he whispered—a tiny sound, coming from so great a body. "We must find out who."

Does it matter? Irrith wondered. Her muscles were wound so tight she thought her bones might snap. *We are out of time.*

The comet—and the Dragon it carried—had returned.

PART SIX

Dissolutio

Winter 1759

Substance and form in me are but a name,
For neither of the two I rightly claim,
A spirit less, and yet such force enjoy,
As all material beings shall destroy.

—"A Riddle,"
attributed to Elizabeth Carter,
The Gentleman's Magazine, November 1734

Distance shrinks to nothing at the touch of eyes. A man in a night-black field, peering up at the sky, seeing its wonders magnified beyond their natural size.

Seeing the comet.

The Dragon coils within its prison. Its being is light, part of the growing brilliance that shrouds the comet's dark core. Matter could not leap the distance between this traveler and that night-dark field, but light can, light does.

Freedom awaits.

Freedom, yes—but little more. There is no power there. Grass, and trees, and the man with the watching eyes; these things could be burnt, and there would be joy in that.

The Dragon wants more than joy.

It wants the city, and the shadow beneath it.

Patience. After so many years, the beast has learned its meaning. The light streams outward now, a banner through the void; it is a declaration of war, growing brighter with each passing instant. Other eyes will come, forging links between Earth and the far-distant comet, and in time one will—must— lead to the Dragon's prey.

It can wait.

For now.

"It was a German." For once Galen came in without pausing for a bow, brandishing the folded letter Wilhas had given him. "Johann Palitzsch, in Saxony. A gentleman farmer, if you can believe it; he practices astronomy as a pastime."

The people assembled to hear him were a motley sort of war council, seated around the chamber's grand table. Peregrin and his lieutenant Sir Cerenel, representing those who were prepared to fight. Cuddy for the dwarves, who were still in their workroom, swearing over Niklas's most recent attempt at a trap. The alchemical scholars: Dr. Andrews and Lady Feidelm, Wrain and the exhausted Savennis, and even the genie Abd ar-Rashid. Irrith. Rosamund Goodemeade. And Lune herself, who stood tensely behind her own chair, gloved hands resting on its back.

The Queen said, "And nothing has happened to him."

She phrased it as a statement, but the tension in her eyes said she wasn't certain. Galen hastened to reassure her. "Nothing at all, or the Hanoverian fae would have said. The Dragon did not leap down."

Lune let her breath out slowly, good hand relaxing. "Then that is our first question answered. Either it needs a closer approach to Earth, or it does indeed want this place, and will not settle for another. Though I wouldn't test that with a sighting by anyone in England, whether at Greenwich or not."

Which led all eyes to Irrith. The sprite grinned, though it was a strained thing. "They'd be lucky to find the moon, through the clouds we have right now."

Galen returned her smile. "Lord Macclesfield says Messier has been complaining since November that the skies above Paris are very frequently cloudy. He's scarce been able to take any observations at all."

"But will it *hold*?" Wrain asked.

Irrith frowned in doubt. With this meeting being held in Lune's council chamber, Ktistes could not join them; the sprite was the only one speaking for the clouds. "How much longer do we need them?"

Once Galen would have needed to consult his notes, but at this point the dates were engraved in his memory. "Perihelion is mid-March. We can't be sure how long the comet will remain visible afterward, though. To be safe, call it three months, the inverse of Palitzsch's sighting. Can we stay hidden until Midsummer?"

The sprite chewed on her lower lip. Her hands were clasped around her knees, and her shoulders hunched inward. "Maybe," she said, drawing the word out. "I'll have to ask Ktistes. But we *might* be able to hold it that long."

Sighs of relief sounded all around the room, from almost everyone there. Not Irrith, though, or Galen, or Lune.

The Queen met his eyes, and he saw his own thoughts mirrored in her. *They think we can avoid the question. Put it off until the next century.* And perhaps they could, if the clouds held. But they both knew the risk of complacency: all it took was one slip, one tear in the veil, and they could find themselves facing a battle for which they were unprepared.

No, it's more than that. Even if we knew for sure . . . Lune is done with waiting. And so am I.

The time has come to face our enemy.

The thought should have terrified him. In some respects, it did. But Galen discovered, to his surprise, that even fear could not last forever. The omen in the night garden, Palitzsch's sighting of the comet, lanced a wound that had festered for years. He no longer had to dread this moment. It had come, at long last, and now they would make their answer.

Lune straightened, and with that simple motion a regal mantle settled over her shoulders. Here in the crowded council chamber, she commanded as much respect as she would have done seated on her throne. "Thank you, Dame Irrith. Warn us if that cover seems in danger of breaking."

Her eyes sought out and held every person in the room, from Dr. Andrews to Wrain. "Understand this: we mean to answer this threat. We hide, not like mice, hoping the eagle will pass us over, but like cats, awaiting the best moment to strike.

"Lord Galen estimates our danger shall last at least until Midsummer. I say now that we will not wait that long. Sir Peregrin, how ready are your knights?"

The Captain of the Onyx Guard stood and bowed. "Your Grace, they would fight today if you called upon them."

The imperious demeanor softened a bit, and she gave her captain a wry look. "I'm sure they would. But how stands their skill?"

"They're ready," he assured her. "Spear-knights and others alike. They'll train from now until you need them, because a soldier must always keep his skills in practice; but if they were to fight today, I would send them into battle with pride."

"Good. You are our third line of defense; the clouds are the first. Which brings us to the alchemists." Lune looked to Dr. Andrews. Galen held his breath, wondering if she was about to do something terribly foolish. He almost melted in relief when she said, "Lord Galen and I set you the task of finding a suitable procedure to refine sophic mercury. Do you have one yet?"

Thin to begin with, Andrews had worn down to a skeleton held together by little more than passionate hope. His febrile eyes shifted restlessly, unable to hold Lune's gaze. "I'm not sure, madam. There are still fundamental questions—"

"Dr. Andrews," Galen broke in, before the man could say anything injudicious in front of the others. "I understand your uncertainty, but the time for hedging is past. You needn't say it will be ready tomorrow. In a few weeks—perhaps mid-February—the comet will draw too close behind the sun for anyone to see it, even with a telescope; the clouds can protect us until then. After that, I doubt if anyone will be able to sight it until perihelion at the earliest, in mid-March. That gives you more than two months. Can you be prepared by then?"

The doctor licked his lips, then said, "Yes."

Andrews's answer might be a guess, rather than a promise, but Galen counted it as victory nonetheless. Without a date to aim for, the scholars could ponder their questions endlessly, never arriving at a firm conclusion. Placing a boundary would do them good. And if the procedure were truly not ready then, they could always extend the time—so long as the clouds held out.

"You have until perihelion, then," Galen said. "After that, the comet will draw nearer to the Earth, and our danger will be at its greatest. As soon as you are ready, we will dismiss the clouds, call the Dragon down, and end this."

Andrews nodded, and wiped sweat from his pale brow.

Lune still stood alone, behind her chair. Galen circled the table and positioned himself at her side. For once—perhaps for the first time—it felt right. Queen and Prince, shoulder to shoulder, against the threats that faced their court.

Their court. His as well as hers.

"Until March, then," Lune said. "May Fate and Faerie bless us all."

The Onyx Hall, London: January 25, 1759

If, upon her arrival in the Onyx Hall, anyone had asked Irrith how she would spend her final weeks before the confrontation with the comet, she would have confidently predicted a wild adventure through the streets of London, visiting taverns and shops and the houses of mortals, enjoying the city as if she might never see it again.

Instead she divided her time between the Temple of Arms and Dr. Andrews's laboratory, wishing she could be of greater use in either place. But she had done her part; their first defense was holding, and others were far more qualified to contribute to the second and third than she was. Especially on the alchemical side. Galen had abandoned her bed, though, and the laboratory was the surest place to find him.

Him, and half the Onyx Hall. An exaggeration, of course,

but right now the room held Galen and Dr. Andrews, Wrain and poor Savennis, Lady Feidelm and Abd ar-Rashid. Even Podder had been pressed into service; when Irrith entered, he sat with a penknife and a pile of quills, carving each to a fresh point.

It wasn't entirely true Irrith was of no use. "Lune's had word from the Cour du Lys," she announced to the various mortals and fae. "Messier thinks he's spotted the comet from Paris."

Galen slammed shut the book he'd been consulting. "Damnation. Is it public yet?"

Irrith grinned. "No. The French king—the faerie one—has done Lune a favor. Delisle, the fellow in charge of the observatory at Cluny, has told Messier not to announce anything just yet. Messier's furious."

"Good," Galen said, fingers curling around the book's edge. "The silence, not the fury. The fewer people who are aware of this, the better."

She smiled at him, but in his distraction, he didn't return it. What his scruples over marriage had failed to accomplish, the sighting of the comet had done; Galen had little time for anything but preparation these days.

No one did. Irrith hadn't realized just how complicated this "alchemical plan" would turn out to be. She wandered toward Abd ar-Rashid and stood frowning over the Arab's shoulder. He was sketching something with a careful hand, but she could make no sense of it. "What is that?" she asked.

The genie answered without looking up. "We need a vessel, an alembic, in which to effect our work. The intent is to use the Monument to the Great Fire, the chamber in its base."

That explained the general shape, but—"What about that stuff at the top?"

The pen lifted from its line and paused. "Mirrors," Abd ar-Rashid said. His accent had improved to the point that she could detect impatience in the answer. "And lenses. I am told that observation from London will bring the Dragon down, but the Monument is a zenith telescope; it cannot be pointed at its target. Since the comet will not pass directly above, we must direct the observer's gaze."

She could understand the difficulty easily enough, but not Abd ar-Rashid's sketch of a possible answer. Much simpler was the question Dr. Andrews asked of the room at large, utterly without warning. "What happens when a faerie dies?"

Podder dropped his penknife. Irrith said, "How do you mean?"

The doctor had been frowning over some notes in his hand. Now he put them down and frowned at the wall across from him instead. "*After* a faerie dies, I should say. Suppose this Dragon is killed, instead of trapped or transformed. Will its body decay, according to the ordinary way of such things?"

That, at least, was a topic Irrith was qualified to speak on. "It won't rot, no. They just fall to dust over time, bones and all."

"Not dust," Wrain corrected her. "Nothingness."

She stuck her tongue out at him. "I meant it poetically."

"And sometimes it takes no time at all," Feidelm added. "The body just vanishes."

"I suppose that explains why no one has ever found a faerie graveyard," Andrews mused. He tapped his cheek with the ragged end of his quill. "And the spirits?"

"They die, too," Wrain said.

He sounded grim, as most faeries did when they spoke of their own deaths. *We don't like thinking of it—that our eternity may see an end.* For some reason it was even more disturbing now, in this well-lit room, than it had been on All Hallows' Eve. Hugging herself, Irrith said, "Not always, though. Don't some faeries go on?"

"Where? To Heaven, whose Master does not love us? Or down below, where the devils have their day? Perhaps you think they go into Faerie." Wrain's snort showed what he thought of that. "Superstitious nonsense, told by frightened fae who wish to believe they can look forward to something after."

It stung Irrith, less because she believed it herself than because Lune did. "Her Majesty said she saw a faerie go elsewhere, once."

"Oh? To where? And how did she know it was so?"

Irrith fiddled with a nearby microscope. "She didn't say."

Andrews seemed obscurely pleased. He jotted a series of notes in a nearby book, lips moving in a soundless mutter. Sometimes the man disturbed Irrith, and not just because he was dying; his passion for ideas bordered on the unnatural.

She wished for a different subject, one that would not make her think of Aspell and Lune. A diversion presented itself, in the form of the Prince, who was sitting bolt upright with the book forgotten in his hands. "Galen? What is it?"

He didn't seem to hear her at first. Then she moved in front of him, and he shifted and came awake. "Have you thought of something?" Irrith asked.

"Vanishing." He pronounced the word as if it were an epiphany, but she shook her head, not understanding. "Like Lady Feidelm said. Sometimes the body just vanishes. Why?"

"Lune said it happened to the faerie she was talking about," Irrith said, remembering. "The one she thought went . . . elsewhere."

"Yes! Precisely! What if that's it? What if the fae who vanish are the ones who go on instead of ending?"

His excited cry had everyone's attention now. Dr. Andrews said, "Some property of aether, perhaps—"

Galen's hands flew through the air, cutting him off. "No, no—well, yes, perhaps, but not the way you're thinking. You gave a lecture on this yourself, Dr. Andrews; don't you remember? At Mrs. Vesey's house. On Cartesian philosophy, the separation of Mind and Body. What if that's one of the laws that differs here, in faerie spaces—or more to the point, with faerie bodies?"

Irrith struggled to understand him, because this had animated him so greatly. "You mean that minds and bodies aren't separate? *Our* minds and bodies aren't?"

"Spirit as matter." Galen seized her by the arms, the first touch they'd shared since Delphia Northwood came into the Onyx Hall. "This, right here—*this is you,* Irrith. No division. In elemental terms, oh, I don't know . . . perhaps faerie matter is simply an idea the faerie mind imposes upon the aether. Or something. It might explain what a glamour is, where it comes from. But when a faerie is killed, body and spirit die together, because they're no different, and what's left behind soon falls to nothingness. When the spirit goes elsewhere, though . . ."

"The body vanishes," Irrith whispered.

Feidelm drew near, the tall sidhe towering over Irrith and Galen both. "It would explain why the Dragon survived all attempts to kill it. We've said before: its spirit is powerful. *That* is what we must kill."

Irrith still wasn't sure whether the idea was too far beyond her to comprehend, or so simple she didn't understand why Galen hadn't seen it before. But the part about death . . . that was another matter entirely. Wrain's doubt had faded into thoughtful consideration. Savennis was staring at his own arm as if he'd never seen it before. Abd ar-Rashid looked worried, and she didn't know why.

Andrews had gone so pale she thought he might fall over, but his eyes glittered like diamonds. "Perfect," he breathed.

Galen turned sharply, releasing Irrith's arms. "What do you mean?"

"Oh—" Andrews blinked, then brought out his handkerchief to dab at his perpetually sweaty face. "If you are right . . . the Dragon has no body at present, as I understand it. Yes? So as long as we keep it away from any source of aether, it will continue to be bodiless."

"Keep it away from faerie spaces, you mean," Galen said.

Irrith shook her head. "No, I don't think so. The Dragon was born above, in the Fire. Remember? So it—"

The words stuck in her throat, choking her. "Oh, Blood and Bone." Faerie profanity wasn't enough. "Oh, *Hell*."

They were all staring at her, until she had to fight not to squirm. "Isn't it in those books of yours? All that alchemical gibberish? As above, so below. And the other way around, too. The Onyx Hall echoing into London, with aether or whatever else. I think—I think we *made* the Dragon." Just as Carline had said.

Andrews spat a curse and flung his handkerchief away. But he seemed curiously abstracted and calm as he said, "Then it will have to be done quickly. If we can get pure mercury into the base of the Monument, then break the clouds and call the sulphur down, so that they join before either has a chance to become contaminated . . . perhaps if we lined the chamber with iron?"

The others began to argue theories, a conversation to which Irrith could add nothing. For once, she was glad of it. A knot of cold had formed in the pit of her stomach. Never mind alchemy; all she could think about was Aspell's plan.

If Lune is devoured by the Dragon . . .

It meant the same thing it always had, really. When fae died, that was it; if there were exceptions, they were rare, and hadn't Lune said that sometimes she liked the thought of a true end? But Galen's notion, putting an explanation to something Irrith usually preferred not to think about at all, somehow made it a dozen times more horrifying. The Dragon wouldn't just be eating Lune's body; it would consume her spirit.

Irrith wished, suddenly and fiercely, that the fae had someone to pray to as the mortals prayed to their Heavenly Father. They swore by Mab, one of the ancient powers of Faerie, but that wasn't the same thing; she didn't watch over them and help them when they needed it. And that was what Irrith wanted right now, someone to beg for aid, so that Galen and Dr. Andrews and all the rest of these clever minds would find a way to make this work, ensuring it never came to that dreadful pass.

I'd ask Galen to pray, but I doubt the Almighty is much interested in helping fae.

But maybe for the sake of London, He would take an interest. She would ask Galen later. At some point when they were alone together—if they ever were, again.

"I'll go tell Lune," she offered, into the chatter of the others. Only Feidelm seemed to hear her, nodding before answering some point Andrews had made. Forlorn in the face of their excitement, Irrith sighed and went back to the Queen.

St. James' Park, Westminster: February 12, 1759

"If chill fogs prevented Britons from walking in the park," Delphia had said to her mother that noon, "we should never make use of them at all."

She was not the only one to hold that view, it seemed, for she and Galen were far from alone in St. James' Park. They had even seen the Duchess of Portland walking with a friend, despite the dreary weather. The months of gray had worn on everyone's mind, until everyone was desperate for light, however weak. And truth be told, he was something grateful for the fog; it meant Mrs. Northwood fell back and wrapped herself in her cloak, muttering peevishly to herself, leaving the two of them with freedom to speak more frankly—so long as they were careful.

Such freedom was hard to come by these days. With Delphia about to leave her natal household, her liberty to spend time at Mrs. Vesey's was much curtailed; and now there lay the great weight of a secret between them, a joy to share, but not one they could often indulge. Delphia had tithed some bread to the Onyx Hall, and in exchange Lady Yfaen came calling upon her when possible. It was her primary source of contact with the fae.

Delphia said, "I hear you've made some great philosophical discovery."

He blushed and looked down—never a wise idea, in St. James' Park, where it was easier to ignore the things one might step in than to try and avoid them all. Cows and deer roamed the park freely, with inevitable consequences. "Not so great; there are still a number of things we're uncertain of. Though we needn't try to answer them all in the next month, thank Mab."

A smile darted across her features at the name. "They have you well trained, don't they? I have an advantage in that respect, I suppose; gently reared maidens are not supposed to take the Lord's name in vain, and my mother reared me as gently as she could." They walked in silence for a while, nodding to those they passed, and when they were once more safe from being overheard she asked, "How long have you been among them?"

Irrith had asked him the same question, nearly a year ago. Galen could not help but feel a pang at the thought of the sprite. He'd hurt her when he drew back, much to his surprise; he'd thought himself nothing but a toy for her, that she would tire of soon enough. But with Delphia brought into the world of the fae, he could not in good conscience go on sharing Irrith's bed.

"Four years or so," he said, straightening his gloves to hide the discomfort of his thoughts. "Though I had my first sight of them some months before that."

"And how long have you been struggling with the problem of this comet?"

Against his will, his gaze went upward. The clouds were as thick as ever, and he thanked God and Mab alike for that, depressing as they were. "Myself? Four years or so. For them, however, it's been more than fifty years."

Delphia shivered. He doubted it was from the chill. "That long. I can't imagine living that way—not for decades on end."

"They don't see time as we do," Galen said. While true, it wasn't the whole of the truth. The long wait *had* worn on the fae, he thought. They were accustomed to passing eternity with little attention to the years, counting few things in any increment smaller than "an age." For half a century now, however, they'd lived with one eye on the calendar. The strain showed. Podder, who had been servant to seven Princes of the Stone, had vanished last week. He wasn't the only one to go.

"I confess," Delphia said, "I did not expect them to have philosophers and scholars. When I thought of such creatures at all, I associated them with—oh, I don't know. Flowers and butter churns, I suppose."

"Those things have their place; I should introduce you to the Goodemeades. But the fae copy anything they like, and ignore whatever they don't. They're very curious creatures, Delphia," Galen said. The name had grown more comfortable over the months, though he took care never to use it around anyone who might find the familiarity inappropriate. "You would like Lady Feidelm, I think; she, too, is very interested in learning."

Delphia smiled, tugging her cloak more firmly around herself. "Never mind the faerie *court* beneath London's feet; you have a university down there."

His laugh was too loud; a guilty glance over his shoulder told him Mrs. Northwood had overheard. But what, he asked himself, would she do? Call off the wedding? The marriage settlement was signed, and the ceremony planned for a month hence; she would not undo it all just because her daughter and future son-in-law seemed to be sharing a private joke. "With tedious lectures and the granting of empty degrees? I think not."

"An academy, then, such as Plato had in Athens. After all, you said yourself that there are unanswered questions yet. Surely you won't abandon them just because a star is no longer about to fall on your head."

Now it was his turn to shiver, and she placed a hand on his arm. "I'm sorry. I should not jest about something that worries you so much."

He laid his own hand over hers in reply, before they moved apart once more, Delphia tucking her arm back into the shelter of her cloak. For all that Galen appreciated the semisolitude that being outside gave them, he was beginning to grow chilled; they could not stay out here much longer.

Delphia might have been thinking the same thing, for she said, "I will be glad when we are wed, and can spend time in company with one another—or even go missing for a few hours—without raising suspicion." Then she blushed and said, "I—that is not to suggest that my *only* reason is—"

Galen drew her arm out again, bringing them both to a halt in the grass and turning Delphia to face him. Before Mrs. Northwood could catch up to them, he placed a kiss on the hand of his soon-to-be bride, and said, "I understand. And I feel the same. Be patient but a little while longer, Miss Northwood, and you shall have what you desire."

The Onyx Hall, London: March 12, 1759

The laboratory was empty when Irrith came in. Abd ar-Rashid was in Wapping, talking to the Dutch Jew who had made their bowl, arranging for lenses and mirrors. Wrain and Lady Feidelm were also above, examining the Monument to the Great Fire, seeing if they could somehow shield the chamber in its base from aethereal contamination.

Galen was at home with his family, for tomorrow he would be married.

Irrith had expected to find Savennis or Dr. Andrews, though. Without them, the abandoned laboratory seemed forlorn. Paper lay scattered everywhere, with notes scribbled in half a dozen different languages and hands. Shelves meant for books were all but bare, their former occupants tottering in piles on the tables and floor. Cold ashes filled the hearth, with no Podder to see to them.

Irrith trailed her fingers over a microscope, a pendulum, some chemical apparatus whose purpose she'd never learned. She picked up a sheet whose top read *Extraction of Sophic Mercury* in large letters; the rest of it was blank. It flutttered from her hand to the floor.

This wasn't what she'd imagined. In the long ages of her life, she'd seen every kind of struggle from a knife in the back to armies at war, but never one fought so much in the mind. It might yet come down to armies, of course; that was what Peregrin's spear-knights were for. But Galen and his scholars were trying to defeat the Dragon with nothing more than ideas: a kind of war she'd never seen before.

In a moment of rare carelessness, she'd left the door open behind her. How long Irrith hadn't been alone, she couldn't say, but she turned to find Lune standing in the opening.

Irrith jumped, of course, and her hand went into her pocket, gripping the pistol she always carried these days. There was a hawthorn box in her other pocket, its friendly wood shielding her against the three iron balls within. If the clouds failed suddenly and the Dragon came roaring down, she would be prepared.

But it was Lune, not the Dragon. Once her nerves had calmed, Irrith remembered to curtsy. "Your Majesty." Then she peered out the door, into the empty corridor beyond. "You're . . . alone?"

Lune smiled, with rueful amusement, and closed the door behind her. "I am. After so many years, even I forget there was a time I walked this realm alone, without ladies and footmen and all the other pomp that attends a Queen. I wanted to speak to Dr. Andrews privately—but it seems he's not here."

"I think he went home."

"Good." Lune picked up a mortar and pestle, studied its contents, set it down again. "Galen said he was having difficulty persuading him to do so."

"He's dying," Irrith said bluntly. "And he thinks being here can save him, at least for a while. But I think it's sending him a little mad."

The silver eyes darkened. "Gertrude is very apprehensive of that danger. But Galen argued, and I agreed, that Dr. Andrews's condition made it worth the risk; we needed his mind, and he would not have long to run mad."

Needed. Lune spoke as if the matter were done. "Are we ready, then? I know about the Monument plan, but have they found their mercury?"

"They found it long ago," Lune murmured, and her lips tightened. On most fae, it would have been nothing, but on her it was a like a banner, advertising her distress. "But there is . . . a problem."

They had a source for the sophic mercury? This was the first Irrith had heard of it—though admittedly, she hardly understood the scholars' debates. She knew they wanted to draw it out of some water-dwelling faeries, but there was, as Lune said, some problem. Irrith furrowed her brow, trying to remember.

Then she succeeded, and wished she hadn't. "They're afraid it would kill the river fae."

Lune's lips tightened again. For a moment she was like a statue, frozen and mute; then she inhaled and answered with a simple truth. "Not the river fae. Me."

Irrith gaped. No one had breathed a word of this, not in all the time she'd spent in the laboratory—well, of course they hadn't. Who would say such a thing, any more than they had to? But a thousand things made more sense now, that she hadn't understood when Wrain muttered them, or Feidelm lapsed into language so abstract she could have been talking about anything at all.

A thousand things—and chief among them, the desperation in Galen's eyes. He wanted to save the Onyx Hall, of course, but sometimes it took on a sharper edge, and now Irrith knew why.

She studied Lune, marking the hollows under her high cheekbones, the sharp line of the muscles in her neck. Fading, yes—but slowly. She could hold on for a very long time. If there was good reason to. "Galen would die to save this place," Irrith said, and then corrected herself. "To save *you*. I don't think you would die for him . . . but would you do it for London, and the Onyx Hall?"

Lune stood silent, head bowed, long-fingered hands folded across the stomacher of her simple dress. Irrith could never have asked her this if there were servants present, or even waiting outside the door, but it was just the two of them, and for this brief span she could speak to the elfin woman, rather than the sovereign. The distinction was important to her, though she could not have said why.

"There have been times when I almost did," Lune said finally, not lifting her head. "I held back because in the end, I believed my death—or even my abdication—would create more problems than it would solve. There are fae here who share my ideals, but none of them, I think, could manage this court. And those who could rule effectively would not do so in a manner I can accept.

"So when it was merely the arguments of the Sanists, it was easy to say *no*. But now there is the Dragon. And now . . . I do not know."

Irrith's hands curled into fists. She was vividly aware of her fingers, bones, joints—her body. Her *self*. No separation between the two. "Maybe you wouldn't die, though. I don't really understand what they've been talking about, but it sounds like what they're after is just you in a different form, your soul separated from the aether that makes you solid. So you wouldn't really be dead, would you? You'd just be . . . different."

The two of them stared at each other, neither one moving, as if both were struck by the same thought. Lune said, "The philosopher's stone—"

"*Would* it be a stone?" Irrith asked, still not blinking. "Galen told me the alchemists thought it would be some kind of powder, red or shining or whatever—but how would they know? None of them ever made it, not truly. And we aren't working with metals, are we?" They were working with spirits. The Dragon's, and Lune's.

Wouldn't the result be a spirit, too?

The words seemed to float up out of Lune, without any effort on her part. "I want to save the Onyx Hall."

"And the Dragon wants to destroy it," Irrith finished. "Which one of you wins?"

Her answer was the fear in those silver eyes. Lune was strong and determined, yes. But strong enough to defeat the Dragon?

"We could be wrong," Lune said carefully. "This is mere speculation, and neither of us is a scholar. Nevertheless . . ." Her shoulders went back, and the elfin woman was gone; in her place stood the Queen. "I hardly need tell you not to speak of this to anyone. I will consult with Galen—no, he is occupied. Another, then. I thank you, Irrith; you've given me much to think about."

She swept out the door, leaving Irrith alone once more in the laboratory. Staring blindly at the far wall, she sank into a cross-legged position on the floor.

The philosopher's stone might not be their salvation after all. Which left them with what? Aspell's plan of sacrifice?

A chill sank into Irrith's bones. Until Lune brought it up, she hadn't given much thought to the question of what would happen to the Onyx Court if its Queen . . . went away. The Hall, yes; but not the court itself, the fae and mortals, with all their conflicting desires. Who would hold them together in Lune's absence? Who *could*?

Aspell, maybe. But he showed no sign of wanting it; from what Irrith had seen, he was a Sanist only with reluctance, because the situation forced him to it. So who, then? One of the others in the coffeehouse that day?

She didn't even know who they were—much less what ambition hid beneath their masks. And the more she thought about it, the more fear tightened her muscles. The Lord Keeper might insist he would do nothing against the Queen's will, but those unknown others. . . .

Irrith paced with small, tight strides, thinking. If she tried to ask Aspell for their names, he wouldn't tell her; he'd think she was preparing to betray them. And maybe she was. But there was someone else she could ask—someone who might know, who could be intimidated into telling, and who wouldn't much care what happened afterward.

Irrith went to hunt Carline.

Feidelm sat in perfect silence for a full minute after Lune shared what she and Irrith had discussed. The sidhe's vivid eyes grew distant; when they sharpened once more, frustrated regret filled them. "Now of all times, I wish I still had my prophetic gift. I could look to the future and tell you if that danger is real."

Such favors had been precisely what lost her that gift. Tensions between mortal England and Ireland rose and fell, but never subsided entirely, and that colored relations between their faerie courts, as well. The King and Queen of Connacht did not want one of their seers constantly lending aid to Lune, even if the Onyx Court no longer meddled in national politics as it once did.

Reminding Feidelm of that would do no good at all. "You have more gifts than just foresight," Lune said. "What does your wisdom tell you?"

The Irish faerie bent her head, gripping her hands together. "That you and Dame Irrith are right—and even if it's unsure, we cannot risk it." She sighed, knuckles tensing. "We struggled so hard with the question of *how* to do this thing that we could not spare thought for what would happen afterward. But we should have done."

The brilliance of the idea had carried them all away. Not just to stop an evil, but to turn it to good. It meant more to Galen than it did to the fae, who were already immortal; and it meant the most of all to Dr. Andrews, whose life might be saved by this means.

Lune asked, "Is Dr. Andrews at home now?"

Feidelm nodded. "With Savennis, I think. The last I heard, he insisted he'd conceived of a way to extract sophic mercury, without harming the source; Savennis was trying to find a river nymph to assist them." She exhaled, not quite a laugh. "I don't know what they think they're doing. Nothing Andrews says about it makes the slightest bit of sense. He may have gone mad in truth."

Staring at his own death so near—any man might lose his wits, even without the touch of faerie. And now Lune would have to crush his final hope.

It would be better if she waited for Galen, though. Not only did she wish to avoid undermining his authority as Prince, he was friendly with Dr. Andrews, more than any of the fae were; that might make this less cruel. In the meantime—

Feidelm straightened her shoulders under Lune's gaze. "I know. Wrain and I will go into the Calendar Room. We won't give up. If this can be made safe, we'll find a way; or we'll find something else."

They still had the clouds. They still had time.

Sothings Park, Highgate: March 13, 1759

At the wedding breakfast after the ceremony, the loudest talk was of the St. Clair estate in Essex, and how it would be opened for the first time in years so that Galen and the new Mrs. St. Clair could reside there. His father and Mr. Northwood were already discussing investments, which would multiply Delphia's dowry for such renovations while still keeping portions safe for Galen's sisters, and Irene was telling anyone who would listen that her brother should breed horses once he had his own estate; but Aldgrange was the subject of immediate interest, for it was agreed upon by both families that the happy pair should remove from London at the first opportunity, and enjoy themselves in the countryside.

Fortunately, "the first opportunity" was months off yet. Aldgrange needed a good deal of cleaning and repair before it would be suitable to inhabit. Galen and Delphia would be going nowhere before the end of the Season.

In the interim, they would reside at Sothings Park, with Mr. Northwood paying for their keep there. Galen had to admit it would be both easier and more pleasant than living under his father's eye. Strange as it sounded, he was master of his own household now; if he devoted his hours to the Onyx Hall, he need answer to no one other than Delphia. And she understood.

I made the right decision, telling her. Tension might grip his heart as they walked through the gardens after breakfast, but at least none of it arose from secrecy.

As if thinking of that tension, Delphia tilted her head back and shaded her eyes with one hand, searching the clouded heavens. "Even if the skies were clear," Galen said, "you wouldn't be able to see it. It's too near the sun."

She lowered her hand. "Perihelion—am I right?"

"Yes." Today, the comet stood at its closest approach to the sun. In the following days, it would draw toward the Earth. Pamphlet writers and half-literate preachers had been prophesying a resulting doom for years; Galen wondered sometimes whether they had somehow divined the faerie threat. Or perhaps some Sanist had told them, in order to undermine the Queen. A fiery conflagration, destroying all life upon the Earth . . . he prayed it would not come to that.

This was a miserable topic to consider on his wedding day. "We're quite safe at the moment," Galen said. "Even telescopes cannot find the comet, even in clear skies. Let us turn to happier topics—ones, perhaps, that do not touch on the world below."

They rounded a hedge, and found Lune waiting for them.

The faerie Queen stood unmasked in the center of the path, silver hair shining despite the cloudy light. The sight of her sent a lance through Galen's heart: today of all days, to face the creature he adored, with his new wife upon his arm.

His pain was all the worse because Lune had obviously caused it unthinking. "I came to deliver my good wishes to you both," she said, inclining her head toward Galen and Delphia in turn.

If she was here, showing her true self, there must be half a dozen fae elsewhere in the gardens, keeping watch to ensure no one else wandered by. And more keeping her secret back in the Onyx Hall, so the Sanists would not know she'd gone. All that effort, just for good wishes. Lune truly considered it that important, to come and congratulate them on their wedding day?

Congratulations, and something more. "I have gifts to bestow upon you," Lune said. Her hands were empty; did some lady or hob lurk in the hedge, ready to hand her things as needed? No, her gifts were of an intangible sort. "For the two of you together, a promise of blessing. You need not fear losing children to illness; they will never want for good health."

Gertrude had once said the Queen did that for all her Princes' children. Fae almost never had any of their own, so the offspring of mortals were priceless wonders in their eyes. Galen bowed, murmuring thanks, and Delphia echoed him.

The Queen looked next to the new bride. "For Mrs. St. Clair, a position in my household as lady of the bedchamber—the first mortal ever to be offered such a place."

Delphia's eyes widened. Galen doubted she had expected anything at all, not for herself in particular; certainly she hadn't expected this. Ladies of the bedchamber were few in number, and close to the Queen. Even Irrith was not counted among them. Delphia sank into a belated curtsy, this one deeper than the last, and stammered new thanks.

Then it was Galen's turn. He knew Lune had promised a wedding gift, but what she might choose to give him, he could not begin to guess.

"I considered many things for you, Lord Galen," she said softly. Sorrow touched the edges of her mouth, so faintly that one who had not studied her face for years would not have seen it. "In the end, I could think of no thing better than this: to say that you may have one boon of me. Whatever you ask—whatever might please you on this day—I will grant it to you."

His heart ached so fiercely he thought it might stop. Galen

was perversely glad of the pain; it kept him from speaking the words that leapt into his mind.

Give me one more kiss from your lips, as I had when you made me Prince.

He would rather have died than said it, with Delphia standing at his side. By the time his throat had opened enough to speak, he'd conquered the impulse—but that left him with nothing to say. What could he ask of her, that he wanted badly enough to spend her boon upon it? Everything he could think of was too trivial, or else would cause Delphia grief. *I want to choose something neither will despise me for. Something they can be proud of.*

Both of them, Delphia as well as Lune. While there was no romance between him and his new wife, there *was* friendship, and he wanted to be worthy of it.

Those thoughts, here in the garden of Sothings Park where he had made certain promises to Delphia, gave him the inspiration he needed. "Your Grace," Galen said formally, "I would like to form an academy in the Onyx Hall."

Now all three of them had been surprised this day. "An academy?"

He heard the soft breath of Delphia's delighted laugh, and took heart. "Yes. A society of those who take interest in the nature of your world. An institution that might draw to it learned minds from all lands, mortals and fae alike, for the purpose of understanding the sort of questions we've begun to ponder this last year."

Baffled though she was, Lune nodded. "If that is what you desire—then certainly." Her expression turned speculative. "In fact, it might be of some help to Ktistes, whose efforts have been sadly neglected while we addressed the problem of the comet. I wonder—"

Then she broke off with a laugh. "No. The academy, yes; but I will not trap you here discussing troubles. Not on such a happy occasion." Lune approached, holding out her slender hands; Galen took one, and Delphia the other. "My felicitations to you both, Lord Galen, Lady Delphia. Enjoy your wedding day, and may many more days of joy follow it."

Despite the myriad of good reasons he had to refrain—his

wife's presence; the formality of the moment—Galen murmured what he had never dared voice before, not to the Queen's face. "Thank you . . . Lune."

The Turk's Head, Bow Street: March 15, 1759

Irrith was not at all sure of the directions she'd been given. Bow Street was easy enough to find, and a carved Turk's head hung above the lintel of one well-lit door, but the interior looked like a coffeehouse—not the place she sought. London had plenty of Turk's Heads, most of them selling coffee; perhaps she'd been directed to the wrong place.

Still, she went inside, and was accosted before she'd gone three steps. "How can I be of service, my fine young sir?"

Irrith transferred her suspicion to the smiling man at her elbow. "I don't think you can. I'm looking for a bath-house."

His smile only broadened. "Why, it's here, good sir!" One hand swept an inviting arc toward a door in the far wall. "The bagnio is right this way. Though I regret to say that this evening it is occupied by a party of illustrious gentlemen and their companions. I would be happy, though, to serve you an excellent supper, and some—"

Her glare stopped him before he could say "coffee." *Gentlemen and their "companions"? I'm in the right place, sure enough.* But not well-enough dressed to pretend she belonged with illustrious folk. And she wasn't good enough to lie her way past, even if she changed her glamour.

A simple faerie charm did just as well. Irrith dug around in her pocket and produced a golden guinea. The man's eyes bid fair to pop out of his head at the sight of it; she wondered wryly if they would sink back into his skull when he found a dead leaf tomorrow. "I bear a gift for one of the ladies," Irrith said, patting her other pocket. "On behalf of my master. I won't impose on them long."

The man made the coin vanish so fast he might have been a faerie himself, and laid a sly finger along his nose. "For Kitty Fisher, perhaps? She made quite a name for herself by that riding accident in the Mall—I've heard two songs about it already. Quite the beauty they say she is, sir, if you don't mind my saying so. Your master will have to strive against some important men to win her charms, though." And so saying, he opened the door to the bagnio.

Now it was Irrith's eyes that threatened to fall out of her head. Oh, she'd heard of these places, but had been so occupied with other matters that she never found the time to visit one. She found herself in the midst of an Oriental dream. Tiled pools, coyly separated by carved screens, sent steam wreathing through the air—a wholly inadequate veil to cover the many half-clad or altogether naked people lounging about the space.

Not so many, she realized once her initial startlement passed. Perhaps a dozen in all: three ladies, and the rest men, all enjoying a thorough debauch. One fellow floated blissfully in a pool; two others sprawled with wine and candied fruit, conversing upon some topic with much laughter. A blonde woman sat on the back of a fourth, kneading his shoulders while she whispered in his ear. The other two ladies—to grant them a title they did not deserve—were dallying upon cushions with the remaining men. And it was there, of course, that Irrith found her target.

Once again, Carline had made no particular effort to disguise herself, aside from a thin veneer of mortality. No reason she should; her lush beauty was perfectly suited for this kind of pastime. Seduction had always been her favorite game, and she played it very well. Irrith was not surprised that her last farewell to London should be a night in a bagnio with as many handsome and wealthy men as she could manage.

Her dark-haired friend was devoting her attention to a rather unhandsome fellow, with a wide mouth and unfortunately bulbous eyes. *He must have a great deal of wealth,* Irrith thought cynically. Carline had taken the finest of the set, a strong-jawed man with shoulders that would look well in a tight coat and looked even better out of one. He so occupied her that she didn't look up as Irrith approached.

The unhandsome one did, though, and frowned. His companion wrinkled her upturned nose. "A friend of yours, George?"

He shook his head. Irrith offered a deep bow to them all and thought fast. The "gift" had just been an idea to get her past the owner of the bagnio, but now she had more attention than she wanted, and no good way out of it. "Good evening, my most excellent lords," she said, delaying while she scrambled for a fresh idea. Sweat was already soaking through her shirt into her coat, and nervousness did not help. "I've come in search of a, er, a lady—"

Derisive laughter greeted her stammering statement. "Miss Fisher," one of the men said in cool tones, "is not available this evening. As you can no doubt see." He gestured at the woman with the upturned nose.

"Not her," Irrith said, and pointed at Carline. "That's the one I seek. My master sent me with a gift for her."

Carline still had not looked up from her giggling play with the broad-shouldered man. "Tom," the ugly George called, and Kitty Fisher jabbed the fellow with her toe. "Competition for your Caroline's charms."

The two broke apart, and Carline, pouting, finally turned to face Irrith. The sprite watched as understanding came to her, stage by stage: she saw first a gentleman, then someone under a glamour, and then apprehension settled in. Not knowing who lay beneath the disguise, she would be fearing the worst—as if Lune had the attention to spare for one turncoat faerie lady on her way out of London.

But Irrith could use that fear. Her hand brushed her pocket, and a dreadful notion came to her. Bowing to the broad-shouldered Tom, she said, "May I present the gift to her?"

He scowled, but Kitty jabbed him again. "Go on, Tom. Or are you afraid your, ah, *purse* isn't deep enough to keep her?"

His scowl shifted targets, but George lifted a quelling hand, and Tom slid backward with ill grace, leaving Carline alone on her couch.

Irrith knelt before the faerie lady and pulled the box from her pocket. Then cupping it in her hands so no one but Carline could see, she cracked the lid upward.

All the blood drained from Carline's face. While Kitty and the others hooted and began speculating about the gift, Irrith murmured, "Five minutes of your time—and a bit of information. Then you can go wherever you please."

For a moment it seemed Carline would be unable to move. Then she shoved herself off the couch so fast Irrith almost fell onto her rump. "Five minutes," she said in a strangled voice. "No more." And she stalked into the far corner of the bagnio, bare feet thudding hard against the floor.

The laughter faded, and Tom regarded Irrith with undisguised suspicion. "Pardon me," she said, and went hastily after Carline before anyone could decide to interfere.

Carline waited with her arms crossed tight beneath her breasts, straining the damp fabric of her shift. Had Irrith been interested in such things, it might have been an effective distraction, but Carline hardly seemed to be trying. "Who sent you?" she demanded, before Irrith had even come to a halt.

"That doesn't matter. So long as you tell me what I want to know, there won't be any need for what's in that box." If Carline were thinking at all clearly, she would know that iron shot in a box was little threat; and loading the pistol in Irrith's other pocket would give her time to get away. But she had been drinking a great deal—for days now, if her servant was to be believed—and fear was louder than common sense.

Carline swallowed hard. "If you shoot me . . . these are important men, you know."

"I'm not going to shoot you," Irrith said impatiently. "All you have to do is tell me: who are the Sanists? Not the folk who read *The Ash and Thorn* and get into fights in the Crow's Head; I mean the leaders, the ones who are plotting. They wear glamours when they meet, but I'd wager my entire cabinet that at least a few of them were your supporters when you wanted to be Queen. Who are they?"

The tension faded minutely from her hunched shoulders at the reference to a cabinet. "Irrith?"

Blood and Bone. She gritted her teeth. "Names, Carline. You're leaving anyway; it doesn't matter what you say now. I need to know who they are."

Carline cast a swift glance over her shoulder at the others, who weren't pretending not to watch. Kitty was whispering into George's ear. "Nianna Chrysanthe supported me. Hafdean, who keeps the Crow's Head. The fetch Nithen. Valentin Aspell."

She tried to imagine any of those under the glamours at the Grecian. "Wait—Aspell? He was working with you, that long ago?"

The lady's entire body stiffened. All artifice and pleasantry vanished.

"What do you mean, he supported you? What was he doing? Tell me!"

Muscles stood out in Carline's lovely face, her jaw clenching tight. Her eyes blazed out of that rigid mask, as if trying to communicate by passion alone.

Irrith had to fight to draw breath. "You—you're under an oath, aren't you." No response, but of course there wouldn't be. Fae could not break their sworn words, and Carline had given hers to Aspell. Some loophole allowed her to let slip that he'd supported her—Irrith was sure that had been deliberate—but nothing more.

The sprite's mind felt like it was moving three times faster than normal. "He did more than just encourage you. He *helped* you. In ways he didn't dare let Lune find out about, so he made you swear." The answer was obvious, now that she looked for it. "He told you about the London Stone."

Carline couldn't say anything to confirm or deny it, but her expression gave way to pity, and she put one hand on Irrith's shoulder. "You've fallen into politics again, haven't you? Poor fool. I wish you well in escaping whatever net has you now, as you escaped mine. There are some in the Onyx Hall who could stand to suffer the consequences of it."

Irrith didn't pull free. "But I—I was with them. The things I did, the things I told them—if I tell Lune—"

The fallen lady smiled bitterly. "Yes. Oaths are one way to bind people, but guilt is another. Betray them, and you betray yourself. Especially after your history with me, which will not look good at all. Be glad you have a merciful Queen. She will likely only exile you."

I'll lose London. The thought hurt, but Irrith was fiercely glad to realize that it didn't matter. And not because of the

Dragon; even if there was no other danger, she would tell Lune. She was done helping Valentin Aspell.

"Enjoy France," Irrith said. Then she walked very fast out of the bagnio, past the owner in his coffeehouse, and once she was out in the street she began to run.

Memory: December 21, 1705

"It's been tried, Valentin." Carline blew her breath out in a theatrical display of frustration. "You're not the sort of faerie who forgets yesterday as soon as the next day begins. People have tried to usurp the throne of the Onyx Hall before, and failed."

The serpentine lord had draped himself over her most comfortable chair in a posture that seemed to require joints where ordinary beings did not have them. "And people have also succeeded. Lune did it. Or have *you* forgotten your history? She wasn't always Queen of this court, Carline. Have you never asked yourself how that change came about?"

Glaring at him, Carline sank gracefully onto her second-best chair. "Invidiana died. If you're advocating regicide, you can leave my chambers now. I have no stomach for blood."

He uncoiled his arm from the back of his seat and leaned forward with an intense air. "It doesn't require blood. All it requires is to make the realm recognize you as its sovereign."

She threw her head back in a laugh. The ceiling of her chamber was an intricate lacework of black stone; she addressed it whimsically. "Oh great Onyx Hall—will you make me your Queen?"

"You're speaking to the wrong part," Aspell said. "Surely you've heard the rumors. To control the Onyx Hall, you need the London Stone."

Her laughter faded away. Carline lowered her head, and found the Lord Keeper smiling. Nervousness made her play with one of the bows that crossed her stomacher; then she made herself stop. "More easily said than done. Its location is the most closely guarded secret in this place." She bit her lip. "Do you . . . ?"

"Know where it is? No. As you said, it's closely guarded. The Queen and Lord Joseph know, of course. I believe the Goodemeades do as well, for all the use *that* is. Sir Cunobel and Sir Cerenel were there when Lune claimed the Hall for herself; they might know."

The lady scowled. "Cunobel's long since vanished into Scotland, and Cerenel—hah. You'd have better luck forcing blood from a stone."

"And one other," Aspell said. "More easily squeezed than a stone. Dame Irrith."

The rustic little sprite from Berkshire. That showed real promise, Carline thought, running one fingernail over her painted lip. Unlikely that she could be persuaded or bought— but the poor, simple creature was not beyond manipulation, however much she liked to think so. Friendship would be the easiest way. Irrith distrusted courtiers, but responded well to friends.

But not if their generosity seemed too out of place. Carline fixed a suspicious eye on Valentin Aspell. "Why offer me this help?"

He shrugged and leaned back once more, this time settling into a watchful posture. "I have my reasons."

"Come, Valentin—you needn't be coy. We've sworn each other to secrecy, and I of all people am not likely to throw stones at a little naked ambition." She rose and drew near him, trailing one hand over the shoulder of his coat. "You're already Lord Keeper, so it must be something greater you want, that Lune will never give you . . . King, perhaps? Do you wish to rule at my side?"

He laid his fingers over her own, cool and dry. "I believe you'll need a mortal in that position. Lune is overfond of them, but her insistence on replacing Princes as soon as possible makes me suspect there's more to it than mere attachment."

"That isn't a denial."

The light from the fireplace cast his eyes into shadow. "I have my reasons, Carline. Leave it at that."

Doubt curled in Carline's heart. Even with so easy a target

as Irrith, there was risk. And were she to be caught, the oaths she and the Lord Keeper had sworn to each other would make it hard for her to accuse him. Once she found the London Stone for him, she might discover her use had run out.

Or something else. Aspell's motivations had never been clear to her. He enjoyed power, but was content to bide his time until those above him precipitated their own fall. If he did anything to hasten that, she'd never caught him at it.

Until now. The change bothered her, because she didn't know its cause.

She would have to be wary of him. Whatever game Aspell was playing, she did not intend to let it take her by surprise.

The Onyx Hall, London: March 15, 1759

"He said he intended nothing against your will." The memory stung bitterly in her mind. "And I *believed* him."

The elfin woman Irrith had spoken to in Dr. Andrews's deserted laboratory was gone; the creature she faced now was every inch the Queen of the Onyx Hall. Lune sat with rigid posture, hands unnaturally still on the arms of her chair, flanked by Sir Peregrin Thorne and Dame Segraine. The Queen had listened without comment to the tale of Irrith's involvement with the Sanists; now she sat silent a moment longer, eyes as flat and inexpressive as two silver coins.

Sir Peregrin asked coldly, "And what was your part to be in all of this?"

Irrith was already kneeling; now she ducked her chin and dug her fingers into the midnight carpet. "He—he said the idea would need to be in her Grace's mind already, so that she'd make the decision quickly when the time came."

A soft, sharp exhalation: the first sound Lune had made since Irrith began. "Perhaps he spoke the truth, then," she said, with a razor edge of irony. "My will; my decision to die. Once he'd arranged for it to be so."

"You give him too much credit, madam," Segraine muttered. Irrith had asked her to be here for this audience. Lune might be merciful as Queens went, but Irrith wanted a friend present regardless. "He'll have weighed Irrith to an ounce before he said anything to her. He knows she would never agree to outright regicide. But just because he said all those fine words doesn't mean he wouldn't hurl you into the Dragon's maw if you decided the wrong way."

Irrith's gut twisted. *Still like a babe in the wood.* Still a puppet to be danced about by courtiers. Carline used friendship to snare her; Aspell had used her ideals. Pretending all the time that he wanted what she did, when in truth his treason began long before the Onyx Hall began to crumble.

She bowed her head even farther. "Your Majesty . . . what are you going to do?"

Leather creaked as Lune flexed her good hand. "Sanist sentiment is widespread in some parts of the Onyx Court. Eliminating their leading cabal won't change that—though it would at least prevent what you've described. Unfortunately, Lord Valentin led my efforts to uncover that cabal. Thanks to him, we have nothing better than suspicion, and your word that he is their leader. We have no firm accusation to level against him, that would carry weight in a trial."

What do you need a trial for? Just kill him! But Irrith had reason to be grateful for the Queen's sense of justice, and her mimicry of mortal customs in reaching it. "Your Grace, I meant—what are you going to do with me?"

Sir Peregrin made a brusque sound that might have been either a growl or an angry laugh. Irrith did not dare look up at Segraine. She could feel the pressure of Lune's gaze upon her. *This is what he wanted me to be afraid of. And I am. Bad enough I went with him, but much worse that I stayed silent. That I let months go by without telling her.*

"Why did you meet with the Sanists?"

Irrith could read nothing out of that question; Lune was too good at keeping her thoughts from her voice. Not that she would have had any other answer to give, regardless of the Queen's state of mind. All she had was the truth. "Because the monarch *is* the realm. I don't think it's fading because you're wounded, madam, but—I don't know if it can be repaired so long as it has a mistress who isn't whole."

That was definitely a growl from Sir Peregrin. Lune, however, gave a quiet and weary reply. "Neither do I. I'm not ready to give up yet, though."

"You shouldn't!" It burst out without any polite address at all, and jerked Irrith upright as if someone had pulled on a string. Sitting back on her heels, hands clenching, she said, "He wants you to think you should. All of them do, all the Sanists, and they're too eager to accept the easy answer, rather than looking for something else. But Aspell's the heart of it. Don't wait for a trial; give me permission, and I'll go stab him this very moment."

The Queen laughed, as much from startlement as anything else. "A very kind offer. Unfortunately, it's one I can't accept. That would make him a martyr, and encourage the others. Not only do you not have my permission, Irrith, you have our royal command that you are *not* to murder Valentin Aspell."

Irrith hung her head. "Yes, madam."

"As for your punishment," Lune said, and paused.

Even though the sprite knew she should keep silent, she said it anyway. "I don't have any right to ask for this, but—if you're going to exile me, then please, let me stay long enough to face the Dragon."

Sir Peregrin made a disbelieving sound. Lune said, "My subjects slip away in the night, and you ask to stay." Despite everything, a bright edge lightened her voice. "Very well, Dame Irrith. For now, your punishment is that you are forbidden to depart until we have disposed of the Dragon. After that, we shall decide further."

The Onyx Hall, London: March 16, 1759

The Queen forbade her to kill Aspell, but not to plot other things.

Irrith perched atop a flying buttress, watching the door to Valentin Aspell's chambers. She'd been up there for a while, considering her options. Part of her was tempted to stab him anyway; it might be worth guaranteeing her exile, just to get rid of him.

That shouldn't be her first move, though. At present she was contemplating breaking in and seeing what she could find, but she suspected someone had already done that on Lune's behalf. Besides, Irrith wouldn't know what to look for. The Lord Keeper would hardly leave a notebook lying around with *PLANS FOR TREASON* written in large letters across the top.

Sitting here made her feel better, though. More fixed upon her purpose, which was to find proof that could be used to put an end to Valentin Aspell.

Could she lie to him? Make some pretense of— no, she dismissed the thought before she even completed it. Irrith was no good at masquerade, and she knew it.

They said Lune was very good at it indeed before she became Queen, disguising herself as a human woman for months on end. Some said that was why she had such strange mortal notions—that even the "safe" bread of the tithe left a taint of mortality, if eaten for long enough. Irrith thought it had more to do with loving a human man, but perhaps the two went hand in hand.

Distraction, all of that, from the fact that she didn't know what to do. Irrith was jarred out of it by movement below.

She had spied on people from the concealment of trees, and this was not so different. Her blood quickened as she recognized the thrumpin from the Crow's Head, the Sanist who helped start that brawl. He knocked on Aspell's door, and handed a folded slip of paper to the hob who answered.

Irrith leaned forward, hoping for something of interest, but the hob merely bowed and closed the door, and the thrumpin went away. Frustrated, she smacked one hand against the stone. Seeing Aspell receive a message from a known Sanist was no use at—

The door opened again, and Aspell emerged.

Despite herself, Irrith grinned. She might not be much of a liar, nor a thief, nor a knight—but trailing someone in secret? *That, I can do.*

She went from buttress to buttress until she reached the end of the gallery. Then, unfortunately, she had to drop to the floor, which meant following at a greater distance, with a charm to silence her feet. Aspell had cast no such thing, which made her frown. If he wasn't bothering to be secret, then maybe this was nothing to do with the Sanists, thrumpin or no thrumpin.

Her mind was so on that question, and on the challenge of neither losing her quarry nor betraying herself to him, that she paid little attention to their path. With a start, she realized they had passed the only remaining branch in the corridors, and that only one thing lay ahead.

The Newgate entrance.

Blood and Bone! Aspell was going above. No need to hide that—it was ordinary enough—and once up there, easy enough to give the slip to any pursuers. And Irrith, searching desperately through her pockets, realized what bread she had was in Ktistes's pavilion.

Aspell went into the chamber. She drew close, into the shadow of one of the pillars supporting the arch, and saw him don a glamour. Then the air whispered, ghost-quiet, as he stepped onto the roundel and floated upward.

Irrith gritted her teeth. *I should let him go. Too hard to follow him, too dangerous, and what proof have I it's even worth the risk?*

Proof didn't matter. Only the possibility. In her heart, Irrith had sworn she'd find a reason to take Aspell down. It was the only way to purge her own guilt.

Cursing softly, Irrith began to build her own glamour.

Newgate and Holborn: March 16, 1759

Luck seemed to be smiling and spitting upon her by turns. First it sent the thrumpin to Aspell; then it put no bread in her pocket. Now it gave her the gift of a city in the dark of night, when almost no one would be on the streets to wave iron or invoke the Almighty, and by doing so shatter Irrith's unprotected glamour. Still, she wondered what ill luck would follow in turn.

She got her answer when, out of habit, she glanced up to judge the time.

A waning moon shone in the sky, its light breaking through wisps of cloud.

Irrith's heart tried to burst right through her ribs. She actually pressed her hands to her breast, as if that would help her slow its sudden pounding. Hemmed in by walls, she could see only a little of the heavens; the rest looked to still be shrouded in clouds. Hadn't Galen said the comet was near the sun right now? The sun was hours from rising. The comet couldn't possibly be visible. They were still safe.

But the clouds had begun to fail.

Irrith forced herself to concentrate. She could do nothing about that right now, and if she didn't move, she was going to lose the one thing she *could* do. Where had Aspell gone?

Fortunately, the likely guess turned out to be the right one. The Newgate entrance, like the Fish Street arch, saw a great deal of use these days, thanks to the growth of Westminster and the areas between, and there was a gleam of flame headed down Snow Hill. Aspell, and someone else—a human, it looked like, carrying a link to light his way. A real human, not a faerie under a glamour. He must have been waiting for the Lord Keeper, and that was the content of the thrumpin's note.

Grinning, Irrith followed. Soon they were on the much wider street of Holborn, and still going west. If they were going to some secret meeting, it could be anywhere in Holborn or the north of Westminster, but it certainly wasn't in the coffeehouse Aspell had taken her to before. *Too easy to guess, probably. He thinks like a spy, well enough not to repeat himself.*

Suddenly fearful, she cast a glance behind her, but saw no one. Of course not: he was still Lune's Lord Keeper, with no reason to think the Queen suspected him of anything. And the link-bearer glanced back occasionally, but with that light in his eyes, he hadn't a chance of spotting her. Irrith had spent long enough in the city to be almost as good at hiding as she was in the Vale—except when the occasional bit of passing iron made her queasy.

When they turned right at last, her heart began pounding almost as hard as it had upon seeing the moon. She'd been down this road, twice before. Once with Segraine, and once following Galen.

They were going to Red Lion Square.

In the dark of night, when no one was around to see. Irrith quickened her step, risking them seeing her. Aspell had spoken so much of last resorts—but they had another, didn't they? The alchemical plan. She'd told him about it herself. Only she hadn't told him everything: the role Lune might play, and the possible danger they'd uncovered. Whether the scholars had settled the question of the philosopher's stone, Irrith didn't know, but it didn't matter. So far as Aspell knew, alchemy held a way to save the Onyx Hall, without harm to Lune.

Unless he and the brawny man with him did something to prevent it.

In her haste, Irrith almost fell prey to an easy threat. A constable coming down a crossing street made her pull back into the shadows, crouching and holding her breath. Fortunately he was a lazy fellow, whistling as his own yawning link-boy trotted on ahead, making no real effort to see beyond its smoky light. By the time he passed, though, Aspell and his man were already in Red Lion Square.

She peered carefully around the corner of a building and saw nothing but an empty square. Coming farther out, she studied the front of Andrews's house. The blue door was black and silent, and the shutters were closed against the night.

The lock on the front door was beyond her abilities, and the shutters of the ground floor windows out of reach thanks to the open space of the area. How was she to get in?

Against her will, Irrith's gaze went downward, and she cringed in dread.

The area. It lay at the bottom of a set of steps giving access to the cellar, where the kitchens would be located. *Those* shutters, she might be able to open.

But first she would have to get past the iron railings that helpfully prevented passersby from falling down the steps.

She'd come this far. Even now, Aspell and that man might be creeping into Dr. Andrews's bedchamber, putting an end to the old man before consumption could. And then what he knew would die with him.

Thinking about it wouldn't make the task any easier. Biting down on her own hand, Irrith forced herself down the steps, feeling her glamour crumble around her. *Don't think about the iron fencing you in. Don't think about how one careless brush of your elbow could—oh,* Mab—*don't think about it, just keep moving . . .*

She had to remove her hand from her mouth when she reached the bottom, so she could deal with the window. The slender knife she kept inside her coat was perfect for sliding in between the shutters, fumbling around until she felt the latch lift. When she drew it back, though, the faerie silver of its blade had dulled and blackened, from the iron of the shutter nails. Gagging, Irrith took hold of the wood with her fingertips and pulled it back, until the panels swung clear. Then she was shoving at the window's lower sash, sliding it upward, hardly caring how much noise she made, until she could squirm through the gap and into the cellar beyond.

It wasn't much better here. Iron screamed at her from all over the kitchen: pots, hooks, more things than she wanted to think about. Irrith stumbled forward blindly, and gagged when her hand touched a hinge. Stifling her cries, she dragged the door open and fell out into the blessed darkness of the passage. She fled to the base of the stairs and stood there gasping, cradling her stinging hand. *I'm a fool. A reckless fool.*

Carline's mocking voice sounded in her head. *And what will you do when you go upstairs, little sprite? Attack those two, all on your own?*

Yes, if I must. She had her pistol. But only iron shot. Could she even bear to load the gun?

It was that or the knife, and that would mean going within reach of the link-bearer's brawny arms. But even as Irrith marshaled the will to go upstairs, she heard something that stopped her where she stood.

Voices. Valentin Aspell's, sibilant and oily, recognizable

anywhere. And a hoarse, whispery reply, coming from a chest that could no longer manage anything more.

Dr. Andrews.

"Will you live until the morning?" the Lord Keeper asked cynically.

"I will. I must." A pause for coughing. "I have not endured this long only to die now."

"We'll need bread."

Irrith tensed. Bread would be in the kitchen. But it seemed Andrews was prepared, for she heard a soft *clink,* as of a bowl placed on the floor. "Or should it be the doorstep?" Aspell must have shaken his head, for Andrews recited the rote phrases, tithing bread to the fae. When it was done, Andrews said, "Send your people in pairs. I don't want suspicion."

"Dr. Andrews," Valentin Aspell said, with an edge sharp enough to draw blood, "do not presume to tell me my business."

Footsteps, and the front door opening and closing. He was gone.

Irrith sank onto the bottom step, mouth open. *What was that?*

She didn't have long to wonder. More footsteps, these light and uncertain, but headed toward the head of the stairs. *Blood and Bone!* She couldn't go back into the kitchen—not with all that iron—

Her eyes had adjusted enough to the darkness that she saw a second door, close by her hand. Irrith pushed this one open and slipped through, praying there would not be another world of iron behind it.

The chamber smelled of alcohol and less pleasant things, but no iron scraped across her nerves. Unfortunately, luck was spitting upon her again; light came through the gap of the door, heralding an approaching candle. Irrith's hand bumped a table, and she dove underneath it just before the candle entered the room.

Andrews was dressed, despite the black hour. She watched his feet shuffle unsteadily around the room, light blooming in his wake, as he lit a set of lamps. It revealed two more tables apart from the one she hid under, all three of them large, heavy things, and shelves along the walls. Then the rustle of paper, as he turned the pages of a book.

Pressed into the corner of the walls, concealed by the table, Irrith wondered what to do. Stand up and announce herself? But then she would have to explain what she was doing in Andrews's cellar, and whether she'd heard that strange and worrisome conversation. Any kind of cooperation between him and the Sanists troubled her. How could Aspell—

Her entire face creased into a silent wail. *My fault. Again. I told him about the alchemical plan; he must have gone to Dr. Andrews. But what are they planning?*

Gentle tinkling: the doctor was ringing a bell. A moment later, he repeated it, more insistently. She heard him cough, then mutter something too faint to be made out. His feet shuffled from the room, and back up the stairs. Blessing whatever servant was failing to respond, Irrith slipped from under the table, intending to escape while she could.

Horror turned her to stone.

One of the other tables held a crumbled, indistinct shape, so far gone all that could be told was that it had once been very small. The other was much newer: a river nymph, pale and cold and unmoving.

And the third . . .

Irrith staggered away from the table that had sheltered her. Savennis's clouded eyes stared blindly at the ceiling, as if refusing to look at the gaping hole in his chest. Alcohol, and less pleasant things: she'd been smelling old blood. It stained the table, the shackles that held Savennis, the cracks between the stone flags of the floor, where no amount of scrubbing could remove it.

Her mind refused to put the pieces together, the corpses and the blood and the knives, the rowan chains no faerie could break and the jars of alcohol holding things she didn't want to recognize. Dr. Andrews. Valentin Aspell. There was a picture here, but she could not see it around the scream that filled her mind.

She ran. Even iron couldn't keep her out of the kitchen, her one route to safety; she was through the window and up the stairs before she knew she was moving, running away from Red Lion Square, back to something like safety.

But time had passed; people were beginning to move, in the murky predawn light. She tried to put up a glamour, lost it before she'd gone ten steps. Irrith snatched desperately at everything she knew of London, every black alley and hidden nook, every series of rooftops that afforded her a road away from where people could see. She had to make it back to the Onyx Hall. Had to stop Aspell, whatever he was planning for the morning. She *had to.*

She made it down Holborn, past the flat new space of the Fleet Market where sellers were beginning to set up their wares, through the broken mouth of Newgate, until she was on the roof of the pawnbroker's that held the hidden entrance.

Church bells caught her there, and she fell.

The Onyx Hall, London: March 16, 1759

The usher, it seemed, had been given new instructions. "Lord Galen, Prince of the Stone, and his wife Lady Delphia!"

The lady in question colored at the unaccustomed title, but sallied bravely forward with her arm in his. Galen nodded at the curtsies and bows they received, and approached Lune in her chair of estate. "Lord Galen," the Queen said, with a smile that warmed her worried eyes. "We did not expect to see you here so soon after your wedding."

"The comet may still be concealed in the light of the sun," Galen said, "but that's no excuse for laziness on my part. And my lady wife was eager to spend more time in the Onyx Hall." Now that she could do so with greater ease. No one could object if Mr. and Mrs. St. Clair chose to wander off in each other's company.

"Lady Delphia," Lune said, and received another curtsy in reply. "If you are so eager, then we'll put you into the keeping of Lady Amadea, our chamberlain, who will acquaint you with the other ladies."

Amadea seemed pleased enough, though some of the others

were clearly not so sure. Galen kissed his wife's hand and let her go. She would do well enough in the Lady Chamberlain's company.

A brief exchange was occurring at the door behind him, someone handing a note to the usher, who passed it to a nearby lord, who brought it to Lune with a bow. The Queen unfolded it, and Galen saw surprise break over her like a wave. "Lord Galen, if you would—"

He followed her into the small privy chamber beyond. His curiosity didn't last long; Lune said in a voice that carried no farther than the two of them, "Dr. Andrews says he has succeeded at last. Sophic mercury, extracted in a form we can use, like drawing blood from a patient. He's invited me to Red Lion Square to see."

"Only you?"

"You, Lord Galen, are supposed to be at Sothings Park still, enjoying your connubial bliss. No doubt a letter is seeking you there, without result. In a moment we'll go back out, and my courtiers will hear me send you to Holborn, to consult with Dr. Andrews."

Amusement rippled inside him. It felt good; the knot of tension that had bound his heart since Abd ar-Rashid first brought up the moon queen was coming untied at last. Lune did not seem so relieved, but her determination was unmistakable. "I'll find you waiting for me in Newgate, won't I?"

"I thought the Fleet Market would be an appropriate rendezvous. Meet me there in half an hour."

Red Lion Square, Holborn: March 16, 1759

They shared a carriage, knees almost brushing in its close confines, and arrived at Dr. Andrews's house a little before noon. The footman escorted them up to the drawing room on the piano nobile. This was where Andrews had displayed his menagerie, before illness forced him to disband it. The room was less comfortable than the back parlor, and despite the chill in the air, no fire burnt in the grate: an unusual piece of carelessness, from Andrews's usually scrupulous servants. Nor was Andrews there.

They heard the man's coughing before he entered the room. Galen was appalled. Andrews had finally agreed to spend less time in the Onyx Hall, for the sake of his mind; it seemed his body had paid the price. Or perhaps this decline would have happened anyway, his health finally abandoning the fight against the disease that was killing him. He should have been in bed, enduring his last days in what comfort could be managed, but it seemed his will was too strong to allow him that surrender.

Lune saw it, too. She swept past Galen and took Dr. Andrews by the arm, helping him into a chair. "Thank you," the man whispered, his voice a ghost of what it had been before.

Then he saw Galen, and surprise sparked another bout of coughing. When it ended, Andrews rasped, "Mr. St. Clair— you were supposed to be at Sothings Park."

"I came to see the mercury," Galen said, his own voice as hushed as if he stood at someone's deathbed.

Andrews shook his head. "I don't have it yet."

Lune and Galen exchanged looks of mutual confusion. "But your letter said—"

"Need you." He pointed at Lune. "It won't work with a nymph. We need the connection to the Onyx Hall. Just as the Dragon acquired an association with air by its transmission to the comet, so are you completed by your realm."

"Dr. Andrews, *no*." It hurt all the more because Galen had believed their problem finished at last. "If this mercury depends on a connection to the Onyx Hall, it cannot be used; the power of the Hall is exactly what the Dragon desires. You would give our enemy precisely the thing we fight to keep it *from*."

Andrews's breath rattled audibly in his chest, and he clutched his ever-present handkerchief as if it were the only thing anchoring his spirit to his body. "There is no other choice, Mr. St. Clair. If the Dragon's power is as great as you say, then it must be matched by a source equally strong; only the Onyx Hall will suffice. Else sulphur will obliterate mercury and the work will be lost."

Galen rose slowly to his feet. His entire body was trembling, and the dark, bare space of the drawing room seemed to be closing in on him, narrowing his world to himself and Dr. Andrews alone. He didn't want to ask, but he had to; the salvation of London depended on it. "How—how would the extraction be done?"

The dying man finally met Galen's eyes, and what he saw revealed there struck him dumb with horror.

Andrews whispered, "I'm sorry."

The doors to the drawing room opened. In came six people Galen didn't recognize: ordinary laboring men, or so they appeared to be, except he knew without question that they were fae under glamour.

Sanists.

"There is no drawing of blood," Andrews said. "No extraction of the necessary element without harm to the patient. I tried, Mr. St. Clair, but they all died. If there was any other way, I swear to you, I would use it, but—"

"Dr. Andrews." Lune spoke his name, but addressed all of them, with courage and dignity that would give the hardest assassin pause. "I understand your desperation, but you must listen to me. The philosopher's stone is not your salvation. Not if it is created from the Dragon. It's a creature of destruction; even if you take me, with all the power of the Onyx Hall behind me, I won't be able to stop it."

Andrews shivered. "But it's perfection. It *creates* perfection."

"And so it may do—by annihilating that which is not perfect." Lune spread her arms, seeming to encompass the entire city within her embrace. "After London burnt, men submitted plans to the King, grand designs for transforming it into the jewel of Europe, sweeping away the old tangle of streets to create something better. They failed. But if London were to burn again—why, then, they would have another chance. Dr. Andrews, you *cannot* do this. It will destroy us all."

For one timeless, breathless moment, Galen thought she had persuaded him. Andrews's mouth wavered, uncertainty breaking through the desperation.

Then the doctor made his choice.

What he would have said to excuse it, Galen never learned. He charged forward, blindly, but one of the Sanists was there before he got two steps, grabbing him and wrestling him back. Another trapped Lune with brawny arms. "You shouldn't have come, Mr. St. Clair," Dr. Andrews gasped, in between coughs. "I meant to spare you this. I'm sorry. I'm sorry . . ."

Galen screamed. It didn't last more than a heartbeat before silence blanketed the room. A third Sanist came forward with rowan-wood shackles to bind Lune's good and crippled hands together. Her silver eyes sought him out, and their touch pierced Galen to the bone.

Still screaming, feeling it tear out of his chest even if nothing reached his ears, Galen fought like a wild animal. He clawed free of his captor and snatched the nearest thing that came to hand, his chair, swinging it like a tavern brawler. The Sanist knocked it aside contemptuously and punched him in the face. Light burst all across Galen's vision. He felt the wall beneath his hands, holding him up; then a second blow struck him in the stomach, driving all the air from him, knocking him back. He raised his hands in feeble defense, but it did him no good as the fist came at him a third time.

This one sent him staggering backward, out of control, and into the window.

Glass shattered against his back. The wooden sill caught his knees; Galen threw his hand out, trying to catch himself. Pain flared across his palm—he lost his grip—then he was tumbling over the projecting lintel of the front door below, scrabbling for purchase on its edge and then slipping free. Galen hit the front steps and went sprawling in the street.

He looked up to see his captor's face at the window, staring in surprised fury. Gasping for air that would not come, Galen staggered to his feet and ran, limping, for the corner of the square. No shouts came from behind him—of course not, the silencing charm—but he ran as if the hounds of Hell chased him, because soon they would. Out onto Holborn, and there was a hackney; he flung himself into the carriage, ignoring the startled protests of the man inside, and rattled away into the faceless masses of the street, where no pursuer could find him.

Newgate, London: March 16, 1759

When the hackney driver stopped to throw him out, Galen poured the entire contents of his purse into the man's hands, demanding he be taken back to the City.

Only after he staggered out again in Newgate Street, wrapping his handkerchief around his bleeding left hand, did he realize his error. This was the obvious entrance to seek if he were returning to the Onyx Hall. Galen whirled in the narrow alley, trying to look in all directions at once, and nearly fell.

Then he looked up, and he *did* fall, straight into the mud.

A hand dangled over the edge of the roof, at the back of the pawnbroker's. An unmoving hand, he realized—a hand too delicate to belong to anyone human. Galen lurched to his feet and crept forward, half-crouched, ready to run again.

When the fingers did not so much as twitch, he climbed onto a crate, and looked over the edge of the roof.

Irrith lay unconscious, sprawled across the tiles of the building's back extension. Galen thought she was dead. Her skin held a gray pallor, as if the light of her soul had almost gone out. But when he cradled her face in his hands, she stirred, ever so faintly.

Favoring his gashed palm, Galen pulled her awkwardly forward, dragging her off the roof. The contents of her pockets rained down, making hazards for his feet, but he managed to lift her onto his shoulder and carry her to the ground. Had the Sanists attacked her? But if so, why had they left her alive?

The flapping of wings gave him half a second of warning. Galen had just enough time to lay Irrith down before the approaching faerie transformed in midair, falling out of the sky to land in humanlike form. She was a sharp-faced creature, none Galen knew by name, but her predatory leer told her intent clearly enough. And she stood between him and the relative safety of the street.

Ever since fleeing Red Lion Square, the shame of having abandoned Lune had burnt Galen alive. Now Irrith lay helpless in the mud at his feet. Once the goblin woman finished with him, the sprite would not last long.

No.

That single word was the only clear thought in Galen's head as he lunged for the fallen contents of Irrith's pockets. It gave him speed: he came up with the pistol in his hands just before the goblin reached him, and fired from a mere foot away.

The hammer of the gun snapped down—and nothing happened.

She'd slid to a halt in a vain attempt to dodge. Now she laughed and raised her claws.

Galen struck her in the head with the empty pistol. The goblin staggered. He struck her again, a third time, a fourth, beating her down into the mud, until his sweaty grip failed and the gun flew from his grip. But by then the goblin wasn't moving.

He didn't trust it. Any moment now she would rise again, and then he would be doomed, because he was no soldier or brawler; he was a gentleman, and had never come closer to battle than his fencing lessons as a youth.

Galen dragged Irrith out of the mud. How he fit both of them into the cramped alcove of the entrance, he would never know; but a moment later they were in the relative safety of the Onyx Hall, and then he began shouting for help.

The Onyx Hall, London: March 16, 1759

His cries seemed to have summoned fae out of every crevice of the Hall, and half of them were now crowding into the room. Galen didn't even know where they were; it was some courtier's chambers, he thought. Whatever had been nearest when help came running. But the result was chaos, and they were *wasting time.*

He bellowed loud enough to make Gertrude drop the bandage she was wrapping around his hand, and was rewarded with a ragged fall into silence. *"Out,"* he snarled. "I need Sir Peregrin and Sir Cerenel—the Goodemeades can stay—and the scholars, get me Lady Feidelm, Abd ar-Rashid, any of them you can find. Everyone else, *get out."*

Sir Adenant took up his orders and repeated them, herding almost everyone from the room. Now Galen could see Rosamund, crouching over Irrith, trying to chafe warmth back into the sprite's limp hands. "What's wrong with her?"

"Iron," the brownie said, not looking up. "And holy things, and everything else. She was up there without bread, Galen, I don't know for how long."

Would she recover? He couldn't spare the time for that worry, not right now. Gertrude tied off the bandage as Sir Peregrin came in with his lieutenant. Abd ar-Rashid was not far behind. Good enough to start with.

Galen told them of Red Lion Square. He wanted to be concise, but every word made his face ache, and his thoughts kept scattering to the four winds; Gertrude pressed a cup of mead into his good hand, and he drank it down, shaking almost badly enough to choke. Where were the rest of the scholars? Abd ar-Rashid shook his head when Galen asked. "Lady Feidelm and Wrain are in the Calendar Room. I cannot find Savennis."

"He's dead."

The paper-thin whisper came from Irrith. Rosamund had tucked her into the bed of the courtier whose chambers they'd usurped, where she looked like a small child, wasted by illness. Her shifting eyes had dulled to a flat, muddy green. "In the cellar. Andrews was experimenting. They're all dead."

I tried, Mr. St. Clair, but they all died.

The doctor's words echoed in his head. The vivisected salamander, the laboratory beneath Andrews's house—the questions about what happened when a faerie died. *Christ. Lune.*

Galen stumbled blindly toward the door. "We have to go *now*. She—she may already be dead . . ."

Cerenel caught him before he could get far. Rosamund hurried to his side, with hasty words of comfort. "She isn't, lad; you'd know if she were. The Hall would tell you. But you have to plan before you go rushing in, because of a surety they'll be waiting for you."

"We don't have the time!"

Abd ar-Rashid's accented voice brought him down to earth,

unreasonably calm in the face of his own panic. "I think perhaps we do. If I understand Dr. Andrews well enough."

Galen stopped fighting Cerenel's hands. "What do you mean?"

The genie folded his arms, frowning. "He seeks the moon queen, yes? Then he will want the moon. Full would be best, but he has missed that; he will not wait for it to come again. But the . . . extraction will be tonight."

"Then why snatch her now?" Peregrin demanded. "When it gives us time to respond?"

"Because he needs time to prepare."

Cerenel allowed Galen to step back. The pause had checked the fire in his veins; now, at last, he began to feel the beating he'd taken, the throbbing heat of his hand, the protests of his right ankle when he put weight on it. But the mead gave him the strength to keep going.

Everyone was looking at him. Prince of the Stone, and in Lune's absence, the voice of authority in the Onyx Hall.

He tried to focus, past the unpleasant pulsating of his bruised face. Abd ar-Rashid's calm response to Peregrin sounded plausible, but he suspected it was more of a guess than the genie admitted. If the extraction was now . . .

"Lune was supposed to go alone," he mumbled, mostly to himself. "Not with me."

"Aspell must know she's been sneaking out of the Hall," Irrith said, struggling to sit up, against Gertrude's insistence.

"Aspell? The Lord Keeper?"

Peregrin's teeth bared in a snarl. "The Sanist. Dame Irrith told us, while you were away."

The knight likely didn't mean it as an accusation, but it cut Galen nonetheless. Irrith brushed lank hair from her face and said, "I followed him to Dr. Andrews's house. I didn't know what they were planning, but I was trying to get back here to warn the Queen."

They shared the same shame, the same failure. He saw it in her face, as no doubt she saw it in his.

So the intent had been for the Queen to go in secret, by herself, or at most with one attendant. There was no reason to suspect Dr. Andrews, and no reason to take a guard. By the time her absence was remarked, and her location determined, it would be too late.

"But they know now that we know," Galen said. He lowered himself stiffly into the nearest chair. "Andrews won't use his cellar laboratory. By now they'll be gone. But to where?"

Silence. The assembled fae looked from one to another, seeking answers, finding none.

Andrews had nowhere else to go, not that Galen knew of. He could not kill a faerie woman inside the house of the Royal Society. "Does Aspell have any familiar haunts, outside the Hall?"

More silence, shaking heads. It sparked Galen's anger. "Come on! There must be something. Where can they be safe? Abd ar-Rashid, give me the alchemical answer. What place is best for the work he intends to do?"

The genie closed his eyes and began to murmur to himself in rapid Arabic, unintelligible to them all. Then, still without looking, he changed to English. "Ablution. Washing the material in mercurial waters to reach albedo, the white stage before the creation of the stone. He will need to purify her . . . he would not have done this in his house, I think, even without being found. He needs a source of water, away from iron or other things that will harm her."

Galen's mind offered up an enormous list of water sources in London. "The ponds in St. James' Park. The Chelsea Reservoirs. The Serpentine. Not Holywell—the New River Head—"

"No," Rosamund murmured, cutting him short. "Think, Galen. The Thames."

The answer so obvious, he overlooked it. Abd ar-Rashid's lip curled delicately. "It is an open sewer. Not clean at all."

"But the heart of London, and connected to the Onyx Hall," Galen said. "Which is part of what Andrews is relying upon. Rosamund is right: he will use the Thames."

Abd ar-Rashid was right, though, about the state of the waters. Somewhere upriver, then, where they were less fouled. Galen thought back to his Vauxhall visits, what he had seen from the barge. Westminster—no, too many wharves. The swampy banks of Lambeth, perhaps. Or Vauxhall itself? But while all of that, strictly speaking, fell under Lune's authority—which extended to more than just the Onyx Hall itself—the farther he went, the farther he took her from the London Stone, and the heart of her realm. And Aspell knew about the Stone. Surely he would have told Andrews.

Galen stared blankly at the far wall, seeing in his mind's eye the journey upriver. The wharves floating by, the fine houses along the Strand, the Palace of Westminster.

Upriver and down. Cleansing before the extraction. No one place would serve, but . . .

"What about a barge?"

A gleam came into Abd ar-Rashid's dark eyes. He shared a little bit of Dr. Andrews's flaw, Galen thought, the willingness to love an idea for its own beauty, without concern for its consequences. "A moving laboratory, for the volatile principle. Yes, it would do well."

Very well indeed—if they weren't speaking of Lune's death. "Starting upriver, where the waters are cleaner, and floating down. If it's her connection to the Onyx Hall he wants, then the—the *extraction* will happen in the City. Beneath the moon, I suppose." Galen swallowed down bile.

Peregrin said, "Assuming all this speculation is correct. We have nothing but logic to support it."

Gertrude had convinced Irrith to lie down again, or perhaps simple exhaustion had done it for her. The brownie said, "Might be we have a way to tell. I don't know how far it goes, but—the Thames is connected to the Onyx Hall, and so are the Prince and Queen. If she's on the river, he might be able to tell. Once she's close enough, anyway."

The Onyx Hall. A quiet presence in the back of Galen's mind, grown familiar enough that he rarely thought of it. Could he use it to find the Queen?

He could certainly try. "In the meanwhile," Galen said, "we assume nothing. Sir Peregrin, I'll tell the Lord Treasurer to provide whatever's needed. Search this city from one end to the other. If Lune is anywhere within London, find her—before tonight."

"I'd bring you with me, but you need to rest."

Irrith shook her head—or at least rolled it on her pillow, the best she could do. "Not even if I could, Galen. Carline almost tricked me once into telling her where the London Stone lay. I'm happier not knowing where it is now." So long as there were vipers like Aspell in the Hall, she wanted to know nothing that could betray it.

He squeezed her limp hand. Even that light pressure forced her bones together—as it had always done, no doubt, but now she was aware of it, as she was aware of the fragility of her entire body. Irrith felt as if she'd been pounded, head to toe, with an iron club, and one more blow could break her. "I'm sorry," he said.

She wasn't sure either of them knew what precisely he was apologizing for. An unaccustomed prickling stung her eyes. "Galen—I think Podder was in that cellar. He didn't run away."

It barely touched him; his fear and rage for Lune left little room for anything else. But Galen nodded. Then, when neither of them could think of anything further to say, he turned to go.

When he was halfway to the door, his wife came into the room.

Delphia Northwood—no, Delphia *St. Clair*—gasped at the sight of her new husband. Irrith had no idea what Galen had been up to while she lay unconscious in Newgate, but his shirt was filthy, the back of his coat was slashed to ribbons, and his face was beginning to bruise beneath the blood. Small wonder the woman was horrified. "What in Heaven's—"

He held up his left hand, seemed to notice the bandage on it, and replaced it with his right. "Delphia, I'm sorry; I don't have time to explain. I have to find Lune. Something terrible has happened, and I . . . I need to be Prince right now."

Irrith watched the words settle over Delphia St. Clair. Did the woman see the difference in Galen, beneath the blood and the bandages? *I need to be Prince right now.* He *was* the Prince, maybe for the first time ever. Not merely standing at Lune's side, fulfilling his duties as required, but making decisions, giving orders. The change showed in his posture, the set of his jaw. The challenge had come—the crisis, not just the creeping threat of the comet—and he had stepped up to meet it.

As a Prince of the Stone should.

Delphia let him go, with only a brief touch of her hand on his shoulder. Then she stood, eyes cast down, in silence, and Irrith would have wagered all her remaining bread that the woman thought she was alone in the room.

But Gertrude would come back in a moment with mead for Irrith, and then it would be embarrassing to admit she'd listened to that exchange without saying anything. *I could pretend to be asleep.*

Instead she cleared her throat, and watched Delphia try to jump out of her skin. "It won't end, you know," Irrith said. "This fight, yes—one way or another, it will be over tonight. But it will always be true that Galen has to be Prince. He'll always be running off, and leaving you behind." Not just for Lune's sake, but for the entire Onyx Court.

The mortal woman came forward one slow step at a time, hands clasped over her skirts. She studied Irrith with curious eyes, and a hint of compassion. But only a hint; the rest was steel.

"I am not left behind," Delphia St. Clair said. "I'm a lady of the bedchamber to the Queen. I'll make my own place here in this court, and when my husband goes to do his duty, I will not resent him for it."

Irrith managed a weak smile. She *did* like this woman, who commanded admiration instead of pity. "Well said. If you really do mean it, then I suggest you go above, where your words won't hurt us . . . and pray you still have a queen to serve tomorrow."

In a tiny alcove well concealed in the Onyx Hall, Galen stood with both hands upraised, clutching the rough surface of the London Stone.

It looked like nothing: a rounded stub of a crude pillar,

protruding from the ceiling above, its tip deeply grooved by the abuse of centuries. Its significance to London above was half-forgotten, even as the Stone itself was half worn away.

But in the shadowy reflection that was the Onyx Hall, there was no place of greater significance. This was the axis, the point where the two worlds fused into one, and Galen could touch his entire realm with his mind.

The Hall, fraying and fading in scattered patches. The wall, fragmented more with every passing year. The hill of St. Paul's Cathedral in the west; the hill of the Tower in the east. The Walbrook, running buried beneath the City, from the north down to the greater waters of the Thames in the south.

The Thames.

This was where Galen directed his thoughts, striving outward, seeking the Hall's other half. He devoted some attention to the waters downriver, and more to the ground of the streets above, in case Lune should be there; but the greater part of his being he sent upriver, past the Fleet, past the Strand, past Westminster, stretching himself farther and farther as he went, desperately grasping for any tremor that might indicate the presence of the Queen.

He held the image of her before him like a beacon, shining silver and pure. The moon queen, as Dr. Andrews had said. A goddess beyond his reach, but perhaps this once he could serve her as she deserved, saving her from those who would cut that glory out of her flesh and feed it to the fire.

Before she could be saved, she must be found.

Farther. And farther. And *farther,* his spirit strained to the breaking point.

There.

The River Thames, London: March 17, 1759

The barge approached Westminster just after midnight, floating silently on the black waters of the Thames. Even the watermen who managed the craft worked without sound, going about their tasks like automata, their minds fogged by their faerie passengers. They took only as much notice of those passengers as was needed to avoid tripping over them, and no notice at all of the canvas-roofed cabin in the center of the deck, where a cool light unlike any lamp's flame shone.

The fae were silent, too, until the thrumpin Orlegg elbowed his neighbor and pointed at a shadow on the water up ahead. "Glamour. Big one, on Westminster Bridge."

All the faerie company, save those inside the cabin, squinted through the darkness to pierce the effect. The first one to succeed snorted. "Swopped the arches half a step, all the way across. Seems they don't mind risking their Queen drowning."

Orlegg growled. "They know we're coming."

The Sanists moved quickly. One charmed the watermen, persuading them to steer the barge straight for what appeared to be a solid stone pier. Another cracked the door to the cabin and whispered to those inside. Orlegg mustered the rest in preparation for battle.

The loyalists would not give up their wounded Queen without a fight—and so the Sanists would give them one.

All along the Strand, the wide road leading from Westminster to the City, folk waited in shadows. The Lord Treasurer had all but emptied his domain, armoring fae for the long night of readiness. A company had concealed itself in the alcoves of Westminster Bridge, hoping to catch the barge in its deceptive glamour, so they could swarm down on it from above; so far all they had caught were two little scullers, ferrying gentlemen home from their late-night pleasures.

But if fae rode upon the barge, that trap would do little good. And so the rest of the Onyx Hall's fighting force, all those loyal to the Queen, strung themselves along the Strand, waiting to converge upon their target.

As soon as they found it.

Segraine's blade hissed from its scabbard and swung before Irrith could even leap back. The point came to rest just against the side of her neck. "Blood and Bone—Irrith! What in Mab's name are you doing here?"

The sprite pushed the sword away with two careful fingers. "Rescuing the Queen."

"Over my dead body—or your own, more like. You can barely stand."

"But I *can* stand," Irrith pointed out, and began loading her pistol. Elfshot only; the iron in her pocket, she was saving for the Dragon. "Unless you want to waste time dragging me back to the Hall, I'm here to stay."

The lady knight ground her teeth. "Irrith, we can do this without you—"

"It's my fault, all right? I'm the one who told Aspell what Andrews was doing, and if it weren't for me—"

She never got a chance to say how things might have been different. Bonecruncher clapped one taloned hand over her mouth. "If it weren't for you, we might have a chance of avoiding the constables," the barguest hissed in her ear. "Leave or be quiet, but if you go on shouting like that, I'll drown you in the Thames myself."

Mute, Irrith met Segraine's eyes. The knight clenched her teeth, but nodded. Bonecruncher dropped his hand, Irrith loaded her second pistol, and they waited for the barge to come.

In the black waters of the Thames, more shadows moved.

The fae of the river, nymphs and asrai and draca, found less and less joy in the city these past years. Their land-dwelling kindred could retreat from the filth of London into the Onyx Hall, but living in Queenhithe's subterranean mirror was like living in a pond. Out here in the river, they had to contend with all the refuse of the mortals, and waters that grew fouler every year.

Tonight, however, they swam without complaint. They flooded out the Queenhithe entrance and formed a line across the river, sweeping upstream in search of the barge. There were other craft upon the Thames, of course. The larger ships, however, were confined downriver by the ancient stones of the London Bridge, and at this hour of the night, only a few small wherries plied the surface. Their search was—should have been—easy.

But they were not the only shadows in the water.

There was no warning. Just a claw, snaking out of nowhere to snatch an asrai and drag her down. Underwater, she could not scream; she vanished without a sound.

A draca was the next target, and he dodged not quite rapidly enough. Blood bloomed in the murk, and then he saw his enemy.

Blacktooth Meg cared little for the politics of the Onyx Hall. All she knew was rage. The poisoned Fleet, long choked with garbage and offal, corpses and shit, had turned the foul river hag even fouler, until all she wanted to do was rend and destroy. Valentin Aspell offered her a chance to do so. She merely had to venture out of her waters into the Thames, and prevent the fae there from swimming upstream.

Battle churned in the darkness below, invisible to those above. Even the water-dwelling fae could scarcely see their enemy before she closed with them. But one nymph broke free, driving herself upstream with frantic speed, desperate to carry out her sworn task.

She didn't have to go far. Under cover of darkness and charms, the barge had come nearly to the mouth of the Fleet, and the boundary of the Onyx Hall.

Hands made clumsy with panic tore at the box tied to her waist. Then the lid was open, and the will-o'-the-wisp sprang out, erupting from the water into the air above, marking the target for those who waited to attack.

The sky was too dangerous for large forces on any night other than All Hallows' Eve. But birds attracted no notice, especially against the dark background of the clouds. Their sharp eyes picked out the flare of light on the river below, and they screamed a warning through the air.

A lone horseman came galloping through the sky, downriver from Westminster Bridge. The tatterfoal stretched his legs to their fullest, angling downward to seek out the barge, and his rider Sir Cerenel dropped the reins to ready the weapon he held.

Not all of the jotun ice had gone into the spear for the Dragon. Leaning sideways out of the saddle, the elf-knight hurled a shard into the river below.

It struck the water and sank halfway in. No farther: by then the river had frozen around it, ice crystalling outward in all directions, even down to the soft mud of the bed, trapping the barge just short of the mouth of the Fleet.

And forming a bridge from one bank to the other, a road for the rescuers to ride.

Galen had positioned himself in the timber yard off Dorset Street, scant yards from the open bank of the Fleet. Sir Peregrin let him do it because the Captain believed they would catch the barge much farther upriver. But Galen thought, when he saw the ice race across the surface of the Thames, that some dismal part of himself had always believed it would come to this, the last, desperate chance to save Lune.

He heard the clatter of hooves and feet approaching down Temple Street, the company that had waited in the King's Bench Walk, but he could not wait for them, not even half a moment. Spurring the brag he rode, Galen charged out onto the ice.

The surface was treacherous beyond belief, crazed from the unnatural speed of its freezing, but slick all the same. His mount screamed and went down twenty feet from the barge, sending Galen flying across the ice, out of control. But it also saved the Prince; when a goblin leapt over the gunwale, sword in hand, the attacker's feet went out from under him, too.

A bullet chipped the ice near Galen's head. Someone on the barge was more clever. The Prince half-crawled, half-slid into the shelter of the vessel's wooden side, and snatched up the sword the goblin had dropped. The creature tried to run at him, but by then the rest of Galen's company was there; Sir Adenant rode him down.

Behind them came Segraine's company, marked by the

flaming eyes of Bonecruncher. And Irrith, corpse-pale as if she might collapse, but lifting her pistol to fire at a Sanist.

Galen gritted his teeth and rose, clawing his way over the barge's edge. Gunfire still cracked around him, but they couldn't afford to lose a second, lest Andrews decide he'd come close enough to his goal. The Prince came aboard to find himself facing a blank-eyed waterman. A blade flashing out from behind the man told him a fae was using the mortal as cover. But the strike was made half-blind, and Galen dodged it easily, shoving the waterman backward. *There— the cabin—*

Cool light radiated upward as someone dragged free the canvas that served in place of a roof. Heart in his mouth, Galen looked upward.

Clouds still covered most of the sky, but ragged patches had appeared here and there, and one of them revealed the moon.

Only the raw scratch of his throat told him he was screaming. Galen threw himself forward, using the sword as much like a bludgeon as a blade, not caring who he drove through or how. More fae swarmed onto the barge with him, but the Sanists stood ready, and the confines of the deck limited the opposing numbers to something like equality. Then the thrumpin in front of him went down with a howl, and Galen saw Irrith, crouched low with a knife at hamstring height. "Come on!" she shouted, and snatched without success at the handle of the cabin door.

She got out of the way just in time to avoid Galen's rush. He hit the door with the shoulder bruised last fall, and felt the jolt all the way across his body, but the cabin was a flimsy thing. The latch snapped, dropping Galen through into the room beyond.

He knew what he would see even before he regained his feet. Valentin Aspell, leaping in front of Galen with a hiss. Dr. Andrews, looking like Death itself in the cold faerie light.

And Lune, chained by rowan to the table on which she lay, naked and vulnerable to the knife.

The faerie lights dimmed without warning. Aspell flinched involuntarily, one hand flying to shield his face, as three small, dark spheres struck him and fell to the boards. In that moment Galen leapt; he'd lost his sword somewhere, but he still had his weight, and it was enough to send Aspell crashing backward in the cramped space, into Dr. Andrews.

They went down in a heap, all three of them, and the knife clattered loose. Then someone else was there—Peregrin, dragging Aspell free and wrestling him to the boards, snarling curses in his ear.

No one had to do the same to Andrews. The mortal lay gasping, too weak to even cough. Galen crawled off him and stood, glaring down without pity. Only by a supreme effort of will did he keep from stamping on the hand that had held the knife.

But a whimper distracted him from vengeance. Lune twitched weakly against her bonds, until Irrith crawled forward and retrieved the three iron bullets she'd thrown at Aspell, stowing them once more in their hawthorn case. Galen shrugged out of his tattered coat and flung it over the Queen, giving her a measure of decency as he found and pulled free the pins that held her rowan chains.

The barge shifted beneath his feet. Someone had retrieved the jotun ice; the river was beginning to thaw once more. Galen helped Lune to her feet, supporting her out onto the open deck, and gave her reluctantly to Sir Cerenel, whose tatterfoal would carry her to immediate safety. They'd clearly fed her no bread, needing her faerie soul pure, and Galen suspected Andrews had done something more; the Queen's knees were as weak as a newborn child's. But she had the strength to press her lips to Galen's cheek and murmur half-coherent thanks, before she was gone.

He turned back to see Irrith sprawled in the cabin doorway, hawthorn box dangling loosely from her fingers. The sprite turned dulled eyes up to him and said, "We did it."

Galen was too weary to do more than nod. Looking past Irrith to the huddled form of Dr. Andrews, he thought, *Yes. We saved Lune.*

But we've lost the philosopher's stone.

Red Lion Square, Holborn: March 18, 1759

The weak rasp of Dr. Andrews's breathing was the only sound in the room. Outside, the world went on, heedless of the comet in the sky above, and the acts it had inspired. The clouds still held, but imperfectly; the protection they had given these long months was failing at last.

The man in the bed would not live to see it end.

Galen said, "Why did you do it?"

He thought at first that Andrews was coughing. It turned out to be a laugh, bitter as gall. "Why. You stand there, watching me die, and you ask *why*."

To save his own life, of course. "For that, you would murder an innocent woman. And not just her, but Savennis, Podder—"

"I tried everything, Mr. St. Clair." Andrews lay limp beneath his sheets, unable even to lift his hands now. "If I could have done it some other way, I would have. But the sands of my hourglass had nearly run out. When the Lord Keeper came to me, offering his aid . . ." He had to pause for breath. "The others were tests of my method. I had to be sure it would work. Once I was—then yes. To save myself, and this city, and all of mankind, I would kill. Who would not?"

Galen thought of what Lune had said. That the Dragon would bring perfection through destruction. How many would such a creature truly save?

It didn't matter. "I wouldn't," Galen said. "No moral man would."

Andrews didn't answer. After a few moments of waiting, Galen realized he would not speak again. The Prince stood and watched in silence as the wasted chest rose and fell, until it moved no more.

Then he went downstairs to tell Dr. Andrews's faithful, unquestioning servants that their master was dead at last.

PART SEVEN

Calcinatio

Spring 1759

'Tis Saturn's offspring who keeps a well in wch
drown Mars & then Saturn behold his face in't wch
will seem fresh & young when ye souls of both are
blended together, for each need be amended by
th'other. Then a star shall fall into ye well.

—Isaac Newton,
unpublished alchemical notes

The sun has come and gone, growing from a spark to a sphere of undying flame. Now it recedes into the dark once more.

And still the Dragon waits.

Impatience rages as brightly as its light. The greater brilliance of the sun briefly severed the links between the Dragon and the Earth; the eyes were gone, and even its own straining efforts could not make out the distant speck of its target. It thought, then, that it had lost its chance. When contact returned, it almost leapt down, to gorge upon the first thing it found.

Almost. Almost. But the promise of power is enough to hold it in check.

Not for much longer, though. Its instinct to destroy is too intense. If it cannot have the city, and the shadow, and the ones who banished it to the cold black sky, it will take something else instead. Grow strong once more, stronger than it ever was, until it consumes everything.

Then it will have power, and all the world besides.

Valentin Aspell seemed far more serene than he had any right to be. The treasonous Lord Keeper was sitting at his ease in a chair when the jailer unlocked the door to his cell; they had permitted him that much comfort, though there was little else in this bare stone room, beneath the Tower of London. Upon seeing Lune and her escort, he rose and sank to one elegant knee. "Your Majesty."

The Queen stopped a little way into the room, letting Sir Peregrin and Sir Cerenel keep between her and the prisoner. Irrith was glad to remain at her side. Aspell's eyes did no more than flicker briefly in her direction, but it was more than enough; Irrith shivered, and wished she hadn't come. Lune needed her, though. Whatever Dr. Andrews had done, she'd been days in recovering from it; he hadn't weakened her so much as . . . detached her. The effort of will had been visible, every time Lune concentrated on their words, moved her body, spoke. Irrith wondered privately—and would never ask anyone—whether it was true that too much mortal bread, even of the safe, tithed kind, could tinct a faerie, and whether Andrews had washed that from her. What human qualities Lune had taken on might be gone from her now.

She certainly did not look human as she regarded the kneeling Aspell. She let the silence grow, heartbeat by heartbeat, until Irrith herself wanted to say something just to break it; and then she said, "Tell me why I should not execute you."

There were many answers Aspell could have made. It wasn't Lune's customary way; it would anger the Sanists; he held some last weapon or offer that made it wiser—or at least more useful—to keep him alive.

Instead he replied, "Because everything I have done, I have done for the good of the Onyx Hall."

Irrith couldn't prevent herself from making a startled and disbelieving noise. Aspell's courtesy was too good for him to lift his head; he remained kneeling, eyes on the cold black floor of his cell. Lune waited until the sound faded before saying, "If your crimes consisted only of my abduction and intended murder for Andrews's scheme, I might believe you. If they extended no further than to what Dame Irrith has told me, your plan to sacrifice me to the Dragon, your current involvement with the Sanist conspiracy, I might still believe you. But your guilt is older than that, Aspell. You plotted with Carline even before the Hall began to fray." She paused, then asked, "Do you deny it?"

"No, your Grace. But I maintain my defense."

"Putting Carline on the throne would be good for the Onyx Hall?" The question burst out of Irrith before she could stop it. Lune made no attempt to stop her. "She would have been a *terrible* queen! And you know it!"

Aspell hesitated. His calmness was no act, Irrith realized; this wasn't some political game. He truly meant what he said. "Madam, with your permission, I would answer Dame Irrith's accusation."

Lune only moved one hand, but Aspell must have seen it, for he went on. "Carline was . . . not ideal, it's true. But she had this virtue over others who might have been more suitable: she could have been controlled. So long as she had her entertainments, she would have been willing to give me free rein in the Onyx Hall."

"And that was what you wanted, wasn't it."

"Not at all—not if I could have the world according to my preferences. The power I have now—had—pleased me very well. But others who might have taken the throne would have been equally flawed, and far less biddable."

Irrith wanted to shove past Cerenel and strangle him. *This is what I hate the most—forked tongues speaking treason and patriotism at the same time. All the twists, all the lies, until even the liar believes his own words.* "Is that how you see your Queen? Unbiddable and flawed?"

"Yes." The word was cold and uncompromising. "Your Grace . . . you have been flawed since the iron knife first entered your shoulder."

Before the Dragon burnt her hand, before the first bit of the Onyx Hall began to crumble away. Before Irrith had ever met London's Queen. Lune said, "And yet you served me, even though I was wounded, never to heal."

A ripple in Aspell's shoulders, a serpentine shrug. "At first it didn't seem to matter. This place is an exception to many rules of faerie-kind; you could have been another. But then Lady Feidelm warned us of the comet's return, and I foresaw a second destruction. To speak bluntly, madam—for I think I have nothing to lose by doing so—had you done as you should, you would have sought out and prepared a successor, to give the Onyx Hall a monarch who is whole. Your continuing refusal to do so, and your failure to dispose of either of the threats that imperils this realm, convinced me there was no other choice."

"No other choice than regicide." Irrith spat the word like the poison it was.

He lifted his head to regard her. As he said, he had nothing to lose by the discourtesy. "When it offers the one plausible chance to save the Hall—yes. With regret. Time forced my hand, you see. Dr. Andrews's plan struck me as far more likely to succeed than my own, but he hovered at the edge of his own grave; if it were to be done, it had to be done *then,* without time to persuade her Majesty into cooperation." He sighed. "I threw the dice, and failed."

With a soul-deep chill, Irrith realized what lay beneath his calm. *He has nothing to lose—not just because Lune may execute him, but because he believes this whole realm is now doomed.*

And what did the Queen believe? Only Lune herself knew; the silver eyes gave nothing away. Irrith couldn't decide which was worse: naked ambition, or this double-knotted rhetoric, laying a road that led sanely and inevitably to horrifying treason.

Aspell bowed his head once more, dismissing Irrith. "You asked, your Grace, why you should not execute me. That is the defense I offer. The preservation of the Onyx Hall requires your removal, and so I pursued it. I renounce nothing I have done, though I regret the clumsy and ineffective manner of its doing. I await your sentence."

Irrith would have killed him, without hesitation. Yes, fae bred rarely, and yes, killing Aspell would likely obliterate his spirit forever—she didn't *care*. He was a traitor, and if lopping his head off angered the Sanists, so be it; they could handle the rebellion once they'd disposed of the Dragon.

Unless it destroyed them all, in which case, no sense wasting effort on the Sanists now.

But Irrith wasn't Lune, with her responsibilities and knowledge of politics and, perhaps, queerly human notions. If she still had them.

The Queen said, "You will face a formal trial, so that all my subjects may know that the Sanist conspiracy, in its extremity, resorted to attempted regicide. But the sentence will be mine to pronounce—and I will not kill you, Aspell."

His shoulders trembled. This might not be mercy; there were fates less pleasant than death.

"Nor," the Queen went on, "will I exile you, to foment trouble abroad. I think rather to return to an older way.

"Niklas von das Ticken has failed to make a functional Dragon-cage, but he assures me he can imprison an ordinary faerie, in a manner more secure—but less cruel—than the iron we used upon that beast. You, Valentin Aspell, will sleep for one hundred years, in such manner as to ensure that no one can free you before your sentence is done."

Irrith realized the intention even as Lune said it. "By the time you wake," the Queen said, "I expect we will have resolved this issue. Either the Onyx Hall will be whole once more, or I will no longer be its mistress. Either way, your concerns will be laid to rest."

Aspell said nothing. What reply could he make? Thanking her would have been absurd; anything else would have been an invitation to greater harshness. For her own part, Irrith thought it as good as any other path out of this situation, and better than some. Lune had passed far harsher sentences before.

She followed the Queen out of Aspell's cell, listening as the heavy bronze door clanged shut behind them, and shivered at the sound. *Will there be an Onyx Hall waiting for him in a hundred years?*

Rose House, Islington: April 4, 1759

Galen was surprised to receive a message at Sothings Park, summoning him to Islington. True, he hadn't been to see the Goodemeades in quite some time, but it hardly seemed to matter. He'd been so occupied with the refinement of the alchemical plan that he'd had little time to spare for political lessons from the brownies.

Could I have prevented Aspell's treason, if I hadn't been distracted? Instead of wasting his time on Andrews's mad scheme. He would never know, and doubting did no one any good.

At least he could take a carriage. The Northwoods kept one at Sothings Park, and it was his to use as he pleased. On a sudden inspiration, he sought out Delphia, who was deep in discussion with the housekeeper, and looked more than happy to be rescued. "I must go to Islington on business, and I thought you might like to accompany me, to visit with some friends."

He laid faint stress on that final word. It had almost become a code between them, a way of referring to the faerie court when others were around. Delphia had met the Goodemeades in the Onyx Hall, but never seen their home; she smiled at the suggestion. "Let me change into a dress suitable for visiting, and I shall."

Let the servants think him besotted with his new wife, eager to spend absurd amounts of time in her company. Galen didn't care. Once Delphia knew the way into Rose House, she could visit on her own.

He assisted her up into the carriage, waving the footman

away, then followed her in. Delphia waited until they were rolling down the drive before she said, "The clouds are breaking up."

So she'd noticed him looking upward. An ordinary person would still call the days cloudy; Galen heard no end of complaints from family and friends about the relentlessly gray weather. But the clouds were bunching up now, rather than forming an unbroken ceiling; sometimes there was even a patch of clear blue. Galen said, "We might have another month left. If we're lucky." Lune was attempting to contact the Greeks again, but Galen doubted it would do much good. Sooner or later, the clouds would fail.

Delphia fiddled with her gloves. She'd been in the Onyx Hall long enough for the fear to infect her, as it did all the rest of the court. "What will you do?"

Galen stared out the window, trying not to pay attention to the sky. "Fight. It's all we *can* do, now."

Country lanes brought them to Islington, and to the busy Angel Inn. Delphia made no comment, but only watched with interest, as Galen led her to the rosebush and spoke to it. He bowed her down the uncovered staircase, then followed her into the house below.

"Lady Delphia!" The brownies were all smiles and curtsies and offers of refreshment; in return, his wife was all admiration of their comfortable home. Gertrude in particular warmed to the compliments, and soon offered to show her guest the other rooms, leaving Galen alone with Rosamund.

The instant they were gone, the smile fell off the little hob's face as if it had never been. "Quickly," Rosamund said, "while Gertrude has her occupied. Oh, Galen—I fear this was *not* the time to bring her here."

She gestured, and the worn carpet obediently folded itself out of the way, revealing floorboards polished by centuries of feet. "I'm sorry," Galen said, nonplussed. He could not imagine what Rosamund might be doing. "I—I merely thought to show her your home—"

"On any other day, yes, of course. But the Queen needs to speak with you privately. Go on; I'll find something to tell your lady wife."

As Rosamund spoke, the worn planks of the floor flexed aside much as the carpet had, disclosing a second staircase. Galen didn't have long to wonder at it; the brownie gestured impatiently—not to say commandingly—and so he went down, into a small chamber whose existence he'd never suspected.

The floorboards sealed above him so rapidly they almost knocked his hat off, and he heard the soft rustle of the carpet sliding back into place. A murmur of voices told him Gertrude and Delphia had returned, and then he had no thoughts for the people above, for he found others waiting below.

Lune sat with her Lady Chamberlain in front of a small hearth. "We can speak," she said, though she kept her voice low. "This room protects the secrets of those within it."

He followed the wave of her hand upward, and saw that a network of roots spread across the ceiling, except at the top of the staircase. Their rough surface was studded with tiny flowers—roses. The same yellow as those on the bush above. "*Sub rosa,*" Galen breathed, understanding. An ancient emblem of secrecy. No doubt among fae, it was more than a mere symbol.

Why had Lune called him here?

The question chilled him. They had talked of delicate matters before, and never needed any privacy greater than that afforded by the Onyx Hall and Lune's guards. He doubted it was merely the shock of Aspell's treason, either.

What could she possibly have to say, that required such powerful security?

It could only concern one matter. Galen made his bow out of habit, then stood gripping his hat in one hand. Lune indicated a chair left for him, but he ignored it. "We've lost, haven't we. The clouds can't be restored."

"No," Lune admitted. "Irrith and Ktistes have sent Il Veloce out with his pipes; he's trying to shepherd the clouds into position so they block sight of the comet, at least. That's all we can do. But no, Galen: we haven't lost."

Hope surged in his heart. The other face of the coin, which he hadn't even let himself consider: the comet, yes, but good news instead of bad. "Then we have a plan?" Wrain and

Lady Feidelm had emerged from the Calendar Room a few days before, but been closeted with the Queen ever since.

Lune nodded, serene and unreadable as he'd ever seen her. It was Amadea who betrayed concern. The Lady Chamberlain clearly didn't know what her Queen meant—but she just as clearly feared it would be nothing good. And seeing her apprehension, Galen feared it, too.

Lune said, "It . . . is not a certain thing. Peregrin's spearknights will do what they can; it may be enough. But Wrain says, and I concur, that the Dragon's spirit—and therefore its body—is too strong to be defeated in such fashion. Therefore we need some other position we may fall back on, should it come to pass that they fail."

The formal cadences of her speech wound his nerves tight. She spoke this way in two circumstances, Galen realized: when she held court, and when the burden of her thoughts was so heavy as to be shared only with reluctance.

In other words, when she was afraid.

She saw him realize it, too. Their eyes met, and she discarded formality for simple, horrifying bluntness. "If we cannot kill the Dragon, then I will give myself up to it."

"*No!*" Galen leapt forward, hat falling from his hand. "No, Lune, you cannot—"

"Why not?"

"Because that's what Aspell wanted!"

"And perhaps he was right." She didn't move from her chair, not even to stand; for once he towered over her, and it felt wrong. "A last resort. A choice between my own death, and the death of my realm—not just the Onyx Hall, but London as well. Thousands of mortals, *hundreds* of thousands, who for years now have dreaded a fiery death at the comet's return, without ever knowing why. Should I stand living, when that disaster comes?"

Galen's hands ached. He'd clenched them into fists, without any target to use them on. "What if it fails, though? What if we lose you and the Hall both?"

The peaceful acceptance in Lune's eyes terrified him. "Then at least I will have done everything I can."

Even unto the sacrifice of her soul, obliterated by the Dragon. Galen felt too light, as if he would drift away; his breath was coming too fast. Had his shouts carried above, or had the watchful roses kept his cries from Delphia's ears? He wondered if the Goodemeades knew of this. They were Lune's friends, beyond the bond of subject to sovereign; surely they could not stand by while she proposed such madness!

But they know her. Perhaps they know she won't be dissuaded.

He shoved that thought away with almost physical force. The Lady Chamberlain, when he looked to her for help, sat white-faced and staring. Lune laid one hand on hers. "You know why you're here, Amadea. I won't leave the Onyx Hall without a mistress. If it comes to this pass, I'll renounce my claim, and you must take it in my place."

Her mouth says if; *her mind says* when. Amadea shook her head, little more than a tremble. Lune's hand tightened. "You must. The court needs a Queen—a Queen, I think, and not a King, because it also needs a Prince of the Stone." She transferred her attention to Galen once more. "She will need your help."

He backed up a step, then another. His own head was moving, back and forth, slow denial. "No."

"Galen, we have no choice."

"Yes. We do. Or at least I do." He should have been rigid with tension, but he wasn't. His body felt loose, supple. Ready to spring. "It would be an insult to the men who have gone before me if I let you die while I still lived."

"Galen—"

He stopped her with one hand. "No. I swear by Oak and Ash and Thorn that I will give my life before I let you die."

An echo of his oaths, when he became Prince of the Stone. Lune's face paled to pure white. Galen bowed to her, then went up the staircase, through the hidden opening, past the Goodemeades and Delphia, and out of Rose House, and he did not look back.

The Onyx Hall, London: April 6, 1759

"Begging your pardon, your Majesty—you're an *idiot*."

Lune didn't flinch at the accusation, much less protest. Irrith would have gone on even if the Onyx Guard were there with swords out to stop her. "You know what he's like. You know he's in love with you. And you thought he'd stand by while you put yourself in danger?"

More than just danger, but neither of them would say it directly. Not here, inside the Onyx Hall. Irrith had heard it from the Goodemeades. If she could have gone to the cells beneath the Tower and dragged Aspell out of his hundred-year-sleep, she would have spit in his face. *He's still succeeded, even after being defeated.*

And Irrith herself was partly to blame. She was the real idiot. Not the Queen.

Me and Galen. We're both too stupid to be let out without keepers.

They were alone in the chamber, with strict guard on the door outside. Lune sat with her head bowed, but in thought, not penitence. Her slender hands rested atop the pillar-and-claw table at her side, as if she were sitting for a portrait—probably some study in melancholy.

"Do you love him?"

The question rocked Irrith back on her heels. "Who? Galen?"

The Queen nodded.

"No. I don't."

One pale finger tapped against the table's pearly surface. After a strange pause, during which Irrith could not begin to guess the thoughts in her head, Lune said, "You've been his lover, though."

Most of the Onyx Hall probably knew, without need for royal spies. "I was. Until he got married. He means to keep faith with his wife."

"But he doesn't love her." Lune shifted, leaning back in her chair, still thoughtful. It wasn't idle thought: she was more like an owl, searching out suitable prey. "I've watched them closely, because I hoped he might, but no. They feel nothing more than friendship for each other. In time it might grow to love . . . but not soon enough."

Irrith regretted it even as she asked, "Soon enough for what?"

The Queen's mouth settled into a line Irrith had seen before, determination in the face of impossibility. "To save him. He might not throw his life away if he felt it would hurt another. Unfortunately, he's done his duty by his family—their wealth is restored—and he has no children yet. I am the only one he loves, and he knows too well that I do not love him back. I would regret his passing, but not deeply enough."

Her silver regard settled on Irrith, who suddenly felt like the mouse the owl had been waiting for. "You could make that choice."

To love him. It *was* a choice, on the part of the fae; that was why they adored stories of mortal passion. The notion that love could strike without warning and sweep away all reason was alien, baffling. Fondness could happen that way, even infatuation, but not love. That required a conscious decision to give over one's heart.

She'd wondered, ever since she met this Queen who loved a mortal man, what it would be like.

But she also knew the price.

"Tell me this," Irrith said, crossing her arms and tucking her elbows close against her body, as if to warm the chill inside. "What Dr. Andrews did to you, that 'cleansing.' Did it take away the grief you feel for Michael Deven?"

The first Prince of the Stone, dead these hundred years and more. Lune said, "No."

So even alchemy could not end the mourning of a faerie who gave her heart. Irrith shook her head. "Then no. I won't. Even if it did stop him, I'd have at most, what—fifty years more? Sixty, if his health is very good? Then an eternity of grief. And he would hate me for having made him choose between me and you." If it was even a choice. Just because one person loved, didn't mean the other would. Galen's fruitless devotion proved that.

Something finally broke through the serenity Lune had maintained all this time, ever since her rescue from Dr. Andrews's knife. "He'll throw his life away," she said, helplessly. "For no better reason than to save himself from watching me die."

Much as Lune herself proposed to do. But it wasn't a fair comparison; she at least had some hope of appeasing the Dragon, even if only for a while.

"Stop him," Lune said. "Please, Irrith. I cannot."

The only way to stop him would be to find a better answer. One that didn't end in either a dead Queen or a dead Prince, much less both.

Irrith didn't know if such an answer existed. But it wouldn't do any good to say that, and so she answered, "I will."

Great Marlborough Street, Soho: April 9, 1759

A few awkward conversations at Royal Society meetings and the dinners beforehand did not a true acquaintance make. Galen cared little for such niceties, though—not now. As soon as he discovered Henry Cavendish's address, he went there straightaway, and made it clear to the servants that he would not be put off. "I must see Mr. Cavendish on a matter of most urgent business. He is the only man who can help me." *I only pray that he can.*

Henry lodged with his father, Lord Charles, and so the footman was accustomed to far more important visitors; he was not easily impressed. But at Galen's insistence, he did bear word to the young master that a very determined madman was at the door.

And whether by his determination or his target's pity, Galen won through. Soon he was shown into a small parlor, where he tried not to wear a hole in the carpet with pacing before Henry Cavendish came in. The man was as shabby as ever; Galen only prayed it would be easier to get him to speak in this more private setting. "Mr. Cavendish," he said as he made a perfunctory bow, "I apologize for the vehemence of my approach, but I have a very great problem, and little time in which to solve it. I must beg you to tell me everything you know about phlogiston."

Cavendish was taken aback. Whatever business he'd believed brought Galen to his door, surely it hadn't been this. It might have been surprise more than the stammer that made him hesitate in saying, "Phlogiston? Ah, yes—" His high-pitched voice went even higher, and the next words took forever to come out. "You said you could get a sample."

Ages ago, at dinner in the Mitre Tavern. Just before he revealed the Onyx Court to Dr. Andrews. Galen cursed his choice: what might have been achieved had he trusted this young man, instead of the mad consumptive?

Possibly nothing. It might even have been worse. It was too late, regardless; the fae would never tolerate him bringing a second philosopher among them. Not now, with the end so near at hand. Cavendish would have to work blind. "I—yes. I have. That is, I *think* I have," he cautioned, as his host came alive with curiosity. "I'm not certain. But what I have is *extremely* dangerous, Mr. Cavendish—very destructive—and I must find a way to render it safe again, before it can do more harm."

"Let us go, then!" All hint of a stammer had vanished, along with Cavendish's awkward shyness; he even tried to grab Galen by the arm.

Galen pulled back. "No. My apologies, Mr. Cavendish, but—" He floundered for an excuse. "Its destructive potential is too great. I mean no offense to you, but if anyone else learned how to isolate phlogiston, *before* I discover a means of securing it again, the consequences could be disastrous."

An ordinary man would have been offended; Cavendish was already lost in his own thoughts, talking to himself. "So far as we understand it, phlogiston exists in all combustible materials. When they burn, the phlogiston is released into the air. If you burn a candle in a sealed jar, in time it goes out; this, I think, is because the air has absorbed all the phlogiston it can hold."

"How does it get into those materials in the first place?"

Cavendish shook his head. "I don't know." He began to

pace, chewing on one knuckle in what looked like a habitual gesture. "Perhaps trees produce it as they grow? . . . but that does you no good; you don't want to make *more*. Not yet, at any rate."

Galen twisted his fingers together. He'd forgotten gloves, and even his walking stick; he wished desperately for something to occupy his nervous hands. "Then to break it down instead. But no—it's elemental; it can't be broken into other substances. What about its opposite?"

"Opposite?"

"As in alchemy. Fire was opposed by water, cold and wet instead of hot and dry. What would that be, in modern terms? Not water itself, I know that much; it must be something else, more fundamental, perhaps some quality *in* water, that would be antithetical to phlogiston."

But Cavendish was already waving for him to stop. "No, no. As you said—that's alchemy. And it doesn't work. Phlogiston has no 'opposite,' not that I'm aware of; for it to have an opposite, it would have to exist within a scheme like Aristotle's, tidy and patterned. But the world is not so."

Not this world. Galen's throat seemed to be closing, making it hard to swallow, cutting off his air. Only in faerie science was there such patterning, and it had pointed to the answer: Lune. The moon queen; sophic mercury. But that would kill her, and then they would face the Dragon, perfected and unstoppable.

Cavendish suddenly bounced where he stood, a stiff-legged hop that would have been comical had Galen been less desperate. "Saturating the air! If phlogiston moves from wood to air, and stops when the air is saturated, then perhaps it could be contained by material already filled to the brim with it."

"Wood?"

The young philosopher shook both hands by his head, as if warding off distraction. "Too fragile. Gold? Though how you'd get the substance inside, I'm not sure. Draw it into something lacking phlogiston, I suppose, but then you'd lose the purity. If you would let me see your sample—"

Gold. Not iron. Galen had no idea if it would work, but Cavendish had told him what he needed to know; the container had to be something saturated with fire. And the fae had gold they said was drawn from the sun itself. If anything would suffice . . .

"Thank you, Mr. Cavendish," he said, the words almost tumbling over each other in his rush to get them out. "I must go, my apologies, but I'll let you know what happens—this has given me an idea—"

With Cavendish's protests following him, Galen fled out the door and downstairs, running to find the dwarves.

Cinnamon Street, Wapping: April 12, 1759

Irrith hadn't been in the eastern parts of London for a hundred years. There was a lot *more* of eastern London now, and while she'd seen it from the air when she rode with the Queen on All Hallows' Eve, going through it on foot was rather different. She passed all manner of strange people, scarcely one in five an Englishman, or so it seemed: Irish, Negroes, Lascars, and more, living cheek by jowl among the workshops that served the docks and the ships crowding the river.

She didn't know her way around, and she didn't know where to go, either. It took more than an hour of questioning before someone could point her to the shop of the Jew Schuyler. It was her one hint of direction: Abd ar-Rashid lived near the Dutchman who made the lenses and mirrors for the Monument, and the bowl they used to summon the clouds. No one had seen the genie since Dr. Andrews died, and so she had to find him the hard way.

The girl inside the shop listened to Irrith silently, as the sprite tried to describe the bowl; then she vanished, still without a word, through the curtain behind the counter. A moment later, a gray-haired Jew came out. "Why do you look for him?" Schuyler asked, wariness clear even through his accent.

"I need his help," Irrith said, realizing too late that she might have sounded more sympathetic as a woman. Schuyler looked as if he expected Irrith to assault the Arab when she found him. *Around here, that's probably a fair fear.* The docks were just a stone's throw away, with all their drunken sailors.

After a moment Schuyler jerked his thumb to the side. "End of the street. There is a house with lascars in it; he lives on the top floor."

She found the dark-skinned sailors, and the staircase that served their house. Irrith took the steps three at a time, and pounded on the door at the top.

The man who opened it didn't look like an Arab. Nor did he seem quite like a fae; whatever Abd ar-Rashid did to disguise himself, it didn't feel the same as an English glamour. But she knew it was an illusion, and knew it was him.

And he knew it was her—or at least a faerie. He backed up sharply. Irrith held her hands out, soothingly. "It's me. Irrith. I'm just here to ask you something."

The strange-looking man hesitated, but finally beckoned her in, and closed the door behind her.

"It would have been a lot easier to find you if you hadn't vanished," Irrith said, glancing around. The genie appeared to live in a single room, with few possessions: a narrow bed, a few cushions, a shelf of books. She supposed exotic silks were unlikely, if he was trying to live as an Englishman, or whatever he was supposed to be. His clothing wasn't English, though it was less showy than what he normally wore.

"I know," he said, and his voice was the same, accent and all. "That was the hope."

She turned to face him, surprised. "You didn't want to be found? Why?"

His illusion didn't drop away like a glamour, either. His flesh looked like it was shifting, rippling into a different shape, and darkening as it went. It steadied into the genie's familiar face, and a frown. "I suggested alchemy to the Prince, and to Dr. Andrews. I determined the best source for sophic mercury. I helped devise a plan for the use of that mercury. I, a foreigner, did all these things, and because of it, Dr. Andrews attempted to murder your Queen. And you ask why I wish not to be found?"

Irrith hadn't thought of that. Neither Galen nor Lune

blamed him, so far as she knew, and no one else had said anything in her hearing—but then, she hadn't spent any time listening for it, either.

She ducked her chin, embarrassed. "How long will you hide for?"

"There is a ship leaving for Cairo in five days."

"Cairo? Where is—" It didn't matter where Cairo was. "You're *leaving*?"

He nodded.

"What, you're just going to run away? Better hope we can keep the clouds up for five more days; otherwise your ship may burn before you can get on it." The floorboards creaked mightily beneath Irrith's feet as she stamped toward him. "You'd best not hope to come back, either. Because if you run away, people really *will* think you had something to do with Dr. Andrews's plan."

The genie was at least a foot taller; he held his ground as she glared up at him. "They already do. How can I convince them otherwise?"

He wanted to. She heard it in his voice, and she believed it. Irrith's anger melted away, and left behind something like her usual grin. "You can help me. Which is what I came for in the first place. There's a challenge on, to see who can throw their life away more uselessly, the Queen or the Prince. I'm trying to stop them. But right now, our only other plan is to stab the Dragon with a big icy spear. We need something better."

Abd ar-Rashid frowned thoughtfully and moved away, pulling two battered cushions from inside the chest at the foot of his bed. He gestured for Irrith to sit on one, and by the time she'd done so, a coffee urn and two bowls had appeared from nowhere. Sighing inside, she accepted one, and hoped he would get distracted before she had to drink it.

"Beyond the spear," she said, "there are two other possible plans. One is that Galen thinks gold could be used to trap the Dragon. I don't quite understand his argument, but it has to do with that flodgy—oh, I can never remember the word—"

"Phlogiston," he murmured.

"Yes, that. Some philosopher Galen knows says it goes into

materials that aren't already full of it, and so if we trapped it in something already full of fire, it wouldn't be able to go anywhere. They're planning to use sun-gold."

The genie's frown deepened, and he cupped his coffee as if it held the answer. "Because gold does not calcine. It melts, though, and very easily. This trap might work for a time, yes—but not for long."

As Irrith had feared. "Can you find a way to keep it from melting?"

"In the time we have? I doubt it very much."

We. He wasn't getting on that ship to Cairo, Irrith suspected. Not unless the Onyx Court was destroyed in the next five days. "The other possibility is the philosopher's stone. Even if we had sophic mercury, though, the Queen's afraid it would just create a Dragon *nobody* can destroy, that would still burn down London."

Abd ar-Rashid jerked, and his coffee almost slopped onto the floor. "But—the philosopher's stone is perfection. Something that *brings* perfection to others. Surely—"

Irrith raised her eyebrows. "Do you want to gamble London's future on 'surely'? Maybe the best way to perfect things is to destroy them, so something better can be built in their place."

Alarm filled the genie's dark eyes. "I had not thought of that."

None of you did. That was the problem with bringing scholars together. Clever as they were, sometimes they forgot their ideas were more than pretty shapes in their minds.

He sipped his drink, frowning once more. "No, we do not want a perfect Dragon. Even supposing we had the mercury with which to make one."

They wanted the opposite. And that gave Irrith an idea so startling, she spilled her own coffee. It scalded her hands, but she hardly noticed. "What if we went the other way?"

"What do you mean?"

"Alchemy perfects things, right?" She put down her cup before she could lose the rest of its contents. "What if you went the other way? Reverse alchemy. Use it to make something *im*perfect. We've said all along that the Dragon is too powerful to be killed. But if we can weaken it, make it vulnerable—"

It was wild speculation, and maybe complete nonsense. The genie's eyes widened, though, and he fair floated up from the cushion on which he sat. His mind had gone elsewhere, and his body only followed. "Combine it with something that is *not* pure. The alchemists combined many impure things, misunderstanding their own work, and achieved no particular result—but they were working with mute substances, not things of faerie." His gaze sharpened, as if his mind had come back from a voyage into possibility. "I do not know if it would work."

Irrith bit her lip so hard it almost bled. "It must." The alternative was too dreadful to think of. Lune dead, or Galen, or both. *We have to try.*

The Onyx Hall, London: April 13, 1759

Galen came through the front door of his chambers and stood blankly for a moment. The hearth was cold and black; the only illumination came from a faerie light, that whisked back to its sconce when its limited awareness realized someone had entered. Beyond that, the room lay still.

Of course. Edward was at Sothings Park. Podder was dead, and the knights who guarded Galen below didn't know he'd returned. In his absence, charms were enough to protect his chambers, while the knights prepared for battle.

He should light a fire. The Onyx Hall was a chilly place, and the gloom pressed in on him. But he was still standing there when he felt eyes upon him.

Galen turned and found Irrith in the open doorway. His heart skipped a beat at the sight of her. She'd discarded the civilized fashions of the Onyx Hall for rougher garb—perhaps what she wore in the Vale. A short tunic over hose, displaying a figure that, while slender, was not boyish. She shifted from one foot to the other, hands tugging at the hem of the tunic, and said, "I . . . was looking for you."

Waiting for him, judging by how quickly she'd appeared. Galen reached the obvious conclusion. "Are you leaving?"

Startlement pulled her straight. "What? No! Is that how you think of me, as someone who runs away?"

He remembered her charging across the ice, pistol in hand, to free Lune. The marks of her exposure in the world above had largely faded now, but there was still a hollowness to her, shadows in her cheeks and along the line of her collarbone. No, she was not the sort to run away.

"I'm sorry," Galen said, turning back toward the hearth. It was easy enough to do his servants' work, here in this faerie palace; all it took was a whispered request, and fire bloomed in the empty grate. "I've been with the von das Tickens. The news isn't good. Niklas says gold would only hold the Dragon a little while, before it melted."

Irrith closed the door behind her. "Abd ar-Rashid said the same thing. But he suggested—well, I did, but he agreed—that we might be able to weaken the Dragon by doing the alchemical thing badly. On purpose. Combining it with something impure, to make it imperfect. And therefore vulnerable."

Silence followed, in which Galen fancied he could hear the beating of both their hearts. The pieces hovered in his mind, not quite coming together. A vessel of sun-gold. Filled with something lacking in phlogiston, that would draw the Dragon in, as air was drawn into a vessel from which it had been pumped. Something impure, so they could enact the "chemical wedding" of the philosophers, with opposite intent.

But what thing?

"Water and earth," Irrith said, like a schoolboy recalling his—her—lessons. "Cold and wet. It has to have no fire in it, but it also has to be flawed. *Not* Lune. Something that's vulnerable."

"Something," Galen whispered, "that is mortal."

Her mouth fell open by degrees, as if all the world had slowed. Irrith stood perfectly still at the edge of the carpet, not breathing. Any more than Galen was.

"Mortal," he repeated, more strongly. "Bind the Dragon's spirit into a vessel that can be destroyed—that can be *killed*. You might not even have to do anything; the mere presence of such power might annihilate the vessel, and by doing so, take the Dragon with it." How could the words be so steady, so calm, as if he were speaking of philosophy only, with no application to life?

Irrith's voice was not so steady. "There are plenty of stray dogs in Lo . . ."

She couldn't even finish it. Galen was shaking his head. "No. It needs more than a dog."

"Then a beggar. Plenty of those, too. Snatch one off any street corner—"

"An innocent?" he demanded. His own calm slipped. "Someone ignorant of this world, this war, tied down for the slaughter without even knowing why? I'll be damned first! It must be someone willing, Irrith."

His declaration hung in the air. She could make the tally as well as he could. Edward Thorne was half-faerie. Mrs. Vesey? Delphia? There were others in the Hall or associated with it, various lovers and pets of faerie courtiers, many of them with no awareness of the larger faerie world, its politics and dangers. It would be his duty as Prince to go among them, to question one after another, asking who would lay down his life for the good of London.

And perhaps one might agree. Perhaps.

But he could never bring himself to ask.

She shook her head, a tiny movement at first, then a more vehement one. "No, Galen."

"I am willing," he said, and if it was ragged, it was also true.

"No, no, *no*—" Irrith spun and crossed the room, hands in the air as if to ward off his statement, and then without warning she seized the nearest thing that came to hand and hurled it across the room. Porcelain shattered against the far wall. "No! You aren't going to do it!"

"Yes. I am." Peculiar joy was filling the hole inside him, driving back the fear. "Who better, Irrith? If the Prince will not sacrifice himself for the good of his people, who will? I'll renounce my connection to the Hall—"

The firelight caught Irrith's face, revealing fury. "Do you think this will make her love you?"

The chain of her question dragged him back to earth. "What?"

"Lune. That's why you're doing this, isn't it? Because you love her, and you want some grand gesture to show it, saving the Onyx Court single-handed. You think she'll finally love you, then. You're an *idiot,* Galen. Her heart was given centuries ago, and not to you."

He flinched. It struck too near the mark. He *had* dreamt like that, too many times, but such dreams could not survive the light of day. "No. I—I know she will never love me."

"Then what?" Her contempt lashed out like a whip. "That when you're gone, she'll understand? These years you've been in the Hall, worshipping at her feet, laughed at by all the courtiers who have seen it a thousand times before, a poor little mortal pining for his faerie lover. But once you're *dead,* oh, yes, *then* we'll understand. We'll see what your devotion was worth.

"You won't be here to see it, though. Because you'll be gone. Do you imagine yourself looking down from Heaven, seeing us all mourn you as you deserve?" Irrith's eyes blazed green, burning with inhuman light. *"What makes you think you're going to Heaven at all?"*

Galen's heart pounded once, hard enough to shake his entire body, and then it stopped.

The sprite's slender frame was rigid with emotion. The only thing moving was her breast, heaving with her shallow gasps. Then it slowed, and Irrith said, more quietly but with no less force, "I don't know your divine Master. But I know this much: he does not love suicides. And what would you call it, when a man embraces death for love of a faerie queen?"

He had no answers. His heart was beating again, but he could not draw breath. Her questions rang in his head, the echoes multiplying instead of fading out, and all he could see was Irrith's green eyes, shifting as no human eyes could.

And Lune's face, the perfect portrait that had resided in his memory since he first saw her above Southwark, shining in the night sky. His goddess.

Irrith opened her mouth, as if to say something more. But no sound came out, and then she spun away and was gone, slamming the door shut behind her, leaving him alone with the silent fire.

The Onyx Hall, London: April 15, 1759

It was not the Queen's mourning night, but the great garden of the Onyx Hall was empty. At Lune's request, even Ktistes had departed, leaving her alone with the trees and grass, fountains and stream, and the faerie lights blazing the image of a comet across the ceiling above.

She walked without purpose, without seeing, up one path and down another, lost in the maze of her own thoughts. In nearly one hundred and seventy years of rule, Lune had faced many challenges to the Onyx Hall and her rule over it. More than once she had thought herself at the end of that road, doomed to lose her realm, her sovereignty, or even her life. And always she had found a way to continue.

Always—until now.

The weight of the Dragon already lay upon her. She remembered that searing touch, the annihilating force of its attention. Soon she would feel it anew. The last clouds were shredding; they would not endure until the end of the month. The reports from Paris were that Messier was having difficulty sighting the comet, obscured as it was in the morning twilight, and soon he might lose it entirely; but after that it would reappear in the evening sky. They would face the Dragon whether they were ready or not.

She was not alone after all. Someone was waiting on the path ahead.

Galen.

The meticulous elegance of his apparel set off a warning bell in her mind. She'd seen such a thing before—had done it herself. He dressed with care because it was a form of armor, a way of preparing for battle.

They had not spoken to one another directly since he fled Rose House. She knew what battle he expected, and was prepared for it.

But Galen surprised her by bowing, with the same flawless care that marked his appearance. "Your Grace, I bring you good tidings. I know how to kill the Dragon."

Kill. Not trap, or banish, or appease. End. And ensure their safety forever.

So why did the Prince not look happier?

Formality rose, unbidden, to her lips; she dismissed it. That was the game he wanted to play, and she didn't trust it. Instead she asked directly, "How?"

"It requires a little preparation," he said. "With your permission, Abd ar-Rashid and I will enter the Calendar Room for that purpose—though I know we can ill afford to lose eleven days. But the principle, madam, is sound.

"Much of it will be the prior plan. We will use the Monument to summon the Dragon down into the chamber in its base. This will be armored in gold, to prevent it from fleeing while an alchemical conjunction is performed. But not with sophic mercury: instead we will bind it into mortal form. If this does not immediately result in the death of that host, and therefore the death of the Dragon, then it will at least be vulnerable, as it was not before." He bowed again. "Your Grace, I will undertake this duty myself."

Duty. Binding. Elegant words, to blunt the raw edge of his meaning.

He still intended to die.

Galen didn't flinch away from her gaze. He'd gotten better at lying, but not perfected the art. There was fear beneath the surface, whose existence he was doing his best not to show.

Fear held in check by certainty. The principle *was* sound. Every detail of their predicament was too firmly graven into Lune's mind for her to delude herself on that front; offering herself up to the Dragon as appeasement was a weak possibility at best. Even Aspell had known that. Binding the Dragon to mortality stood a far better chance of success.

He hadn't come here expecting argument, she realized. The armor was not for her. It was for himself, to hold the fear at bay.

She wondered if he had chosen his moment deliberately, tracking her movement through the garden until she came to this point, or whether it was pure chance that put them near the twin obelisks. Michael Deven's grave, and the memorial to her past Princes.

All of them died eventually. Some from illness, others from misfortune; one had given his life to prepare them for the Dragon's return. None of them could live forever.

But she hadn't expected to lose Galen so soon.

She had not answered him. He was stiff as a pike, still where he had been when she stopped, awaiting the answer they both knew she had to give.

Before she could give it, though—"What of your family?"

It was cruel, but necessary. His calm cracked a little. "My sisters," he said, with a hint of unsteadiness, "have been taken care of. Delphia's jointure is provided for by our marriage settlement."

A lawyer's reply, which told her the answer to her real question. "You have not told her yet."

His jaw trembled, then firmed. "No. But I will."

Lune could not guess how the woman would take it. Delphia was too unfamiliar to her still. But the considerations of one mortal woman would not change their circumstances— nor, she suspected, Galen's determination. He would do this come Hell itself.

And she had no reason strong enough to refuse him.

"Then make your preparations, Lord Galen," she said formally, acknowledging him with a curtsy, Queen to Prince. "The resources of this court are at your disposal."

Memory: April 15, 1756

"I think the one thing worse than locking myself in that room for months on end," Cuddy said, "would be locking myself in that room for months on end to do *mathematics*."

The puck's voice echoed down the corridor as Lune approached. She hid a smile before she came through the pillars into the dwarves' workshop. Some fae, like the von das Tickens, might have a great deal of love for craftsmanship, but none of them enjoyed mathematics. Even those mad brothers did their work by instinct, not calculation. For that, they needed a mortal.

Eleven days ago, Cuddy and the dwarves had carried stacks of books into the great clock's chamber: instructions in algebra, elementary works on the calculus, and Newton's great *Principia Mathematica*; Flamsteed's observations from 1682; Halley's *Astronomiae cometicae synopsis,* which had started their troubles to begin with. There were rumors that a French mathematician would be attempting to calculate the comet's orbit and perihelion, but Lune and her court could not afford to wait. The Calendar Room was the only solution, and so Lord Hamilton had offered himself for this herculean task. He knew little of that branch of learning, but that was nothing sufficient study outside of time could not mend.

She'd given him her most heartfelt thanks before he went in, and would do so again when he came out. To be locked inside, alone, with only the great clock for company . . . Cuddy's jest aside, even the work could not be enough to distract a man from that dread presence. She hoped Hamilton would not come stumbling out in a few moments to say he could not do it, that he'd only lasted three days and accomplished nothing at all.

The time had come to find out. Wilhas took hold of the sundial on the door and dragged the portal open.

At first she thought Hamilton's slow, shuffling steps a sign of mere exhaustion. He could not have slept well, inside the Calendar Room. But then he came forward, into the illumination of the workshop's faerie lights, and she saw his head. Not a wig; he'd taken none into the room. Those long, ragged locks were his own hair—and snow-white.

The Prince of the Stone lifted his head, revealing his time-worn face to the world.

Lune's breath withered in her throat. *Mortal. He is mortal. Time outside of time—we knew he wouldn't need food, but we did not think of aging.*

How long was he in there?

Hamilton extended one wrinkled hand. The papers in it trembled, until Lune took them. "Perihelion on March thirteenth, 1759," he said, in a reed-thin voice that had spoken only to the walls for years. "The French will need more than one mathematician if they want their answer before the comet has come and gone; the work is enormous. I fear I took too long learning the calculus—it was hard to concentrate in there—"

He staggered. Everyone had been standing like stone, but now Wilhas leapt into the chamber and came back with a chair. Its cushion was worn beyond threadbare, its padding flattened until it was almost as hard as the wood. Hamilton collapsed into it with a motion that spoke of endless, horrifying habit.

Lune sank into a crouch before him, papers forgotten in her hand. A single glance had shown her the unsteady scrawl, replacing his old, meticulous writing. "Hamilton—did you not *realize*?"

His gaze fixed on her. With a chill she had not felt since she took the throne, Lune saw a familiar madness in his eyes. He had aged as if in the mortal world, but his mind suffered the effects of too long in a faerie realm. Or perhaps it was only the isolation, and the inevitable ticking of the clock.

"I did," he said gently, as if speaking to a child. "But by the time I did . . . it was already too late to go back to my old life. Years had passed. People would wonder. So I decided to finish the work. But it was hard, and sometimes I forgot what I was doing . . ."

Cuddy's feet scuffed against the floor as he shifted his weight. Hamilton glared at him. "The numbers are right, though," the Prince insisted, with something like his old strength. "I made sure of that. Only when I had the same result three times in a row did I come out."

Lune tasted ashes. Hamilton had not been the youngest Prince she ever chose, but even accounting for the effect of his broken health, he must have been inside for at least twenty years. Probably more. Six years her Prince, and he would not live to see a seventh. She'd feared losing a consort to the Dragon, but she'd never imagined it would happen like this.

He laid his shaking hand atop hers, where it rested on one

skirt-shrouded knee. "I'll help you look," he promised, with sincerity that brought tears to her eyes. "There were some likely lads in the court. They're still here, yes? They haven't gone away?"

"No, Hamilton," she whispered. "They haven't gone away."

The old Prince nodded, white hair falling in a curtain around his face. "One of them will do well, I'm sure. One of them will do very well indeed."

The Onyx Hall, London: April 30, 1759

The workshop was silent, the tools cleared away. Even the clocks had been allowed to run down, their hands stopped at odd hours. Most of the Onyx Court waited in the great presence chamber, filling the space before the Queen's silver throne and the Prince's chair of estate, gathered to hear their rulers speak. And soon enough that time would come.

Once the door to the Calendar Room opened.

The escort waited in silence: dwarves, scholars, an honor guard of knights, and three women. Irrith and Delphia St. Clair flanked Lune on either side, and none of the three met the others' eyes. *Once we divided him among us,* Irrith thought, bones aching with tension. *Now he belongs to none of us.*

Lune was, or at least seemed, her usual self: serene as the moon, and as cool. Delphia presented a stony mask to the world. Surely she hadn't expected to be widowed scarcely a month after marriage. *It won't end,* Irrith had said to her, the night they went to rescue the Queen. *He'll always be running off, and leaving you behind.* Where he ran to now, no man returned.

A hard knot lodged in her own throat, hurting every time she swallowed. Often as she reminded herself that Galen was mortal, and mortals died, the knot refused to go away. It was fury, and betrayal, and fear; and it was grief, too, which made her angriest of all. She shouldn't have to suffer that when she hadn't chosen to love him. He should mean nothing to her, one more broken doll, gone a bit too soon.

She knew it was a lie, though. Lune mourned all her Princes, not just the one she loved. Not as deeply, and as time passed they would fade from her mind; but any faerie who lived closely with mortals, mimicked their ways, ate their bread, felt at least a touch of loss when the close ones passed on. Next year Irrith's grief would be forgotten.

But it hurt *now,* and she hated it.

The sundial began to spin. Cuddy stepped forward and grasped its angled style, throwing his slender weight backward to help drag the door open.

Only one other mortal had ever gone inside that chamber and closed the door behind him. Irrith had heard the story of Hamilton Birch in gruesome detail, since Galen went into the room; her mind had conjured up plenty of possibilities for what would emerge today.

Abd ar-Rashid stepped through the portal first. If the strain of the chamber had told upon him, he gave no sign. But he nodded to Lune, and then Galen came out.

The Prince looked almost unchanged. No lines in his face, no white in his hair. It would be easy to imagine the Calendar Room had no effect upon him—easy, until one looked in his eyes. There Irrith saw changes for which there were no words. He was older in mind, if not in body, and he'd left part of himself in the Calendar Room. Everything in him that was fire.

Galen bowed to the Queen and said, "I am ready."

Both rigidity and nervous fidgeting were gone from his body. He stood with his hands loose at his sides, his breathing slow and measured. Like a man ready for battle—

No. There would be no battle; only surrender and death. He stood like a martyr, ready for the lions.

Lune asked quietly, "Do you wish the services of a priest?"

Irrith choked. Had Galen told her? The horrific words she'd flung at him, telling him he was damned to Hell—the Prince was shaking his head. "No," he said, equally quiet. "I have been in meditation for days now, preparing. I must not lose this. Let us speak to the court, and be done."

The Queen did not press the question again. Throat aching with unsaid words, Irrith followed the small procession out of the workshop, toward the great presence chamber, where Galen would be made Prince no more.

It had been done once before, Irrith knew, divesting a Prince of his title. Michael Deven gave over the position before his own death, so that "Prince of the Stone" would be an office passed from man to man, rather than a privilege belonging to him alone.

But there was no replacement waiting for Galen. Amadea had spent the past eleven days assembling a list; there were possibilities. None were gentlemen. Lune would choose from among them after this was done—if there was still an Onyx Hall left.

Galen surrendered to Lune the London Sword, the central piece of their royal regalia. She released him from his obligations as Prince, with many fine phrases. All of it was for show. Many of the watching fae knew by now about the London Stone, if not where its faerie side lay; they knew the true release would come in that hidden chamber, where Lune had once bound Galen to the keystone of their realm. Even Michael Deven had never renounced that bond. But this ceremony served its own purpose, because the enchantments of the Hall were not the only things that needed to bid the Prince farewell.

Lune faced her court and spoke, pitching her voice so it carried to the far corners of the chamber, and up into the crystal panes high above. "Once the sun sets, we will be redeemed from the threat that has haunted us since the days of Charles II. Galen St. Clair, though Prince no more, will render unto us the greatest gift any man can bestow. He will lay down his life, binding the spirit of fire to his own mortality, and in doing so will destroy it. Remember this. Remember him. Let the Onyx Hall honor his sacrifice, until the last stone falls, and the last faerie departs from England's shores."

The wave spread outward from the dais, fae kneeling upon the cold marble. Perfect silence followed in their wake, as if all the court held its breath. Then footsteps: uneven, two no longer walking as one. Hand in hand, Galen and the Queen descended and crossed the chamber, going out through the great bronze portal, which shut behind them with a sound like the closing of a mausoleum door.

The Monument, London: April 30, 1759

The sun died a bloody death on the eastern horizon, staining the last remaining shreds of cloud with crimson light. London still bustled with evening activity, carters and porters and housewives exchanging familiar curses, but it was distant and muffled. Magic as strong as that used to hide the Moor Fields for Midsummer cloaked this little yard, clearing it for the use of the fae.

The Monument to the Great Fire of London dominated the space, its squat, square base ringed about with carving. Three sides bore Latin inscriptions; the fourth bore an elaborate allegory of the City's destruction. Irrith had paced past it six times already, and hated the work more with each turn. That stiff image did not begin to describe the infernal horror of those days.

But it was easier to look at the carvings than the pillar above. The Monument soared two hundred and two feet into the darkening air, an enormous, isolated column, crowned with an urn of gilt-bronze flames. Tiny shadows moved up there: the von das Tickens, placing the lenses and mirrors Schuyler had made for this purpose. The comet, they said, haunted the southern horizon, beneath the constellation of Hydra, just on the edge of twilight. Once they arranged their equipment and opened the hatch in the urn, they would banish the few remaining clouds; and then someone would be able to look up from the bottom chamber and see the comet.

Galen would be able to look. Irrith's gut twisted into a knot.

The spear-knights waited on the paving stones of the Monument Yard, armed and armored and protected by the tithe.

Bonecruncher led a troop of goblins in support. They, like Irrith, carried guns loaded with iron shot, and knives made from leftover slivers of the jotun ice. The rest of the Onyx Guard were stationed at the entrances to the palace, in case all failed, and the beast escaped them. If Galen's own mortality didn't kill the Dragon, they would.

They hoped.

Irrith halted near the door into the Monument, because there was movement at the edge of the yard. The procession was a small one: just Lune, Sir Peregrin Thorne, his half-human son Edward, and Galen. No Delphia St. Clair. Irrith didn't blame her for not coming to watch her husband die.

Galen wore only a shirt and knee breeches, stockings and shoes; no coat, no waistcoat, no wig. In the light of the lantern Edward held, the chestnut tint of his hair was stronger than ever. Irrith stared as if she would memorize it, to be recalled a century from now, and then she closed her eyes in stark refusal. *No. Let it go.*

The light dimmed. She opened her eyes to see Edward extinguishing the lantern, and the knights and goblins saluting. Belatedly, she did the same. Lune pressed her lips to Galen's brow. Only that; no final words. Perhaps she'd said them below, when they were alone in the chamber of the London Stone. Or perhaps there was nothing she *could* say.

The former Prince hesitated. For a moment, Irrith thought he was about to speak; then she thought he was about to refuse. She froze, torn between terror and hope.

Galen spun without warning and strode toward the Monument. The others were standing a little distance away, and so they were behind him; Irrith, waiting near the door, saw his face.

Fear. The white line of his lips, the desperate set of his jaw, the tendons rising sharply from the open collar of his shirt. What Galen hid from the others, Irrith saw: the terror of a man walking to his death.

Tears obliterated her vision, and then he was gone.

———

He'd walked the path a thousand times in his mind.

Through the door, into the cramped space beyond. To his left, one set of stairs: barely wide enough for two people to pass, leading upward to the viewing platform and the urn of flames. To his right, a second set: rougher and narrower, leading downward into darkness.

He took the second path.

A dozen steps, then a sharp turn, then five more. Galen descended carefully; they dared send no faerie light with him, and he hadn't thought to ask for a candle. The chamber at the bottom was stiflingly close, almost small enough to span with his arms. The ceiling curved into a shallow dome, with a round opening in the center. By the faint light filtering in from above, Galen positioned himself beneath the opening, and looked upward.

The sun-gold sheathing the walls, marked with alchemical symbols, was invisible in the gloom. Through the opening, though, he could see the stairs, curving around and around, more than three hundred steps in total. The hatch at the top, concealed within the urn, was still closed. But soon enough the von das Tickens would open it, and then he would look through the lenses and mirrors to the comet whose return Halley had predicted more than fifty years ago.

He would see the Dragon, and the Dragon would see him.

The warmth of the sun-gold did not touch the coldness inside. Abd ar-Rashid had prepared him inside the Calendar Room: congelation, distillation, fermentation, conjunction, separation, dissolution. Alchemical processes, their order reversed, while Galen purged all things of fire from his body and spirit. There was no anger in him, no desire for action; he was an empty vessel, awaiting the annihilating light.

But fear was not a thing of fire. And so the fear remained.

Three hundred steps and more, a spiral path to Heaven. Galen stood in the darkness below. It was fitting, really. Irrith's words had cut deeply because they were true. All of this had come about because he loved Lune. Because of her, he returned to London, following his heart instead of his duty to his family. Because of her, he searched the city high and low until he found a door to her hidden realm. He accepted the title of Prince, which he never deserved to bear; he betrayed the loyalty he owed to Delphia, in spirit if not in deed. None of it was righteous. And now he sought his own death.

I am damning myself to Hell.

No priest's absolution could change that. No penance in advance could ameliorate the sin committed afterward, the willing suicide. The Dragon's fire would be only a foretaste of the fires that waited for him after judgment. Irrith was right about every part of it.

Yet here he stood, beneath the Monument, hearing the metallic clang of the dwarves working high above. Because when Irrith left him, he stood in the silence of his chambers, tears wet on his face, and he thought about London, and the Onyx Court. Fae and mortals who would suffer, perhaps die, if the Dragon were not stopped. The Goodemeades and Abd ar-Rashid. Edward and Mrs. Vesey. Lady Feidelm, Wrain, Sir Peregrin Thorne. His sisters. Delphia. Irrith.

Lune.

If he refused this choice, then they all burnt. Better to die now than to let that happen.

Even if it meant going to Hell.

He accepted it, embraced it, clasped the notion to him with desperate strength, lest his nerve break and he flee. Light flooded down the shaft: the hatch was open. The gold about him began to glow, alchemical emblems glittering with cold radiance, turning the chamber into a trap, and a vessel of transformation. Galen flung his arms wide, flung his head back, stared up toward the waiting sky.

Come on. Come to me. Let us be each other's death.

His entire body was shaking, trembling like a leaf in the wind. Tears ran down his face, and he clenched his jaw so hard his teeth ached with the strain. *This is it. My last moment, and I'm weeping, because I'm going to Hell—oh, God—*

He could see nothing through the tears. But he felt the moment the connection formed: a terrible awareness, inhuman beyond anything the Onyx Hall contained. Vast, and distant, but filled with a malevolence that did not forget. The clouds had broken, and the comet blazed in the sky, and the Dragon *saw him*.

His own keening filled his ears. *God, please save me, Christ, oh* Christ—

Light pierced the sky, a lance from horizon to lens to mirror, downward through the pillar, and Galen screamed.

All of them flinched when the scream came. It tore into Irrith like a serrated knife, a sound no mortal throat should produce, a sound that would stay with her until the end of her immortal span.

And then it stopped.

She blinked away the ghost of that flaring light and saw the spear-knights set themselves, great pike of ice raised. No one knew for sure what would happen now. The simple fact of being bound to mortality might kill the Dragon on the spot—or flames might come pouring out the door, the pillar itself exploding into a hail of shattered stone, as the golden prison failed and the beast broke free. They had to wait, until their enemy emerged or enough time had passed that someone dared brave the interior, descending to see if Galen St. Clair was dead.

Noise from inside: the scuff of a shoe, short gasps of breath. And then Galen stumbled out the door and staggered down the two steps, falling on his knees before them.

Sir Peregrin stood with one fist raised, ready to give the signal.

Galen's voice was a ragged thing, torn by his unbearable scream. *"Where did it go?"*

Irrith's heart thumped painfully in her chest. The spear-knights were too disciplined to look away from the body they expected to be their target, but Peregrin's gaze snapped to Lune, who stood well back, one hand pressed to her breast. The Queen wet her lips, lowered her hand, and said, "What do you mean? What happened?"

Galen shook his head. His fingers splayed hard against the paving-stone, knuckles white. "I don't know. It came down the pillar—I felt it—then *through* me." His body twisted in a half cough, half retch. "I think it went down. Into the Calendar Room."

Which lay directly below the Monument. Horror rose like bile in Irrith's throat. What little color was in the Queen's face drained away. It wasn't a proper entrance, not like the others; that opening only admitted moonlight, the ray from which the great clock's pendulum hung. The Dragon shouldn't have been able to escape that way.

Shouldn't and *couldn't* were two different things.

Breath drawing in a sharp gasp, Lune closed her eyes, no doubt seeking within. She shook her head. "It's too difficult to sense from up here. The Calendar Room doesn't exist entirely within the Hall. We have to get below. If we can trap it there—"

Peregrin was already snapping orders. The guards on the entrances, under Segraine's command, must draw inward like a net, seeking to catch the Dragon if it escaped the Calendar Room. Cerenel and the other spear-knights set off for the Billingsgate entrance at a run.

Lune hesitated. Her eyes were open again, and they rested on Galen, still hunched on the ground before the Monument. He had one palm braced against his thigh, trying to rise, but his entire body shook with the effort.

He was no longer Prince. If Lune had to summon the power of the Onyx Hall against the Dragon, he could do nothing to help her. He couldn't even stand, let alone fight.

Yet he was trying to rise.

Irrith stepped forward and faced the Queen. "I'll carry him if I have to. You get below. Galen and I will find you there."

One curt nod; that was all Lune could spare. Then she hiked up her skirts and ran.

"Can you make it to Billingsgate?" Irrith asked, alone with Galen in the Monument Yard. "Or do I have to carry you after all?"

He'd forced himself to his feet, but still stood half-bent, shoulders trembling. In the privacy of her mind, Irrith placed a wager on "carry." But Galen shook his head. "Not Billings-gate."

"What?"

Another wracking cough. When it ended, Galen rasped, "Have to defend from the center. London Stone. It's an entrance, too. Might still answer to me."

An entrance. She shouldn't be surprised: that was the central point, where faerie and mortal London merged into one. Galen was already staggering past the Monument's base, stumbling like a gin-soaked beggar, but moving with speed. The mortal face of the London Stone was almost as close as Billingsgate. Irrith hurried after him, flinging a concealment over them both, so that no one would try to stop the half-dressed man and the faerie that was chasing him.

They dodged the carts and carriages, sedan chairs and people on foot that still crowded Fish Street Hill, then turned onto the lane that became Cannon Street a little farther down. Irrith could see the spire of St. Swithin's up ahead, hard by the Stone, which lay now on the north side of the street. They were almost there when Galen's foot caught against something in the muck and he went down again, collapsing heavily to the ground.

"Hang your pride," Irrith muttered, and caught up to the fallen man. She could at least support him, if not carry him. Before Galen could protest, she slipped one arm under his chest and lifted him to his feet.

His skin burnt hot through the thin fabric of his shirt.

"You're feverish," she said, foolishly—and then she saw his eyes.

Pupil, iris, and white: all gone, replaced by blazing flame.

Instinct sent her leaping backward, an instant before his hand could close on her throat. Curses flooded through her mind, panicked and incoherent. This wasn't the Dragon they'd fought before, the ravening, near-mindless beast, its cunning limited only to destruction. No, they'd given it a human mind, a clever one. A mind that knew all about the Onyx Hall: not just its power but its secrets, from the Calendar Room to the truth of the London Stone.

The beast that wore Galen's body shuddered, an inhuman, spine-twisting ripple. Irrith flinched on instinct, remembering that motion from the infernal days of the Fire—

But nothing happened.

She smelled smoke, the dreadfully appealing scent of meat on the spit—but no flames leapt out at her. The blazing eyes widened. Then the Dragon, realizing its powers were limited by human flesh, did the only thing it could.

It ran for the Stone.

Irrith hurled herself after. She was the faster of the two, and knocked her quarry sprawling a second time. They narrowly missed a maid, sleepily yawning her way down the dark street. An inhuman snarl rose from Galen's throat, and a foot slammed into her face, hard enough that Irrith saw stars. She rolled free, then forced herself to her feet once more, because a single thought survived the impact of his foot: *I have to keep it from the Stone.*

They were already at Abchurch Lane. Irrith snatched out one of her pistols and fired, but running spoiled her aim; her shot chipped the front of a shop. Swearing, she dragged out the other and halted for an instant, concentrating on Galen's back.

Her second shot flew more true—but not true enough. It struck his hip, spinning him into the brick wall at his side, scarcely three paces from his goal.

Irrith was already running again. She dropped both spent pistols to the ground and drew her last weapon, the knife of jotun ice. He knocked her aside as she came near, but the blow served her purposes well enough; it threw her that last bit of distance, putting her between Galen and the London Stone.

No. It isn't Galen. Galen died inside the Monument.

But to her horror, she saw something of him in the twisted snarl on his face. "Irrith," he said, spitting her name like a curse. "Traitor one day, faithful the next. Can't you change your mind one more time? For me?"

She tightened her grip on the knife. Its cold seared her hand; the Dragon kept well clear of it as he pushed himself away from the wall. His shirt was beginning to smoke, tiny flames curling up where his skin pressed against the fabric. "Odd," she said breathlessly, trying to delay long enough for her still-spinning head to settle. The Stone was a hard presence just behind her back. If he got so much as a finger on it . . . "You know the things Galen knows—knew—and yet you don't know me at all."

He laughed, and the sound itself burnt her. "Don't I? I know you're a coward. You could have loved me, but you were too afraid. Not of the grief—of the possibility that your love would never be returned. That even that ultimate gift couldn't draw me away from my hopeless devotion to Lune, and you would be left as I was, groveling after someone forever out of your reach."

"Don't say that word," Irrith snarled, past the choking knot in her throat. "*I*. You aren't Galen."

"Half of me is."

"The body means nothing."

"All of the body; half of the spirit. That's what the alchemy meant, Irrith. A wedding of two separate spirits into one, cleaving unto each other like man and wife. Though in this case, the man *is* the wife." The Dragon twisted Galen's mouth into a travesty of a smile. "He welcomed the fire in like a demon lover."

Fire that was burning his body up from the inside. They weren't wrong; the conjunction had weakened the Dragon. Might even kill it, in time. But how long would that take?

She saw again the terror in Galen's face, as he went to his death. *Walking into Hell with his eyes wide open.* Could the torments of damnation be any worse than this, his spirit shackled to a creature that would destroy those he loved?

As if it could read her thoughts, the Dragon grinned and spread Galen's arms wide. "Do you think death will free him? We are one spirit now. Kill him, send him to Hell, and I will go with him, for I *am* Galen St. Clair."

They both lunged.

The Dragon was ready for Irrith, because it knew her, as Galen had known her. One searing arm came across to block her thrust. But Galen knew weapons as a gentleman did, with rules and courtesy and honor, and he couldn't block what he didn't expect.

Irrith's right hand was knocked out of line—but the knife wasn't there anymore. Their joined momentum brought them crashing together hard, her slight weight against Galen's searing body, and her left hand brought the blade up and into his chest.

They staggered, scant inches from the Stone. Then Irrith set her feet and drove him back, slamming his rigid frame against the brick wall behind. Elemental ice and elemental fire warred, sending waves of heat and cold radiating outward, until she wanted to scream and flee to safety. But she hung on, sinking the knife hilt-deep into his ribs, glaring into those eyes of flame, until the light in them flickered and died, leaving behind pits of black ash. When Irrith let go, the body fell limply to the ground. The knife-hilt clattered free, its blade melted away.

She stood gasping, shaking, staring at the corpse of Galen St. Clair.

His blind face seemed to stare at her in accusation. Pain twisted inside her, sharper than the vanished knife. *I'm sorry. I'm so sorry. I didn't love you*—I couldn't.

If she had loved him, she could never have killed him.

Slowly Irrith became aware of eyes on her. No one stood near, but mortals were watching from a safe distance, peering through shutters and half-cracked doors, whispering to each other in the shadows. From farther off she heard shouts and running footsteps: a constable, no doubt. Her concealment had fallen at some point, and now she stood over a dead man's body, with her faerie face bared to the world.

She could not leave him there, lying in the filth of the street. Clenching her jaw, Irrith bent and took hold of Galen's lifeless, unresisting hand. With an effort, she heaved him over her shoulder, then built another concealment for them both. It was hard, with so many people watching, but the darkness helped; she slipped away down Cannon Street, carrying the dead Prince, taking him home to rest.

The Onyx Hall, London: May 1, 1759

Fae knew little of funerals. Those mortals who died among them were generally deposited back in the world they'd come from, in their beds or in a gutter, according to the kindness of the one who put them there. The fae did not bury their own dead. There was no need, when their bodies fell so soon to nothingness, the spirits that shaped them gone to oblivion.

The Princes of the Stone were always returned to their families, to be buried with Christian rites. Only Michael Deven lay interred in the ground of the Onyx Hall, beneath a stand of ever-blooming apple trees in the night garden, forever close to the faerie Queen who loved him.

Michael Deven—and now Galen St. Clair.

For him, the fae gathered in solemn observance, lining the path through the night garden. Or at least as close to solemnity as they could manage: some were puzzled by this semimortal ceremony, and some showed too-sharp curiosity in his death, fascinated by the experience that came among them so rarely. But knights of the Onyx Guard stood sentinel along the path, and Bonecruncher's loyal goblins lurked behind; anyone who thought to profane the Prince's funeral vanished instantly from view, with a minimum of fuss.

The pall-shrouded bier came through the arch, borne on a tatterfoal-drawn open carriage. Preceding it was an honor guard of five elf-knights and one half-mortal valet; Edward Thorne and his father Sir Peregrin led the way, side by side. The plaintive sound of a flute threaded through the quiet air, marking time for their slow procession. Fae knelt as they went by. The bier crossed the Walbrook, passed under the drooping branches of willow trees, and came among new mourners: the mortals of the Onyx Hall, all those who had been under Galen's authority as Prince. They rarely gathered in one place, those mortals, and made an odd assortment standing together. Men of all classes, from the wealthy through to lawyers and artisans, laborers and the humble poor. Women, some beautiful, some scarred by disease. Old and young, and a large knot of children, lured away into a realm of wonder, their eyes wide as they watched grief go by.

At last the procession reached its end: the obelisk listing Princes of the Stone. A small flame burnt in its base, and a new line had been chiseled into the plaque:

Mr. Galen St. Clair   1756–1759

A small group waited there. Mrs. Vesey supported Delphia St. Clair, who wore mourning sewn for her by the finest faerie seamstresses. Lune stood alone, dressed in the same white she wore every October, when she came to grieve for Michael Deven.

And Irrith, clad in green, the executioner attending the funeral.

The honor guard lifted the carriage's burden down to the grass. Irrith stared at the pall draped over the coffin, grateful for its presence. She preferred to remember the man she'd first seen, extending his hand to the muddy, swearing sprite who had just fallen through the Newgate entrance; but every time she blinked, she saw the gaping voids of Galen's eyes, burnt out by the Dragon. And nothing could block her ears to the memory of that searing voice, taunting her with the inexorable truth. *Kill him, send him to Hell, and I will go with him, for I am Galen St. Clair.*

They had saved the Onyx Hall, but nothing could rob the beast of that victory.

Galen's family would bury a manikin disguised as their son and brother, thinking Galen the victim of some illness or misfortune. Irrith hadn't inquired after the lie. There would be Christian rites then, but they could hardly say any here, in the heart of the Onyx Hall. Delphia had not pressed for any. She understood what this court had meant to Galen, and where he would wish to be buried.

Once the bearers folded the pall and retired into a line, Lune came forward, and laid her hand upon the grass.

They weren't certain if she could do this, without a Prince's aid. It might come to shovels after all, the indignity of digging a grave and piling the dirt atop the coffin. The Hall answered to Queen and Prince together, a faerie and a mortal. But either Lune could in this small way command it alone, or the palace recognized the interment of its former master, for after a few breathless moments, the bier began to sink beneath the earth. The grass closed over the coffin's lid, and still the Queen knelt; then, at last, she let her breath out and stood.

No more ceremony than that—but Lune looked to each of them, and repeated the words she'd spoken in the great presence chamber. "Remember him."

Irrith, hearing the Dragon's laughter in her mind, wished she could forget.

Word came that evening, from someone's mortal pet: a Londoner named John Bevis had sighted the comet on the night of April thirtieth.

The people of London had all but forgotten Halley's prediction. Their fears of fiery demise had flared too soon, sparked by the false alarm of the comet two years ago; the ongoing inability of their astronomers to sight the returning comet had slain the last of their fears. It was just a star now, trailing its diminished tail, an object of astronomical curiosity and little more.

The message was brought to Lune in her privy chamber, where she sat with only the Goodemeades for company. Most of her court was above, in the Moor Fields, celebrating May Day and their release from fifty years of fear. No Sanist concern kept Lune below, not this time; she simply could not join their revelry. Not while she wore her gown of mourning white.

She thanked the usher who brought the message and dismissed him, then lapsed once more into silence.

The two brownies had kept her company before, permitting her quiet and melancholy when she needed it. If they spoke, it was because they thought it necessary. Still, that didn't prevent a surge of resentment when Gertrude said, "You should go to them."

Leaving aside the fact that she didn't wish to go anywhere at all—"Them?"

"Irrith and Delphia."

Lune passed one weary hand over her eyes. "Mrs. St. Clair

will not wish to see me, I think, nor anyone of this world. Not after what we've done to her husband."

"Then you haven't come to know her very well," Rosamund said. "She's here, in the Onyx Hall. Right now. But if you leave her alone, then pretty soon you'll lose her. And Irrith's thinking of leaving for the Vale. So if you want to keep either of them in your court, you should go to them."

The Goodemeades were the only two who could speak so bluntly to her. The two of them, and the Prince of the Stone. Galen never availed himself of that privilege, too awed by her—too worshipful—to presume such familiarity. She'd hoped that in time his awe would fade to something more comfortable.

But his time was cut too short.

"Find them," Lune said. "We will meet in private."

The parlor of Galen's chambers still lay as it had days before, with chairs turned toward the hearth, a book open facedown on a table, fragments of porcelain strewn across the floor. It was easy to believe the Prince might walk through the door at any moment. Coming here was painful, but Lune thought it the right choice. There was no hiding from his ghost. Better to face it directly.

Delphia's face showed the marks of sleeplessness and tears, though she was composed now, like a painting of grief. Irrith's countenance was formed of something colder and more brittle: marble, perhaps, veined with flaws, that would shatter under the wrong tap of the hammer.

Lune had offered her formal condolences to Delphia before, in full view of her court; now she offered her informal sympathy. "I lack the words to tell you how grateful I am to Galen. That's little comfort to you, I'm sure; no doubt you wish he were still alive. Or even that he'd never wed you at all, so that you'd be spared this sudden loss, and the knowledge of how it came about."

The young widow shook her head. "The loss, yes. Galen was a good man, and I mourn his passing. But had I not wed him, I would have faced something much worse; and more, I would never have known of this world." She hesitated. "I—I know you permitted me among you because of him. If it would be possible, though, I'd like to stay."

It had never occurred to Lune that Delphia might think her place revoked. *It occurred to Rosamund and Gertrude, though.* She blessed the absent brownies for their insight. "Galen may have been the means by which you came to our attention, but that does not make you his servant, to be turned out once he is gone. You will always be welcome among us, Lady Delphia."

The woman's plain face flushed a delicate pink. Brushing one hand over the book that lay upon the table, she said, "Indeed, if it isn't too presumptuous . . . the academy Galen suggested to you, on our wedding day. He and I had spoken of it before. I'd like to see that done."

Faerie and mortal scholars, furthering the work Galen had begun here. Dr. Andrews was dead, and Savennis, but there were others. If Delphia would work with an Arab, Lune suspected Abd ar-Rashid would be happy to lend his aid. "Granted, and with pleasure." It would be a more fitting memorial than a simple flame.

Through this all, Irrith had stood stiffly to one side, with none of the loose grace that characterized her usual posture. Her hands fiddled with a shard of porcelain, collected from the floor. Lune searched for the right words, that wouldn't shatter her composure. "Irrith . . . I'll understand if you wish to leave. The deed you performed on this court's behalf is not one that people can praise, however necessary it was. But know that you, too, are always welcome here, if you wish to return." There was no question now of punishing her for the Sanist affair, even if Lune had intended to.

The sprite nodded, saying nothing. What haunted her? It wasn't the agony of a heart lost to death; Lune was sure of that much. Yet some shadow hung over Irrith, its claws hooked deep.

Hoping to draw the sprite out, she said gently, "Indeed, I owe you a great debt. Ask anything of me, and it will be yours." Save the abdication of her throne—but after Valentin Aspell, Irrith would never ask it.

Unfortunately, the effect was not what she intended. The green eyes sickened, and Irrith dropped her chin. "You can't give me what I want, your Grace."

"Perhaps another could?" The sprite shook her head, a quick jerk with hunched shoulders. Refusal of more than just that possibility. "We've known each other for a century, Irrith. Whatever it is, you needn't fear saying it in front of me."

"Not you." The wince that followed made it clear that had slipped out against her will.

There were only three of them in the room, and Delphia could count as well as any. With the abruptness of a woman who must force the words out of her mouth, she said, "The ladies of this court gossip, in the manner of ladies everywhere. I know you shared his bed. And I—I won't begrudge you your grief."

The sprite shook her head vehemently, auburn tangles whipping. "No. I didn't love him. Not in the way that we do—not *real* love, the sort that hurts forever."

But there was grief in her voice, even if it was of a transient kind. Delphia, folding her hands like one at prayer, offered up a misplaced mortal reassurance. "We may comfort ourselves that he is with—that he is in a better place now."

It was the wrong thing to say. Not just a Christian comfort, and meaningless to fae; no, this was the hammer stroke, shattering Irrith's mask and laying bare the horror beneath it. "No, he isn't! He killed himself, and now he's in *Hell*!"

The word rang through the room like a thunderclap—and then the air changed.

Irrith thought at first that tears were blurring her vision. And so they were; but the shape remained even when she blinked the moisture away.

It formed above the carpet, in the center of the triangle the three of them created. White mist at first, almost too faint to see; then it thickened, solidified, color seeping through it like slow dye, never quite attaining the vibrancy of life.

Delphia sank to the floor in shock, and Irrith almost did the same.

Those bound to the fae sometimes lingered among them after death.

The ghost of Galen St. Clair seemed puzzled at first, unsure of where he was. Then he saw Delphia on the floor; then Irrith and Lune, standing to either side. He turned from one to the other, half-drifting, and Irrith's heart tried to burst from relief when she saw his eyes, clear of any flame.

"The Dragon," he whispered.

She had to try three times before the word came out. "Dead. Do—do you remember?"

The question sent a shudder down his spine. Galen was dressed as he had been in death, free from all the armor of elegance, but his shirt was whole; no mark of the beast's flame showed on him anywhere. "I . . . I remember pain."

"You were burning," Irrith said, voice wavering so badly it was almost unintelligible. "It would have killed you eventually. And maybe that would have killed the Dragon. But I—"

"Destruction." Galen might not have heard anything she said; he was lost in the fog of his own memories. "For its own sake, at first; that was the fire of the Dragon. Then destruction for the sake of making others suffer. And that was *my* fire."

His gaze pinned Irrith, swift as an arrow. "I hurt you."

She shook her head so hard, pain flared in her neck. "No. That wasn't you."

"It was. The me that was the Dragon. The two of us as one . . ." He trailed one ghostly hand across his chest, where she had stabbed him. "The ice put out the flames. I think some part of it is still in me—I remember the comet, and the vastness of space. But there is no more fire."

The tears were coming again. She'd done this much for him, then: that beast would not add to his torments. Scant comfort.

The ghostly substance of Galen's body rippled, then firmed once more. Looking around as if seeing his surroundings for the first time, he said, "I thought I would be in Hell."

Lune smiled. A strange radiance had suffused her: serenity, unshakeable as the foundations of the earth. "No, Galen. Your soul is not bound for Hell."

"But he *killed* himself," Irrith said. "Even I know where suicides go."

Delphia pushed herself to her feet, careful as a cripple walking for the first time. She said, "I won't quote the words of scripture directly, not in this place—but it tells us the greatest love of all is to give up one's life for the sake of others."

"For the sake of faeries." The words tasted bitter in Irrith's mouth, all the more so because she wanted to hope, and didn't dare. "We don't matter, in Heaven's eyes."

"Yes, we do." The joy in Lune's smile was like nothing Irrith had ever seen before. "We are not creatures of Heaven, but when love joins our two worlds, even the angels do not condemn it. I have seen it myself, long ago."

She sounded like a madwoman. The shining certainty in her eyes, though, dissolved the ache that had lodged within Irrith's breast since Galen first offered himself for the sacrifice. *He isn't damned. He's given up his life—but not his soul.*

Through her own dignified tears, Delphia said, "Go on, Galen. Heaven awaits you."

He hesitated. Irrith thought some lingering fear held him back, until he shook his head.

"I don't want to leave you."

To leave Lune—but he said it to all three of them, his wife, his lover, and his Queen. Irrith's throat closed, with sudden hope. "He's a ghost," she said, as if no one had noticed. "Haunting the palace. He doesn't have to go anywhere, does he?"

She looked hopefully to Lune as she said it, but saw the elfin woman's radiance dim. "Have to—no. But Galen . . . do not trap yourself in that fashion."

"It isn't a trap if I choose it," he said, and all the passion of his soul was in those words.

Sorrow touched Lune's lips. The fading that had come upon her, the exhaustion of the Onyx Hall's decline, had only made her beauty more poignant. "But think of what you are choosing. For today, it would be a blessing; you would remain among those you love. What of tomorrow, though, and the next day, and all the days to come? Forever adrift in these halls, as mortals pass and faerie memory dissolves into forgetfulness, until even your friends scarcely remember who you are and why they once cared for you."

Irrith wanted to insist it would not be so. But then she thought of past Princes—or tried to. Lord Antony, Jack Ellin, Lord Joseph. The names were there when she reached for them, and even the faces; that was not how fae forgot. When she tried to recall Jack's sense of humour, though, or the respect she felt for Lord Joseph when he heard the news of the comet's return . . . nothing. They might have been people from a history book, not men she'd known.

That would happen to Galen, too. The only way to hold on to such memories was to love. And then his lingering would be an endless source of pain to them both.

"This place would become a prison to you," Lune said, softly, regretfully. "Do not condemn yourself to that Hell."

His face was taut as if he would weep, but death had robbed him of all tears. "I cannot abandon this place, though. If I knew all danger had passed—the Dragon is gone, but the enchantments are still fraying. How can I leave you to face that alone?"

He couldn't go, and he couldn't stay. Irrith remembered the moans of the ghosts on All Hallows' Eve—then thought of other ghosts. The ones they didn't sweep away each year.

"Then come back," she said.

No one understood her. Irrith fumbled for an explanation. "There's a manor house in Berkshire that's haunted by the ghost of some lady. Not all the time; just on the night of her wedding. I have no idea where she goes the rest of the time, but couldn't Galen do that? Come back once a year—at least until this place is safe?" Until the desire binding him to this world faded enough for him to let go.

Lune didn't answer immediately. She turned instead to Delphia. Any normal woman might have argued, out of confusion or piety or simple instinct, but Galen had married one who understood; she nodded. Then Lune said, "I cannot promise it will be so; that, I fear, lies beyond me. But I can leave the door open. If you wish to return, nothing here will prevent you."

It wasn't certainty. It was enough for Galen, though. A smile broke across his face, like dawn breaking clear after the endless months of clouds. The image spread across Irrith's memory like a balm, blotting out the horror of Cannon Street and the black holes of his eyes, and the relief brought her almost to tears. "Good-bye—for now," she whispered, and heard Delphia and Lune echo her with their own farewells.

And the light grew. It came from everywhere and nowhere, shining through the fading substance of Galen's ghostly body. It should have burnt, like church bells and prayers; Irrith felt in it that same holy force, the touch of the divine. It *could* have burnt, if it chose. But the light passed through her without harm, shining in the depths of London's faerie realm, and then it was gone, as if it had never been.

Irrith drew in a deep breath, let it out slowly, and said to the Queen, "Yes. I'll stay."

EPILOGUE

Royal Observatory, Greenwich: October 6, 1835

Frederick Parsons stepped away from the eyepiece and grinned. "And there it is. Just like it was seventy-six years ago."

His companion raised both eyebrows dryly. "Not *just* like, I should think. May I see?"

Frederick waved him forward. His companion had to bend farther to reach the eyepiece, but despite the discomfort, stayed in that position for a long time, studying the heavens above.

Far in the distance—unimaginably far, though not incalculably so—a "star" blazed across the sky. They weren't the only curiosity-seekers at Greenwich, come to observe the return of Halley's famed comet, but they were the only ones to bring their own telescope. The Royal Observatory yet remained far enough outside of London's gaslights and filthy smoke to be a good point from which to see such wonders.

Other comets came and went, of course, but they didn't interest Frederick as this one did. He'd been born only twenty-four years before: far too recently to have seen its last apparition, and far too long ago to have any hope of seeing the next one. This was his only chance to observe the comet that had nearly destroyed London.

His companion had watched it from France, though. Yvoir had spied on the great Charles Messier himself, and sneaked an opportunity to use the astronomer's own equipment one night when Messier lay coughing in bed. He claimed to have sensed the malevolent presence of the Dragon, but Frederick thought the faerie was making it up.

"We should figure out some way to drag Master Ktistes up

here," Frederick said, bored with watching Yvoir watch the sky. "You could put a glamour on him, to hide the horse body."

"Hiding it doesn't make it go away," Yvoir said, still hunched over. "I don't fancy putting him on a steamboat for a jaunt down the river. Besides, it hardly matters now. This is a historical curiosity, nothing more. The academy has other concerns."

Frederick sniffed, doing his best impression of a stuffy old man. "There's no respect for history nowadays—not even for our poor martyred founder." He dug a stone out of the dirt with the toe of his shoe. "They say he haunts the Hall, you know. But I don't believe it."

"Lady Delphia believed," the French faerie told him. "And since she was the patroness of the Galenic Academy, I would say you're the one with no respect for history, my friend." He straightened at last, with faerie suppleness that even Frederick's young joints could envy.

At least until impatience banished it. Frederick said, "Very well; we've seen the comet. Now can we go back? Wrain claims he finally has a working model of his aetheric engine, and I don't want to miss the chance to laugh at him when it fails again."

Together the faerie and the mortal packed up their telescope and then raced down the steep slope of the observatory's hill, running by the light of the full moon and the stars, and the wandering star of the comet, trailing its bright banner across the sky.

ACKNOWLEDGMENTS

Like the other Onyx Court books, *A Star Shall Fall* owes a great deal to the people who assisted me in my research. In London, that included Mick Pedroli of Dennis Severs House, for advice on living in an eighteenth-century style; Eleanor John of the Geffrye Museum, for answers about house furnishings; Rupert Baker and Felicity Henderson of the Royal Society Library, for fetching out comet books and many dusty volumes of Royal Society minutes; Dr. Rebekah Higgitt and Dr. Jonathan Betts of the Royal Observatory, Greenwich, for assistance with the history of the observatory and horology respectively; Susan Kirby, Alan Lilly, and Mimi Kalema of Tower Bridge Authority, for letting me into the basement of the Monument very early on a Saturday morning; and Dr. Kari Sperring and her husband, Phil Nanson, for touring me around Cambridge and even taking me punting.

I also needed a great deal of help via e-mail, on a variety of arcane topics. John Pritchard sent me a fabulous diagram of the Monument; Ian Walden advised me about local flora; Farah Mendlesohn was my go-to woman for Jewish history; Ricardo Barros of the Mercurius Company helped me figure out eighteenth-century dancing; Rev. Devin McLachlan did the same for eighteenth-century Anglican theology; and Dr. Erin Smith made the astronomy go. For information on Ottoman Arabic society, the Arabic language, and the nature of genies, I owe thanks to Yonatan Zunger, Saladin Ahmed, and Rabeya Merenkov. Sherwood Smith did the German translations for me, and Aliette de Bodard not only knew what iatrochemistry was, but could tell me how to say it in French.

The late-night conversations this time were with Adrienne Lipoma and my husband, Kyle Niedzwiecki, with an assist from Jennie Kaye. They very kindly let me talk at them endlessly about the book, and provided more than one useful suggestion.

And then there are all the authors who wrote books I made use of. They are too many to list here, but as always, the bibliography is available on my Web site, www.swantower.com.

Turn the page for a preview of

A Natural History of Dragons

A Memoir by Lady Trent

MARIE BRENNAN

Available in February 2013 from
Tom Doherty Associates

TOR® A TOR BOOK

FOREWORD

Not a day goes by that the post does not bring me at least one letter from a young person (or sometimes one not so young) who wishes to follow in my footsteps and become a dragon naturalist. Nowadays, of course, the field is quite respectable, with university courses and intellectual societies putting out fat volumes titled *Proceedings of* some meeting or other. Those interested in respectable things, however, attend my lectures. The ones who write to me invariably want to hear about my adventures: my escape from captivity in the swamps of Mouleen, or my role in the great Battle of Keonga, or (most frequently) my flight to the inhospitable heights of the Mrtyahaima peaks, the only place on earth where the secrets of dragonkind could be unlocked.

Even the most dedicated of letter writers could not hope to answer all these queries personally. I have therefore accepted the offer from Messrs. Carrigdon & Rudge to publish a series of memoirs, chronicling the more interesting portions of my life. By and large these shall focus on those expeditions that led to the discovery for which I have become so famous, but there shall also be occasional digressions into matters more entertaining, personal, or even (yes) salacious. One benefit of being an old woman now, and moreover one who has been called a "national treasure," is that there are very few who can tell me what I may and may not write.

Be warned, then: the collected volumes of this series will contain frozen mountains, foetid swamps, hostile foreigners, hostile fellow countrymen, the occasional hostile family member, bad decisions, misadventures in orienteering, diseases of an unromantic sort, and a plenitude of mud. You continue at your own risk. It is not for the faint of heart—no more so than the study of dragons itself. But such study offers rewards beyond compare: to stand in a dragon's presence, even for the briefest of moments—even at the risk of one's life—is a delight that, once experienced, can never be forgotten. If my humble words convey even a fraction of that wonder, I will rest content.

We must, of course, begin at the beginning, before the series of discoveries and innovations that transformed the world into the one you, dear reader, know so well. In this ancient and nearly forgotten age lie the modest origins of my immodest career: my childhood and my first foreign expedition, to the mountains of Vystrana. The basic facts of this expedition have long since become common knowledge, but there is much more to the tale than you have heard.

> Isabella, Lady Trent
> Casselthwaite, Linshire
> 11 Floris, 1895

ONE

Greenie—An unfortunate incident with a dove—
My obsession with wings—My family—The influence of
Sir Richard Edgeworth

When I was seven I found a sparkling lying dead on a bench at the edge of the woods, which formed the back boundary of our garden, that the groundskeeper had not yet cleared away. With much excitement, I brought it for my mother to see, but by the time I reached her it had mostly collapsed into ash in my hands. Mama exclaimed in distaste and sent me to wash.

Our cook, a tall and gangly woman who nonetheless produced the most amazing soups and soufflés (thus putting the lie to the notion that one cannot trust a slender cook), was the one who showed me the secret of preserving sparklings after death. She kept one on her dresser top, which she brought out for me to see when I arrived in her kitchen, much cast down from the loss of the sparkling and from my mother's chastisement. "However did you keep it?" I asked her, wiping away my tears. "Mine fell all to pieces."

"Vinegar," she said, and that one word set me upon the path that led to where I stand today.

If found soon enough after death, a sparkling (as many of the readers of this volume no doubt know) may be preserved by embalming it in vinegar. I sailed forth into our gardens in determined search, a jar of vinegar crammed into one of my dress pockets so the skirt hung all askew. The first one I found lost its right wing in the process of preservation, but before the week was out I had an intact specimen: a sparkling an inch and a half in length, his scales a deep emerald in color. With the boundless ingenuity of a child, I named him Greenie, and he sits on a shelf in my study to this day, tiny wings outspread.

Sparklings were not the only things I collected in those days. I was forever bringing home other insects and beetles (for back then we classified sparklings as an insect species that simply resembled dragons, which today we know to be untrue), and many other things besides: interesting rocks, discarded bird feathers, fragments of eggshell, bones of all kinds. Mama threw fits until I formed a pact with my maid that she would not breathe a word of my treasures, and I would give her an extra hour a week during which she could sit down and rest her feet. Thereafter my collections hid in cigar boxes and the like, tucked safely into my closets where my mother would not go.

No doubt some of my inclinations came about because I was the sole daughter in a set of six children. Surrounded as I was by boys, and with our house rather isolated in the countryside of Tamshire, I quite believed that collecting odd things was what children did, regardless of sex. My mother's attempts to educate me otherwise left little mark, I fear. Some of my interest also came from my father, who like any gentleman in those days kept himself moderately informed of developments in all fields: law, theology, economics, natural history, and more.

The remainder of it, I fancy, was inborn curiosity. I would sit in the kitchen (where I was permitted to be, if not encouraged, only because it meant I was not outside getting dirty and ruining my dresses) and ask the cook questions as she stripped a chicken carcass for the soup. "Why do chickens have wishbones?" I asked her one day.

One of the kitchen maids answered me, in the fatuous tone of an adult addressing a child. "To make wishes on!" she said brightly, handing me one that had already been dried. "You take one side of it—"

"I know what we *do* with them," I said impatiently, cutting her off without much tact. "That's not what chickens have them for, though, or surely the chicken would have wished not to end up in the pot for our supper."

"Heavens, child, I don't know what they grow them for," the cook said. "But you find them in all kinds of birds—chickens, turkeys, geese, pigeons, and the like."

The notion that all birds should share this feature was intriguing, something I had never before considered. My curiosity soon drove me to an act that I blush to think upon today, not for the act itself (as I have done similar things many times since then, if in a more meticulous and scholarly fashion), but for the surreptitious and naive manner in which I carried it out.

In my wanderings one day, I found a dove that had fallen dead under a hedgerow. I immediately remembered what the cook had said, that all birds had wishbones. She had not named doves in her list, but doves were birds, were they not? Perhaps I might learn what they were for, as I could not learn when I watched the footman carve up a goose at the dinner table.

I took the dove's body and hid it behind the hayrick next to the barn, then stole inside and pinched a penknife from Andrew, the brother immediately senior to me, without him knowing. Once outside again, I settled down to my study of the dove.

I was organized, if not perfectly sensible, in my approach to the work. I had seen the maids plucking birds for the cook, so I understood that the first step was to remove the feathers—a task which proved harder than I had expected, and appallingly messy. It did accord me a chance, though, to see how the shaft of the feather fitted into its follicle (a word I did not know at the time), and the different kinds of feathers.

When the bird was more or less naked, I spent some time moving its wings and feet about, seeing how they operated—and, in truth, steeling myself for what I had determined to do next. Eventually curiosity won out over squeamishness, and I took my brother's penknife, set it against the skin of the bird's belly, and cut.

The smell was tremendous—in retrospect, I'm sure I perforated the bowel—but my fascination held. I examined the gobbets of flesh that came out, unsure what most of them were, for to me livers and kidneys were things I had only ever seen on a supper plate. I recognized the intestines, however, and made a judicious guess at the lungs and heart. Squeamishness overcome, I continued my work, peeling back the skin, prying away muscles, seeing how it all connected. I uncovered the bones, one by one, marveling at the delicacy of the wings, the wide keel of the sternum.

I had just discovered the wishbone when I heard a shout behind me and turned to see a stable boy staring at me in horror.

While he bolted off, I frantically began trying to cover my mess, dragging hay over the dismembered body of the dove, but so distressed was I that the main result was to make myself look even worse than before. By the time Mama arrived on the scene, I was covered in blood and bits of dove flesh, feathers and hay, and more than a few tears.

I will not tax my readers with a detailed description of the treatment I received at that point; the more adventurous among you have no doubt experienced similar chastisement after your own escapades. In the end I found myself in my father's study, standing clean and shamefaced on his Akhian carpet.

"Isabella," he said, his voice forbidding, "what possessed you to do such a thing?"

Out it all came, in a flood of words, about the dove I had found (I assured him, over and over again, that it had been dead when I came upon it, that I most certainly had not killed it) and about my curiosity regarding the wishbone—on and on I went, until Papa came forward and knelt before me, putting one hand on my shoulder and stopping me at last.

"You wanted to know how it worked?" he asked.

I nodded, not trusting myself to speak again lest the flood pick up where it had left off.

He sighed. "Your behavior was not appropriate for a young lady. Do you understand that?" I nodded. "Let's make certain you remember it, then." With one hand he turned me about, and with the other he administered three brisk smacks to my bottom, which started the tears afresh. When I had myself under control once more, I found that he had left me to compose myself and gone to the wall of his study. The shelves there were lined with books, some, I fancied, weighing as much as I did myself. (This was pure fancy, of course; the weightiest book in my library now, my own *De Draconum Varietatibus,* weighs a mere ten pounds.)

The volume he took down was much lighter, if rather thicker than one would normally give to a seven-year-old child. He pressed it into my hands, saying, "Your lady mother would not be happy to see you with this, I imagine, but I had rather you learn it from a book than from experimentation. Run along, now, and don't show that to her."

I curtsied and fled.

Like Greenie, that book still sits on my shelf. My father had given me Gotherham's *Avian Anatomy,* and though our understanding of the subject has improved a great deal since Gotherham's day, it was a good introduction for me at the time. The text was only half-comprehensible to me, but I devoured the half I could understand and contemplated the rest in fascinated perplexity. Best of all were the diagrams, thin, meticulous drawings of avian skeletons and musculature. From this book I learned that the function of the wishbone (or, more properly, the *furcula*) is to strengthen the thoracic skeleton of birds and provide attachment points for wing muscles.

It seemed so simple, so obvious: all birds had wishbones, because all birds flew. (At the time I was not aware of ostriches, and neither was Gotherham.) Hardly a brilliant conclusion in the field of natural history, but to me it was brilliant indeed, and opened up a world I had never considered before: a world in which one could observe patterns and their circumstances, and from these derive information not obvious to the unaided eye.

Wings, truly, were my first obsession. I did not much discriminate in those days as to whether the wings in question belonged to a dove or a sparkling or a butterfly; the point was that these beings flew, and for that I adored them. I might mention, however, that although Mr. Gotherham's text concerns itself with birds, he does make the occasional, tantalizing reference to analogous structures or behaviors in dragonkind. Since (as I have said before) sparklings were then classed as a variety of insect, this might count as my first introduction to the wonder of dragons.

I should speak at least in passing of my family, for without them I would not have become the woman I am today.

Of my mother I expect you have some sense already; she was an upright and proper woman of her class and did the best she could to teach me ladylike ways, but no one can achieve the impossible. Any faults in my character must not be laid at her feet. As for my father, his business interests kept him from home often, and so to me he was a more distant figure, and perhaps more tolerant because of it. He had the luxury of seeing my misbehaviors as charming quirks of his daughter's nature, while my mother faced the messes and ruined clothing those quirks produced. I looked upon him as one might a minor pagan god, earnestly desiring his goodwill but never quite certain how to propitiate him.

Where siblings are concerned, I was, as I have said, the fourth in a set of six children, and the only daughter. Most of my brothers, while of personal significance to me, will not feature much in this tale; their lives have not been much intertwined with my career.

The exception is Andrew, whom I have already mentioned; he is the one from whom I pinched the penknife. He, more than any, was my earnest partner in all the things of which my mother despaired. When Andrew heard of my bloody endeavors behind the hayrick, he was impressed as only an eight-year-old boy can be and insisted I keep the knife as a trophy of my deeds. That, I no longer have; it deserves a place of honor alongside Greenie and Gotherham, but I lost it in the swamps of Mouleen. Not before it saved my life, however, cutting me free of the vines in which my Labane captors had bound me, and so I am forever grateful to Andrew for the gift.

I am also grateful for his assistance during our childhood years, exercising a boy's privileges on my behalf. When our father was out of town, Andrew would borrow books out of his study for my use. Texts I myself would never have been permitted to read thus found their way into my room, where I hid them between the mattresses and behind my wardrobe. My new maid had too great a terror of being found off her feet to agree to the old deal, but she was amenable to sweets, and so we settled on a new arrangement, and I read long into the night on more than one occasion.

The books he took on my behalf, of course, were nearly all of natural history. My horizons expanded from their winged beginnings to creatures of all kinds: mammals and fish, insects and reptiles, plants of a hundred sorts, for in those days our knowledge was still general enough that one person might be expected to familiarize himself (or in my case, herself) with the entire field.

Some of the books mentioned dragons. They never did so in more than passing asides, brief paragraphs that did little more than develop my appetite for information. In several places, however, I came across references to a particular work: Sir Richard Edgeworth's *A Natural History of Dragons*. Carrigdon & Rudge were soon to be reprinting it, as I learned from their autumn catalog; I risked a great deal by sneaking into my father's study so as to find that pamphlet and leave it open to the page announcing the reprint. It described *A Natural History of Dragons* as "the most indispensable reference on dragonkind available in our tongue"; surely that would be enough to entice my father's eye.

My gamble paid off, for it was in the next delivery of books we received. I could not have it right away—Andrew would not borrow anything our father had yet to read—and I nearly went mad with waiting. Early in winter, though, Andrew passed me the book in a corridor, saying, "He finished it yesterday. Don't let anyone see you with it."

I was on my way to the parlor for my weekly lesson on the pianoforte, and if I went back up to my room I would be late. Instead I hurried onward and concealed the book under a cushion mere heartbeats before my teacher entered. I gave him my best curtsy and thereafter struggled mightily not to look toward the divan, from which I could feel the unread book taunting me. (I would say my playing suffered from the distraction, but it is difficult for something so dire to grow worse. Although I appreciate music, to this day I could not carry a tune if you tied it around my wrist for safekeeping.)

Once I escaped from my lesson, I began in on the book straightaway and hardly paused except to hide it when necessary. I imagine it is not so well known today as it was then, having been supplanted by other, more complete works, so it may be difficult for my readers to imagine how wondrous it seemed to me at the time. Edgeworth's identifying criteria for "true dragons" were a useful starting point for many of us, and his listing of qualifying species is all the more impressive for having been assembled through correspondence with missionaries and traders, rather than through firsthand observation. He also addressed the issue of "lesser dragonkind," namely, those creatures such as wyverns that failed one criterion or another, yet appeared (by the theories of the period) to be branches of the same family tree.

The influence this book had upon me may be expressed by saying that I read it straight through four times, for once was certainly not enough. Just as some girl-children of that age go mad for horses and equestrian pursuits, so did I become dragon-mad. That phrase described me well, for it led not only to the premier focus of my adult life (which has included more than a few actions here and there that might be deemed deranged), but more directly to the action I engaged in shortly after my fourteenth birthday.

TOR

Award-winning authors
Compelling stories

Please join us at the website
below for more information
about this author and other great
Tor selections, and to sign up for
our monthly newsletter!

www.tor-forge.com